Milly J ... hor from L ...hire. ...ngs card copy ...umnist, after-dinner speaker and winner of *Come Dine ...Me* Barnsley. When not working, her hobbies include: sailing on big ships, hobnobbing with the transatlantic wrestling community, buying red lipsticks, listening to very loud rock music, admiring owls and trying to resist buying crap from eBay.

She lives with her two sons, Teddy the Eurasier and a quartet of decrepit cats near her mam and dad in Barnsley, South Yorkshire. She is a proud patron of Haworthcatrescue.org and 'The Well', a complementary therapy centre associated with Barnsley Hospital. *An Autumn Crush* is her sixth book.

Visit her at *www.millyjohnson.com*

Also by Milly Johnson

The Yorkshire Pudding Club

The Birds & the Bees

A Spring Affair

A Summer Fling

Here Come the Girls

milly johnson

An Autumn Crush

SIMON &
SCHUSTER

London · New York · Sydney · Toronto

A CBS COMPANY

First published in Great Britain by Simon & Schuster UK Ltd, 2011
A CBS COMPANY

1 3 5 7 9 10 8 6 4 2

Simon & Schuster UK Ltd
1st Floor
222 Gray's Inn Road
London WC1X 8HB

www.simonsays.co.uk

Simon & Schuster Australia
Sydney

A CIP catalogue record for this book is available
from the British Library

ISBN 978–1–84983–203–8

Typeset in Bembo by Hewer Text UK Ltd, Edinburgh
Printed and bound in Great Britain by CPI Cox & Wyman,
Reading, Berkshire RG1 8EX

This book is dedicated to my greetings card copywriting 'brothers': Paul Sear, Alec Sillifant, Fraz Worth, Pete Allwright and Tony Husband. Boys, I absolutely adore you xx

Love is a fruit in season at all times, and within the reach of every hand.

Mother Teresa

An Autumn Crush

August

'Before the reward there must be labor. You plant before you harvest. You sow in tears before you reap joy.'

Ralph Ransom

Chapter 1

Things had been going swimmingly with Miss One O'Clock. Juliet and Coco were united in their decision, and both prided themselves on their razor-like intuition. She was fragrant, unlike Miss Twelve O'Clock, who drifted into the flat on the crest of a wave of armpit smell – and she had laughter lines, unlike Miss Half-Past Eleven who'd had so much Botox she looked like she'd escaped from Madame Tussauds. And she was well into her thirties, unlike Misses Ten Forty-Five and Five Past Nine, who were far too young and silly. Anyone who couldn't remember *The Karate Kid* first time around was deffo off the list. She was beautifully plump and buxom too, unlike the heroin-chic-thin Miss Half-Past Twelve. Yep, the fact that Miss One O'Clock looked as if she would happily share a midnight cheesecake was the best indication yet of a good egg. People who relished their grub were more likely to have an accompanying joie de vivre than those who ate merely to fuel their bodies, Juliet believed. She sighed with relief that her search for a suitable flat-mate was finally drawing to a close, because trying to find someone to share your home and bills with when you were older and fussier had been the biggest imaginable pain in the bum.

Then Juliet offered her a chocolate digestive.

'I don't eat those,' said Miss One O'Clock, her face

contorting like Mr Bean's. 'They contain animal fats. And I'm a vegan.'

She made the word sound like she was from another planet, which in Juliet's eyes she might as well have been. Vegans, Vulcans – no difference, give or take the pointy ears. Pure unadulterated aliens. Juliet and Coco exchanged knowing glances. Aw God, another one bites the dust, they said to each other via the language of eyeballs. Coco knew that Juliet would sooner have shared her flat with Harold Shipman than a vegan. She wouldn't want someone glaring at her as if she was a mass murderer for enjoying a bacon buttie, with full-on Lurpak, or plodding around in sheepskin slippers.

Miss One O'Clock's whole demeanour had changed now she was in the presence of established carnivores and milk-slurpers, and there was no point in going on with the interview. She gave Juliet and Coco a Siberian-winter smile goodbye and toddled off in her plastic shoes.

'How can anyone get an arse on them that big just by eating celery?' Juliet marvelled, when the door was firmly shut.

'Beats me,' said her friend Coco, primping his dark brown New Romantic curls and pursing his full red lips in camp puzzlement. He was long and stick-thin himself, but Juliet forgave him that because he had always eaten like a starving horse. He just had an enviable metabolism. 'Of course, if you'd had me as a flat-mate, you wouldn't have any of this to go through.'

'Coco,' said Juliet firmly, 'you and me not living together equals friendship. You and me living together equals me kicking your head in or you scratching my eyes out. I could not share a flat with you. Ever. And you could NOT share a flat with me.' She employed the two words she always did when this argument reared up, as it had done quite a lot recently. 'Remember Majorca?'

Two weeks in Spain with Coco and their mutual friend Hattie had been the best fun, but Juliet knew then that she could never have shared a flat with a man so anal about cleaning. And seeing as Hattie then ran off with Juliet's husband Roger, *she* wasn't in the running to be her flat-sharer either. Good luck to them anyway. Because underneath her ex-husband's charming, shining veneer lay a dark soul heavily marinated in 'miserable bastard'.

Which is why, having lived with him for six years, a man whose smile had ended up in a kidney dish with his tonsils at age ten, there was no way Juliet would *ever* take the business of choosing who to live with – flat-mate or partner – lightly again. The non-negotiable criteria were: smile-ability, body shape and that old stand-by, intuition. Juliet had no intention of sharing living space with anyone who tutted if she happened to stuff something in her mouth that didn't include the whole five-a-day fruit and veg cocktail.

There were just two possible candidates left to see. Until Miss Two O'Clock arrived, Juliet and Coco killed time with three thousand calories'-worth of Thorntons.

Andrea arrived at two on the dot. The punctuality was impressive, but sadly little else about her was. She looked as if she had just caught a Tardis from 1962. She was willowy with angular features and wore a floaty frock in bogey-green and matching love beads, had a dated perm that made her look as if she'd been electrocuted, and she stank of very strong patchouli oil, which set Coco off on a coughing fit when he got a lungful at the door. He judged people by their fragrance. Scents had always been a passion of his and he owned a bijou fragrance shop in town: Coco's Perfume Palace. He knew and loved his subject, but patchouli was right up there with Tweed and Charlie, and one notch down from Devon Violets.

Andrea immediately crossed to the far corner of the room and started clapping her hands up in the air.

'You have a lot of negative energy stored in this space,' she said, with the same level of distaste one would have used on finding mouse turds in the biscuit tin. 'And is that a *bin* I see next to your dining-table?' She made a few 'deary-me' tuts and carried on clapping.

'Would you like a coffee?' asked Coco, his eyes watering from the strain of keeping his laughter under rein.

'Black. And only if it's Fair Trade,' said Andrea, swishing her way back to the sofa. 'Has this flat ever been smudged?'

Juliet looked blankly back at her, not having a clue what she was on about.

'It's been blurred a few times,' offered Coco. 'After a few bottles of Shiraz.'

'The energy residues badly need purifying,' sniffed Andrea, ignoring his joke. Then she twisted her head sharply to her side and spoke to an invisible presence. 'Yes, I totally agree.'

Coco ran into the kitchen and stuffed a tea-towel in his mouth. He found a sachet of Fair Trade coffee in Juliet's cupboard after a forage. It had come free with a magazine.

'So . . .' began Juliet with a forced smile, though knowing inside she was on a highway to nowhere with this one. She just wanted someone normal, for God's sake. Was that too much to ask? 'Where are you living now?'

'Myrtle Grove, off Huddersfield Road,' replied Andrea, her eyes roving the room as if following something flying around it. 'Have you ever cleansed your chakras?'

Cleansed me what? thought Juliet. Sounded too much like that colonic hosepipe up the bum thing for comfort.

'Raven is asking me to ask you,' Andrea smiled, turning her attention full on Juliet now.

'Raven?' asked Juliet, trying to ignore the sight of Coco's head poking out of the kitchen doorway behind Andrea, with a towel jammed in his jaws.

'My spirit guide,' replied Andrea. 'He's a Red Indian Blackfoot chief. I consult him in all things.'

This really was too much.

'Er, does *he* want a coffee?' asked Juliet with wide innocent grey eyes. She heard a shriek from the kitchen as some of Coco's hysteria escaped through the towel.

Andrea sighed and lifted up her bag which looked as if it had been home-made out of a couple of carpet tiles. Her nose was wrinkled up as if someone had just stuck a rotting fish under it.

'I'm sorry. We couldn't settle here. I can see that from the colour of your aura which is very blue-grey. I don't think we would get on; you're obviously not receptive to new ideas.'

Juliet bounced to her feet. 'Oh, what a shame. You're right though – traditional to the last, that's me. You're obviously a very perceptive lady.'

'I am indeed. I am totally at one with myself.' Then Andrea strolled out of the flat very regally, without a backward glance or a goodbye.

'Silly cow,' said Juliet, as the door hit the catch. 'And she had appalling manners.'

'What was all that about?' A very puce-faced Coco strode into the same corner of the lounge which Andrea had recently vacated and started clapping his hands together like a flamenco dancer with severe anger management issues. 'Feng Shui?'

'Feng Shite, you mean. I haven't a frigging clue what she was on about,' tutted Juliet.

'And that smell, ugh! It's worse than the devil's arse.' Coco wafted the air trying to rid it of the strong scent.

'Anyway, I for one was glad that "Dances with Ravens", or whatever he was called, put her off the place. He'd have only set fire to the curtains with his smoke signals. I ask you, Coco, is there anyone normal left in this world?'

'Me!' Coco grinned.

'I rest my case.'

There had been hardly anything to do to the flat when Juliet bought it from the middle-aged Armstrongs, just after her divorce in February, with the rather nice proceeds from selling her share of the marital home to Roger. 'Two substantial bedrooms, airy, spacious lounge with applaudable dining area, newly refurbished kitchen, Hollywood-style bathroom and generous storage cupboards,' the estate agent had bragged.

You could tell a dominant female had lived here before Juliet got her paws on the place. Mrs Armstrong must have wielded a whip over Mr Armstrong every evening and week-end with insatiable demands for shelves and stripped wood and wrought-iron curtain rails. And at the end of a hardworking day, it appeared they retired to their separate bedrooms with not even the prospect of a 'thank you' bonk for him. And just when Mrs A. had got it to her ideal, she spots a bigger place and poor old Mr A. has to start realizing her laminate-floor dreams all over again. But this flat was perfect enough for Juliet. It had lots of space and nice high ceilings, which was handy when you had a freaky-tall family like she had. And though the mortgage was a stretch – as was to be expected for a quality pad in such a nice area – a flat-mate would alleviate that problem.

The Armstrongs had put it on the market for a not-too-greedy price in the hope of a quick sale, which Juliet was in a perfect position to take advantage of. It was just a bit empty. Not furniture-wise but company-wise: nice girly Black Forest gateau in the middle of the night, face packs at nine o'clock, borrow your nail varnish, sloppy video with smouldering-gorgeous Darcy-like hero to fantasize about, bottle of Cab Sav and a curry sort of company. The sort of camaraderie she and Caroline and Tina had relished at college before they all grew up too much and found they didn't have anything in common any more – not even enough to want to swap a Christmas card. Juliet tried not to think about Hattie, who had been her friend forever. She hadn't even admitted to Coco how much Hattie's deception had hurt her. She had her reputation as a hard, brazen bitch to consider.

So, a classified ad went into both the *South Yorkshire Herald* and the *Barnsley Chronicle*. She drafted: *Flat-mate wanted for good-hearted, big-bummed, smiley, smart, bossy, dirty-joke-loving, chocolate-eating thirty-four-year-old. Candidates must not mind nosy Irish parents popping around far too often for comfort and a massive, genial but bloody clumsy twerp of a twin brother who is wont to annoying one with his repertoire of wrestling holds and kitchen creations being more or less permanently present in abode.*

Then, on second thoughts, she went for a heavily abridged version so as not to alarm. *Thirtysomething female flat-mate wanted to share a very smart second-floor flat with easygoing professional lady (straight). Own large, sunny room, quiet but central location. 3, Blackberry Court.*

'What if Miss Three O'Clock is as bad as the rest?' asked Coco, taking a peek at his watch.

'I don't know, struggle on with the mortgage by myself. What else can I do?'

'You overstretched yourself with this place, lovely as it is. Another coffee?'

'Go on then,' said Juliet. 'And don't lecture me.'

'I could move in tomorrow,' Coco threw over his shoulder.

'I'd rather cut my own foot off and eat it in a French stick.'

'Well, we haven't had a rabid religious nutter yet. Maybe, in five minutes' time, we will be thrilled with a medley of tambourine songs and some tin-rattling.'

'I wouldn't be at all surprised,' sighed Juliet.

By quarter past three, no one had turned up. Coco was just about to say, 'Well, that's that then,' when the entryphone buzzed.

'Hello,' said a breathless voice when Juliet picked it up. 'I'm so sorry I'm late. I've just had to take a hedgehog to the vet's.'

'Do come up,' said Juliet, through a rictus smile. She turned to Coco and shook her head. 'I give up. It's not religion, it's hedgehogs. And she sounds a posh one.'

'Oh dear Christ.' Coco raised his eyes heavenward. 'Bring back Big Chief Clapping Corners.'

Juliet opened the door. 'Please come in,' she said, and she stood aside to let Florence, who preferred to be called Floz, Cherrydale in and gave her a good look up and down from behind. She was tiny, height-wise – about five-foot two – with long wavy dark-red hair and a fifties-style curvy silhouette. From the front she was awfully pink-faced from rushing up the stairs. She also looked too meek and mild for Juliet's tastes, and as if she'd not exactly been at the front of the queue when they were giving out a sense of humour. And she had the accent of a wing-commander. Great, Juliet thought. This one was probably a right snob who would look down on everything. What a waste of a chuffing day off work for both herself and Coco this was turning out to be.

'I'm so sorry again that I'm late,' Floz repeated. 'I had to stop the traffic to pick up this little limping hedgehog and it didn't go down particularly well with one shouty man. I couldn't have left him hobbling like that. The hedgehog, not the shouty man, I mean.'

'You're here now,' super-smiled Juliet, thinking, Here we go again.

Whilst she put the kettle on for the hundredth time that day, Coco gave a still shaky Floz the guided tour. The vacant room was the smaller of the two bedrooms, but it was still gigantic compared to Floz's present arrangements, apparently. It was L-shaped too, and the 'L' part would be perfect for her as Floz worked from home and needed a mini-office.

They moved to the lounge to have coffee then. As she drifted past Coco, he caught the gentlest scent of late-summer strawberries from her. His smile curved upwards in response to it. Floz set her handbag down on the sofa and it toppled off and out fell, amongst the other handbag detritus, a tiny book – *The Art of Being Happily Single*.

Floz looked mortified. 'I'm so sorry again. I'm such a klutz.' Her cheeks re-flared up like red traffic-lights and Juliet felt a sudden and surprising wave of pity. But it was Coco who rescued her.

'I've read loads of those sorts of books,' he said warmly as Floz got all flustery trying to stuff all her things back in. '*The Rules, Women Who Love Too Much, Get Rid of Him . . .*'

'. . . *Women Are From Venus, Men Are Up Their Own Anuses . . .*' put in Juliet.

'. . . *He's Not That Into You,*' said Coco, with a sad sigh. '*Why Men Lie and Women Cry . . .*'

'*How to Find a Man Who Isn't a Complete Berk,*' Floz added. And she smiled and suddenly looked like a different person. One with a 1,000-watt lightbulb inside that had suddenly been switched on. Even her eyes were smiling. Mischievous bright green and shining, they were the eyes of a small child beaming out: 'I've got a frog in my pocket.'

Juliet's intuition tore up the list with all other possible candidates on it and threw it behind her because of that smile. *Yep*, it said. *She'll do.* The crazy hedgehog-rescuer with the very nice speaking voice and self-help book in her bag was The One.

She proffered the chocolate digestives and Floz took one with a very smiley 'Oooh' of delight. The deal was sealed.

And that was how, by seven o'clock that night, Floz Cherrydale had introduced her suitcases and her boxes to the floor of her new bedroom and was sitting on her new flat-mate's sofa picking from the Great Wall takeaway menu, watching *Emmerdale* and drinking celebratory measures of Baileys.

Chapter 2

Juliet's phone rang just as she had taken her coat off in the office. It was Coco, being his deliciously nosy self ringing her, as he liked to, five minutes before he opened up his Perfume Palace in the town-centre shopping mall.

'So how was your first night with your new flatty then? Anything happen after I left?'

'Like what?' teased Juliet.

'Any goss?'

'Like what?'

'Ooh, you are awkward this morning. Is this what you're going to be like now you've got a *new friend*?'

Juliet laughed. 'That is *so* rich coming from someone who drops me like a hot brick when he's got the tiniest glimmer of a love interest.'

'I can't help it if I'm an obsessive,' sniffed Coco. 'Doesn't she speak nicely? Not like you, you common tart. Ooh, and what perfume does she wear?'

'How the bloody hell do I know?'

'Whatever it was, it had a hint of strawberries in it. Delightful.' He made a mental note to ask Floz the next time he saw her.

'I think Floz must like strawberries. She's got little pictures of them on her wall, and when she opens her door, the smell of them wafts out of her room.'

'Aw bless,' smiled Coco. He knew that anyone who smelled like Floz Cherrydale could be nothing other than a darling soul.

'I don't suppose you've heard anything from Darren?' Juliet asked softly.

'Nope, still nothing,' said Coco, his smile falling to the ground on hearing his last lover's name. 'That's three weeks, six days and fourteen hours now. Not that I'm counting. I still think he will ring. My intuition is strongly telling me that I'm on his mind.'

'No, sweetheart, I don't think you are,' replied Juliet. She wasn't the sort of person to lie to Coco and give him false hope. What would be the point of that? When a man was full on with his attentions then suddenly disappeared and didn't answer phone calls or texts, he was not going to suddenly reappear with a viable excuse. Unless he had died – then he was still unlikely to turn up.

'Okay,' said Coco, trying not to give way to an inner surge of rising emotion. 'Change of subject. What do you know about Floz so far then?'

'Not that much,' said Juliet. 'She's single, as you might have gathered from that book she dropped, works from home making up jokes and poems for the greetings-card industry, drives a Renault – all boring stuff.'

'That it?'

''Fraid so for now, kiddo. No doubt we'll get to know more in time,' said Juliet. 'I like her. We had coffee together this morning. She gets up quite early to start work.'

'Such a shame she isn't Guy's type,' said Coco, who never missed a good match-making opportunity.

'I thought exactly the same,' sighed Juliet.

Yes, it was a shame that Floz was so small and red-haired and eggshell crushable. Had she been tall and statuesque and blonde, Juliet would have grabbed her brother and frog-marched him over to the flat to meet Floz five minutes after she moved in.

'You could have gone double-dating,' said Coco, with glee. 'Floz and Guy and you and Piers.'

'Oh, don't get me going. He'll be here any minute, breathing the same air as me.' Juliet melted at the thought of having a little bit of her boss inside her – even if it was just his exhaled breath in her lungs.

'I've been thinking,' said Coco. 'How about something to occupy the time between now and you becoming Mrs Winstanley-Black?'

Ooh, that sounded good, thought Juliet. She mouthed the words 'Juliet Winstanley-Black' and thought it made her sound like a magistrate. 'Like what?'

'Internet dating.'

'Internet dating?' echoed Juliet. 'What's brought this on?'

'I'm bored,' said Coco. 'I'm seeing all the same faces at all the same clubs and I want some fresh meat.'

'Get to Barry the Butcher's then on Lamb Street.'

'Ho ho. Marlene my Deputy Manager met her fiancé online. And her cousin is going out with an architect that she met on the same Singlebods site. So they aren't all *Jeremy Kyle* rejects that sign up to these things. Oh come on, it'll be fun. And I need something to take my mind off Darren.'

At that moment Juliet heard the velvet voice of Piers Winstanley-Black say 'Good morning' to the receptionist.

'Okay, count me in,' hurried Juliet. 'Laters. He's here,' and she had just enough time to end the call, run her fingers through her long, black sheen of hair and stick out her tits.

Amanda and Daphne, who shared the same office, were also having a quick hair-primp and straightening their backs. Would he come in and choose one to go upstairs to his office to 'take something down'? they all hoped collectively.

Piers Winstanley-Black. Owner of a prestigious family hyphen and, as from four years ago, partner at Butters, Black & Lofthouse where Juliet had worked since leaving college and was now the most efficient legal secretary in the history of the place. Not that it stood her in good stead with 'the boy from Ipanema' as her twin brother Guy called Piers. Just like the song, Piers Winstanley-Black was tall and tanned and long and lovely with a flashing white smile that made Simon Cowell's look grey by comparison. He drove fast cars, wore sharp suits that accentuated his broad shoulders and trim gym-toned waist, hand-made shoes and expensive Italian aftershave of which Coco would have mightily approved. Despite being months away from turning forty, he had never married – although Juliet suspected he had a little black book full of women just waiting for him to call and propose. He emerged every so often from his own arse to acknowledge his gorgeousness and witness himself sending a million champagne bubbles of erotic shivers down female spines. He did well to milk it now for all it was worth, since in ten years' time, Juliet thought, he might have jowls like a Basset Hound and a bald patch the size of Mars.

Despite all three women having puffed themselves up with breathless anticipation, his eyes didn't even touch any of them as he passed by the open door. There was obviously a long wait to be had until Juliet could carve her double-barrel onto their joint four-poster bedhead.

Daphne let her breath out. 'If I were only twenty years younger . . .'

'You'd still be fifteen years too old for his tastes,' laughed Juliet. 'Even Amanda is too old and she's twenty-five.'

'Tell me about it,' huffed Amanda. 'Plus he likes blondes with legs up to the ceiling and boobies like beachballs.' At four foot eleven with short dark hair and a AA chest, she knew that Piers Winstanley-Black was more likely to look at blonde Daphne than her.

'If I roll my boobs up from my knees, I might be able to turn his eye,' chuckled Daphne.

'Daf, don't be gross. And I do believe it's your turn to put on the kettle,' said Juliet, in her best mock-authoritarian voice.

'Aye, lass,' said Daphne, getting to her feet. 'A cup of tea instead of sex. Story of my life.'

'And sadly mine,' replied Juliet, wondering what the magic key was to make Piers Winstanley-Black see her with man eyes. There had to be a key – with men there always was.

Chapter 3

Juliet's parents managed to restrain themselves until Sunday before they called by on the ridiculous pretext of borrowing a hammer.

'Dad, you've got more hammers than B and Q and Wickes put together!' laughed Juliet down the door entryphone.

'Yes, but I can't find my pin hammer anywhere,' said Perry Miller. His real name was Percy but the last person ever to call him that was a horrible old nun, Headmistress of Holy Family Infant School, County Cork.

'And it takes two of you to come over and carry it back, does it?' Juliet went on, winking over at Floz.

'Oh, let them in and stop teasing,' said Floz, whose eyes lit up like green emeralds when she smiled. 'They just want to make sure you haven't opened up your home to a homicidal maniac.'

'Come on up then,' sighed Juliet, pressing the lock-release button. 'I'll put the kettle on.'

Floz braced herself for their scrutiny. Years of shutting herself away at home to work had made her shy of strangers. She really need not have worried though, because Perry and Grainne Miller breezed into the flat, embraced her like a long-lost daughter, and soon they were all sitting at the dining-table sharing a pot of tea and a tin full of

date-and-walnut scones which Grainne – 'Call me Gron' –
had brought over.

Grainne and Perry were a very tall couple and Juliet was
physically like both of them. She had her father's cheeky grey
eyes and high cheekbones and her mother's large generous
mouth and sexy small gap between her front teeth. Grainne's
hair was short and greying now, but it had been long and jet
black in her youth; curly though, where Juliet's was poker
straight. Perry had a lovely thick head of snow-white hair and
the air of a very calm and gentle person.

'So, what is it you do for a job then, Floz?' asked Perry,
looking over at the tower of notebooks on the dining-table
which she had been perusing that morning.

'Don't be so nosy, Perry,' Grainne admonished him, her soft
Irish accent as strong now as it was when she moved to Barnsley
forty-five years ago.

'I'm not being nosy,' said the placid Perry. 'It's called making
conversation.'

'I don't mind answering,' Floz said and laughed. 'I'm a
freelance greetings-card copywriter.' She was forced to elaborate in response to the blank looks the Miller elders gave
her. 'Basically, I sit at my computer and churn out jokes and
rhymes day after day. The greetings-card companies buy
them from me.'

'Well, would you believe that?' said Grainne. 'I never
thought before who writes all the stuff you get on cards.'

'Mum will have bankrolled your companies in her time,'
said Juliet. 'She sends cards for any occasion. "Congratulations
on getting rid of your big spot". "Sorry to hear you've fallen
downstairs and bust your skull open". "Well done on throwing
your scumbag of a husband out of your life".'

Grainne jumped up and went over to the handbag she'd left
with her coat by the door.

'That reminds me.' She came back holding a red envelope

which she presented to Floz. 'It's a "Welcome to your new home" card,' she beamed.

'See?' said Juliet. 'QED!'

'Thank you, that's very kind of you,' smiled Floz, wondering whether to open it in front of everyone or save it until later. She decided on the former as Grainne was waiting with a wide arc of grinning anticipation on her face. Inside the envelope was a card with a big bun on the front with doors and windows in it. Inside, the message read: *Welcome to your new home, with lots of love from Grainne, Perry and Guy Miller.*

'Thank you, that's very thoughtful of you,' said Floz. 'Is Guy the cat?' She knew that the Millers had a cat because there was a photograph of her father holding one on Juliet's kitchen noticeboard. An ancient black cat, with one eye and no teeth. Obviously Guy wasn't the cat, from the hilarity that comment caused.

'He's my twin brother,' said Juliet. 'He lives with Mum and Dad.'

'Well, he lives in the granny flat adjoining our house,' added Grainne. 'I'm not sure he'd like to be classed as still living with his parents.'

Juliet turned in her seat and fiddled in the drawer of the dresser behind her. 'Look, this is him,' and she handed over a photograph of herself standing in between two huge men dressed in wrestling gear – one with flowing white-blond hair, and with a fur waistcoat on, the other with jet-black floppy curls and Perry's grey eyes, fringed with thick, dark lashes. Floz gulped. Square-jawed, tall, muscular Guy Miller was an absolute hunk. She felt her heartbeat quicken inside her.

'That's Steve Feast, Guy's best friend.' Juliet pointed to the blond man. She said his name in such a way that Floz guessed he wasn't one of her bosom buddies. 'And that is my brother. Where is Guy by the way, Mum? He's not been around yet for me to introduce him to Floz.'

'He's been working flat out at the restaurant,' replied Grainne. 'Poor boy is exhausted. That Kenny is a bloody slave-driver! I don't know why Guy doesn't tell him to stick his job.' Grainne's blood began to boil when she thought about the many liberties Kenny Moulding took with her son, making him work such long shifts.

'Oh now, Gron, the man has been good to Guy in his own way. He's always paid him very well for his services,' countered Perry, taking his pipe out of his pocket and clenching it between his teeth. He didn't light it in anyone else's house, he just liked the comfort of it on his lip.

Grainne huffed. 'Money is not everything, Perry. It doesn't buy you happiness.'

'Yes, I totally agree with you on that, my dear Gron. Still, it's nice to have. Oils the wheels of living.' Perry disarmed his wife with a smile. Floz thought it might be impossible to have an argument with such a calm and diplomatic man. He should have been serving in international peace-keeping missions. 'So how many card firms do you actually work for then?' Perry continued quizzing Floz.

'Seven,' Floz answered. 'Though I get a weekly brief from a firm called "Status Kwo" and they're the main suppliers of my bread and butter.'

'What do you do then? Do they send you some pictures and you have to write around them?'

'Sometimes,' said Floz. She picked up a file and opened it to show Perry pages full of thumbnail black and white images. 'They send me these pictures on a disk and I write copy for them, depending on what occasion they've asked me for. For instance, this picture of a woman swigging back a glass of wine – well, I could marry that to some copy for Mother's Day about a mum going for it and over-celebrating, or it could be a best friend card, about only drinking on days with an "a" in them, or it could be a Get Well card about eating grapes to get better but only when fermented and bottled. That sort of thing. Sometimes . . .' She rifled through the file for another brief '. . . all I get is an instruction to write rhymes for Father's Day or Valentine's Day. Then I'll send them in and their illustrators work around what I've written.'

'What a nice job. Is it well paid?'

'Perry Miller! You are obsessed with money today.' Grainne was disgusted her husband would be so cheeky as to ask that.

'It pays the bills,' replied Floz, grinning at Grainne's comical display of embarrassment. But she also knew they must all be thinking that it couldn't pay that much if she was in her mid-thirties and having to share a rented flat. She didn't enlighten them with details about her circumstances, but moved quickly on to show Perry an example of her weekly briefs from Lee Status – loony maverick owner of Status Kwo.

Juliet was on her third thickly buttered scone by now.

'Who made these, you or Guy?' she asked her mother through a mouthful of crumbs.

'You've answered your own question by eating them, dear,' said Perry. 'Your mother only makes scones for smash and grab robbers who are in short supply of bricks.'

'Cheeky thing, you are,' said Grainne, giving him a sharp but good-humoured nudge. 'Aye, Guy made a batch for you when he came in from work last night.'

'That was kind of him,' said Floz, wishing he could have delivered them in person.

'He bakes to unwind,' confided Grainne, her voice tight-ening as conversation touched upon the restaurant again. 'And my God does he need to unwind when he comes in from that place. After tomorrow he's taking a couple of days off, thank goodness.'

Floz took another bite of scone and thought that any man who baked like this had to be a catch. It was a long time since she had felt even a single butterfly in her stomach. But if Guy

Miller was anything like as good-looking in the flesh as he was in his photograph, Floz knew she'd be contending with butter-flies the size of eagles flapping around in her gut when they eventually met.

She couldn't have been more wrong if she'd tried.

Chapter 4

Guy Miller wasn't just tired, he was exhausted. He couldn't remember the last time he'd had a day off from working in the kitchens in the Burgerov restaurant. The owner Kenny Moulding was taking the piss, he knew. He had thrown most of the responsibility for his restaurant onto Guy with the excuse that he was a top-notch co-ordinator, but Guy had stopped buying into Kenny's flattery years ago. Guy knew he ran the business because Kenny couldn't be arsed – and though Kenny did pay him well, it wasn't nearly enough for the burden he shouldered. If he lost Guy, he would be totally stuffed. Also, there were three areas where Kenny refused to relinquish control: employing new staff, sacking his incompetent cheap labour, and the buying of foodstuffs from dodgy traders who arrived at the back door with hoods up and faces down. Kenny loved a bargain, which was what he said to justify being a total cheapskate. In fact, Kenny Moulding made Ebenezer Scrooge look like the Secret Millionaire.

Guy had been so run-down lately that Kenny was forced to give him some long-overdue days off. Anyway, Guy needed to seriously recharge his batteries before honouring his promise to help his best mate Steve out the next night. Steve was a self-employed plasterer by trade but it wasn't in that capacity that Guy would be assisting him. Steve's real passion was wrestling and he was a part-time amateur grappler who dreamed of working with the huge stars of GWE – Global Wrestling Enterprises – in America, where wrestling was still a seriously popular business. When Steve performed in the ring, he imagined that the billionaire bigshot promoter Will Milburn was out there in the shadows, talent-spotting – and so he gave every show his all.

Guy looked around at the kitchen staff pretending to clean up the work surfaces. He dreaded to think what would happen over the next couple of days when he was absent. He was tired from constantly picking them up on their hygiene skills, or lack of them. The only one he never had to nag was Gina. She was long and leggy and pretty and blonde and three years younger than him; in fact, Gina was everything on paper that would have made his ideal girlfriend. He knew that she stared at him with her big blue eyes when she felt it was safe to do so, because he had caught her off-guard a few times. And though he thought she was a nice girl, he wasn't drawn to look at her with any eyes other than those of an employer. Guy wasn't vain but it couldn't have been more obvious that Gina fancied the pants off him, and he often wished he felt something for her. Why couldn't people just switch on attraction? It would make life so much easier.

'Varto, why are you cleaning that work surface with the same cloth you've just used on the raw-meat board?' Guy tried to yell but he was too tired to raise much volume. How the heck someone hadn't died of salmonella in this place was anyone's guess. Varto was the oldest member of Kenny's cheap labour crew and more useless than the rest of them put together. Not half an hour ago, he had signed for and accepted a consignment of lamb which had arrived at the back door from a man with a balaclava on. It stank. Guy had gone as ballistic as his heavily depleted energy levels would allow and thrown the rancid meat in the wheelie bin. He had then poured the cheap washing-up liquid that Kenny bought in all over it so that Kenny wouldn't make Varto take it out again after Guy had left. And still he worried that Varto would do exactly that and wash it off and put it on the menu tomorrow.

Kenny Moulding had made a lot of money from cheap-meat burger and hot-dog stalls over the years. Certainly enough for him to have a holiday home in Dorset and a small boat, but not enough to spend on decent kitchen equipment or replacing the hideously tatty restaurant furniture. 'Make do and mend' was Kenny's philosophy, although if he had used that with his missus, he'd have been divorced before he even got to the end of the sentence. Burgerov was in a fabulous location, at the lip of the countryside in the quiet hamlet of Lower Hoodley, but it was near enough to town so that a taxi didn't cost a fortune. Its menu was surprisingly popular, but only because Guy worked long hours and far above the call of duty to make as much of a silk purse as he could out of the sow's ear of a place. Guy could do wonders with a rubbish cut of meat – he often fantasized about what he could do given quality cooking facilities, prime ingredients and some half-competent staff.

Once upon a time there had been a semblance of quality workers in Burgerov, but Kenny's increasing meanness had driven them all away and Kenny, who had less and less interest in the place as time passed, wasn't bothered about replacing quality with the same. He was setting on workers who couldn't tell one end of a spatula from another and considered it a breach of their human rights if they didn't have a fag break every ten minutes. Plus Glenys the cleaner was off with cystitis so they were all having to take over her duties too as Kenny hadn't arranged any cover.

Guy called goodnight and left his crew to finish off cleaning and clearing up, knowing that as soon as he was out of the door, they would down tools and light up cigarettes. All except dutiful Gina. But, for once, Guy switched off worrying about the place as soon as he got into his car. His brain was addled.

It was ridiculously chilly for an August night; maybe the meat-man had a balaclava on for warmth and not for disguise. Guy hated this time of year, when summer segued into brown, dark autumn – the season when things died and memories of sad times flooded back to him. In fact, he preferred to work stupid hours in these months. Filling his days with hard labour didn't allow him space to dredge up the past. Instead, unwelcome thoughts skittered across his brain like rusty leaves caught in the breeze, but did not settle. He wished he could have emptied his head of everything.

So exhausted was Guy that he failed to notice the *For Sale* sign that had been erected outside the gate of the old cottage on the road out to Maltstone, although, to be fair, the wind had blown it half into one of the overgrown conifers. Had he seen that, maybe it would have given him something far nicer to focus upon, because Guy Miller had been waiting for Hallow's Cottage to come onto the market ever since he was a little boy. And when he decided to make a detour and call in for a coffee with his sister, he had also forgotten that she had a new flat-mate and let himself in with his own key as usual.

Floz had just come out of the bath when she saw the door of the flat swing open. She expected to see Juliet home from the work schmooze she was going to. Instead, in strode a man, a huge man, with black wavy hair and the same grey eyes as Juliet and her father and the same full mouth as Grainne Miller. Her first thought was, Wow – it's Juliet's brother. Her second was, Yikes, I've got no make-up on, wet hair wrapped up in a towel, and am in my Dalmatian spotty dressing-gown. Not only that, but she had got shampoo in her eyes and had been rubbing them so much she just knew they'd be puffy and red.

Guy had but one thought when he saw Floz for the first time. *Lacey Robinson*. He gulped at the initial resemblance between the small woman in front of him and his old crush, and it threw him totally off-balance.

'Sorry,' he said, 'I forgot you were here. Floz, isn't it?'

'Er, yes,' said Floz, pulling her robe further around her. 'You must be . . .'

But Guy was already retreating to the door with the speed of a greyhound on amphetamines. And in his haste to get away from the scene, he fell backwards over a footstool, careered into a coffee-table and sent everything on it flying onto the carpet. Then, like a one-man *Carry On* film, he righted himself so quickly that he banged his head on the lampshade above him.

'Gotta go, sorry again,' he said, leaving Floz with the distinct impression that she must look like Linda Blair in *The Exorcist* as he slammed the door.

Floz stood open-mouthed. Jeez, am I that hideous? The sudden stab of hurt she felt exploded into a burst of anger. *How bloody rude!* She didn't care how much of a hunk he was physically; personality-wise he wasn't much of a gentleman. Then again, hadn't she learned by now that whenever she emerged from her shell, lured by a scent of love in the air, all she found was that some fist was waiting to smack her in the face and send her even further back inside it again?

Romantic thoughts of Guy Miller would no longer be allowed entry.

Chapter 5

Steve dialled on his phone and waited to see if she would pick up. She did and he breathed a sigh of relief that she hadn't fallen downstairs or turned on the oven and forgotten about it and burned the house down.

'Hello, who is it?' said a gruff, slurred voice.

'Hiya, Mum, it's me. How are you?'

'*Who* is it?'

'It's me, Steve. Mum, how are you?'

'I'm all right,' said the voice. 'Why wouldn't I be?' She was drunk. It was ten o'clock in the morning and she was plastered. After so many years it shouldn't have surprised him, but it still did.

'I'll be there in an hour. Do you need any shopping?'

'Just the usual.'

'Mum, I can't. You know I can't.' Steve's heart sank.

'Then don't bother coming,' and the phone line went dead.

Steve arrived at his mother's house an hour later hating himself for including the quarter bottle of vodka with the shopping. It was the smallest size he could find, and he knew she wouldn't acknowledge his existence otherwise.

The semi adjoining his mum's couldn't have been more different. Sarah Burrows's house had spotless windows, pretty curtains and a neat and tidy garden, with no trace of the usual sofas/car parts that posed as garden ornaments for many houses on this roughest end of the Ketherwood estate. And on the scrubbed step sat a small ten-year-old boy with a Barnsley foot-ball shirt on.

'Wotcher Denny,' smiled Steve. 'Nearly didn't recognize you there. Where's your specs, kiddo?'

'They got broke,' replied young Denny. The closer Steve got to him, the more Steve could see he had faint bruising on his eye too.

'You been scrapping?' asked Steve, a little concerned, because Denny Burrows wasn't a fighting lad. The Burrows didn't belong on this estate. Sarah Burrows was a hard-work-ing cleaner, a decent lass, and Denny was a quiet lad, always with a book in his hand.

Denny didn't answer him, just dropped his head. Steve strode over the fence and sat down next to the young boy on the step.

'You all right, son?' he asked.

'Yeah course,' said Denny, trying not to look obvious as he wiped away some water from his eyes.

'Oh hello, Steve,' said Sarah Burrows, appearing from behind them in the doorway. 'Do you want a cuppa? Denny – do you want some pop, love?'

Denny nodded and didn't speak, because his voice was all choked up. Steve didn't want to put Sarah to any trouble but he wanted to winkle out of young Denny what was up, so he said, 'Tell you what, make that two pops, will you, Sarah? Please.'

When Sarah had disappeared back into the kitchen, Steve left it for half a minute or so then nudged Denny.

'Come on then, kid. Tell your Uncle Steve what's up.'

'Nowt's up,' said Denny.

'You can tell me, you know.'

Denny opened his mouth as if he wanted to say something, then clamped it shut again.

'There's nowt.'

'Yes, there is,' said Sarah, appearing with two long tumblers of Diet Coke. 'I'm worried sick. It's an evil bastard by the name of Tommy Paget. This is the fifth time Denny's glasses have been broken this year. I didn't know any of this was going on until his eye got bashed. Then I found his little body's covered in bruises.'

'Denny, you've got to bash him back, son,' said Steve, putting an arm around the lad and feeling how small he was when he squashed him into his side.

'There's four of them,' put in Sarah. 'A gang. And the chuffing headmaster is about as much use as a chocolate chip pan. He's promised there will be no more incidences, but I'm sceptical. I'm keeping Denny off school for a few days because he's not sleeping. What state is that for a ten-year-old kid to be in?'

'Where's he live, this Tommy Paget?'

'Ooh no, Steve, you can't say anything to kids these days because it just makes them do it all the more,' said Sarah quickly.

'I'm not going to. I'm just asking where he lives.'

'Other side of the estate. Bridge Avenue. Number ninety-five, I think. You might know his dad – Artie Paget. Fancied himself as a bit of a boxer, once upon a time.'

'Artie Paget's his dad?' Oh yes, Steve knew Artie Paget all right.

'It's a horrible feeling, not being able to protect your own.' Sarah shook her head slowly from side to side. She looked totally worn out.

'You shouldn't be on this estate, love,' said Steve, looking around at the bloody awful place.

'You're telling me. I've had our name down for a transfer for well over two years now. I probably don't make as much fuss as some. *He who speaks loudest, gets heard first*, don't they say? But at least I can keep an eye on your mum for you whilst I'm here. She sometimes lets me in.'

Steve smiled sadly. 'Thanks so much, Sarah.'

'I wish I could do more,' Sarah replied with a heavy sigh.

'I know what you mean.' It was ironic how Christine Feast clung to her right to destroy herself with cheap booze. Life was so precious and yet Christine Feast had never seemed to want it.

Steve drained his pop and gave young Denny an affectionate nudge before stretching to his feet. 'You have any more trouble, you tell me,' Steve said. 'I'll teach you some self-defence moves.'

'I've just started karate,' said Denny proudly, sniffing back the last of his tears because he felt better now, having Steve on his side. 'I go on Wednesday nights.'

'Big Jim's on Buckley Street?'

'That's the place,' said Sarah.

'He taught me as well,' said Steve. 'He's a good teacher, is Jim. If you tell him you know me, he'll give you a bit of a discount.'

'I don't like to be cheeky,' Sarah bristled. Steve smiled at the proud young woman and wished his mam had an ounce of her dignity.

'Sod that,' he said, knowing that Sarah didn't have a lot of money to spare. 'Have you got all your gear yet?'

'He said I can do it in my tracksuit for now,' said Den.

'Here.' Steve delved into his pocket and pulled out a few notes. 'Go and get yourself kitted out.'

'Don't you dare take that money, Dennis,' said Sarah, leaping to stop the transfer of funds.

'It's not for you, it's for the bairn.' Steve pushed the notes into Denny's hand. 'Go on, you take it, son. A bloke once did the same for me as I'm doing for young Dennis,' Steve lied, to protect Sarah's pride. He too had been in his tracksuit until he was given the cast-off karate suit from Jim's own son.

'It's an interest-free loan. I want it back when you get your black belt, okay?'

Steve wouldn't take no for an answer. Sarah begrudgingly gave him an annoyed thank you. She never had been a sponger. The little she had, she had earned herself.

Steve climbed over the adjoining fence and took a fortifying breath before trying the handle on his mum's front door.

She sometimes forgot to lock it – something else he worried constantly about. He pushed open the door, steeling himself for what he'd find inside. He could smell smoky grime in the air. The central heating was on boiling, which warmed up the awful odours but didn't blend them. They circulated around each other instead like some weird plug-in air-freshener: cigarettes, sweat, something rotten – and yet he'd cleaned up only a couple of days ago, emptied the bins and left the place smelling half-decent.

'Hello, Mum,' said Steve tenderly, awakening her from a nap. Christine Feast was sitting upright on the sofa, swaddled in a blanket. Her eyes slowly opened and her head turned in his direction but she viewed him with as much emotion as she would a lampstand.

Her hair, which had been grey for as long as he could remember, was so thin these days. He wanted to brush it so it was neat around her face, but he'd tried that before and she wouldn't let him.

'I've brought you some things. There's an egg mayo sandwich here. Your favourite.' He reached in the carrier bag and pulled out a fresh, brown bap.

'I'm not hungry,' she said. Her eyelids started falling again. She was drunk, of course. He couldn't remember the last time he'd seen her sober. Her body clock didn't work any more; she dozed for a few hours, drank, dozed again, drank some more . . . sometimes she made it to the bathroom, sometimes she didn't.

She told her son to sod off when he tried to clean up a bit for her; she wouldn't let him take her to the doctor and resisted all attempts to let him lift her up from the sofa so she could change out of her urine-soaked clothes. Social Services wouldn't interfere and now Steve didn't know what to do other than come around and just hope for a miracle. The shop on the corner would not refuse her alcohol, however much Steve had begged them. Christine also paid the older kids on the estate to buy it for her.

'I'm wrestling tonight,' he said. It was as if she was in a coma and the only way to reach her was by talking normally, willing her to wake up and respond. She never did. 'I'm the good guy. The Angel.'

He sat with her for an hour and talked and she heard nothing. Then he put some money in her hand in the hope that she wouldn't buy drink with it. But he knew she would.

Chapter 6

As Guy, resplendent in swirling villain's black cape and black satin shorts, cut through the cheering, jeering crowd, arthritic old pensioners sprang up, agile as athletes, pushing to the aisles to batter him with their handbags. He ran the gauntlet, spitting and snarling, then climbed cockily through the ropes into the ring, took off his plastic crown, ripped off his cape and handed them to the assistant's waiting hands.

'Ladies and gentlemen, tonight for your entertainment,' began the dramatic, broad Yorkshire build-up over the PA system, 'it's the mad, it's the bad, it's the dangerous, the one you love to hate, the one and only CRUSHER KINGSTONE,' the name being drowned in a fresh crescendo of jeering as the massive, black-haired lad sprang forwards into the centre of the ring. There waiting for him, in white shorts with wings attached to his shoulders, was a silver-blond man standing nose to nose with him at six foot four exactly.

'And D and E Wrestling Entertainment is proud to present his opponent, the magnificent, the angelic, the good, the beautiful, the divine and the heavenly STEEEVE ANGEL.'

The mood of the crowd turned to one of cheering as the huge muscular angel-man raised his hand and greeted the throng before taking off his wings and handing them to the same ring assistant for safe-keeping.

The referee, Little Eric, stretched up to his full height of five foot three, and pulled down on the two large men's shoulders.

'Now, lads, I want a good, fair fight – and remember, Angel, you're going down in the third from a Boston Crab. Best of luck, lads. Give 'em a good show, for fuck's sake.'

Steve nodded and smiled widely at Guy, proffering his hand. Guy snarled and slapped it away, prompting every able-bodied pensioner in the hall to rise to his or her feet in a chaotic Mexican wave of gravelly boos and gnarled old fists.

'There's plenty of time before that Boston Crab, so you watch yourself,' whispered Steve, squaring up.

'Do your worst!' said Guy, reaching over and throttling him with no further warning.

It was a short but thrilling bout. As the first-aiders carried off a damaged Angel, dramatically howling on a stretcher that his back was broken, Guy strolled around the ring sponging up the jeers before braving the run through the passionately angry throng back to the safety of the changing rooms. Steve hopped off the stretcher just before the bearers turfed him off as they would need to be back at ringside shortly to carry off Tarzan and the Apeman after being walloped by the Pogmoor Brothers.

'Thanks! You nearly broke my spine that time,' Steve said to Guy, reaching round to rub his aching back. 'I much prefer it when I'm the Dark Angel and you're Guido Goodguy. You're a nasty bugger when you're the villain – worse than Alberto Masserati.'

Guy grinned at the mention of the infamously brutal local wrestler. 'If you can't stand the heat, get out of the kitchen, as we say in my profession.'

'Your ear's bleeding,' said Steve.

'Aye, I thought it was sore,' said Guy, rubbing it and then checking his finger. 'One of the old ones lamped me when I ran off. I swear they still put bricks in their handbags.'

They shipped the OAPs in from all over the place when

there was a bout anywhere within reasonable travelling distance, and for a couple of hours they became spring chickens again, before reverting to the knackered old cocks and hens who climbed wearily on the bus back to their residential homes. How they had got away with never having to stop a match for someone to be carted off with a heart attack, was anyone's guess. Steve liked them, though. He loved that he was partly responsible for awakening that old passion in them, even if it lasted just long enough to boil a soft egg. Most of them remembered the glory days of British wrestling, and these evenings were a hark back to their youthful past.

Every Christmas Guy and Steve, the Pogmoor Brothers tag team, Big Bad Davy, Klondyke Kevin and some of the other wrestlers took chocolates and a few bottles of beer and wine up to Daffodil House near Penistone and saw these same crazed old buggers from their audiences sitting in their chairs, staring at TV screens and into space as if their spirits had been stored in mothballs until the next outing to the Centennial Rooms Wrestling Nights. No, Steve never minded if they loved him or hated him when he was grappling in character, just that they enjoyed him.

'Seriously, mate, thanks for stepping in,' said Steve. 'I know you're not getting much time off at the moment.'

'Ah, don't worry.' Guy waved the thanks away. 'Couldn't see you without a partner tonight, could I?'

Little Derek the promoter was a man down thanks to Flamboyant Fred Zeppelin's broken wrist. He was lucky to get only that, as he sustained it during a bout with Alberto Masserati, who ignored whatever stage directions Little Eric and Little Derek gave out and always went for the kill. Alberto turned into a borderline sadist once he was in that ring. In fact, no one would get in with him, except big Fred, because he was so fearsome. And yet out of the ring Alberto was a mild-mannered family man who ran a small but jovial pub and loved nothing better than to cook and entertain and watch opera.

There might have been a lot of theatre in wrestling, but injuries were common. A large part of it was 'stage-managed', but when a thirty-stone Apeman did a body-slam on his contender, there was no guarantee it wouldn't at the very least crack a rib.

'Pint?' said Steve, rubbing the towel quickly over his platinum hair after a freezing shower. It looked like it was heavily peroxided, but it was totally natural. His paternal grandfather had been Swedish – though Steve had never met him – and handed the white-blond gene in its entirety to his only grandson. It caught and possessively held any light and illuminated him so much, it made him look as if he was wearing a halo. After a bout once, when his on-stage persona was Thor Svensson, the Viking Warrior, a drunken bird had said to him: 'Ooooh, you look like an Angel.' Then she threw up all over his 120-quid brand new trainers.

All things in consideration, he liked the name and used it from then on.

'Then you can tell me what's going on in your tiny brain,' Steve continued.

Guy stopped momentarily from combing his black waves in the mirror he always had to bend to see in. He had been about to tell Steve about meeting Floz, then thought better of it.

'Nothing's going on in my brain.'

Steve huffed. 'Yeh, and I'm Ronnie Corbett!' Guy carried on combing. 'You've gone quiet and are doing that Heathcliff glowering thing. You always do that when you've got something on your mind.'

'You sound like our Juliet,' replied Guy, since she had been the first to comment that her twin brother turned into a mean and moody Heathcliff when his thoughts were preoccupied.

Steve knew he'd probably be able to winkle it out of Guy over a pint and thought he'd change the subject for now.

'So, what's Ju's new flat-mate like then?'

Guy groaned and shook his head.

'That bad eh?' Steve grimaced.

'Oh boy,' said Guy, throwing the comb into his holdall. It missed. He muttered an expletive as he bent to pick it up.

'What the hell is up with you?' prodded Steve.

They were interrupted by Little Derek, the promoter, who came into the changing rooms waving two brown envelopes.

'Nice work, Steve! Fifty quid and an extra ten for your expenses. Next bout will be back here on Tuesday the thirty-first. I'll ring you with the details. Good to see you back, Guy. You up for some more, lad?'

'Nope,' said Guy definitively. 'This was a favour to Steve. I'm too busy, Derek.'

Derek smiled paternally. He had been involved in the business since he was a teenager and clung to the illusion that it was on the brink of a massive comeback. He would never admit to himself that the wrestling game was dead in this country. Each bout had to be expertly stage-managed to get the punters in, playing on their nostalgia for better days with larger-than-life characters such as Giant Haystacks, Catweazle, Big Daddy, 'Rollerball' Rocco, Jim Breaks: the guys everyone loved to love and loved to hate. Derek couldn't remember how many times he and Guy had had this same conversation: that he was only doing 'this last one' to help Steve out, and it would be his last. It never was his last. He knew he'd get a few more fights out of him if Steve was stuck for a partner.

'Trust me,' said Derek. 'It's only a matter of time before we catch up with the Americans, and the home of wrestling returns to Britain. And I'll be ready when it does. Millionaires, those wrestlers are out there – millionaires and superstars. And when I get rich, you'll get rich.' He presumed everyone was as focused on money as he was. It wouldn't have occurred to him that the lads wrestled for the love of it. 'I have to keep my little girl in designer gear.'

'Oh yes, your Chianti. How . . . how is she . . . Chianti?'

said Steve, doing a very bad impression of nonchalance as his voice always tended to rise three octaves on her name whilst the rest of the sentence stayed in bass. He sounded like a yodeller who has had too much schnapps.

'Someone mention me?' Right on cue, glossy Chianti Parkin, the twenty-five-year-old daughter of Little Derek, appeared in the doorway with her skinny legs, pneumatic breasts and long tumbles of golden hair extensions, courtesy of some poor woman in Russia trading her locks in for the price of a couple of loaves of bread.

'Oh hi, Chianti, are you well?' asked Steve, scratching the back of his neck nervously.

'Yeah, I'm great,' replied Chianti, whilst chewing the life out of her gum. She afforded Steve a second of her attention then flicked her eyes away from him and back to Little Derek.

'Just came to say I'm off, Dad. Wayne's here to pick me up.'

'Goodbye, love. Have a good night,' said Little Derek softly and proudly, and he kissed his daughter on her cheek. Steve watched Chianti turn and sashay off in her thigh-length boots and short, swingy skirt. A low animal growl rose in his throat and he swallowed it quickly.

'She's off to Four Trees tonight. You know, that fancy restaurant out on the Pennines with the long waiting list. Some businessman or other – Wayne. Big flash car he's got, obviously. She won't look at anything less than a personalized number-plate. Course he won't last, they never do. Use and abuse, that's our Chianti.' Derek sighed fondly at his daughter's sadistic tendencies towards men, then snapped back to business. 'Anyway – got to dash. Tata, lads, and thanks. Good one.' He gave them a thumbs-up and disappeared back to the front of house to watch the tag teams then the final act, Grim Reaper (whose entrance in a cloud of dry ice always raised the blood pressure of the pensioners by three zillion per cent, submit to twenty-two-stone Jeff Leppard's stranglehold. The old ones liked to see the Grim Reaper defeated.

'Chianti Parkin.' Steve's sigh said it all.

'You can do better than her,' Guy replied. Chianti Parkin didn't do much for him. She gave off a very cold vibe – and Steve needed someone soft and warm and a nest-builder to make up for all that he had missed. He couldn't imagine Chianti in an apron rustling him up a shepherd's pie and welcoming him home from work each night with open arms.

'How's your mum?' was Guy's next question.

Steve sighed again – a heavy, sad sigh this time. 'The same, really. I went up today but she was out of it. Then again last week I took her some fish and chips and she wolfed the lot. It was just nice to see her eat something.'

Guy knew that Steve would have seen that as a result. Christine Feast sometimes wouldn't even let her son into the house. It all depended on how paranoid she felt at the time. Christine had been a chronic alcoholic since Steve was a small child. She came from a family of drinkers and didn't fight the pattern.

'She's the size of a baby bird,' Steve went on, wrestling with the tremor in his voice. Then he coughed and batted thoughts of his mum out of his brain for now. 'Anyway, never mind about me and mine, we're going for a beer and you're going to tell me why you've been walking around like Adrian frigging Mole all night.' He bet it was woman trouble. And Steve knew all about woman trouble. Chianti was less attainable than Kylie Minogue.

Like the whole Miller family, Steve wished that Guy would find a good woman and settle down. He was sure and steady and built for having a family to work for and enjoy. And he really deserved a bit of happiness after all the shit he had been through. Different sort of shit to what he himself had been through, but shit all the same.

Guy swung his giant holdall over his shoulder. 'If I tell you, not a word, and I mean not one bloody word to Juliet.'

'You can trust me to be discreet,' returned Steve, mortally affronted.

'Aye, well I can't trust *her*,' said Guy. In the School of Indiscretion, his twin sister was Headmistress. A horrible memory flashed past of his secret Valentine's card to Michaela Hall being outed (design courtesy of *Blue Peter* two nights previously: cornflakes packet, sticky-back plastic, school glue, red poster paint and Trill budgie food). He couldn't listen to Chrissie Hynde singing 'Talk of the Town' without breaking out into a cold sweat.

'So, what have I not to tell Juliet then?' said Steve, at the end of his patience. He pushed open the door which creaked arthritically and they walked out into the warm mid-August night air.

'It's this new flat-mate of Juliet's. I made a right arse of myself last night in front of her.'

'Oh aye, what did you do? Trip over the coffee-table and land at her feet?' Steve laughed.

The look that Guy threw him told him he wasn't far off the truth.

Steve listened to Guy's recollection of their first meeting. The way Floz looked small and vulnerable, snuggled up in a spotty dressing-gown, and how, just for a moment, he'd had a panicky flashback to Lacey. And he finished up by telling Steve how he'd made the most unchivalrous and puerile exit imaginable.

'It's not exactly a big deal, is it?' said Steve. He knew Guy's type of woman – long and leggy with golden hair, give or take the unfortunate blip that was tiny, dark Lacey Robinson. 'Anyway, why are you so bothered what a short bird dressed up like a Dalmatian thinks of you?'

Guy exhaled a long, heavy breath. 'Because she was bloody gorgeous.'

Chapter 7

Just as Guy was admitting to Steve how blown away he had been by the sight of her even with no make-up and big red eyes, Floz's mobile rang and she picked it up immediately on seeing the name on the screen.

'I need ten really saucy Valentine's cards prontissimo,' said Lee Status, his voice breezing down the line with his usual confidence. 'At least two blow-job jokes and a few "nice-tits" poems, if you don't mind.'

Floz laughed. 'No worries, Lee. When do you want them for?'

'Yesterday.'

'Don't you want any nice, sweet, secret-admirer ones?' suggested Floz.

'Nope. The youth of today are sexually aggressive and don't bother with foreplay. They head straight for the genitals.'

'Okay,' sighed Floz. 'I'll have them done for you tonight.'

'Thursday morning's the deadline really,' he said, and the phone cut off immediately. Lee Status was a busy man with no time for excess chit-chat.

Her head didn't begin whirring into action straight away, as it usually did after a brief was received. Instead Floz wondered how she would feel receiving a card telling her that she had nice tits. She must be getting terribly old because it wouldn't really have made her melt, even if George Clooney had sent it to her. Surely Valentine's cards should be romantic, not too slushy, with a soupçon of spice – like the one Nick had sent from Canada. A white background with a tiny heart on the front and inside the words: *I just want to pick you up, bring you over here and love you.* Her own heart flared at the thought of it and she stamped it down again. No point in nudging those thoughts back to life.

She'd not really understood what had happened there. Why a romance full of such honesty and promise had just ended so abruptly, why he wouldn't answer his phone or reply to her emails. It had been eighteen months since he cut off all contact but, as she found out, from her thoughts merely brushing against the memory of that card, the hurt lingered still.

She obviously scared men. She only had to think back to the previous evening and that first encounter with Guy Miller. It had taken mere seconds of being in her presence to have him tearing off at warp speed with such a look of horror on his face that she'd had to check in the mirror to make sure she hadn't suddenly grown snakes on her head. That scene had haunted her ever since. Had he seen the flash of attraction in her eyes and been revolted by it? Or scared he'd be turned into stone? Well, just in case, the next time she encountered the big twerp, she would show him that his idiotic behaviour hadn't affected her in the slightest and that she had no designs on him whatso-ever. She would be as aloof as an ice-queen.

She opened up a file on her laptop and named it *Val-risqué* then let her mind wander down the avenue of smutty jokes. Not for the first time she thought that maybe her destiny was to write about love for other people, and never receive it herself.

Chapter 8

Juliet floated through the front door of Blackberry Court the next evening with Coco 'in tow'. She had just spent the last hour in the illustrious personal space of Piers Winstanley-Black and his cloud of expensive aftershave. She was sure his pupils were dilated when they made contact over the *Brownlee vs Goldman* file. It wasn't her imagination, he was edging closer to her net, she could feel it. But like a patient fisherman, she would wait until her trout came near enough to tickle.

And to top a very nice day, the delicious aroma of stew curled up Juliet's nostrils as she pushed open the flat door.

'Oh. My. God. What is that beautiful smell?'

'Beef hash and dumplings,' answered Floz, who was sitting at the dining-table scribbling work-notes. 'I made enough for a few helpings if you're interested.'

'Oh, you divine creature,' said Coco, kicking off his shoes. 'I'm deffo staying for tea. I've only had a Crunch Corner all day. Are we having cake afterwards? I should have desserts to hand at all times with my sugar levels. Marlene's off sick and we had a right rush on so I couldn't even run out to Greggs.'

'I knew you'd be a perfect flat-mate, Floz,' smiled Juliet, sliding off her stilettos and wiggling her toes. And that was the truth too. This was only Floz's seventh evening in Blackberry Court but it seemed as if she had been there forever. The flat felt warmer and it was so nice to come home to the lights on and company and smells like these.

'I thought Guy had been round again and brought us dinner,' said Juliet. She saw a little head-shake from Floz when she mentioned his name and wondered why they seemed to have taken such an instant aversion to each other. She didn't expect them to start snogging when they met, but neither did she expect whatever had happened at their initial meet to scar them both for life.

When Floz mentioned that Guy had popped around on Monday night, she hadn't said much more than he had forgotten she had moved in and was embarrassed by that. No, he hadn't introduced himself properly, in fact he had been in and out within a minute. Yes, Floz had presumed from his physique and looks that he was Juliet's twin and not some burglar who happened to have a key. Juliet noticed how clipped Floz's tone was as she recounted the story. For whatever reason, she hadn't been impressed by Guy. Juliet wondered if he had had his scary Heathcliff face on when they met.

Juliet being Juliet had then rung Guy on his mobile and demanded to know why he hadn't told her he'd been around and met her new flat-mate.

'I've been too busy!' he snapped.

'What – helping *Steve Feast* out with his stupid wrestling?' huffed Juliet. She had a special tone reserved for her brother's best friend – one of disdain and dislike, but tempered with the slightest begrudging gratitude for all he had done for Guy in his dark days.

'Anyway, what did you think?' she went on.

'Think about what?' hedged Guy, not wanting to get drawn into verdicts.

'Floz – what did you think about her?'

'I didn't think anything about her,' said Guy. 'She was half-undressed when I burst in so I made my excuses and left.'

And he refused to be drawn on any more detail than that. From this, Juliet deduced that Floz hadn't made an impression on him either. Which was a shame because he was far too nice to be alone and it might have been good for them both if there had been a mutual attraction. Even if Guy was the boy she used to batter with her Tiny Tears doll and fight with over their jointly owned Stylophone. (She always won, despite the size difference because it was imprinted in his DNA: 'Thou shalt always be gentle with the fairer sex.')

There were so many ostentatious sods out there charming the drawers off women – and gay men, as Juliet had seen with the disaster that was Coco's love-life – with frilly false promises that Guy and his quiet non-flash solidity was totally over-looked. Correction, with his height and build he couldn't fail to pull in a first glance, but he never managed to secure the second – and that was the important one.

Juliet popped the cork out of a bottle of Cab Sav and poured three generous glasses.

'Here, stop working and have a swig,' she said, nosying over Floz's shoulder. 'What are you writing?'

'Valentine's cards,' replied Floz. 'Smutty ones for Status Kwo.'

' "I think you're super smashing, I just love you to bits. I cannot wait to kiss you. And squeeze your gorgeous XXXs",' Coco read over her other shoulder. 'What a brilliant job you have, Floz.'

'Not exactly Keats, is it?' she smiled back at him.

'It would work for me,' mused Juliet. 'If Piers Winstanley-Black sent it, anyway.'

'Who's Piers Winstanley-Black?' asked Floz.

'You haven't told her about PWB yet?' Coco feigned a faint. 'You must be the only person in the universe who isn't aware of his name.'

'Ignore him. Piers is only the most gorgeous man in the universe,' replied Juliet with a girly sigh. 'Solicitor, thirty-nine wonderful years old, eyes the colour of a Caribbean sea and lips like red pillows.'

'Yuk,' said Coco. 'You were doing so well until you got to the lips part, Ju.'

'Single?' enquired Floz.

'Absolutely,' said Juliet with vehemence. 'I don't lust after any taken property. Not after what happened to me.'

'What happened to you, Juliet?'

'You haven't told her that either!' gasped Coco. He sank onto the sofa and got ready for the floorshow.

'Where to begin?' laughed Juliet, reaching in the drawer behind her and pulling out a half-eaten box of Thorntons which she handed over to Floz to choose from. Even in that they matched – Juliet preferred all the pralines, Floz didn't. Jack Sprat and his wife didn't have anything on them.

'Well, I was married to Roger for six years,' Juliet began. 'Last July – two weeks after our anniversary, when he bonked me in every room of our brand new three-bedroomed house – I came home early from work to find him rather courteously preparing to pack a suitcase for me.'

Floz's mouth dropped open.

'Apparently, our marriage was over. And it was all my fault.' There was a brief pause whilst Juliet grabbed a couple of pralines and Floz's mouth sprang further open. 'Roger explained that all the little things that had once attracted him to me had become big things that revolted him. Somewhere along the line I had ceased to be amusing and become raucous. Stopped being saucy and become vulgar. I was no longer a voluptuous goddess but a fat cow. That was the reason, he said, why he was having an affair with my best friend, Hattie.'

'*Our* best friend,' amended Coco. 'We had all been at school together since nursery. I couldn't believe I hadn't spotted it. My intuition is usually as sharp as Sinbad the sailor's cutlass.'

'Blimey,' said Floz, for want of a better word. 'What did you do?' She wouldn't have fancied being the 'best friend' after Juliet had found that out.

'I let him have his say, of course,' purred Juliet, in the manner of Fenella Fielding in *Carry On Screaming*. 'Then I grabbed him by the scruff of the neck and chucked him and the empty suitcase out of the front door. Then I threw the contents of his wardrobe out of the bedroom window for him so *he* could pack *his* suitcase instead of mine. Oh, then I rang one of the solicitors I work with.'

Karren Brookside was an evil Bitch Queen from hell. She didn't just get blood for her (female only) clients, she got the veins, arteries, all internal organs and both testicles. Then she served them up on gold plates with a nice 1945 Château Pétrus. Karren Brookside made Hannibal Lecter look like Anne of Green Gables.

'Roger's balls were in his wallet – so that was the best place to kick him,' said Juliet, who seemed to be enjoying the story of her divorce. 'He was begging me to take him back and forget and forgive everything after a month of Karren's savagery.'

'But you didn't?'

'No, I did not,' replied Juliet, horrified that Floz had even considered she might. Unlike her brother, Juliet had always had a great sense of self-worth, and woe betide anyone who tried to mess with her.

Juliet had made her errors with men in the past, but once she had realized she wasn't top of their agenda, she had cut and run. Her first boyfriend, Pete, was a nice enough bloke but when she twigged that all those cosy nights in were because he didn't want his mates to realize he was seeing a rather large lady, he was history. Then there was Gary, who never turned up without bringing chocolates and spent a fortune on taking her out for meals, insisting she have dessert. She thought she had landed a lottery win to find a man who celebrated her curves so enthusiastically. Then she discovered his secret stash of American videos: huge women-whales being fed cream cakes, unable to move and totally dependent on their feeder. After finishing with him, it took her weeks to look an eclair in the face again.

'What about you, Floz?' asked Coco. 'How's your love-life been?'

Floz looked a bit shy to have the spotlight shone on her.

'Couple of boyfriends in my teens but nothing that serious, married for ten years to Chris. We just drifted apart and divorced three years ago.'

That was a bit boring, thought both Juliet and Coco, who had been hoping for more of a trade-off of information. Coco pressed for more.

'How do you just drift apart?'

'I don't know. We just fell out of love with each other.' Floz shrugged shyly.

'No one since?' poked Juliet.

'No one,' replied Floz too quickly. 'What about you? Anyone since Roger?'

'No,' said Juliet flatly. 'No, no one since him – I've been saving myself for Piers Winstanley-Black. But a year is a long time to go without sex. If we ever do get it together he'll find my fanny full of cobwebs,' she chuckled, making Coco shriek with disgust. 'I don't know how you've done three years of celibacy, Floz.'

'I've only done a month,' said Coco. 'And that's been bad enough.'

'What's your story, Coco?' asked Floz. 'Is that your real name?'

'It is now,' he nodded. 'You can tell her if you like, Ju.'

Coco covered his ears whilst Juliet leaned over to Floz and whispered, 'His real name is Raymond, but he hates it. One must only ever refer to him as Coco.'

'Ah, I see,' said Floz, who couldn't think of anyone who

looked less like a Raymond. Probably because one of her head-masters had been called that and he was a huge, square man who played rugby and spoke with a Lee Marvin voice. 'Is that because you've got eyes the colour of cocoa?'

'Floz, I'm in love with you,' said Coco, clasping his hands together with delight. 'What a lovely thing to say.'

'No, it's because he wants to be Coco Chanel,' said Juliet. 'His shop is covered with pictures of her. Plus it's his favourite perfume.'

'Anyway, back to my love-life: awful.' Coco ripped a tissue out of a nearby box.

'He falls in love at the drop of a hat. And they're all dysfunctional bastards,' cut in Juliet. 'He couldn't pick a good man if he landed in his lap with a recommendation from God Himself.'

'I don't know what happened with Darren,' said Coco. 'One minute everything was fine, the next he wouldn't answer my texts or take my phone calls. He just disappeared. No explanation, no goodbye – nothing.' His eyes filled up with bright tears.

'Silence is a cruel weapon to use,' Floz said gently.

'I know,' agreed Juliet. 'Not having the decency to say "we're over" to someone is gutless and vicious. And Darren would have known that Coco would rip himself apart over it to find the reason why it happened. Not that he cared enough to spare him that.'

'You'll have heard this before, but you really are worth more than that sort of treatment.' Floz's voice was soft and kind. 'It's not respectful – and do you really want a man who treats you with such little thought?'

'I know,' said Coco, dabbing his eyes. 'At least, my head knows, my heart has a little catching up to do. Of course, he may just be taking some time away to sort his feelings out. Men are like elastic bands, apparently . . .'

'Coco, what possible excuse could he have? Unless he was the new Terry Waite and had both hands tied to a radiator by international terrorists, there is absolutely no excuse at all for that sort of crap behaviour,' said Juliet, a little impatiently now because they'd had this conversation too many times. 'I can't understand why you'd want him back anyway. If he did have the absolute cheek to turn up in your life again, I would tell him to f—'

Coco clamped his hands over his ears as Juliet launched into a diatribe.

'Closure helps to move us on,' said Floz, counterbalancing Juliet's Ian Paisley-type rant with her own softer perspective. 'It's hard when you don't get it.'

'Coco, I've told you before: if they don't give you closure, you have to take it for yourself. His gutless, bastard silence is all the sign of closure that you need.' Aware that her words were hard, Juliet put her arm around Coco and pulled him into her shoulder. 'Floz is right, you are worth so much more. And your dream man is out there somewhere with your name tattooed on his arse.'

Coco half-laughed, half-cried at that.

'Least he wasn't a pervert like the one before.' Juliet winked at Floz. She knew telling that particular story would cheer Coco up.

'Perfume rep. Courted me, moved in with me and then decided he wasn't sure if he was fully gay. He wanted to sleep with a woman to see if he'd like it. How bloody disgusting can you get,' snarled Coco through gritted teeth.

It made Floz giggle to see Coco shivering at the thought of such a major perversion.

'I think we all need a decent boyfriend,' Juliet said, remembering Coco's recent idea. '*Yeeesss* indeedy. Let's sign onto a site and find some hot males. They are as rare as rocking-horse dung at this age.' She made a grab for her laptop on the bookshelf, opened it and logged on.

'Try *singlebods.com*,' chirped Coco. 'That's what Marlene used. She said it's the best one at the moment.'

'So you don't fancy your brother's friend Steve then?' Floz asked Juliet.

'Steve Feast? You are *so* joking.' Juliet laughed hard. 'He's a complete and utter knob. Always has been.'

'He went to school with us too,' explained Coco. 'He was always pulling Ju's plaits or running off with her hat so she would chase him.'

'And he grew up to be even more puerile,' continued Juliet, topping up the wine glasses. 'I used to see him in pubs picking up two women at once on his shoulders to prove how strong he was or showing off his muscles with cut-off T-shirts.'

'He's all right, really,' put in Coco.

'No he isn't, Coco. He's a big ponce. Always chasing women and none of them stick around very long – which tells you something.'

'He's been a very good friend to Guy,' Coco added – then, from the look that Juliet threw at him, realized he shouldn't have said that. 'Whoops.' He put his fingertips to his lips.

Floz wondered what Coco had said that was so wrong, but didn't feel as if she should ask.

Juliet pulled her focus back to the job in hand. 'Okay. Right, you go first, Floz.'

'Not a chance,' Floz said. Her voice was as firm as her vocal cords would allow. 'I don't want to do internet dating.'

But Juliet didn't hear her. She was on a mission now. 'What's your ideal man look like?' she asked.

'I'm really not interested—'

'Oh please,' said Coco, giddy as a kipper now and clapping his hands excitedly. 'It'll be a laugh, especially if we all do it. We'll put your details in first.'

'Not interested in the slightest.' Floz was adamant. Juliet, however, had a bit of a problem hearing the word 'no'. She tried a different tack to persuade Floz to join in.

'Okay then, humour me: if you were to do this, what would

he look like? I promise I won't do anything with the information. I'm just being nosy.'

'Promise?'

'Promise.'

'Okay then.' Floz tried to think. If she painted her ideal man, Juliet would pick up on the fact that she was describing Guy. Guy who obviously hated her on sight so much that he backed off from her like Count Dracula did from Van Helsing. So she lied and plumped for everything that was *not* Guy sodding Miller. 'Not too tall, fair hair . . . brown eyes.'

'Dress?'

'Suit.'

'Job?'

'Something in an office, I think.'

'Oh please do it with us,' begged Coco. 'It will be such a laugh.'

'No,' said Floz, with steel in her voice. 'But if you two are adamant, then take my advice: be very careful. Don't pick someone too far away to meet up with, and when you do click with someone, arrange to see them as soon as you can. You don't want to fall for someone who doesn't really exist as they paint themselves. Meeting them is the only way to determine if you really fancy each other or not.'

'Oooh, you sound as if you're speaking from experience, Floz,' said Juliet, eyes narrowed suspiciously.

'No,' returned Floz. 'I'm speaking from much reading of magazine articles, much watching of *Jeremy Kyle* and good old-fashioned commonsense. Be very, very careful.'

Floz lay in bed that night unable to get to sleep because something had awoken inside her. Feelings she had pressed down on for so long sprang up like an escapee jack-in-a-box and wouldn't be squashed down again. And it was all Juliet's brother's fault. She couldn't understand why he had affected her so much and why it stung that he had run off like that. How dare he make her feel that bad about herself? She careered between hurt and anger, both emotions keeping away the possibility of any sleep. She hadn't fancied anyone in ages – in fact, she'd wondered if she ever would again. Then in swanned Guy Miller and made her realize that her heart was more than capable of revving up interest in someone. The trouble was, when a heart opened, vulnerability was the first thing to rush in.

The Guy Miller episode combined with the Valentine's brief had stirred up deeper and more dangerous memories. Thoughts of Nick Vermeer had loomed large and colourful in her head again and would not lie still.

Two and a half years ago, she'd signed up for *languagepals.com* only to help brush up on her written German skills and pass some time in the lonely evenings after her divorce. She wasn't looking for romance, especially not on the internet – that infamous playground for charlatans and love-thieves. Then Canadian Nick Vermeer had hooked up with her, offering his services.

Apart from the German, it was obvious from the first that they had nothing in common. He went hunting, owned guns and liked to fish whereas she didn't know one end of a rod from the other. 'I'll teach you,' he promised. He loved the great outdoors but her vision of hell was full of camping equipment. Yet she found herself writing to him, for hours, instant messaging him, then after four months he rang her. She floated for hours after hearing his voice, which was exactly as she wanted it to be: a soft, masculine drawl, confident, witty and very, very sexy.

He sent letters, cards. She reciprocated, sending his letters to a post office box, because he was in the middle of selling his house in Osoyoos, a log cabin on the edge of a forest. From the pictures he sent of the outside, she just knew that the inside would have huge fur throws over the furniture and a log fire burning in it at night.

Then Nick made plans to come over and visit her because

their connection was something mad that had hit him from left field and he needed to discover if the chemistry was as much there in the flesh as it was in their written words and voices. There was never a hint of gratuitous smut in his letters – he was a perfect gentleman – though they brimmed with the promise of passion.

Floz had started researching where to take him when he came over. They talked excitedly on the phone about the lovely restaurants they'd eat in, going to London and taking in a show, and the drives through the countryside they would do. If all went well, he said he would bring Floz over to Canada in the fall, because he said that if she saw it in that season, she would never leave it. Then suddenly, just after Valentine's Day last year, all contact from him ended. Floz had been bereft. She checked Canadian newspaper sites on the net to see if he had been injured or killed, because surely there had to be a serious reason why he wasn't in touch any more – but found nothing. And then she discovered that his profile had been erased from *languagepals.com*.

Yes, she knew exactly what poor Coco was going through. Even now, after all this time, the tears were too close to the surface for comfort when she thought about Nick Vermeer. They had been intensely connected for a year and she still mourned the loss of him from her life. His disappearance had felt like a death.

Chapter 9

Guy nursed his second pint in the Lamp. His body might have been sitting opposite Steve, but his brain was elsewhere.

'You're a right bundle of laughs tonight, considering you're on a night off,' said Steve, polishing off his drink and nudging his empty glass against his friend's. 'Another one?'

'Aye, go on then,' sighed Guy. He might as well stay here with Steve as wander back to the empty flat that was attached to the family home in Maltstone. He had never considered the Rosehip Gardens flat as anything more than a bolt-hole, somewhere to lay his head, despite the fact that he'd been 'laying his head' there for too many years to think about now. The marriage and matrimonial-home thing had eluded him so far. What happened with Lacey, ten years ago, had sent him running from life. He didn't want to get close to a woman again and open himself up to all that potential hurt and confusion and crippling guilt.

Then he had to go and see Floz Cherrydale.

Somehow the combination of that silly dressing-gown, her large watery eyes and a perfumed cloud of strawberries around her had set off a primal explosion inside his chest cavity, sending the blast down to every neurone and blood vessel in his system. He had been knocked sideways into a pit so deep he doubted he'd ever be able to climb out of it.

He had replayed the scene in his head so many times that, had it been videotape, it would have snapped through over-use. His heart was fluttering like a bag of moths as he cringed afresh at the memory of him barging into the coffee-table and sending everything scattering to the floor. He didn't even stop to help clean up.

He exited the memory with a shudder, as Steve returned with two pints.

'You should ask her out,' he said.

'Who?' asked Guy innocently.

'You know who I mean, you berk,' tutted Steve. He was actually quite excited that Guy was fancying someone. He was always trying to get him to go out with Gina, who more or less slavered like a hound over a bone whenever Guy was within touching distance. But after a lifetime of knowing him, Steve was all too aware that Guy was a man of straight lines. He wouldn't have gone out with anyone he didn't fancy. He never had – not even when their hormones were raging as teenagers. Sex and affection were inextricably tangled up for him. But this was encouraging news. Guy had seen the woman once and was already hooked. Love was a curious beast, he had to admit. Then again, that's probably why he was in love with two very different women himself, neither of whom would deign to give him the time of day.

'I know what you're thinking,' Guy went on. 'That I fancy her because my first thought was that she looked like Lacey Robinson. Well, I don't because she doesn't.'

'I wasn't thinking anything of the sort, actually,' Steve defended himself. 'I was, however, thinking that Lacey Robinson shouldn't even be in your brain any more. She's fucked it up quite enough already.'

'She's as short as Lacey, but that's as far as the resemblance goes.'

'Good. Because one Lacey Robinson is enough for one lifetime.'

'Don't,' said Guy quietly. 'She was a damaged soul.'

'I know what she was.' Steve knew that Guy would never talk ill of Lacey Robinson, because he had never managed to quite rid himself of the guilt of not being able to save her from herself. To Guy, Lacey Robinson would always be a vulnerable woman whose heart had been broken one too many times and couldn't live with the pain. To Steve, Lacey Robinson was the equivalent of a suicide bomber. She didn't care how many people she would take down with her when she pressed the final self-destruct button.

'I made such a massive arse of myself in front of Floz.' Guy dropped his head into his hands.

'You need to go back to the flat and act normal, not fall over furniture and run off,' Steve suggested. 'You cocked up the first impression so you need to make a very good second one.'

'Yes, I realise that,' said Guy. 'I don't know what happened to me. She's *so* not my usual type. But it was like . . .' He shook his head because it sounded daft.

'A thunderbolt?' Steve suggested. He knew all about thunderbolts. He'd been hit by a very big one in primary school. He felt its reverberations still.

'Yes,' nodded Guy. 'I've never known anything like it before. I thought when people said they'd fallen in love at first sight, they were just talking bollocks. But that's exactly what it felt like – love at first sight. At least for me. Not quite sure it was the same for Floz.'

Steve's brain started to whirr.

'Your Juliet was on about that damp patch on the kitchen wall. I'll go with you to the flat. We'll check it out with a view to replastering it. That's a genuine reason for calling on them.'

Guy thought it sounded a bit contrived, but Steve was on a roll now. 'Yep, we'll do that. If we say we'll call around tea-time tomorrow, they might ask us to stay for something to eat, then you can have a good natter and show off your charm and wit. And muscles. How can Floz resist?'

'You must keep it secret from Juliet why we're really going,' warned Guy.

'Course I will.' Steve grinned, pleased with his plan. And he was very good at keeping secrets. The one thing Steve had never told Guy was that since they were at primary school, he'd had the biggest crush on Juliet Miller.

Chapter 10

The next morning, Floz spent a few quiet minutes staring out of the window which overlooked the communal gardens whilst she was drinking her second coffee. It was a beautiful mid-August day, bright blue skies and a high sun, yellow as a lemon drop. But there were a few leaves on the turn on the trees, brown splatters amongst the green. The summer was evidently enjoying its last weeks on the year's throne.

Her first job was to send off the saucy Valentine's card copy to Lee Status by email. He rang her within minutes of receiving it.

'Thanks for the Vals, babe. Now, have I got a brilliant emergency brief for you!'

'Do tell,' said Floz, who hoped it was a nice cheery one because she badly needed some light relief after the awful night's sleep she'd had. She'd dreamed of Nick coming back into her life and must have felt real euphoria in her sleep, because when she awoke and realized that it was all a dream, she felt bereft.

'Cards for the terminally ill,' said Lee. ' "Sorry you're dying" et cetera.'

Floz floundered on an answer before finding her voice. 'You are joking! Who'd want to get a card saying "sorry you're dying"?'

Lee ignored her and ploughed on. 'You can really let your

poetic side loose. Don't mention specific illnesses, obviously, just beautiful warm lines like "wishing you strength and guardian angel" bollocks.'

'Lee – are you serious?'

'Absolutely,' said Lee, with glee in his voice. 'The sales figures on our "We'll Meet Again" range are through the roof. People sending cards to dead relatives is the new black. Death is the future. I think it's down to the popularity of these undead teen fiction films.'

Floz had written a lot of the 'We'll Meet Again' verses for the weatherproof laminated cards which were specifically designed to be left on graves.

'There's a bit of difference between a fond verse for a deceased loved one and this new range. I mean, what are you going to call it for a start?'

'Dunno,' mused Lee. ' "Death's Door"? Possibly a bit too harsh. I know, I know – what about "Waiting for God"? Mind you, that could alienate the atheists. Hmmm . . . Anyway, the range title can wait. If you think of one, I'll pay you for it.'

'Okay,' sighed Floz. A job was a job whether it was writing cards for living, dead or dying people.

It took her nearly two hours to write the first poem and be satisfied with it. Then she thought of it sitting in a card shop and the sadness of someone who might buy it, the heartache of the person who might receive it. It wasn't a job that sat well with her at all, however much she needed the money.

Just before she broke for lunch, Floz updated her website. It didn't get a load of hits, but it was a useful tool to advertise herself and her expertise. Gibby, the guy who had set it up for her, had included a page for posting comments. It happened from time to time that she received junk mail that didn't make any sense, and the occasional circulated advert asking her if she wanted to link to a blog about finding sexy housewives in her area, or to grow a bigger penis. But the mail she discovered on her website that day wasn't her regular spam. It was sent anonymously and just said *Glad to see you're doing good, Cherrylips.*

It could have been a coincidence, but she didn't think so. There was only one person who ever called her 'Cherrylips'. Floz carried on writing her poetry, but all through the rest of the day, she wondered if that mail was from *him*. Surely not after a year and a half. But who else could it be? She wondered if by thinking about him she had released some call into the cosmos and he had answered. There were a lot of people out there who wouldn't have called that theory a rubbish one.

Juliet rang her as she was musing over her sandwich.

'Wotcher,' she boomed. 'Is it okay with you if Guy pops by later? With *Steve*.' As she said the latter name, once again the derision crept into her voice.

As Juliet was sneering at the second name, Floz was bristling at the first. She tried to sound casual at the prospect of seeing Guy Miller again.

'Sure,' she said, cool as a cucumber that had been stored in a freezer all night. 'What time will they be coming?'

'I said six, if that's okay with you,' said Juliet.

Floz looked at the clock – that gave her five hours to look as if she hadn't made any effort at all.

'Sure,' she said again, thinking she needed to find a new 'self-assured' word.

'We'll order a curry in,' said Juliet.

'I could throw some pasta together,' suggested Floz quickly. 'Nothing fancy.'

'Ooh, that would be nice,' said Juliet, who preferred home-cooked food to takeaways any day. 'Don't go mad with effort though; it's only Guy and *Steve*.'

'You don't like Steve much, do you?' said Floz.

'Nope,' replied Juliet. 'And you watch yourself, Floz, because he's an absolute dog. However, he's also a damned good plasterer and I need him to sort out my kitchen wall.'

So why was Guy coming as well? Floz asked herself. It wouldn't have taken two people to plaster a crack in the wall. After their rude introduction, she would have thought the flat was the last place he'd want to come with no valid reason. She voiced the question.

'Why is . . . your brother coming up with him?'

'Because the pair of them are joined at the sodding hip,' replied Juliet. 'I'll pick up some wine on the way home. Cheers, babe,' and with that she was off.

Chapter 11

Floz tore around the supermarket and bought breadmaker flour, fresh pasta, a cooked chicken and all sorts of veg to throw into a white wine sauce. For dessert she played it simple: exorbitantly priced raspberries, cream and meringue nests for an Eton Mess – with a kick: she'd add a soupçon of Pernod from Juliet's fancy spirit and liqueur supply. Most of it was unwanted corporate presents, some of it was because Juliet liked to see weird and wacky-looking bottles with coloured contents and couldn't resist snapping up a new novelty one in supermarkets or on holiday.

After all the shopping had been put away in the cupboards, Floz then raced around the flat with a vacuum and afterwards slipped in the bath to soak in something perfumed and to wash her hair. Picking what to wear was a bit of a minefield. A floaty dress signalled that she'd tried too hard, her old jeans and T-shirt: not tried hard enough. After trying on and rejecting half her wardrobe, she settled on a blue hippy top and light-blue jeans, and a coordinating blue-heart necklace. Then she put on an apron and started to prepare the meal.

Floz thought she had got the right dress balance until Juliet arrived home from work and immediately said, 'Ooh, you look nice. But there was no need to dress up for those two, you know.'

'Oh, I didn't dress up,' protested Floz. 'I . . . er . . . spilled some coffee down myself earlier, so I changed my top.' It sounded like the lie it was and Floz cringed, but Juliet didn't seem to notice. She was too busy taking in pasta-sauce-flavoured breaths.

'Smells lovely,' she said. 'You're a good cook, aren't you? I bet you'll even impress Guy.'

'Is Guy a bit of a foodie then?' asked Floz.

'He's a head chef, didn't I tell you?' called Juliet, going into her bedroom to change out of her work suit.

Shit, shit, shit, thought Floz. She knew he worked in a restaurant, but had somehow got it into her head he was a waiter who liked to bake a bit, not a professional cook. And not just a pro but a *head chef*! What a disaster! If he stayed longer than thirty seconds in her presence this time without running off, he was bound to slag off her amateur pasta dish – or worse, throw up. Should she put some herbs in and make the flavour complex? Oh GOD, she wasn't that confident a cook. Why did she have to open her mouth and volunteer to make dinner? They could have had that bought-in curry, as Juliet suggested.

The breadmaker beeped the end of its cycle. Floz peeped in with one eye expecting a sod's law disaster, but no – the loaf was crusty and smelled divine. It just needed a brush over with salted water, some poppy and sesame seeds sprinkled on and fifteen minutes in a hot oven. She busied herself with that whilst Juliet trilled, 'Better get this party started,' behind her bedroom door.

A cuckoo sprang out of the clock on the wall and announced that it was six o'clock. Floz felt stupidly nervous. She almost dropped the bread as the entryphone buzzed to herald that the visitors were here.

'Let them in, Floz, will you?' said Juliet, now in the loo. Floz pretended she hadn't heard. She didn't want to be left alone with Steve, whom she hadn't met, and Guy whom she had met and scared to death. The buzzer sounded again and Juliet emerged from the bathroom just as Floz was heading across the room to it.

'I've got it, no worries,' said Juliet and picked up the door-phone. 'Yep, come on up,' she said into it with easy familiarity.

Outside, Steve wagged his finger at Guy. 'Now remember, be nice and smiley and don't make her feel as if you're terrified of her.'

Guy was trembling with anticipation. Not even the fearsome Alberto Masserati scared him in the ring, but the prospect of seeing Floz again made his knees distinctly wobbly. The door clicked open and Steve pushed it. He didn't let Guy know that he was feeling all hot under the collar too at the prospect of seeing the voluptuous Juliet. Even after all these years, he was still like a jelly in her presence, though he covered it up with a brash show of bravado that she had come to misinterpret.

Steve breezed into the flat first with his usual cocky strut. He went straight over to Juliet, one side of his top lip raising like Elvis's.

'Wotcher, Jules,' he said. 'How's your bits?'

'Hello, Steve,' said Juliet with a flat tone, unimpressed by his cheeky entrance. 'Come and meet Floz. Floz, this is Steve, Steve this is Floz.'

'Oh hi, Floz,' said Steve, holding out an enormous paw. 'I've heard a lot about you.'

'Have you?' asked Juliet quickly.

First mistake. Guy could have murdered him. Luckily Steve was thinking well on his feet today.

'Well, I haven't . . . er . . . obviously, but that's what you say, isn't it?'

'*You* might,' huffed Juliet. God, he really was a jerk. Hand-some, but a total jerk. He always had been. Even at primary school. He was so far up his own arse, he could have played with his tonsils from the inside.

Guy stepped into the room a good few paces behind Steve. 'You two have already met, haven't you?' said Juliet. Guy nodded at Floz, all words suspended in his throat, glued to a ball of nerves that couldn't get past his voice-box. As a result, he was unable to let out the cheery, 'Hi again, Floz. I didn't recognize you with your clothes on – ha!' witty retort that he had practised in his flat. Instead all he managed was a glowering nod. And his Heathcliff face.

And Floz, expecting him to have at least made a bit of an effort with a 'Hi' and a smile, found herself annoyed enough to merely nod in return. She had no intention of putting herself forward for him to knock her back.

'Mmm. I smell cooking,' grinned Steve. 'Great, because I'm starving. Show me where this damp patch of yours is then, Ju.' He made it sound naughty, as if the damp patch was in Juliet's knickers and not on the wall. She expected nothing less of him, though she wouldn't have guessed in a million years that his jokiness was fuelled by the stress of being in her mighty presence.

'Open up the bottles, Floz, will you?' asked Juliet, leaving her brother and Floz in the room together. They were about at ease with each other as a cobra and a mongoose. Floz was grateful to have something to do in uncorking the Cab Sav and the Pinot Grigio. Unfortunately, the cork appeared to have been soaked in concrete for a month before being introduced to the bottle.

Guy wondered if he should wade in and help. He was slightly concerned that to do so might seem cheesily macho, yet on the other hand it seemed very ungentlemanly not to offer and continue to observe her struggling. In the end, seeing as Floz was turning purple, he felt he ought to.

'Can I do that?'

'Yes, please,' said Floz. But as she handed over the corkscrew, it fell and both parties lunged to catch it. This resulted in a head-collision with accompanying sound effect. It was not unlike the noise of a coconut being tapped none too delicately by a lump hammer. Floz yelped, she got the worst of it on the corner of her forehead. She sprang back up, clutching a skull she was convinced would be bleeding if she looked in a mirror.

'Sorry. You okay?' said Guy.

'I'm fine,' said Floz as sparks exploded in her head. She wouldn't have put it past him to have done it deliberately. Maybe it was a twin thing and he felt she was coming between him and his sister so he was trying to kill her.

Guy pulled the cork out effortlessly and hoped it didn't look too cocksure. *Look at how strong I am, and what a soft girly-thing you are!*

'Red or white?' Guy shouted out.

'White!' came a duet from the kitchen.

'Floz?' asked Guy, trying not to look at the swelling that had started to grow on her head.

'Er, red for me,' she said, touching her throbbing skull. 'I'll just go and er . . .' She took her lumpy head and made for the bathroom to assess the damage.

'Should I get some ice?' he started to ask, his voice fading as he realized she hadn't heard him. What next? he thought, as he tipped the bottle, missed the glass and sent red wine splashing all over Juliet's pristine white tablecloth.

Steve led the way out of the kitchen talking plaster-speak. Juliet followed behind him with a dish of pasta, cheese bubbling on top.

'Yeah, I can do that – scratch coat . . . skim . . . trowelling . . .' but if he was hoping to impress Juliet with words like those, he was on stony ground.

'And how much are you going to charge me for it?' asked Juliet in such a way that defied him to ask for any money – as if the honour of doing the job should be enough for any man.

'Oh, I don't know,' mused Steve. 'How about you cook us another meal when I've finished?'

'Okay,' said Juliet, 'you're on. Where's Floz? And what have you done to my tablecloth, Guy? And why is your head bleeding?'

'Floz, er, just went to the bathroom,' said Guy, touching his head and finding blood on his finger. 'We crashed heads.'

'How the chuff could you crash heads?' asked Steve, thinking of the height difference between them. What had she done, stood on a ladder to nut him?

Guy didn't answer as Floz emerged from the bathroom with what looked like the nub of a horn about to burst from her forehead.

'Bloody hell!' said Juliet. 'Let me get you some ice for that.'

'It's fine,' said Floz. 'I think it's got as big as it's going to.'

'Bet you've said that a few times!' laughed Steve. Juliet glared at him and went to the kitchen to wrap up two bags of frozen peas in tea-towels.

'Shall we eat?' Guy said, trying to bring some normality to things when Juliet returned with the giant compresses. Floz pressed hers against her head feeling like a drama queen as Juliet fussed.

'Pass me a plate,' said Steve, digging in his spoon.

'Ooh, that looks down to your usual standard of cooking, Ju,' teased Guy.

'Actually Floz made this,' said Juliet.

' 'Kinell,' said Steve under his breath. If it wasn't enough that his big friend had nutted the bird he fancied, now he had just slagged off her cooking as well.

'Joking. Looks lovely,' said Guy with an exaggerated reflex but it didn't quite come off.

'I won't be insulted if you don't eat it,' Floz said frostily, from behind the bag of peas.

Steve stepped in to rescue the situation with his size thirteens.

'Well, even if it's crap, I'll certainly enjoy it because I'm starving and will eat anything.' Now it was Guy's turn to cringe for her. Between them, they'd have her ringing the Samaritans.

The pasta was lovely though and both Guy and Steve reckoned the only way to get this across was to eat as much as possible as a sign of approval and not trust their mouths in any other way but to chew and issue as many 'mmms' as possible.

'Guess what, we're going internet dating,' Juliet announced.

'Who is?' asked Steve, quickly trying to mask the sudden rush of panic in his voice.

'We are. Floz and Coco and me.'

Floz had a mouthful of bread and couldn't talk through it. She waved the hand not holding the compress to intimate that this was most categorically not true, but Juliet was on a roll.

'A Piers Winstanley-Black clone for me and a blond, short bloke in a suit for Floz.'

'I am not going internet dating,' said Floz, madly chomping through the crust.

'Oh come on, Floz. Mr Right is out there for you somewhere. You've been on the shelf long enough now.'

Juliet chuckled, unaware of how mortified Floz was at Guy thinking she might be going shopping for a man on the net. Although he probably thought she would have to. Especially as Juliet had announced that she had been a love reject for years. Floz started to offer up a stuttering objection. However, she then realized it might come across as 'the lady doth protest too much', so she shut up and displaced her annoyance by pressing the pea-bag extra hard onto her bump.

Guy was trying to look nonchalant but his head was a mass of whirring thoughts. 'The lady doth protest too much,' he deduced. So she was looking for a man? A man who was the exact physical opposite of him. Could he blame her? After he'd almost stoved her skull in, slagged off her cooking and run off like a total dick the other night? He wanted to appear witty and chatty and charming but he couldn't think of a single thing to say at that dinner-table, at least until the raspberry Eton Mess arrived.

'This is very nice,' he said. 'Is it a Pavlova that you dropped on the floor?' He laughed, but was by himself doing so. It hadn't come out as the joke he'd been aiming for if Steve's pained expression was anything to go by. Guy went back to silent Trappist monk mode where he was safest.

They didn't stay for coffee. Guy decided to go for damage limitation and leave the crime scene straight after 'the dropped-on-the-floor Pavlova'.

'Why are we going away so early?' Steve hissed as the flat door shut behind them. 'I thought you wanted to build bridges?'

'I did build a bridge,' sighed Guy. 'And it was just like the one over the River Kwai.'

'Wasn't that the one that got blown up?' Steve puzzled.

Guy gave a heavy nod and turned down the stairs.

Chapter 12

Floz sat in high amusement listening to Coco and Juliet fill in their internet dating questionnaires on Juliet's laptop the next night.

'How ridiculous that you can specify which colour eyes you want your date to have,' said Juliet.

'It is going a bit far,' replied Coco. 'Put me down for the lot. Brown, green, blue, grey, boss-eyed and wonky.'

'Hair colour?'

'Any.'

'Body Art?'

'Any.'

'Salary band?'

Then Coco got fussy. 'Over fifty thousand. I don't want any dole-wallahs.'

'That's high. Why not add the twenty-five to fifty thousand as well?'

'If I must,' sniffed Coco.

'A brief description of yourself,' invited Juliet.

'Hmm, let me think. How about: "Slim, trim, fit, very attractive, *cocoa*-eyed boy with incredible dance-moves and snaky hips, looking for the same for fun and frolics, possibly more with the right person."'

'Snaky hips?' mocked Juliet. 'And fit? When was the last time you did any exercise?'

'I'm naturally a good shape – and supple!' Coco leaped to his feet like Louie Spence on a springboard and started thrusting his groin backwards and forwards. 'I could have taught Michael Jackson a thing or two, had we met – and if he hadn't died, obviously.'

'Yeah, maybe about making Yorkshire puddings, but not dancing,' said Juliet. 'You can't even do the hokey-cokey without putting something out when you should be putting it in.'

'Story of my life,' sighed Coco.

After Juliet had filled in her application, they all went trawling the Singlebods site to look at possible future dates.

'Jesus Christ!' scoffed Coco. 'If he's thirty-five, I'm Cheryl Cole. You don't get jowls like that unless you've been abusing your body for at least fifty years.'

'Look at that one,' giggled Juliet. 'He could eat an apple through a barbed wire fence with those teeth.'

Things weren't that sparkling when they looked through the straight men section either.

'This is the one for you, Ju,' laughed Coco. 'He likes sci-fi, walking in the sunset, holding hands and kissing on the sofa. Yuk.'

'Yes, and look at what he wants from a partner. "Must be between five feet and five feet four, long undyed hair essential, no tattoos or piercings and no make-up please."' Juliet humphed. 'I'd like to meet the man who dared tell me to wear no make-up, fussy fucker!'

Floz would have liked to have been a fly on the wall if Juliet ever did go out on a date with a man like that.

'I feel all depressed now,' said Coco, who had been hoping for a screen full of hunks waiting for him to call. 'I think I'll go home and slit my wrists in a Radox bath.'

'You'd never get the stains out of your pink carpet,' said Juliet. 'Besides, you wouldn't want the paramedics to see you in a bloodbath. Far too unglam.'

'Let's not talk like that,' said Coco, his laughter suddenly drying up. Floz noticed the look that passed between them then, loaded with a private secret. She didn't ask what it was; they would have told her, had they meant her to know.

Juliet said goodbye to Coco with an equally despondent heart. The men on the site made even Steve Feast look interesting.

Just before she went to bed, Floz went to turn her screen off on the corner desk. It was then that she spotted she had another mail via her website address.

Just been looking through the pages of your website. Glad to see you're doing well, Cherrylips. I've missed you.

Floz got a prickly feeling at the back of her neck. It had to be him – it had to be Nick. But why? What did it mean? She knew there would be a third message soon and that her sleep that night would be disturbed. She realized that she hadn't cut him out of her heart as she had convinced herself she had. He was a sleeping dragon within it – and worst of all, that dragon appeared to be waking.

Chapter 13

Kenny Moulding made a beeline for Guy when he showed himself in the kitchen the next morning. He had his customary beige pin-stripe suit on, dark shirt and tie, long slim brown hand-made shoes on his feet. His thick white hair was brushed forward in what he perceived to be a trendy style – which it had been in the 1970s – in order to convince people he was twenty years younger than his true age of sixty-one. His clothes cost a fortune yet he put them together so badly that he always managed to make himself look as if he went shopping in jumble sales. He was to style what the Kray Twins were to French knitting. His trademark Romeo y Julieta cigar was clamped between his cosmetically perfect top and bottom set, and he was holding a folded-up magazine when he dragged Guy's attention away from test-cooking some sausages which were more sawdust than pig. Kenny beckoned the big man into the office with a roll of his arm. His thick gold bracelets jangled as he did so.

'What do you think of this?' Kenny said, throwing down the brochure on top of a box of spongy mushrooms for Guy to pick up and look at. The page featured pictures of a block of apartments by a swimming pool somewhere hot and sunny.

'Tossa,' said Kenny, scratching his chin.

Which is more or less what went through Guy's mind every time he saw the feckless sod.

'Tossa del Mar,' Kenny elaborated, misreading Guy's silence for ignorance. 'Spain.'

'Very nice,' Guy answered.

'I'm selling up and moving there. I've bought that flat on the end with the hanging baskets.'

'Well, good for you,' Guy started. Then he became aware of what Kenny might be telling him. 'Selling up? Your house or the restaurant?' he questioned.

'Both,' said Kenny. 'Had enough of the fucking place. Too much like hard work. I'm getting too old for this catering lark.'

That's rich, thought Guy, considering that on the rare occasions when Kenny deigned to turn up, all he did was sit in his office, read a newspaper and either pick his nose or choose horses to bet on. He had a woman, Sandra, to do the accounts and act as his secretary, and Glenys, the cleaner, who did her best even though she was knocking on for seventy-five. The most stress Kenny had was thinking what to spend his profits on.

'Yep, I'm selling the lot.'

Guy felt the first stirrings of panic. He'd be out of a job. He didn't have as much faith in his abilities as he should have had. And he had a criminal record which wouldn't make him an attractive prospect to a new boss.

'I'm giving you first refusal at buying me out,' said Kenny, relighting his cigar by striking a match on the No Smoking sign.

'Me?'

'Aye – you, lad.'

You're dreaming, aren't you? Guy was about to say, but he knew Kenny wasn't. When Kenny made statements like that, Guy knew he'd done all the groundwork and a solid plan was in the offing. Guy felt a moment of light-headedness at the enormity of what Kenny was suggesting.

'We could bypass all the lying bastard estate agents if you bought it directly from me, lad. Surely you've dreamed of owning your own restaurant?'

Kenny spread his arms wide. Guy took in the bumpy plas-
terwork painted plum-purple with a brown floral border, the
cracked windows, the missing tiles. But, just for a second, he
saw this same room in smooth pastel shades, with a black and
white tiled floor. And the office door swinging open to a
polished stainless steel kitchen. His third eye reached further,
into the body of the restaurant, tall menus on pretty café tables.
He saw heavy drapes at the long, slim windows, heard string
music in the background. Just like a restaurant he had once
wandered into by mistake when he was holidaying in Florence.
He had stood in awe at the perfect shabby-chicness of the
decor: the pale green and cream walls, the beautiful tapestry
drapes. He had known instantly that if he were ever to own a
restaurant, he would make it as serenely atmospheric as that
place. He gave a small laugh to himself. *Florence.* The word
appeared to be haunting him.

'Wheer's me fucking toast?' A big booming voice burst his
thought balloon as some trucker bobbed his head into the
kitchen and bawled at Igor, one of the waiters.

Guy's feet landed back on terra firma with a bump.

'You deserve this place,' said Kenny, with a rare softness to
his rough-edged, fag-ravaged voice. 'You've made me a bomb,
lad. Which is why you can have it at a good price. But only if
you act quick. I don't want to hang about here.'

Guy opened his mouth but nothing came out. He saw
sausages with a high meat content, farm-assured quality lamb,
eggs so fresh the hens hadn't even noticed they were missing
yet. He saw staff with clean aprons and hygiene standards. He
saw returning customers, awards, Michelin stars and no over-
hanging threat from Environmental Health.

'Well?'

Guy had savings. Whether he had enough for what Kenny
would ask for the place remained to be seen, but he was fired
up with a sudden surge of passion. How could he let Burgerov

go to another owner? Someone who might even do the impossible and drop standards even further. Burgerov was his kingdom and he wasn't going to be deposed without a fight.

'Yes,' said Guy, gulping down a big ball of adrenalin.

'Yes what, lad?'

'Yes, I'll buy Burgerov from you, Kenny. Providing the offer's good.'

'It'll be a good one. I promise you that.'

Guy was shivering with anticipation as he took Kenny Moulding's outstretched hand and shook it firmly. He felt the stirring of change in his soul. Change usually unsettled him, but for the first time in ages, Guy Miller felt an inner strength awaken within him and embraced it.

Chapter 14

Coco rang Juliet at work first thing Monday morning.

'Firstly, you've sat on your mobile phone AGAIN and accidentally called me. Will you please take me off speed-dial, Ju. Or lose weight off your arse.'

'Oops, sorry – yes I will. I'll do it now. Take you off speed-dial, that is.'

'You said that last time.'

'Soon as I end the call, I swear. I won't forget again.'

'Good. Anyway, listen to my news – I've got a date!' Coco screamed down the phone so loudly that Juliet had to hold the phone away from her ear before he deafened her.

'From the internet dating site? Already?' said Juliet.

'Yep. Soon as I got home on Friday night, I uploaded my photo and I've had loads of replies. I've chosen one in Bretton. He's gorgeous – ticks every box. I'm meeting him tonight. He's called Gideon and he works with computers. He sounds very brainy. Apparently he has a photographic memory.'

'I hope you've picked somewhere central and well-lit to meet up,' warned Juliet. 'I don't want to read about you dead in a field in tomorrow's newspaper.'

'Well, that would put a dampener on my day if I let it,' huffed Coco. 'Actually I'm meeting him in Papa Giuseppe's in

Barnsley town centre. We both really like Italian. We have so much in common, it's amazing.'

'Report back tomorrow,' Juliet ordered, before slamming the phone down quickly because Piers Winstanley-Black was entering the building. Today he was resplendent in a navy pin-stripe suit. He swaggered in, breezing past her desk, giving the smallest of 'good morning' greetings knowing that his crumb of a salutation was enough to have the office hearts – and pants – melting. Arrogance was coming off him in waves and scored a direct hit on Juliet's libido. If only she could have five minutes in a locked room with him, she grinned to herself, he'd never look at another woman again.

'He is one sexy man,' growled Daphne, pausing from data-inputting. 'What a shame he's not into older women.'

'Or short ones,' added Amanda.

Juliet didn't say anything, she simply mouthed, 'You will be mine,' in the direction of his office.

Just after lunch Juliet sneaked a peek at her date-site web page to find that she had mail. And from the profile pic, he wasn't half bad either. At five feet nine – the same height as she was – he was a bit shorter than she would have liked, but the photo, albeit a bit grainy, showed him to have a nice open smile and well-looked-after teeth.

Hi, the mail began. *I really liked your profile and your photograph. My name is Ralph (pronounced Ralph not Rafe like some pretentious people do!). I have my own small printing business, own house, own teeth, own hair, own limbs and head. Fancy a chat on MSN later?*

Juliet nodded at the screen as if transmitting a yes. Not bad-looking, suit-wearer, good sense of humour, can spell 'pretentious'. It was looking rather promising so far.

Floz had written four poems about dying now and was emotion-ally worn out. There were only so many variations on a theme and she was, like the poor future recipients of the cards, rather near the end. She knew this range would 'die a death'. No one could say that Lee Status wasn't innovative, but this was just too left field to convince her that he had a winner on his hands.

It wasn't the first time Lee had had an extreme idea. The greetings-card market was a broad-minded one, but it only took a prominent news event to alter the tide of buying. No one wanted to buy greetings cards with guns on them any more after all the spree killings there had been in recent years. Lee's greetings-card range based on serial killers was insensitive at the best of times, but his Harold Shipman card with its *The older you get the more attractive I find you* sentiment inside caused outrage, even in the trendy avant garde card shops. Still, Lee was a big believer in 'no press is bad press', and though the cards ended up getting pulped, he still managed to upgrade his Porsche that year to a newer model.

Floz decided that she couldn't write these poems for the terminally ill any more. It was too depressing a job. She sent off what she had written so far to Lee and refreshed her mailbox. And there she saw a name she had never thought she would see again: *Nick Vermeer*.

Floz's skin prickled with a mix of emotions she couldn't define. So it *was* Nick who had been sending her the 'Cherrylips' messages. And now he had contacted her directly. She wanted to double-click and open it but she was scared of the words that would be released. And what they would do to her. She should delete it. The last email she had from him was eighteen months ago. She had carried on writing to him through the summer, hoping to coax a reply from him, but received nothing. Exactly a year ago, she had decided that he was dead to her, and that if he ever deigned to contact her again after so cruelly disappearing, she would delete the email without a second thought. But now, faced with precious contact from him, she could no more have consigned his email to the recycle bin than she could have shaved off her own eyebrows with Juliet's epilator. Slowly she positioned the cursor over the mail and made a double-left click.

Cherrylips

They say every story needs an ending even if its not the happily ever after one.I told you my dad had died,but I'm not sure if I ever told you how.I got to watch my dad battle cancer and lose and the effect that had on my mom.

I was and still am totally entranced by an English girl and now its late enough to let her know.I went for my pre-med the February before last to get ready for a new engineering contract in Cuba.Hit 40+ and they bring up a test that makes you wish you were 39.Results of that,the PSA test and a biopsy said that any relationship that I might have would be short.The big C likes its home too much in my prostate to leave it.I hate short stories that have no happy endings.Did my surgery,did my chemo and promised my mom I would live forever.July this year my follow up said that promise cannot be kept.Acute lymphocytic leukemia hits about one in a thousand who take chemo.Can't win a lottery with those odds but I did it this time.Going for the last kick at the can tomorrow but I've settled my affairs.All except for one. I would have loved the chance to know you better,but that was not to be.My disappearance was me trying to deal with what was happening.How do you explain that to someone far away?I read your website,and try to follow your life from a distance.

I almost got to know a great woman,I regret that I never did.

Nick V

Floz read it again and again. By the middle of the third reading she couldn't see the screen for the tears running out of her eyes. She *knew* after all the exchanges they'd had that he wouldn't have just abandoned her without good reason. They hadn't met, but there had been a long and strong connection between them; they had talked for hours on the phone, written, made plans. They had gotten to really know each other through the power of their words.

Floz knew she had to send a reply back immediately, and the words poured out of her. The portal was open between her and Nick again and she didn't want it to close.

Nick

To hear from you is the worst kind of relief. I wondered so many times what had happened to you, where you were, if you were okay. I've grown into the philosophy over the years that if someone wants to contact you, then they will – if they don't, then they just aren't interested. In your case I went against all my instincts and kept writing because I never expected to like you as much as I did. It was a surprise to discover feelings that ran stupidly deep, considering I'd never met you.

I'm still single, of course. I think I'm too complicated a person to find a match.

I'm edging around the subject because I can't think of a damn suitable thing to say to you. I'm incredibly sorry to hear your news and yet I find myself so touched that you wrote. It's knocked every bit of stuffing out of me.

I would have loved the chance to get to know you better too. I enjoyed writing to you – witty, sexy, intelligent men are very thin on the ground. I think we would have made a formidable couple in a parallel universe – if not a conventional one. But then convention and I have always been

strangers. Who knows where stories end? I've never been
one to believe that all that energy and life disappears into
nothing.

I'll think about you lots, darling. And I wish SO much that
I could have touched you.

Cherrylips xxx

She hit send, not bothering to edit her email but deciding
instead to send the first draft, written with an open heart and
through vision blurred with streaming tears. If there was any
power in words, would he be a little healed by the force of hers?
She hoped so, but knew she was deluding herself. She cried
until her eyes were sore and her tears were spent.

Chapter 15

Guy barked at Varto after catching him picking wax out of his ear and wiping it on his apron. When this place was his, he really was going to kick some ass, but he would keep his take-over quiet for now, as Kenny had requested. However, once his name was on the paperwork, Varto would be booted out along with all the other dross Kenny employed. Guy nursed the secret thrill of being able to fill the place with some really keen staff who wanted to learn from him and not just dollop listeria on a plate. People who got real satisfaction out of food, who wanted to create with it and be proud of it – people who didn't want to poison customers.

He looked up from his reverie and caught Gina staring at him with her baby-blues. She tore them away quickly, embarrassed. He knew she had the hots for him and wished he could feel the same. But life had a habit of not making things that easy.

He wondered if being a restaurant-owner would give him extra attractiveness points in Floz's eyes. Maybe he should suggest a family dinner where he could deliver the news of his impending buyout and cook a fabulous roast for them all? Sunday. He wasn't working Sunday – yes, he would do it then.

Chapter 16

'Are you okay?' asked Juliet.

Floz was going through the motions of being her usual self but there was something not quite right. Juliet wouldn't have been surprised had she looked up and seen a big black cloud over her new friend's head. And her eyes looked a bit glassy, as if she'd been crying recently.

'I'm fine,' said Floz, switching on an instant 3,000-watt smile so bright and perfect it was as plastic as Barbie's knockers.

'Well, you obviously aren't,' said Juliet. 'But I shan't pry. Even though I want to. Glass of red?' She got up from the couch just as the *Emmerdale* music started and headed for the drinks cabinet.

'I'm just a bit tired,' Floz explained. 'I've been doing a really awful brief about sending . . . sending cards to people who are dying.' She tried to hold it together but burst into tears. Her stocks of them had been replenished, it seemed.

'Oh bloody hell. What an awful thing to have to do!' said Juliet, whose curiosity was now totally satisfied. She had sensed almost straight away that Floz was a softie and yep, that must have been truly harrowing for her. She made short work of opening up the bottle of wine and poured two large glasses.

'Thanks,' said Floz, and smiled at her warm concern. She opened her mouth to tell Juliet about Nick, then snapped it shut straight afterwards. It was a miserable subject and a strange one. Juliet might not have understood how close you could grow to someone you had never met, and she didn't want Juliet to think ill of her.

Plus, coming from a military family that moved from house to house, country to country, Floz found it hard to trust and keep friends, having grown accustomed early on to being ripped away from them. But here at Blackberry Court, Juliet felt like the first friend in her life who would be a constant – and as such, her opinion mattered.

'That's lovely,' said Floz, taking a long sip and trying not to think of what Nick's reaction would be to her email, and if he would reply. Her emotions were so raw, it was as if the top layer of her skin had been ripped right away, and it hurt for even breath to brush past.

'I've got something that will cheer you up a bit,' said Juliet. 'I had a text from Guy. He's cooking Sunday lunch at Mum's for us – his flat is far too poky. *Steve* will be there as well, alas.' Again she huffed on that name.

'Lovely,' said Floz, because she couldn't think of anything else to say. Food was the last thing on her mind. And the re-emergence of Nick Vermeer had driven all thoughts of the hunky, Heathcliff-like Guy Miller from her head.

She began to feign tiredness early on so she could make a legitimate break for her computer and write another email. It had started to play on her mind that the one she'd written was pitched wrong. Juliet had plans of her own too, and bade Floz goodnight.

Dearest Nick

I knew as soon as I hit that send button this afternoon that I'd be reprimanding myself all day – have I said too much, have I said enough, have I said the right thing?

I pray I read your email wrong and there is more hope than you can see. And if it makes it easier for you to contact me again, do. Likewise if it doesn't – don't. I understand.

I just wanted to say that my affection for and fascination with you stays with me. Despite the fact that we didn't meet, I feel I know you so well. You were always a hard act to follow. No one even came close, to be honest.

I hope your sisters and your family are giving you comfort and love – I'm sure they are. And I am, of course, just at the end of an email or a phone if there is anything that I can do for you.

Love, Cherrylips xxx

Floz only hoped that the walls were thick enough in the flat for Juliet not to hear her sobbing. Or her heart breaking, because she was sure she had just felt it crack loudly within her chest.

Juliet logged straight onto *singlebods.com* when Floz turned in. She thought she might have a trawl through the site and see if there was anyone living within a ten-mile radius who didn't have two heads.

There were a few messages waiting for her in her 'contact centre'. The first was succinct: *Life is to short, so let's do it alnight.* And accompanying this was the topless profile pic of a grubby-looking man with a face like a pickled, deformed walnut. Juliet grimaced and blocked him from contacting her again. She felt as if she needed a shower simply from looking at his photo. The second was from the sci-fi fan who liked romantic walks and sofa-snogging.

So, did you liked what you saw when you checked me out then I have a supreme package (Juliet doubted that) *so I can see whose viewed me, so I can return the favuor and say hello to them and if I like what I see I can say would you like to come out for a coffee with me we can meet somewere pubic* (she hoped he meant public) *and see were we go from there what about it then hon?*

Apart from the fact that he had never heard of a full-stop, she said to the screen: 'Thanks but no thanks.' She had no intention of dignifying it with a written reply.

The third email was from Ralph.

Hi, just wondered if you were around for a natter. If so, I'll probably be on my computer working this evening so let's hook up on MSN? Here's my email . . .

It was either a crime documentary about the Great Train Robbers on the TV or an evening forging a link with a potential lover. Juliet typed in her request to hook up with Ralph on the net. Two hours later, after a very pleasant virtual chat, she found herself looking forward to dinner with him the following evening.

Chapter 17

Floz awoke late the next morning and could tell she must have been crying in her sleep because her cheek and the pillow beneath it were wet. It was a bitter-sweet experience for the lines of communication between Nick and herself to be open again. As she typed her next email to him, her mind tried to fill in the blanks of the last eighteen months: what he had suffered. The timing was so tragic. Floz thought that if she had been so poorly, she would have wanted to reach out instead, not pull back. But wouldn't that have been selfish and grasping of her – to take a relationship one step further when it had no future? She didn't know. To do what Nick had done required strength that she obviously didn't have. All she did know was that she was grateful Nick had come back into her life and that she doubted she would get any rest until he left it again – for the final time.

Juliet was so excited about the prospect of a real live date that she almost forgot to swoon when Piers Winstanley-Black sauntered into the office. Coco rang from his Perfume Palace just before the clock touched 9 a.m., as was his usual habit.

'Well, how did it go? I've been dying for you to ring me. You must have at least five missed calls from me,' said Juliet excitedly.

'I've only just got in!' said Coco. 'I've been up all night talking!'

'Only talking?'

'Well, and snogging a bit,' said Coco with a blush in his voice.

'Yuk, two men snogging – I'm going to be sick.'

'Oy, cheeky. And he paid for me.'

'What – you charged him to snog you?' teased Juliet.

'Silly. I mean he paid for everything. Wouldn't let me put my hand in my wallet at all. There's a first, I can tell you,' tutted Coco.

'Ooh, that's impressive,' said Juliet, who had never been out on a date with anyone as generous.

'He. Is. Gorgeous. I'm in love.'

'Oh God, here we go again,' said Juliet. 'Anyway, you're not the only one with a date. I've got one as well. Tonight. I'm going shopping at lunchtime if you want to meet me and help me pick a new frock.'

'I can't,' said Coco. 'I've got a delivery coming from the warehouse. I just hope they remember to put that new Beckham perfume in the consignment. I'll go spare if they don't. Anyway, I digress – who's your date with then?'

'Ralph, forty, own house, own printing business and own everything else. Very nice-looking too.'

'Where are you meeting?'

'He's cooking me dinner at his.'

'Oh Ju—'

Juliet had anticipated this and cut him off. 'Don't worry, I'll make sure I leave a trail in case he's a serial killer. I'll give you his full name and address and ring you and Floz when I arrive.'

'Do you have it now? I have a pen and paper handy.'

'Okay, hang on.' Juliet got her diary out of her handbag. 'His name is Ralph Green and his address is ten, Riffington Place.'

'Ten, Riffington Place . . . why does that ring a bell?' mused Coco, scribbling it down.

'Haven't a clue, but he's in the directory because I checked. If that makes you feel any better.'

'This is so not sensible, going to someone's house, you know,' said Coco, his voice weighted with concern. 'There you are telling me to meet a date somewhere safe and then you go and walk into a spider's parlour like a stupid fly.'

'Yes, but I'm a damn big fly who you wouldn't mess with. Plus I've got a good vibe about him. And it was Ralph who said that I should make sure a good friend knew where I'm going.'

'Well, okay then. But we'll have a code and if you're in any trouble at all when I ring to check on you, say the word . . .' He thought hard. 'Ripper.'

'That's going to be a bit obvious, isn't it?' laughed Juliet. 'I'll say "fab", okay?'

'I'm not happy, Ju.'

'Bugger off, you big fairy. I'll be fine.'

Juliet couldn't wait until 7 p.m. She took a long lunch-hour and hit the shops because she was going to buy something clingy and gorgeous for tonight. Sex on a first – blind – date wouldn't be on the cards, but she and Ralph might get carried away and go a little down the foreplay path. Really it was a bit wanton of her going to his house, but she had no doubt that he was a decent guy (she just hoped he wasn't *too* decent). Plus Ralph had told her to make sure her friends knew exactly where she was. Or rather he had 'written' that because they hadn't actually spoken other than on MSN. But how could his voice be anything other than sultry, after looking at that profile picture?

She bought a short satiny shift dress in dark purple and colour-matching wedge shoes in suede. She rang Floz when she got back to the office to tell her about the date, as Floz had still – unusually for her – been asleep when Juliet left for work.

'Floz, I'll be home at five-thirty on the dot and I need some serious time in the bathroom, so if you were thinking of having a bath, will you do me a favour and not?'

'Of course,' said Floz. 'I'll make sure the decks are clear for you. What's he like? Where did you meet him? And where is he taking you?'

'I found him on Singlebods,' said Juliet, anticipating what would come next when she told Floz that she was going to dinner at his house. 'And yes, I'll be careful, and yes, I'll give you his address and phone number and I promise I won't get murdered.'

'Okay,' said Floz, trying to sound a little bit more cheerful and positive than she felt. Because Juliet was at least doing the right thing in moving a cyber-relationship into real life as soon as humanly possible. Cyber-relationships had the potential to wound just as much as real-life ones. Maybe more so because cyber-partners were tailor-made for each other, their faults smoothed out by imaginations hell-bent on wanting to create the perfect being.

Coco rang Juliet mid-afternoon. He wasn't in the best of moods.

'Gideon hasn't rung me.'

'It's only half-past two,' chided Juliet. 'Be patient.'

'He said he would ring me and he hasn't. I can't understand it – we had a lovely night.' Coco was almost in tears.

'Chill, my love,' said Juliet kindly. 'He might be busy or driving. Go and do some work and put him out of your mind.'

'Okay,' said Coco, ringing off.

'Was that Raymond on the phone again?' laughed Daphne, delivering a cup of coffee to Juliet's desk. She had lived on the same street as Coco's family for thirty years and was privy to his real name. She, like Grainne and Perry, had never been able to comfortably think of him as Coco.

'Yep,' said Juliet. 'He's in a flap. He had a date and the guy hasn't phoned him yet.'

'Patience never was his best virtue,' nodded Daphne. 'Harry

didn't contact me for two weeks after our first date. Mind you, he soon bucked up his ideas when he found out that another lad had taken me dancing. He moved like a bloody express train then.'

'How long have you been married now, Daphne?' asked Amanda, taking off her typing headset and joining in the coffee break.

'Twenty-nine years. Pearl celebration on November the twelfth. We're having a do at our Linda's house and you're both invited. She's had a party room extension built,' Daphne added proudly.

'Ooh lovely,' squealed Amanda. 'What made you get married in November though? Wasn't it freezing?'

Daphne shook her head. 'It was the most beautiful late-autumn day. The leaves were blowing in the air like confetti and the sun was like a big scoop of Cream of Cornish. I've always thought autumn was the loveliest season.'

'I suppose it is,' Juliet agreed. She'd never considered how pretty an autumn wedding could be.

Juliet's office phone rang again and interrupted Daphne's trip down a leafy Memory Lane.

'Gideon still hasn't rung,' wailed Coco. 'Why? What's wrong with me? Should I ring him?'

Juliet sighed. She had *sooo* missed Coco's relationship dramatics. Not.

'We got on so well.' There was a tidal wave of sobs building in Coco's voice. 'He can't be another one who just buggers off without warning, can he?'

Juliet bit her tongue because had she said what was on her mind, Coco would have probably been suicidal.

'Darling, if you ring, you'll look intense. You're worth chasing, so let him chase you. You shouldn't have to remind him of your presence because if you're not on his mind, then he's no good for you.'

'But—'

'Just be patient. If he wants to ring you, he will. If he doesn't want to ring you, then he's not the man for you.'

'Bastard!' snapped Coco. 'I'm so cross I could spit.'

'Then go spit,' laughed Juliet gently. 'And keep the faith because someone out there will not let you down.'

As she said the words to Coco, she hoped she sounded more convincing than she felt. Since the betrayal of Hattie and Roger, Juliet had begun to wonder more and more if there was anyone out there to whom she would be able to trust her heart.

Chapter 18

Coco rang Juliet half an hour later to say that even if Gideon did ring now, he could stuff off as he had erased his mobile number from his phone. He rang again just as Juliet was pushing the door open to her flat to say that Gideon had been in touch and explained that he'd been out with a customer all day. Coco was in raptures and Gideon was once again added to his contact list.

'Oh God, it just does not get any easier, this courtship lark,' groaned Juliet, plonking herself next to Floz on the sofa for five minutes before she began the great getting-ready-for-a-date ceremony. 'Coco has been doing my head in all day.' And she went on to explain why Coco had his Calvins in such a twist.

'Poor Coco,' said Floz. 'It's hard opening yourself up and becoming all vulnerable again.'

Juliet sniffed. 'Personally, I don't get the problem. If you have a good time but your date doesn't contact you the next day, they're obviously not interested enough to see you again – simple. If you're worth chasing, they chase.' She raised her hands to gesture how stupidly obvious it was.

'Women are daft for filling in the blanks. "Oh, he hasn't rung me because he's lost his phone," or "He's been kidnapped by aliens," or "He might have been run down". They'll believe anything rather than, "He doesn't want to see me again and daren't tell me". Now I'm putting on the kettle before I jump in the bath. Tea or coffee?'

Floz answered coffee, and was only relieved that she didn't have to enter the argument and explain that sometimes there really were genuine reasons why someone might just cut and go.

She waved Juliet off later and then read the email which had landed an hour ago, but which she wanted to save until she was alone.

Cherrylips

Talked with my mom this morning and cancelled my chemo. No great dispute from my doctor,just said he understood. Going on a family fishing trip up to Warhorse.Too nice a weekend coming up to spend indoors and I've been indoors too much the last while.Sending you this attachment,renamed it but what they going to do about it? And its my view on almost everything.Hope they never turn this into rap,it would end civilization forever.

Wish I could have taken you on a fishing trip,in spite of the fact that I'd have had to worm your hooks,but that's another lifetime away now and some place to dream of for me.Fascination creates more fascination most days.

Nick

Floz remembered how he'd planned to take her fishing one day and then they were going to cook their catches on a barbecue in the woods behind his house. She felt a pain deep inside her. She opened the desk drawer, got out her headphones and plugged them into the side of her computer, then she opened the attachment which had been labelled *What I feel about life now*. The gentle stringed opening of the Louis Armstrong version of 'What a Wonderful World' began and she listened to the lyrics, trying to imagine the mindset of a man who had accepted that he was shortly going to leave it, and she sobbed hard in the empty flat. The sound was that of an animal in pain.

Chapter 19

Coco might have been a 'giddy'un' about Gideon but that was nothing compared to what Juliet had become at the prospect of a man cooking her dinner, which she thought was a very sexy proposal. She had tried not to be stupid and map out the future, but lurid pictures were crossing her mind of a few dates down the line and Ralph taking off her dress and kissing his way down her body with expert skill.

Her SatNav was telling her that she was now turning into Riffington Place. She tried to see the numbers of the houses – 96, 94, 92 – so she still had a way to go to 10. She was in a sedate estate on the outskirts of the village of Lower Hoppleton, one that looked like Pensioners' Land. 38, 36, 34 . . . any minute now. Juliet was nearly exploding with anticipation. 24, 22, 20 . . . She checked the piece of paper again that had Ralph's number written on it. Yep, it was definitely 10.

When she found it, she texted Floz to say she had arrived and then rang Coco.

'Ooh, what's his house like?' said Coco excitedly.

'It's a bungalow and the door has a stained-glass picture of a big bird.'

Coco could read a very unmerry note in her voice. 'What's up with that?'

'Nothing,' said Juliet, who hadn't mentioned the chintzy

frilly curtains at the window, where she had pictured wooden blinds, or the hedge cut into a cockerel shape. Or the gnomes peeping from behind foliage in the garden.

'Go enjoy. Judgeth not a man by his front door,' said Coco. 'Anyway, bugger off, I need to have a shower. You aren't the only one with a date this evening, girl. However, my mobile will be in my pocket at all times if you need me. Remember, "fab" is code red.'

Juliet lifted her bottle of wine and locked the car door. Yes, Coco was right, she was being overly judgemental. She would have had something to moan about if the house had been a scruffy dump with an old car parked in the middle of the garden. Excitement started to surge through her as her heels tappy-tapped on the crazy-paved path. She saw the doorbell was next to a plaque bearing the name of the house – *Holmlea* – which she wished she hadn't seen as its cheesiness made her cringe. She pressed her thumb on the button and a cheap tinkly tune rang out – the first few bars from the theme tune to *EastEnders*. She had a sudden lump of dread in her stomach, which thankfully cleared when she saw the silhouette behind the door which she recognized immediately as handsome Ralph. Then the lump drew back as the door opened and Ralph appeared there, looking older and chunkier than his profile picture, in a dark brown cardigan and matching house slippers. Those photos he posted on his profile had obviously been lucky ones.

Ralph smiled widely at the sight of Juliet and said, in a voice that sounded as if it had been issued from his nose whilst totally bypassing his voice box, 'Come in, dear Juliet, come in. Tea's just about ready.'

Juliet, for all that she wanted to run back to the car, found herself not wanting to be rude after he had gone to the trouble of cooking a meal. She told herself that she would stay an hour – it wouldn't kill her. Ralph moved aside to let her enter and gave her a kiss on the cheek. He smelled nice, at least. He had obviously shaved for the occasion and applied cologne. But was it enough to offset the gnomes and the cardigan and the slippers and the nasally voice?

'Don't be rotten,' said an inner voice of reason. 'Your dad wears those sorts of slippers and the occasional cardigan and they don't make your mum want to throw up. And let's not even talk about your bunny slippers, Juliet Miller.'

Juliet followed Ralph down a short hallway, the walls covered in black and white and sepia family portraits in frames and into a neat square lounge with a tiled fireplace and furnishings in a limited colour palette of browns, beiges and light bile green. A massive old-fashioned radio sat in the corner. It was like something out of the war. She half-expected Vera Lynn to leap out from behind it singing 'White Cliffs of Dover'.

'I thought it was a bit chilly, so I made a fire,' said Ralph and he smiled, and Juliet saw brown bits stuck in his lower teeth. She tried to smile back but her mouth wasn't behaving and it ended up more like a twisted grimace.

'I brought you this,' she said, handing over the wine. He had nice hands at least, she thought as he reached for it, desperately trying to see something positive and make her last the hour.

'Later,' he said. 'I've just brewed a big pot of tea. Can I take your coat?'

'Oh, it's okay, I'll just keep it here, behind me,' said Juliet, removing it. The room was boiling hot with that real fire blazing out. Thanks to the archaic setting, the fire didn't look as cosy as it should have.

'I'll get you some refreshment,' Ralph said, sweeping his eyes quickly and approvingly over her short dress which she could now see was a totally unsuitable buy for this evening. Ralph edged backwards out of the door as if she was the Queen and he daren't turn his back on her. Juliet heard him clattering about in the next room, presumably the kitchen, and realized she'd been naive for taking the way a man wrote emails for his total sum. The Robert De Niro hunk she had visualized had turned out to be Rigsby from *Rising Damp*.

Juliet looked around. The furniture was old-fashioned and dark, polished to a high shine though. The two sofas were bulky with precisely placed cream antimacassars draped over their back and arms. Cushions embroidered with the names *Ralph* and *Mum* were arranged neatly. More old photographs were hung on the walls and there were loads of ornaments on shelves — brass ones and some Spanish dolls in bright dresses in a cabinet along with an old tea-set and the top layer of a very old wedding cake with a faded bride and groom on top. And some bits of porcelain with *Mother* written on them.

'Here we are,' said Ralph, appearing at the door with a tray, which he set on Juliet's lap. There was a dainty china cup of tea on it, a little milk and sugar jug, and a big plate of pie and mash and carrots. And a bottle of brown sauce. 'The pie is my own recipe,' he said with pride.

'Oh lovely,' said Juliet, thrown by yet another vision smashed. She'd expected a three-course meal at a dinner-table and long champagne flutes full of fizz which they'd chink together and toast their first meet.

Juliet was starving and it did look rather good — if plain. She took a forkful of pie, sniffing it surreptitiously for any strange chemical smells which would render her unconscious and unable to ring Floz and Coco after an hour to 'check in'.

Ralph had seated himself on the sofa opposite to her and was watching her chew with open glee. Juliet smiled awkwardly through her mouthful, but Ralph remained there watching her.

'Where's yours?' she asked after a second forkful.

'Oh, I had mine with Mother at five p.m.,' he replied. 'She won't wait and she hates eating alone. I like her to have eaten by five-thirty then she can have her tablet and be asleep by six-thirty. Hopefully all night, although you never can tell these days.' He sighed fondly.

'So, you live with your mother?' said Juliet. Nice as the pie was, she didn't want to sit here eating it alone with a man with bits of meat in his teeth staring at her.

'Yes,' said Ralph. 'She has the back bedroom and I have the front and I work from the third bedroom which is extended out into the garden. I'll show it to you after sweet. I've got a coffee Viennetta.'

Inside Juliet's head, her brain was screaming, 'Help!' Then in her pocket her phone rumbled.

'Oh excuse me,' she said, taking it out and seeing Floz's lovely name flash on the screen.

'Are you all right?' asked her flat-mate. 'I know I said I'd ring after an hour but I thought I'd check on you a little bit earlier than that.'

'You are joking!' said Juliet, grabbing this chance at escape with both hands and feet. 'How did you do that?'

'Do what?' said Floz.

'Have you rung an ambulance? You mustn't move. Stay right where you are. I'm on my way!'

'What?'

Juliet lifted up the tray and stood. As Ralph stood also, Juliet thrust the tray into his hands.

'Oh my God, my mother has just fallen down the stairs. I'll have to go to her. I can't believe it – she hasn't even rung an ambulance. I'm so sorry to cut our evening short after you've gone to all this trouble.'

'Oh it's fine, you must go,' said Ralph, looking crestfallen. 'You have to look after your mother. They're very precious creatures.'

'I'll see myself out. Thank you so much. It was so nice to meet you.'

Juliet dived for the door, hoping it wasn't locked. It wasn't.

The cool air of the evening hit her in the face and she breathed it in gratefully.

Ralph had put the tray down somewhere so he could wave Juliet off. She saw him backlit by the orange hall light, a cardiganned, slippered silhouette. Juliet scrambled into her car wearing her best mum-worried expression and zoomed off. Once around the corner, the tension loosened its grip on her whole body and she drove home in a state of almost kick-back euphoria. She decided that she just might marry Floz Cherrydale when she got home.

Chapter 20

Floz was in her ridiculous Dalmatian-spotted dressing-gown when Juliet barged into the flat, flung her arms around her dainty flat-mate and planted a huge wet kiss on her cheek.

'Florence Cherrydale, I love you and will love you forever,' she gushed.

When Floz could breathe again, after being squashed to within an inch of her life, she asked, 'What on earth happened?'

'Wine – I need wine if I'm doing *Jackanory*,' said Juliet, disappearing into the kitchen and coming out with a bottle and two glasses. It was only a cheap blended red, but it tasted like nectar in her present mental state.

Floz listened as Juliet filled her in on Ralph and his bungalow and tray.

'Ten Riffington Place!' gasped Floz when she heard the address. 'Blimey, that's a bit too near Ten, Rillington Place for my liking.'

'Oh my goodness.' Juliet clamped her hand over her mouth in shock. '*Ten Rillington Place*. I wondered why it sounded a bit familiar. Mind you, Ralph was too wimpy to be a serial killer like Christie.'

'Yes, well, from what I remember about the case, Reginald Christie wasn't exactly a macho man. That's why he gassed his victims first before he . . . he assaulted them. You were reckless,' said Floz. 'Going to a strange man's house was very risky.'

Her voice dropped at the end as she remembered that Nick had at one time been going to come to her flat to stay for a fortnight. But then her mind quickly counteracted that because she and Nick had built a relationship up over many months and got to know each other. No one could keep the pretence up for that long; she would have known if he wasn't genuine and safe.

'I know,' said Juliet. 'But he was harmless, really. And at least a decade older than his photo, I reckon. He made some nice gravy though,' she laughed at the end.

'You shouldn't joke. Some people are very clever at painting portraits of themselves on the net that bear little resemblance to how they are in real life. It's a sea teeming with nutters.'

'Yes, I know,' said Juliet, her laughter subsiding. 'But they can't all be nutters. *I'm* on the site and I'm not a nutter.'

'True,' said Floz. *And neither am I nor is Nick.* 'But it does pay to be careful. You mustn't go to a man's house again on a first date. He could have put drugs or anything in his gravy.'

Juliet smiled at Floz's concern. She was buzzing too much from the relief of getting away to see things darkly. 'Yes, Mum. Coco had a good experience at least, so that bodes well.'

'But, remember, he's just had the one date so far, so let's not jump the gun.'

'Oh, Floz, you're so sceptical,' sighed Juliet. 'Have you had a real hard time with the unfairer sex?'

'No more than any other woman,' said Floz, feeling the conversation was edging too close to things she didn't want to think about and getting ready to deflect Juliet's attention. 'So, will you give internet dating another go or not?'

'I might,' said Juliet. 'At least you meet a wider circle of cardigans and slippers.'

Floz used that as her cue. 'Well, I'll leave you to it and bid you goodnight.'

'Another glass of vino?' Juliet offered.

'Thanks, but I'll pass,' said Floz and feigned a yawn. 'I'm knackered.'

'Okay,' said Juliet. 'I'll go and hunt some more quarry then. Pass me my laptop, would you?'

So whilst Juliet logged on and scrolled through lists of men, Floz retired to her room, turned the light off and quietly turned her PC monitor on. She hoped Juliet wouldn't hear her tapping away on the computer.

Hey Big Man

I think you have your corner at calling the shots now and if you want to go fishing – you go. I hope the sun shines and you catch monsters. Yep, you'd have had to worm my hooks and pass the handkerchief if I thought the fish were in pain, but I'd have made the best picnic basket this side of Venus.
   You idiot – I would have chanced a visit!!!
   Catch me a big one.

Cherrylips xxx

Juliet went back onto Singlebods and found a couple of fresh possibles on the horizon. Ryan, a marketing exec from Sheffield, Jonathan, a web designer from Wakefield, and Brian, a salesman from Rotherham. Juliet opened up chat with all of them. She dropped contact with Jonathan after five minutes when he invited her to view his webcam and she found him sitting at it totally naked. Shame, as he had a gorgeous body, but no one could fancy him more than he fancied himself. Ryan and Brian seemed quite sweet, if not exactly blowing her bra off. They both asked to meet her as soon as possible. She picked Brian for tomorrow and Ryan for Thursday.

Floz woke up at 3 a.m. and made straight for her PC convinced that she would find a reply from Nick, as if she were in tune with him. She had always felt that if they met, they would be the sort of couple who would be able to finish off each other's sentences, know instinctively when the other one was in trouble. *Like your mother and father, Floz?* No, she answered herself. Not like them, because she and Nick would not be obsessed with each other to the exclusion of everyone else. She and Nick would be nothing like them.

She was right – there was a mail from Nick awaiting her.

Cherrylips

Most of me is glad you never did visit.You would have come during the denial,anger,why-me time and I didn't even like me then.The rest of me wishes you had.I sold the place in Osoyoos,but I would drive by sometimes and wonder how it would be if things had turned out differently.Now back in the family fold in Okanagan.

Bye for now

Nick

Floz hit reply immediately and began to type.

3.15am – can you tell I can't sleep?

Dear Nick

I'm SO glad you wrote again to me. I'm reminding you of my mobile number at the bottom of this email. If you should feel you want to ring me – don't hold back.

Catch a huge fish for me. Then throw it back and let it live.

Cherrylips xxx

Chapter 21

'So you had a second date then? How did it go?' Juliet said to an effervescent Coco on the office phone the next morning.

'Fabulously,' beamed Coco. She could tell he was beaming – it was more than obvious. 'He's lovely. And no, I haven't slept with him yet. I want to, but I'm also enjoying getting to know him. Ooh, how grown up do I sound?'

'Very,' said Juliet, impressed. Then she filled him in on her own date, pausing whilst he laughed at the funny bits.

'I'm meeting Brian for drinks at the Old Mill at seven tonight – and Ryan for light supper in the Orchards Hotel near Denby at seven-thirty tomorrow,' said Juliet. 'Both are public and well-lit and there will be no chance of home-made pie on a tray.'

'Good,' said Coco. 'You were lucky. You could have been my first corpse friend.'

'Only you could make that sound a fashionably acceptable thing to be,' giggled Juliet.

Piers Winstanley-Black bobbed his head around the door and indicated that he needed Juliet's assistance.

'Have to go, see ya.' She ended the call to Coco and grabbed her pad and pen. If only the damned man would make a move on her soon and save her from the uncertain waters of internet dating.

'Sorry to interrupt your call just then, Juliet,' said Piers as they climbed the staircase to his office.

'It's fine,' replied Juliet, trying not to sound as breathless as she felt. 'It was just a friend of mine who is driving me slightly potty at the moment.'

It wasn't a firm that frowned on the odd personal call. The solicitors were all very warm and lenient because they knew they had a cracking staff force who worked hard for them, often above and beyond the call of duty.

Piers opened the door for her and as she passed him, his aftershave drifted towards her. She could breathe in his scent all day, every day, and never tire of it.

They sat down at either side of his huge mahogany desk. Piers passed her a written list.

'I'm due in court at ten so I'm sure I can leave all this in your capable hands,' he said. His voice was like honey. She could have listened to his voice all day, every day, whilst she was breathing him in.

'Of course, Piers,' she smiled, taking the list from his large, square hand. He had beautifully kept hands. She could have let him touch her with them all day, every day, whilst she was listening to him and breathing him in. He was so gorgeous, his eyes blue and big enough to swim in – naked. He could have her on the desk right now, if only he'd ask.

But all Piers Winstanley-Black saw when he looked at Juliet was the reliable, smiley female from the office below, not the sexually charged Amazon who might make his heart gallop like a racehorse on a beach.

Yet.

Juliet floated back to her desk, much to the amusement of Amanda and Daphne.

'Well, has he proposed yet?' asked Daphne.

'He wanted to, I could feel it,' replied Juliet dreamily, as she adjusted her magnificent bosom. 'But he's due in court at ten. Another day.'

'Well, give me plenty of notice to get a hat,' chuckled Daphne.

'I'm thinking of an autumn wedding,' sighed Juliet. 'To follow in your footsteps.'

'Anyone want a refill of coffee?' asked Amanda, bringing them down to earth. 'I've got dark chocolate digestives to dunk, unless you're slimming for your nuptials.'

'Maybe just the four then,' said Juliet in her best affected posh voice. 'One wouldn't want to get stuck down the aisle.'

Chapter 22

Cherrylips

I was going through old emails from you last week which I never deleted.Most of my life,I've been a basically decent person,but I wasn't one at that time when I was first diagnozed and cut and ran from you.My intent in getting back in touch was to let you know that the fault was mine in totality. Told my counsellor that I didn't want anyone showing up at midnight to p*ss on my grave.Get a lot of time to reflect on things nowadays.

I live on other people's blood and bottled O2.I breathe like an obscene phone call and I tire out in minutes.No,I won't be phoning you but thank you for the number.I appreciate the offer.

You have always attracted me,totally unlike most of the people I've known.five feet two tall was way too short for someone my height but it began to seem a perfect size.I wanted you to know the impact that you had and the reason that I shutdown.You headed the list of people I needed to contact and apologize to.

Forgot how much of a hold you still have on my heart, Cherrylips.

Last night I realized that it is time to say goodbye.You are the last one.You live well my girl and take great care of a very good person.

Nick

The mail landed whilst Floz was cooking a lunch for herself that she ended up throwing away. Her heart felt so heavy in her chest, and loud, booming out a hard rhythm. It ached for a man she had never met who lived across a very big sea. The distance was doable though, she suddenly thought. If she moved quickly, before there was a distance between them that she could not cross.

Floz pulled up the Google taskbar and started to type in airfares for Kelowna, which she supposed would be the nearest airport to him in Okanagan, not that she had his address there. Then she stopped. She knew enough about Nick to know that there was no way he would see her now when he was weak and ill and not the big strong man who had been going to come over and court her and take her back with him – and love her. The closest she could get to him was when he read her words, and she read his. They were transporters of their feelings to each other's heart. Floz felt weighed down with sadness. She knew that she would have to go to Canada when he was gone and walk in his footsteps. She wouldn't feel as if she had said goodbye until she had.

Juliet arrived at the Old Mill exactly on time and was impressed that Brian was there waiting for her by the gastropub door. He had on a black suit and a red tie and he wore a nice pine-scented aftershave, that Coco would have liked. The good news was that he was impressively tall, the bad – that he was a bit too thin for her tastes, but she told herself off for being ridiculously picky. He had a nice smile, had dressed to impress, and there she was moaning that he was lean and not a tub of lard.

'Hello, Juliet.' He gave her a double-kiss and said how lovely it was to meet her, then he opened the door for her and followed her inside. A big fat tick in the box for that – she liked gentlemen. She was a lot more old-fashioned than people gave her credit for. They presumed because she was big and brash that she would be a die-hard, bra-burning women's libber, but nothing was further from the truth. Juliet Miller was a typically strong woman searching for a man strong enough to take her on and not be threatened by her enough to start whittling away at her fortitude – as Roger and all of her exes had.

Brian bought her a drink, carried it to a nice quiet corner table and asked her if she wanted anything to eat. She didn't, but thought that was sweet of him.

'So, have you been single long?' asked Juliet.

'Four months,' said Brian with a loaded sigh.

Possible point deduction here. 'That's not very long.'

'No, but the marriage had been limping along for a very long time.'

'Ah.'

'She left me for another man,' said Brian, taking a long sip of his half of lager. 'My first wife did the same. I think I'm cursed, to be honest.'

'Oh dear,' said Juliet. 'Anyway—'

'As soon as I filed for divorce, I thought it was time to get out there and find myself a new partner.'

'I'm glad to hear—'

'The financial stuff will take a bit of time to sort out, of course.'

'Yes, it usually—'

'It took me a lot longer to move on with my first divorce. This time it was much easier.'

Juliet opened her mouth to contribute to the conversation, veer it away from ex-wives and onto the here and now, but there was absolutely no gap in Brian's diatribe. Juliet drained

her lager, sat there with an empty glass whilst Brian demon-
strated that he was about as much over his marriage split as the
Clifton Suspension Bridge was over the River Danube.

Though they had both agreed to have one drink together,
an hour and a half had passed and Brian's half a lager remained
unfinished, so she couldn't even offer to get another round in.
Juliet's throat, by this time, had turned to Sahara sand, and as
Brian said, for the umpteenth time, 'It feels good to be over
Janet and have moved on . . .' she heard her own voice crash
into Brian's monologue.

'STOPPP!' She could bear no more, her ears were about to
bleed. She got to her feet and held up her palm as if she were
on traffic duty and halting cars. Brian was shocked into silence
and sat there gaping at her, wondering what could possibly
have led her to roar at him like that.

'Brian, you are a very nice man, but you are so clearly not
over your wife leaving. In fact, I'm not quite sure you ever got
over the first one giving you the heave-ho.'

'I . . . I am,' Brian nodded, but it was a very limp nod.

'No, you are not. Look at my glass! I drained it an hour ago
but you didn't notice. You haven't asked me one single question about myself. You haven't noticed that I'm about to fall
into a coma.'

Brian looked horrified.

'You have talked incessantly *for one and a half hours* about wife
number one – Sue – and wife number two – Janet. I know that
Sue ran off with Robin who fitted your double-glazing and
took Ringo the Vizsla with her when she left. And your jointly
owned Nissan Micra. I know that Janet is presently holidaying in
a cottage in the Dordogne with Neil who is a butcher in
Morrisons. I know that Sue is a size sixteen blonde with an
allergy to Bri-nylon and Janet is a size twelve after losing ten
stone in the past eighteen months through a combination of
salsa-dancing and Weight Watchers. I know she hates marzipan,

fancies George Michael and has a bunion on her left foot the size of Scarborough. So, what do you know about me then?'

'Er . . .'

'Precisely.' Juliet shrugged.

'I'm not ready for the dating game, am I?' gulped Brian, with tears blooming in his eyes.

'In modern parlance, no – are you fuck!'

'I'm so sorry,' said Brian, fumbling in his pocket for tissues. Juliet thought he might have cried into a lot of tissues recently. He blew his nose very loudly, took a deep breath and stood up.

'I'll walk you to your car,' he said.

He gave Juliet a clumsy kiss on the cheek after escorting her out to her Mini.

'Do you think, in a few months, we might meet . . . again?' He looked hopefully at her, but her expression said it all. 'Ah, perhaps not.'

'Good luck, Brian. Don't rush it,' chivvied Juliet. 'You're coming across like a total desperado and a bit of a knob at the moment, if I might be so honest.'

'Yes, yes, I deserve that,' said Brian, sniffling. 'Thank you.'

Juliet slammed her car into first gear and turned on the CD player full blast: AC/DC. She wanted to hear some real, wild men with guts and balls. What a bloody waste of an evening, she said to herself. Still, there was always Ryan tomorrow – third time lucky. And if that failed, well . . . maybe internet dating wasn't for her after all.

Floz was halfway through an email to Nick when Juliet bounced into the flat, dropped her bag, kicked off her shoes and threw herself down on the big, plump sofa.

'Floz, rescue me from tearing out my hair,' she called.

'I'm coming,' said Floz, checking her face in the mirror, making sure she didn't look as down as she felt. 'I was just doing a bit of work. I felt in the mood,' she fibbed.

'I have just been tortured by an hour and a half's worth of stories of ex-wives. I – Juliet Miller – couldn't get a word in edgeways. Can you believe that?'

'That I do not believe,' said Floz. 'I'll put the kettle on.'

'Sod that, get that bottle of Canadian icewine out of the fridge.'

Canadian. There were reminders of Nick everywhere.

Juliet watched Floz go into the kitchen and smiled. She'd only known the woman for a couple of weeks, yet she could see already that they'd be friends forever. Coco was a good friend, but he wasn't a woman and Juliet really missed having a close female *mate* who didn't almost throw up if the conversation turned to menstrual cycles.

The flat had become a much cosier place since Floz moved in, with her cards and computer and her silly spotty dressing-gown and all her lovely strawberry pictures and fruity room-scents. Juliet rather thought that every house should have a 'Floz' in it.

She heard a pop and a shriek from the kitchen. With her feet out of those high heels and a good friend with whom to dissect the evening over a cold glass of fizz, man or no man – life really wasn't that bad at the moment.

Chapter 23

Floz had a much-needed jolly evening listening to Juliet's recounting of her date with Brian. They got the nibbles at ten o'clock and demolished a thin crust ham and pineapple pizza between them. All that laughter tired them out though and by eleven Juliet's eyelids were drooping.

Floz climbed into bed, then climbed straight out again. She needed to finish writing her email to Nick before she went to sleep. There were things she needed to say to him too, whilst she still had the chance.

Dear Nick

If I'm honest, I thought you were the biggest bastard I ever encountered. I couldn't quite believe you'd cut off and go like you did, but then I chided myself into accepting that these internet things were all based on fabrications anyway. I wish I'd known the back story before.

I know you won't phone me again. But I wanted you to have the number – then you had a choice. Anyway, I've never had an obscene phone call – might have been a first. Keep it handy, you might get the urge.

Don't know what it was about you that made you affect me so deeply, especially because we seemed such very different people. You scared me when you first wrote that introductory email, did I ever tell you? I thought if I didn't reply, you'd hunt me down with a crossbow. Months later, all I could think of was that we would have had great sex.

Don't say goodbye until you feel you really have to. I'm clinging on and trying to avoid saying mine. But I will, just in case I never hear from you again because it isn't fair to make you write to me when you need to put the full stop on something and I'm trying to turn it into a comma.

I hope you have gentle days ahead, my love.

Cherrylips xxx

Chapter 24

Guy was writing down a shopping list for Sunday. He'd cook beef. He knew that Floz wasn't a vegetarian. For dessert he'd do the most spectacular thing with strawberries. He knew she loved strawberries because he'd seen the gorgeous little series of strawberry pictures she had on her wall and noticed the scent of them wafting from her room when the door had been ajar.

He had it all planned: first he would wow her with his cooking and smooth repartee at the lunch-table, then he'd make a follow-up call the next day and invite her out to dinner with him.

'Chef, please – you look what I find?' Antonin appeared at the door holding up a dead mouse by its tail. Great, that was all he needed.

As Guy was tearing through cupboards in the restaurant kitchen, trying to find evidence of more mice, Juliet was pulling up in Orchards car park a fashionable five minutes late and driving around hoping to park near to the blue Audi TT which Ryan said he drove.

There it was, and there was Ryan himself looking just like his profile photographs, as tall and broad-shouldered as his description and not a sign of a brown cardigan or slippers.

That's more like it, thought Juliet with a big smile as she got out of her car.

'Ah, Juliet,' grinned Ryan, spotting her and striding over. He gave her a kiss on the cheek and puffed a subtle cloud of lovely aftershave her way.

I'm getting as bad as Coco for going gooey over scents, she giggled to herself. But yep, this was looking very promising so far.

'You are exactly like your profile picture,' Ryan said. His voice was deep and rich too.

'So are you,' said Juliet.

'You'd be surprised how rare that is.' Ryan laughed and it was a nice genuine sound. He held his arm out towards her. 'Shall we?'

They strode forward into the restaurant. Bingo, thought Juliet.

Floz felt claustrophobic in the flat that evening and didn't want to sit in it alone. So she took herself out for a mosey around the supermarket. It was several days since she had crossed the threshold of the flat and she knew that some fresh air would do her good.

She passed the fish counter and thought of Nick fishing with his family that weekend. She put some veg that she didn't really want in her trolley and some herbal Radox in the hope that a hot scented bath might knock her out and counteract her insomnia. Her appetite was zilch and her paltry amount of shopping reflected that. In the magazine aisle a headline caught her eye: THE LOVE OF MY LIFE WAS A MAN I NEVER MET and she pulled her eyes away before she made a fool of herself and starting crying in the middle of Morrisons.

Outside, both the moon and the sun were out, sharing the same sky. The moon was saying goodbye as the sun died for the evening. Even that was painful for Floz to think about.

★

In Orchards, starters had been chosen and enjoyed, main meals finished off, a pleasant carafe of wine shared and coffees halfway imbibed. Juliet was enjoying herself immensely. Ryan was ticking all the boxes so far – he was gallant, attentive, charming, asked questions about her and seemed genuinely interested in the answers, for his pupils were dilated. Great stuff.

'So I have to ask, do you want children?' Ryan asked.

Juliet wasn't sure she'd heard that properly. 'Pardon?'

'What are your views on having children?'

Oh bummer. Well, he was nothing if not direct. 'Erm, I must confess, I don't think I'm cut out for motherhood.'

Juliet imagined that Ryan would stand up then and call the date to a halt. It was obviously a deal-breaker if he had mentioned it on a first date, but she'd had to respond honestly. He didn't make any movements though; he templed his hands and contemplated his next question.

'Theoretically speaking then, since you're not cut out for motherhood, if you found yourself having had "a little accident", what would you do?'

She presumed by 'little accident' he meant pregnancy rather than wetting herself.

'I don't honestly know,' she said with a bemused laugh. 'I don't think I've ever thought about that happening.'

'What do you mean, "you don't know"?' Ryan's lips formed into a smile of strained confusion rather than of humour.

'I mean that I don't honestly know. *Can* you know what you'd do in that situation unless you were actually in it?' replied Juliet, hearing the faint tinkle of a warning bell cranking up in her leetle grey cells.

'Well, would you keep the baby?'

'I don't know.'

'Abort it? Come on, we're talking theoretically and you *have* to make a decision.'

Juliet cleared her throat. They might have been talking theoretically but his body language was signalling that a lot balanced on her answer.

'Really, I don't know.'

'You don't know?' Ryan's whole demeanour changed then. He was no longer bantering metaphorical arguments around. 'You don't *know* if you'd murder your own flesh and blood or not? A foetus is a living thing with all the same rights outside the womb as inside it.'

Juliet put her cup down. She was getting cross at this stupid 'theoretical' argument. It was spoiling their lovely evening. One minute they had been swapping stories about fabulous visits to European capitals, the next they were discussing the murder of foetuses. Her hackles were up now and if he wanted a morality row, then she'd give him one. But she wasn't comfortable talking about what *she* would do, so couched her answer in legal-speak.

'Well, one would have to weigh up certain things. Would the pregnancy involve risk to the physical or mental health of the pregnant mother? Is there a chance that if the child were born, it would suffer from physical or mental abnormalities . . . ?'

'We all know that doctors and clinics liberally interpret the law in this area and "find" reasons to terminate pregnancies where there are none,' Ryan cut in. 'You agree with the principles of abortion then, that much is crystal clear.' All the warmth had dropped from his expression and he was now looking at Juliet as if she was something he had just stood in.

'I didn't say that I agreed with abortion,' protested Juliet, who worked with lawyers all day long and so was well aware how some people could expertly twist things.

'I think you did,' said Ryan. His eyes were big chips of ice now that even the glowing candlelight between them hadn't a cat in hell's chance of defrosting.

'No, I did not say that at all. Anyway, I don't particularly think that abortion is a suitable subject for over dinner.' Juliet swallowed down a few choice swearwords which were rising in her gullet.

'Yes, because obviously the taking of a child's life is not murder when discussed over fucking salmon and mange-tout,' Ryan spat, his voice raised so that the people on the table opposite looked over. 'What sort of an idiot are you?'

'I beg your pardon?' said Juliet. Had he really just said that?

'How can it not be murder?'

'I don't want to talk about this,' said Juliet.

'Oh no, you started it.' Ryan did a strange half-laugh though his eyes looked glassy and dangerous. 'If you take the life of a foetus, it's cold-blooded murder. You tell me one instance where it isn't.'

'No, I shan't,' said Juliet. 'I'm on a first date.'

'And the last with me,' snarled Ryan, pushing his chair with the back of his knees and standing up, struggling quickly into his jacket. More diners were now looking at them. 'It's bitches like you that promote abortion as today's answer to contraception. You're the sort of sanctimonious cow who probably called for Myra Hindley to be hanged without realizing you're as big a murderer yourself!'

Juliet's hand was on her glass of wine and she was a breath away from throwing it in his face. But all her instincts were saying, 'For once, leave it. This man is dangerous.'

Ryan fumbled in his jacket and threw three ten-pound notes on the table.

'That's my share. Pay for your own fucking dinner, you fucking murdering bitch.'

He thundered out of the restaurant leaving Juliet blushing for the first time ever. The waitress came over to see if she was okay and Juliet quickly paid her and left the restaurant feeling a roomful of eyes on her back.

When Juliet reached the sanctity of her car, she thought

how lucky she was that it hadn't been Ryan's house she had agreed to go to for dinner. She really had been stupid. She was shaking hard as she put her key into the car ignition and set off for home. Her foray into the world of internet dating was well and truly over.

Chapter 25

Floz hadn't expected Juliet back so early. The last time they had spoken was a quick check-up call just after Juliet's main meal, when everything was hunky-dory. Juliet came in to find Floz knee-deep in tissues and very red-eyed.

'Floz, what's up?' asked Juliet immediately, her own evening taking second place in importance.

'Oh, I'm fine,' said Floz, scooping up all the spent tissues and trying to plaster on a smile. 'Don't mind me. I've just been watching a weepy film.'

'Liar,' said Juliet. 'What's up?'

Caught on the hop, Floz felt she had no option but to come clean. Sort of.

'Okay. I had an unexpected email from an old . . . flame,' she told Juliet. 'It's just stirred up some emotions inside me.'

'Good or bad ones?' asked Juliet.

'It was lovely to hear from him,' said Floz. 'I'd forgotten how much I liked him.'

'Are you going to meet up?'

'I wish we could,' said Floz, biting her lip. 'He was very special.'

'Well, I would advise you to get straight in there.' Juliet pulled the combs out of her hair and looked at the TV screen. The news was on, another soldier killed in Afghanistan. 'You never know what's around the corner.'

Floz gulped. If only Juliet knew how true that was. 'Anyway, how was the date?'

'Not without a bottle of wine and two glasses,' said Juliet. 'This one was the jewel in the crown.'

When Juliet logged onto Singlebods to show Floz the profile pic of Ryan, she found a long, abusive and aggressively punctuated mail full of the worst swearwords from the man himself. They didn't look as if they could have come from such a nice-looking and friendly smiling man as the three pictures on his profile showed him to be. It was chilling how deceived she had been, and she had always thought her intuition so very reliable. Juliet reported him to the Singlebods administrators, then she deleted her account, despite having a few emails in her box from more interested potential suitors.

'Back to the drawing board,' Juliet decided, hitting the *yes* to *are you sure you want to leave* Singlebods? She'd never been as sure of anything in her life. Somehow, after that night, being single didn't seem so bad.

Chapter 26

They went into town with Coco on Saturday.

'Gideon said I mustn't neglect my friends,' said Coco. 'Which is why you have the pleasure of my company at the moment instead of him.'

'I'm liking this Gideon more and more,' grinned Juliet. 'This is the first man you've not stuck to like Superglue.'

'I might be wrong, yet again, but I'm finding that I want to trust him,' smiled Coco. 'He's taking his mum out for her birthday today. I'm meeting him later on.'

Juliet looked down at Coco's shoes.

'What's up with you?' he asked.

'I was just checking that your feet are on the floor. You appear to be walking on air,' she said.

'I am,' winked Coco, linking both women's arms. 'Like Aled Jones's snowman.'

They went for lunch in the Yorkshire Rose pub in the town centre. It was cheap and cheerful and the meals were freezer-to-microwave, but it was a much nicer affair than the horror of the posh meal at Orchards, thought Juliet. She was still pretty shaken up by mental Ryan, not that she admitted it to the others. Men like that were the obsessive type who turned up on your doorstep and put firebombs through the letterbox. Blimey, she must be getting old, being cowed like that. She couldn't remember the last time anything had scared her. Even she wasn't too big and bold to wish someone would put their arms around her and make her feel protected.

Juliet's way of dealing with the episode was to blast it apart with humour, and over lunch she made the others laugh with predictions on what her future potential dates could have been. An axe-murderer masquerading as a librarian, a suicide bomber who worked in Greggs pastry shop. Floz laughed along with the others, but her mind was never two steps away from Nick. She was sending him her best vibes that he and his family would have a wonderful weekend fishing on a sparkling lake. She could imagine him, tall and rangy, lightly muscular, laughing, cigar clenched between his teeth as he had been in one of the pictures he had sent her. She had burned his cards and photographs a year ago in an attempt to excise him from her life when she believed he had cut her out of it so silently and cruelly.

She pulled herself back into the here and now to order a dessert.

'So where are you going hottie-hunting until Piers casts his beady eye in your direction?' asked Coco.

'God knows,' replied Juliet. 'But if I don't get some sex soon, I'll be jumping on Steve Feast. That's how bad things are.'

'Blimey,' trilled Coco. 'You are in dire straits, darling.'

A text came through on Coco's phone from Gideon saying that he hoped they were all having a lovely lunch and how much he was looking forward to meeting up with Coco later.

'Why can't *I* get someone who pays me attention like that?' snarled Juliet as they left the pub. There was a wailing noise in front of them. A drunk in a shabby suit was causing a bit of hilarity by weaving all over the promenade.

'I bet he's got a profile set up on Singlebods,' said Juliet. 'He'll be a smart executive into amateur dramatics. Self-employed with a brand new Jaguar in the garage.'

Two policemen were heading in the drunk's direction just as he toppled into the photographer's shop window.

'Whoops a daisy,' laughed Juliet.

Oh no, thought Floz. Not this. Not him. This was why she didn't come into the town centre much any more.

'Shall we go back home now?' she said, hanging behind the others.

The policemen had the drunk between them now and were holding him up.

'Two minutes, I just have to go in Boots for some nail glue,' said Juliet.

'I'll meet you outside Thorntons. I want to buy some chocolate,' lied Floz and she zipped off in the opposite direction.

'Come on you.' The drunk's legs buckled and he nearly took one of the policemen down with him.

'I need to talk to that woman,' the drunk slurred, pointing at a giggling teenager with long red hair.

'You can talk to us in the car on the way to the station.'

Coco looked at Juliet. 'What's up with Floz?'

'Old flame back on the scene. Think she's a bit emotional at the moment. Chocolate is exactly what she needs in my opinion. She's been very quiet the past couple of days.'

'Everyone is quiet compared to you, love,' said Coco.

'Cheeky! She keeps bobbing into her room every five minutes then coming out with a face as long as Red Rum's. I presume she's waiting for the mystery man's emails.'

'Doesn't he ring? Or text?' asked Coco.

'How do I know?' laughed Juliet. 'If I knew anything at all about relationships, I wouldn't have been nearly murdered twice in one week.'

'If it's an old flame, he would be more likely to ring, don't you think?' Coco and Juliet stood watching the policemen trying to load the protesting drunk into the car. He was singing now, much to the entertainment of the town-centre shoppers.

His voice was surprisingly clear with a measured vibrato. It was a voice wasted on such a numpty, a few observers thought.

'He might ring during the day when I'm at work so I wouldn't know,' Juliet said, amused by Coco's attempts to turn himself into a detective.

'But if he doesn't ring in the evening . . .' Coco's brain was computing '. . . that says to me that he might be married. Gideon says that a man who prefers to text and email rather than talk has something to hide.'

'Come on, Miss Marple.' Juliet dragged Coco into Boots. She wasn't sure that her friend should sell his Perfume Palace and join the police force just yet.

Across the road, through Thorntons' window, Floz watched the drunk being placed in the back of the police car. He'd lost weight – and teeth. His jaws were hollow now and he looked far older than his age, with his sallow skin and unkempt hair. She couldn't believe that she had once shared a bed with him. He was a tramp now, a drunk at whom people laughed. Once upon a time they had been a couple with a house and jobs and a future. It pierced her that he had chosen this path. Despite everything he had done to her, and the revulsion she felt at seeing him now, she could have cried for him again.

Chapter 27

'So, ready for your lunch with the family and *Steve*?' asked Juliet, with a slight sneer pulling up her top lip.

'What is it with you and him?' said Floz, looping her handbag over her shoulder.

'He's all brawn and no brain.' Juliet tapped the side of her head. 'Find me the polar opposite of Steve Feast and then you'll have someone I'm very interested in.'

'I thought he seemed really nice.' Floz disappeared into the kitchen to get the white wine from the fridge.

'You have only met him once, Floz. I, however, have known him all my life.'

'Your brother obviously doesn't share your feelings.'

'Steve Feast spent more time at our house than his own when he was a kid. Mrs Feast was – and still is, unfortunately – a total piss-head. Steve's father buggered off before he was born. My mam bought him more clothes for school than his own did. But then he was very good to Guy when . . .' She trailed off, as if she had been just been wrenched back from the verbal equivalent of a very large hole.

'When what?' prodded Floz.

Juliet grabbed her coat. 'Oh, nothing really. Guy had a rough time a few years back and Steve helped him through it. So, are we ready for lunch *chez Grainne et Perry* then?'

Yep, thought Floz. Then: This is going to be great, Guy glowering at me, Juliet glowering at Steve . . .

Mr and Mrs Miller lived in a very spacious detached house on the quiet outskirts of Maltstone, a pretty little village with a gothic church and an annual May Day festival. Perry Miller and his late twin brother Stan had owned a successful plastic engineering firm before they sold it for a huge profit and retired. Stan had been the flamboyant director in a suit, Perry – never happier than when he was in his overalls in the engineering toolshop. Grainne Miller had always been content in her role as a home-maker. Only the fact that she was the world's crappest cook stopped her from being Doris Day.

Juliet pushed open the front door to number 1, Rosehip Gardens and stepped into the large square hall immediately followed by Floz. The wonderful aroma of a Sunday lunch hit them both smack in the face. The Miller seniors appeared quickly, arms out ready to greet their daughter and their considerably smaller guest. Grainne gave her a big kiss on the cheek, then, as if she were on a hugging conveyor belt, Floz was passed to Perry and given a squashy hug. They were the sort of people who made her think she had known them forever, and she totally understood why Steve had gravitated to this family if his own had been so cold and dysfunctional. She wanted to smile as soon as she thought about the Millers.

'Where's our Guy?' asked Juliet, stripping off her coat.

'He's in the kitchen,' said Perry, admiring the very nice bottle of Sauvignon Blanc that Floz had just placed into his hands. 'Steven is opening some wine in the lounge – go and say hello.'

'No, thanks,' said Juliet under her breath, but she was forced into meeting him seconds later as Steve rounded the corner with a tray of glasses.

Floz took him in again: the strong lantern chin, the

white-blond hair and eyebrows, whilst his skin was light olive, which set off his ice-blue eyes beautifully. Oh yes, she bet he was an absolute dog with women. Although she did think his eyes were kind, his welcoming smile wide and genuine.

'Steven, put that tray down and come and meet our Floz,' said Perry, putting his arm around the man and pushing him forward.

'We've met, Pez,' Steve answered, putting the tray down on a coffee-table.

'Pez?' Juliet rolled her eyes backwards.

'Nice to see you again, Floz,' said Steve, ignoring her. Steve knew exactly where Guy was coming from with his attraction to Floz. She wasn't beautiful like Chianti Parkin, but she was incredibly sweet-looking – with bright, shiny eyes like waxed leaves.

'Have some wine, Floz,' said Steve, handing her a glass. 'Red okay?'

'Thank you,' replied Floz.

'So, what have you been writing this week?' asked Perry, drawing Floz into conversation whilst Juliet wandered into the kitchen to see Guy in his empire. Pans were bubbling and steaming; Guy was carving the roast beef. Juliet stole a bit and Guy slapped her hand.

'Just testing,' she said, munching merrily. 'Up to your usual standard, I have to say.'

A pan hissed and gravy bubbled over the top of it.

'Oh shit!' said Guy, looking wildly around him for a cloth.

'S'up with you?' Juliet gawped at him. 'You're in a flap. You never get in a flap cooking.'

'I am not in a flap,' growled Guy.

'You all right?'

'Course I'm all right,' said Guy. 'Why wouldn't I be?'

'It's just that . . . I haven't seen much of you recently. And when I do – well, there's me telling Floz what a great laugh you are and you've gone all grumbly like a big disgruntled grizzly bear.'

'I don't think it's right that I visit as much when you have a lodger. She'll want her privacy,' Guy grumbled like a big disgruntled grizzly bear.

'Floz and Steve seem to be getting on rather well,' mused Juliet, stealing a look in the mirror on the kitchen wall which held a reflected view of Steve and Floz talking together in the dining room. 'I reckon there's a spark there.'

Guy dropped a carton of milk and swore and Juliet made a hasty exit. Maybe today her twin would be best left alone.

Steve was leading Floz over to an armchair when Juliet joined them. He was showing off Stripies the family cat: an ancient, one-eyed, one-toothed cat with deformed paws. He looked fiercely feral with his single long canine, but he was as soft as butter.

'Why do you call him Stripies?' asked Floz, seeing as he was all black with not a hint of a stripe anywhere.

Everyone in the room swapped amused glances above Floz's head.

'Ah, there's a story,' said Grainne.

'Actually it's a fact that when black cats are kittens, a lot of them have ghost-stripes on them,' began Perry with a grin. 'They grow out of them soon enough, but they definitely look stripey.'

'Oh I see,' said Floz.

'But that wasn't the reason he got his name,' smiled Perry, being deliberately evasive.

'Oh Dad – tell the story,' urged Juliet with good-humoured impatience. 'Okay, I'll begin. For my nineteenth birthday, Mum and Dad bought me a black fur coat.'

'And a few nights after, Guy runs into the house shouting, "Juliet, give me your coat quick and a black binliner",' Grainne took up the reins of the story. 'And he handed this wet bag over to me and ran out of the house with Juliet's coat and a bin bag.'

Floz looked bemused.

Perry took a few attempts to light the pipe that was now clenched in between his lips. When he had, he carried on with the next part.

'In the bag was a damp, shivering black kitten with strange paws. Turns out that a man called Donald Green had put him in a sack and thrown him in the stream that runs just to the side of Pogley Top Woods. The stream that is known locally as "Pogley Stripe" because it's really more of a ditch with a very shallow *stripe* of water running through it. Hardly more than a dribble. Then this Donald bloke called in the local pub and starting talking about what he'd just done. He thought it was a funny yarn. He had an idea that people would see him as the hard man for doing such a thing.'

'Prick!' interjected Juliet, giving her beloved cat a tickle under his chin.

'And who should be drinking in the pub, but our Guy and Steve,' said Grainne.

'Ah.' Floz was beginning to see the connection now.

'Wait though, there's more to tell.' The story baton passed back to Perry. 'So Guy and Steve straight away leave the pub to go hunting for the cat and find him. The state of the little thing. Pogley Stripe wasn't deep enough to drown him in, but he'd have died of the cold if he hadn't been rescued. Then the boys come home, give us the cat to warm up and grab Juliet's coat, because they've made a plan.'

'We knew that wank— waste of space Don Green always got pi— drunk,' said Steve, trying to mind his Ps and Qs in front of the older Millers. 'So we waited for him.'

'And sure enough, out of the pub he comes,' whispered Perry, milking the drama. 'Drunk as a lord at ten past eleven. And laying in wait for him by the edge of Pogley Top Woods and the Stripe are our heroes Steve and Guy.' Then he started giggling like a schoolboy. It was an infectious sound and set Floz off.

'And Steve puts the bag . . .' began Grainne.

'No, Gron, you're telling the story too quickly!' admonished Perry. 'So, they see Donald Green coming and just as he's in the place where they found the kitten, Guy, clad in Juliet's coat, roars like a lion and grabs Donald Green from behind. And Steve covers the villain of the piece with the binliner and they push him in the ditch. It's only a spit of water, like I said – couldn't drown a man, but I think his trousers were distinctly wet by the time he crawled out. And even today, Donald Green is convinced that he was attacked by the Beast of Pogley. He felt the giant cat's fur, you see. He even got a story printed about it in the *Chronicle*. Obviously he didn't tell them the part about trying to drown the kitten.'

'He ended up giving some money to the RSPCA,' added Grainne. 'Allegedly he still sleeps with the light on.'

'I don't think he's been that way home from the pub since,' giggled Perry.

'What a funny story,' said Floz, giving the old cat a scratch on his head. He really was an ugly creature with his club paws and a greying face, so odd that he was utterly endearing and she could understand why the family loved him so much. Stripies had lived like a king since he entered the Miller portals. He laid claim to the best armchair, ate fresh salmon every Saturday for his tea and he repaid them with the odd knee-sitting, lick and dismembered fieldmouse. He was part of the furniture and no one doubted he would be there forever. Floz thought that Stripies had known more love than a lot of people in this world.

'Do you want a hand, son?' called Grainne in the direction of the kitchen.

'No, I'm fine,' came back the big bass tones of Guy, just

before a clatter of tins and a string of expletives that made everyone swap raised eyebrows.

'Thank goodness we got a taxi – this Rioja is superb. Well done, Dad!' said Juliet, filling up her glass.

Perry gave her a big squeeze and looked at her in such a way that tears blindsided Floz. It cost her a lot of eye-blinking to force them back.

'To the table, boys and girls,' called Grainne.

Perry Miller crooked his arm towards his guest and Floz smiled and threaded her glass-free hand through it. She really had better slow down on the alcohol. This bonhomie was almost painful with its sweetness, although there was always Guy to redress the balance. He made a red-faced entrance carrying a pot of vegetables. He nodded a hello to Floz, barely hunting eye-contact. She prayed he wasn't sitting next to her at the table, or worse – directly across from her. Luckily, when they took their places, she was to find that Guy was heading for the opposite end of the table. She was seated next to Perry and across from Steve and his cheery face.

'You are in for such a treat now,' said Juliet, leaning over the table to Floz. 'Guy is a superb cook.'

Minutes later, the table groaned from the bacchanalian feast of burned honeyed parsnips, cauliflower with an eye-watering Stilton and bacon sauce, sloppy sage mash, baby carrots drowning in butter, over-cooked asparagus, under-cooked sprouts and pine-nuts, liquidy horseradish cream, ultra-thick onion gravy that could have been served in slices, and Yorkshire puddings . . . or were they pancakes? It was as if a three-year-old had got hold of a *Masterclass* recipe book.

'Sorry, folks,' apologized Guy. 'It . . . er . . .'

'Oh, not to worry,' encouraged Perry. 'It all looks jolly fine to me. Tuck in, everyone.' He speared a Yorkshire pudding which was so brittle it shattered over the table en route to his plate.

The beef was good, Guy told himself. Even if it was the only thing that was. He couldn't have been more nervous if he had been cooking for the Sultan of Brunei. In fact, it was worse because he didn't fancy the Sultan of Brunei. And the Sultan of Brunei hadn't been told what a fantastic cook he was with a reputation he sadly had not lived up to on this occasion. He could have died of embarrassment.

'It's great stuff.' Steve stuck his thumb up at Guy and took a forkful of beef. 'Chuffing hell, Guy, that's a fine cut of bull.'

Guy was fidgeting in his seat like Shakin' Stevens, which made Steve want to laugh. If only Floz knew what was making him so nervous.

'When's your next wrestling bout?' asked Juliet. 'Get us a couple of tickets and Floz and I will come and watch you.'

'It's on Tuesday in the Centennial Rooms. I've managed to persuade Guy to fight again because we're a man down.'

'Okay, we'll be there,' said Juliet, taking it as read that Floz would want to go too. She felt her new friend needed cheering up a wee bit.

'Do you come from around here then, Floz?' said Grainne.

Floz finished chewing on a carrot and nodded. 'Higher Hoppleton, originally,' she said.

'Oh, you're posh then,' Steve winked at her across the table.

'Ignore him,' sniffed Juliet. 'He wouldn't know posh if it shoved an olive up his arse.'

'Juliet Miller, you watch your language at my table.' Grainne waved her fork at her daughter.

'Are your parents from Higher Hoppleton, Floz?' asked Perry.

'Dad was, Mum was from York.'

'You must have gone to Penistone High then,' Steve deduced, nearly breaking his tooth on a parsnip.

'No, we moved around a lot. Dad's a Brigadier in the Army.'

'Ah, that's why you have that lovely silky accent,' smiled Grainne.

That also explained why Floz didn't seem to have any close mates, thought Juliet. She'd once worked alongside the daughter of another military man who had told her how a life of being uprooted every few years had affected her ability to make solid and lasting friendships.

'How come you settled back in Barnsley then?'

'I went to Uni in Leeds and I . . . er . . . met my ex-husband there. He was from Barnsley.'

'And you liked it so much, you stayed?' said Perry.

'More or less,' said Floz.

'And where are your parents living now?' asked Perry.

'Stop interrogating the girl.' Grainne told her husband off.

'No, it's okay,' said Floz. She didn't mind. She was flattered that they were taking an interest in her. At this light, non-intrusive level anyway. 'They retired to France.'

'Do you see much of them, then?' asked Grainne.

'No, not really,' replied Floz, feeling the first prickles of discomfort. She knew that a family who were as close as the Millers were to each other would not be able to understand her own family set-up. Juliet and Guy were so obviously products of a loving couple, not an unwanted bombshell of a by-product.

'Oh, that's such a shame,' said Grainne. She opened her mouth to ask another question, but to Floz's great relief, Steve hijacked the course of the conversation.

'So, how's life living with our Juliet then?'

Floz saw Juliet suck in a deep breath of annoyance. She bet her life she was thinking, How dare he refer to me as *our*?

'It's good. We get on really well. I hope.' She looked to Juliet for confirmation. Juliet was eating a mouthful of sprouts and nodded vehemently.

'Rather you living with her than me with all those sprouts she's just eaten,' joked Steve.

'Steven,' Grainne admonished him with a steely look from her grey eyes.

Steve burst into laughter, Perry was chortling, Grainne was stifling a giggle, Floz was smiling – only Juliet, looking murderous, and Guy, preoccupied, didn't join in on the joke. Guy just wanted to rewind the clock and start cooking this meal again. Actually if he could rewind the clock, a better option would be to push the hands of time back to the day when he first walked in on Floz. This really was the most pants meal in history. Could it get any worse?

Steve stretched across the table to reach the black pepper. His sleeve pulled up and revealed the end of the snake tattoo on his arm.

'I'm going to get a tattoo done,' said Juliet, seeing it.

'What do you want one of those for?' asked Guy. 'They're horrible on women.'

From the way Floz dropped her eyes to her food and gulped, Guy just *knew* that Floz must have one. *Oh God!* He heard the slow toll of another dropped clanger.

'What are you two doing for your birthdays this year?'

'Bloody hell, Mum, that's over two months away,' laughed Juliet.

'I was just wondering if you were having a party for your thirty-fifth, because it's a mini-milestone, isn't it? You'll need to get somewhere booked if you haven't already. It's Bonfire Night, remember.'

'Wow, Mum,' gasped Juliet with mock astonishment. 'I'd totally forgotten we were born on November the fifth. Thank you for reminding us.'

'Ooh, will you be getting those Chinese fireworks again, Steven?' asked a delighted Perry.

'Jesus, I hope not,' huffed Juliet. 'They have to be illegal. You could hear them going off in Russia. I bet they thought we were launching a nuclear attack on them.'

'I'll get some, no worries,' grinned Steve. 'I'm seeing Robber Johnny and Billy the Spark next week, so I'll get some ordered.'

'Does everyone you know have a daft name?' tutted Juliet.

Perry clapped his hands together like an excited child. 'What was that huge one called, that we had at the end? It was magnificent. Spread across the sky like a blanket, so it did.'

' "The Big Bugger",' said Steve proudly. 'What a magnificent beast he was.'

'Aye, that was it. "The Big Bugger".' Perry heaved a fond sigh as if he had just been talking about a favourite grandchild.

'Closet arsonists!' Juliet levelled at them. 'What is it about men and fire?'

'You'll have to tell us what you want. I have not a clue what to buy you both these days,' said Grainne.

'I don't know what I want for my birthday this year,' mused Juliet.

Guy wanted Floz for his birthday. Naked. Underneath him and screaming out his name. He had just over two months to make that happen.

'And of course we all know what Guy will be getting for his birthday,' smiled Grainne.

'What?' he gulped. For a moment there, he thought his mother had just seen the film reel of imaginary sex playing in his head.

'Your own restaurant, son,' laughed his mother. 'Cheers!' Everyone followed suit and toasted Guy and his new venture.

'And the very best of luck with that, Guy,' said Perry, raising his glass towards his son. 'But I wish you'd—'

'No,' returned Guy quickly and firmly. His dad had been trying to give him some money towards buying the restaurant. Guy was fiercely independent and had refused it time and time again. He had enough finances in place to take over Burgerov – he didn't need his parents' money for it. Kenny had given him the deal of the century. He obviously needed to get away fast for some reason.

'When do you think you'll take over?' asked Juliet.

'I'm aiming to complete all the paperwork by mid-November at the latest, but it'll be shut for at least a couple of months whilst the builders gut the place. I reckon I'll be up and running by Valentine's Day.'

Guy bit down on a parsnip and nearly broke his jaw. It really was an appalling lunch. And there he was talking about opening his own restaurant. Today he had made Varto's cooking look edible.

'What are you going to call it?' Floz asked timidly.

'I don't know,' said Guy, looking at her and feeling his heart sigh. Her eyes were so very large and green. He ripped his attention away from her before he started blushing like a daft teenager, and addressed the table: 'Any ideas, anyone?'

'Anything but Burgerov!' said Steve. 'Where the hell did Kenny get that name from?'

'He was trying to be funny. I think it was a message to the Tax Office,' Guy replied, rubbing his jaw.

'Well, I hope he isn't leaving to become a stand-up comedian,' said Perry.

'No, Dad, he's leaving to become a professional sunbather.'

'You'll have to make the place your own and call it something nice,' mused Grainne. 'What about "Guy's"?'

'Very original, Gron,' nodded Perry. 'You really have missed your calling in the advertising world.'

Grainne gave her husband a well-humoured frown.

'Will you make a lot of changes?' asked Juliet. 'And will we get freebies?'

'I might throw you the odd bread roll, Ju. And yes – oh boy, I most certainly will make a lot of staff changes,' replied Guy.

'I bet you don't get rid of that Gina,' winked Juliet. 'She's got the hots for you.'

'It's not reciprocated,' said Guy quickly, for Floz's sake.

Floz noted the way he said that and interpreted it as an extra sign that women weren't his favourite beings.

'She's always mooning over you whenever I've been in,' teased Juliet and launched into an exaggerated impersonation of Gina. ' "Oh Guy, will you just help me stir this egg. Oh Guy, will you just help me cut this carrot. Oh Guy, will you just fondle my . . ." '

'Okay okay,' growled Guy. 'I get the point.'

'Ooo-eeerrr. Touchy!'

'She's a good worker,' said Guy. 'That's all.'

'So you won't be getting rid of her?' Juliet folded a slice of meat into her mouth.

'No.'

'I rest my case,' his minx of a sister mumbled smugly.

Guy was going to start another protest but Juliet was a master at contorting things so he decided to leave it. His sister would have made an excellent barrister with her quick – if evil – wit. He just hoped that he had made the point clear to Floz that he didn't fancy Gina in the slightest.

'I hear you're going to be patching Juliet's crack this week, Steven,' said Grainne, not knowing why everyone suddenly started to shove their napkins in their mouths.

'I couldn't get a proper plasterer,' mocked Juliet when she had stopped laughing.

'Ha ha,' said Steve. 'I'll be there tomorrow night at six on the dot. What are you cooking for me?'

'Tripe, shite and onions,' said Juliet. 'We'll have a takeaway. I presume you're coming as well, Guy?'

'If I must,' shrugged Guy, trying to appear nonchalant but ending up like surly Heathcliff again.

Floz had to really beat back the *harrumph* that was fighting to burst from her. No, he really didn't have to feel obliged. Far be it from her to keep him from roaming the windy moors look-ing for dead Catherine Earnshaw.

Guy was used to seeing clean plates when he cooked. He took it hard when food was left – and there was, unfortunately, not a clean plate on the table. Even from Steve, who usually ate everything, however bad it was. He was the only one who had ever cleared a plate when Grainne cooked.

Steve filled everyone's glass up, whilst Guy prepared dessert. At least now he could earn back some points because his strawberry Charlotte Russe, with strawberry coulis and champagne and strawberry cream, was a masterpiece.

'That wasn't half bad,' said Steve, letting loose a very long and space-freeing burp as he ferried in the condiments from the dining-table.

'Yeah right,' huffed Guy.

'Okay, you've done better.'

'I've never done worse.'

'All right, you win. It was pretty bad.'

'The word you are looking for, Steven, is crap. If you'd bought it in my restaurant, you'd never have come again.'

'Take a chill pill, brother.' Steve picked up the dessert plates. 'What are we having next?'

'Something I managed to get right,' said Guy proudly. 'Strawberry Charlotte Russe.'

'Always a winner when you're trying to get into a girl's . . .'

'Girl's what?' boomed Juliet's voice behind him. Steve's arms flew up and the dessert plates jettisoned into space, but somehow miraculously he managed to catch the lot. Had it been an audition for Billy Smart's Circus, he would not only have passed but been upgraded to the star turn.

'Bad books by ruining her diet,' Steve said quickly.

'Who's on a diet?' sneered Juliet. She didn't wait for an answer but turned to Guy and said, 'I came in to help. Shall I take the cream jug?'

'Yes, please,' said Guy. The pressure to impress was telling on him. He had gone very red and hot.

Steve didn't say anything else. He was already in the *Guinness Book of Records* for most feet in one mouth at any one time. Guy carried the dessert through and wallowed in the ripple of joy that the sight of the mighty cake caused.

Except Floz had to pass because she was allergic to strawberries.

'You're *what*?' cried Guy loudly.

'I'm so sorry,' said Floz quietly, feeling an embarrassed flush rising to her cheeks. She had obviously upset him a lot with that revelation, judging by the look on his face. 'I wish I could eat them – I love them, but I can't.' He obviously had a TV chef's temper. They threw people out of their restaurants who criticized their food, didn't they?

'*Shit, shit, shit*,' said Guy under his breath. That was it, surely. That was all that could go wrong.

Wrong.

When Floz nipped to the loo, Perry leaned in close to Juliet. 'Such a lovely girl. Is she single?'

'Well,' began Juliet, checking that Floz was out of earshot, 'she was, but an old flame has just come back on the scene.'

Guy groaned inwardly. What next? Because the way his life ran, there sure as hell would be another nasty ready to manifest itself.

Juliet was half-ratted by the time they'd had coffees, plus a sample or twelve of Grainne's home-made cherry brandy, which was actually quite nice, considering her total inability to cook. Juliet was so mellow that she even let Steve kiss her goodbye on the cheek. Perry and Grainne kissed Floz and told her she was welcome any time. Steve kissed her too and told her that he'd see her tomorrow. Out of all the possible kissing combinations, the only one that didn't happen was one between Guy and Floz. He did a 'how' hand thing, like a rude Red Indian from the kitchen doorway.

Still, she decided not to play his 'I hate you' game and said warmly how much she had enjoyed the food, even though they both knew that was a lie. His mains had left a lot to be desired, and his dessert would have made her whole head itch and her lungs wheeze. She wished she knew why he was so awkward in her presence. The thought even visited her that he had known in advance that she was allergic to strawberries.

'That went well,' said Steve, as Floz and Juliet's taxi trundled off down the road. Guy didn't answer. He was too busy crashing his head against the kitchen wall.

Chapter 28

Not long after the taxi dumped them at the door, Juliet was asleep on the sofa. Floz switched on her monitor to find the welcome sight of another letter from Nick.

Cherrylips

If fish start fan clubs,they will start one for you.Did catch and release,let them know they owed it to you.It was the best time I've had in a long time.If I could have found a cigar,I would have been in paradise.

Sis brought over what pics she has left of me,Mom was over there Thurs. to borrow the pics she had of dad and me.Wish I knew how to tell mom that dad and I will be okay waiting for her and that neither of us ever wanted her to be hurt. Sis says that when the time is right,she'll talk to mom about sending you some.There are a couple of me in militia but they're distant group shots and I can't even pick me out so no point in sending those.Yeah,I was in the militia (Canadian Scottish).This is about the best I can do now.You do get to see me on my first horse and surviving my first suit.

I don't want to leave anyone behind,but I can't take anyone with me.I am going to take the best of the few

options I have left to take.I can't do chemo again knowing
its only meant to buy me a little more time.Maybe its
desertion.I know my mom thinks it is,but at least I'm letting
it kill me and not doing it myself.I am not happy about my
next few months but at least I accept they are going to
happen.

I do wish that things were different,that you had entered
my life sooner and I do regret that it never was,but I can't
change what is.I hurt the most interesting girl I ever knew
by walking away from you and I am stuck with that.

Nick

Attached were two pictures of a boy, one not happy about
being in the sort of frilly-fronted suit that a bingo-caller would
relish, the other of a little boy grinning on a rocking horse.
They were instantly identifiable as younger versions of the man
she remembered from the photographs he had sent her in the
past. Photographs she wished she had kept.

The boy in the photographs made her look at him with a
mother's heart. She imagined what Nick's mother must be
feeling, remembering the son she had seen grow and blossom
only to find that his autumn had come early. There were few
worse curses for a mother than to lose a child.

Chapter 29

Floz slept surprisingly deeply but woke early, which was just as well because Juliet would have slept through her alarm. She was happy to put bacon sandwiches together for them both whilst Juliet tore around getting herself ready.

'Don't forget, we're having a takeaway tonight with Guy and *Steve*,' said Juliet, again with that hint of a scoff in her voice.

'I won't,' said Floz. She was glad about that because she would never cook for that man again. Although, if his attempts yesterday were anything to go by, he had no right to slag off anyone else's cuisine. Her pasta had been far superior to his sprouts. They were harder than Mike Tyson.

Floz felt strangely numb and lonely when Juliet breezed out of the flat. Despite living alone since her divorce, she hadn't felt particularly lonely, but Juliet was such a big presence, it was easy to feel the impact of her not being around.

Lee Status rescued her from any lurking doldrums by ringing just before 9 a.m.

'You sent in some brilliant poetry for ill people, by the way,' he complimented Floz.

'I hope you don't want any more,' she replied.

'No, we've dropped the range,' he said. 'Market research feedback wasn't too favourable. Obviously you'll still get paid.'

Not favourable? What a shocker, thought Floz.

'Lovely brief this week. Everyday humour – nice and easy. Heavy on the farting jokes, please. And I could do with a couple of really good rhymes about turds and bogies.'

Floz nodded. What a way to earn a living was a thought that often crossed her mind in this job.

Juliet was slightly hungover, and not in the best mood to listen to Coco bragging over the phone about what a wonderful weekend he'd had with Gideon. They'd been to the pictures and watched *Harry Potter* whilst sharing a bucket of popcorn.

'Then he came back to mine and set up my new computer for me. And sorted out the cinema surround on my TV. Honestly, Ju, he's an absolute wizard with techno stuff. He's fab, fab, fab. I love him.'

Juliet tipped a couple of Ibuprofen tablets into her mouth. 'I thought you were taking things slowly.'

'This is slow for me!'

'I'm dying to meet him,' said Juliet, trying to sound enthusiastic, but the pain thrumming in her temple was hampering that process.

'Oh you will. He's very shy though.'

'Shy? Not your usual type then.'

'No, he's not my usual type at all,' Coco sighed.

Every one of Coco's exes had been brash and loud and OTT, and no *way* would he have considered going out with a 'computer geek' before. Gideon was a turn up for the books. Juliet wasn't convinced that Coco hadn't been kidnapped by aliens and had his brain rewired. Then again, maybe they were just getting older and their tastes were changing.

'Fancy coming round tonight? We're having a curry with Guy and Steve.'

'Oooh. Steve seems to be coming over quite a bit recently. Do you think he fancies Floz?' gossiped Coco. 'What are they like together? Do they flirt openly?'

Juliet's jaw dropped open. 'They get along very well, I noticed at Mum and Dad's yesterday. Let's watch their body language tonight and compare notes,' she plotted. She would keep her eye on developments between those two, because if Steve Feast hurt lovely Floz, she would kick his nuts so hard, he'd be chewing them like gum.

'Thank you, but I must decline,' Coco said dreamily. 'We're having a romantic night in. I think he might stay over tonight.' He sounded like a giddy teenager. Just like Juliet did when Roger first asked her out. She wondered if she would ever feel like that again. She was getting older and fussier, and nice men who ticked more than one box on her desirable chart were becoming distinctly thin on the ground.

Floz broke off from writing a string of birthday jokes to write to Nick, because a letter was bursting out of her and she needed to keep those lines of communication open for as long as she could.

Hey you

I am so glad you wrote again. Once those goodbyes have been said and are out of the way . . . anything that comes after is a big bonus and I'm drinking in your every word to be honest.

I am SO glad you had a good time at the weekend. I'll expect a Christmas card from the fish but they have such poor memories.

Don't worry about 'us'. You did what you thought was right at the time. I just wish I'd met you in the flesh because you left a crater in me when you stopped writing. I can still recall your confident drawl when you rang, the places we planned to go when you came over. Militia? God – so much I don't know about you. Do you want me to come over – just for a day?

If you don't get any better offers up there, come and say hello when it's my turn. I'll still be single and dreaming of meeting Mr Right, I reckon. I'd like to think we will get to meet – although I'm not sure if you can take guns up there. Hear the trout are good though.

Cherrylips xxx

She hit send, feeling as if she were being ripped to bits from the inside. She couldn't bear it. She pulled the last of the tissues from the box at her side and pressed them to her eyes. Then she took a deep breath, rejoined the real world and threw herself into writing a lot of jokes about bodily functions for Lee Status whilst trying not to think about what might have been, had life been fair.

Chapter 30

Juliet studied the takeaway menu but what she really wanted – which was sex and lots of it – was not featured. The older she got, the more horny she became at ovulation time. She dragged her thoughts from Piers Winstanley-Black and back to choosing between a dopiaza and a rogan josh.

Floz was setting the table. Juliet lifted her eyes from the menu and looked at her new friend. She wondered if Steve really did have the hots for her, and couldn't wait to watch them together that evening. But, also, what was happening with Floz's mystery 'old flame'? He wasn't exactly making her dance around the room with happiness, if their romance was re-blooming.

The entryphone sounded and Juliet buzzed up her brother and Steve, who was dressed in his plastering whites.

'Wotcher,' he greeted with his big cheerful smile. 'Please don't fancy me too much in my work-gear, girls.'

'Come in, shut up and get on with it,' grumped Juliet. He really was a first-class prat. She knew he actually believed that he looked seductive in his plastering whites. It had never crossed her mind that inside that tough shell of his was a bruised little boy wanting to please.

'Thanks, I'll have one sugar in my coffee,' parried Steve.

'Hi, Guy,' said Juliet, ignoring him.

Floz disappeared to the kitchen to make Steve a drink, grateful for the excuse to get out of glowering Guy's way.

Floz took her time making the coffee and stayed to chat to Steve whilst he was plastering. Guy noticed her reluctance to come into the room where he was. He really had alienated her with all his stupid clumsiness, and every attempt he made to put things right only seemed destined to make things worse.

'Here, what do you want?' Juliet shoved the takeaway menu in Guy's hand.

'Let's just get an Indian banquet,' he replied. 'Then we can mix and match.'

'Good idea,' said Juliet, preparing to prod her brother for information. 'Ooh, Steve and Floz are getting on well, aren't they?' She leaned in close to Guy. 'Do you think they fancy each other?'

'Don't be daft,' Guy snapped. A vision of Steve and Floz snogging landed in his brain and he wrestled it out again.

'I might go and have a nosy and see what they're talking about.'

With anyone else, Guy would have told his sister to leave them alone, but he wanted her to go and split up Steve and Floz. He didn't want his friend getting cosy with her. Not that he would ever think that Steve would muscle in on a love-interest of his. He trusted him with his life. After all Steve had done for him in the past, he knew his mate was solid as a rock. Still . . . he remembered what had happened with his sister's husband and *her* best friend.

'How's it going?' said Juliet, appearing in the kitchen doorway to find Floz emptying the dishwasher and Steve cleaning his trowel.

'I've more or less finished. I'll need to paint it when it's dry,' said Steve. 'Alas, Guy forgot to put the paint in his car, the dumb-ass.'

'And I promised you dinner for that!' exclaimed Juliet. 'It's only taken you five minutes.'

'That's because I know what I'm doing, my girl,' winked Steve. 'Have you seen the hourly rates us plasterers charge? You're getting off lightly, honey.'

'I'm not your girl. Or your honey,' Juliet answered rather archly. 'Hurry up and get out of your clothes anyway, I'm starving.'

'Ooh, Juliet, and there's me thinking you didn't fancy me.'

'In your dreams,' Juliet threw behind her as she walked away. The very thought of having a liaison with Steve Feast was enough to bring up her dinner before she'd even eaten it.

While Steve went to change out of his plastering gear, Floz popped into her bedroom to check on her emails, but nothing had arrived, except a brief from another card firm wanting copy written around a series of funny parrot photographs. Juliet was opening up a bottle of Rioja when Floz went back into the dining area and Guy was ringing up the Taj Mahal.

Then Steve joined the table. He'd put on his jeans and a light blue sweater that was the same shade as his eyes. Even Juliet did a double-take when she saw him. She would never tell him that he was good-looking though, even if she thought it. He was up himself enough as it was.

'Oh here, before I forget.' Steve fished in his pocket and brought out a couple of tickets. 'For tomorrow night. Wrestling night in the Centennial Rooms. You are still both coming, aren't you?'

'Yeah, course,' said Juliet, taking them and pinning them to the noticeboard on the wall behind her. 'Thanks for those. Floz can't wait, can you?'

'Sorry – what?' said Floz, hearing her name. She'd been thinking about Nick, trying to imagine what he was doing now. What it must be like to think, That was my last fishing trip? She was dangerously close to tears again.

'I said that you can't wait for the wrestling tomorrow.'

'Absolutely.' Floz pinned a smile onto her lips.

'Guy's the good one tomorrow – Guido Goodguy – and I'll be the Dark Angel,' said Steve.

'It'll be great fun.' Juliet smiled at him. 'I hope Guy kicks the shit out of you.'

'I'm down to win, so no he won't,' said Steve, thinking how deliciously snotty Juliet was. He would love to kiss her full on the mouth and shut her up.

'It'll be here in fifteen minutes,' said Guy, putting down the phone.

'I was just saying, you're the good guy tomorrow and I'm the baddie.'

'Yep,' nodded Guy.

'How come Kenny's let you have all this time off?' asked Juliet. 'I thought you needed to be at least dead before he let you miss a shift.'

'He's keeping me sweet,' said Guy. 'But it's really not worth me taking time off. You should see the mess that happens in my absence. In fact, I'm driving up after I've had my curry to do a spot-check, which is why I'm not drinking.' And he poured himself a glass of tonic water. 'I'm expecting to find chaos.'

Then right on cue, Guy's mobile rumbled in his pocket and he couldn't hit the connect button fast enough for the naff ring-tone not to deafen them all. He had bought it second-hand from eBay and been really pleased with it, except that it insisted on playing a selection of random tunes – and at full volume – from its memory, and all attempts to alter that arrangement failed.

As Right Said Fred told everyone that they were too sexy for their car, Guy could have spontaneously combusted from embarrassment. Consequently, he barked a loud and clipped, 'Hello!' at the caller in an effort to retrieve some machismo.

Wow, thought Floz. Guy Miller really was a grump. And that ring-tone spoke volumes too. Did he really think he was too sexy . . . too sexy for *Wuthering Heights*? Or Emily Brontë?

'You. Are. Joking.' Guy was growling like a werewolf with

PMT. The colour was draining from his face as he spoke. He ended the call and said, 'I'm sorry, I'll have to go. Varto's nearly burned down the sodding kitchen.'

'Oh no, that's a shame,' said Juliet.

'Yes, isn't it?' said Floz with a sigh. Guy cast her a look and she knew he thought she was being sarcastic. He really was determined to see the worst in her.

'I'll get a taxi home later,' said Steve. 'See you tomorrow then, mate. Are you picking me up as usual?'

'Yep. Juliet, I'll drop that paint off in the morning. I've still got my key so I'll just bob in and put it by the door for you.'

'Okay, bro.'

Guy left the flat and headed towards the car. He was going to personally kill Varto when he got hold of him. More for wrecking his evening and his chance to put things on a right footing with Floz than attempting to blow up his future investment. He could feel the fire building up in his brain, ready to shoot down his nose as if he were a murderous dragon.

Chapter 31

Enough food arrived to feed the five thousand. The curries were a bit on the hot side, which led to much wine being quaffed. When Steve went to the fridge to get out another bottle of white, Juliet leaned over to whisper to Floz.

'Do you want me to leave you two alone?' she said.

'What on earth for?' laughed Floz.

'God knows what you might see in him, but—'

'I'll stop you right there.' Floz held up her hand. 'I don't fancy Steve. And I'm damned sure he doesn't fancy me.'

'Sure?' asked Juliet. 'Aw.'

'Absolutely,' nodded Floz. 'I could pass a *Jeremy Kyle* lie-detector on that question as well.'

'Well, I can't say I'm not slightly relieved.' Juliet puffed out her cheeks.

'I think Steve is a darling,' said Floz, checking that he wasn't coming back and could overhear.

'He's all right, I suppose,' conceded Juliet. Then realized she must be half-drunk at least to have said that. An odd moment of clarity told her that she'd been not-liking him for so long it was more habit than anything else.

Another half-glass of white and Floz had to call things a day. She said her goodnights and fell into bed without even checking her emails. She left Steve and Juliet sitting at the table, nibbling poppadoms in a rare state of cordiality.

'Fancy another glass?' said Juliet. 'I can't believe I am saying this, but I'm actually quite enjoying your company, Steven.'

'Likewise,' returned Steve. 'And yep, I'll have another glass with you.'

'Let's see what's on the box,' said Juliet, weaving her way over to the TV and dropping onto the sofa. She flicked through the channels: a documentary about the Boston Strangler, some whales shagging, loads of American teenagers crying in some sort of boot camp for delinquents. None of which would act as a suitably benign background buzz for the present mood. Then she found an old early colour film with a famous actress whose name she would have remembered, had she been sober. She was walking down a sunlit street in New York singing about the end of summer whilst a storm of rusty leaves whirled around her.

'Here you go,' said Steve, handing Juliet a glass of wine and crashing next to her on the big squashy sofa. He was well within her personal space, but she found she didn't actually mind. His leg felt quite nice next to hers – warm and big and muscular firm.

'Floz is nice, isn't she?' said Steve.

'She's lovely,' said Juliet. 'Fancy her, do you?'

'Floz?' said Steve. 'No, I don't fancy her, but I like her.' And he said it in such a considered way that Juliet knew immediately that his answer was a genuine one.

'I think she's a bit down at the moment though. Tomorrow night will be just what she needs – a cheer-up,' said Juliet, cracking into a poppadom.

'I'm having a cheer-up soon,' said Steve. 'I'm going to buy myself a big fuck-off Jag. Or a Merc.'

'You mean a penis extension,' she said. 'You probably need one.'

'Oy, you. I've had no complaints!'

'From your million conquests,' scoffed Juliet.

'I wouldn't say there were quite that many,' said Steve, feeling the temperature between them drop a few degrees and hating that it had.

'Okay then, when was the last time you had sex? With someone else, I mean.'

'I can't remember,' said Steve. 'Ages ago. Too long.'

'Get lost,' Juliet laughed.

'Honest,' said Steve, wriggling on the sofa. 'I'll thank you not to remind me.'

'Snap,' said Juliet, and chinked her glass against his. 'Who was it with? Little Derek's daughter?'

'Chianti Parkin? I wish,' chuckled Steve.

'I'm saving myself for Piers Winstanley-Black,' slurred Juliet. 'He's all my dream hunks rolled into one.'

'He's a tosspot,' said Steve, with more than a hint of jealousy. 'In a couple of years he'll have a head like a boiled egg. Anyway, those legal types get their thrills from doing deals, not doing women.'

'God, I miss sex,' sighed Juliet and drained her glass.

'So do I,' sighed Steve and drained his glass.

Steve turned to look at Juliet, she turned to look at him. And they never did remember who moved first, but suddenly they were kissing ferociously and rolling around in a lot of crushed poppadoms. Then Juliet was pulling him towards her bedroom, ripping off his shirt.

'This would just be sex, obviously. Just a mutual satisfaction of our frustrations.'

'Oh yes, of course,' panted Steve. 'We're just scratching each other's itch.'

They had undressed each other by the time they fell onto Juliet's bed. Steve groaned as his hands smoothed over her soft, velvety skin. Juliet groaned as her hands smoothed over his muscular chest. She wasn't at all sure how she had ended up in a state of sexual desire for her worst enemy, but she wasn't going to let reason butt in and stop what she was doing.

Steve was greedy for her. He'd never had a hard-on like this before. He felt like a bloody animal.

'Not too rough, am I?' he checked.

'Not rough enough, big boy,' she replied.

'How's this then?'

Juliet didn't answer, not coherently anyway. Just a series of high-pitched vowels and small guttural noises, whilst she drove herself onto him.

In the morning Juliet rolled over to see the clock in the pink blush of early daylight pushing through the curtains. Crikey – she'd had two hours' sleep. Steve awoke with her movement. He sleepily pulled her into his chest. As soon as her skin met with his he was rigid.

'This is just sex, remember,' said Juliet.

'Yep, I know,' said Steve, and he slipped effortlessly inside her, doing wonderful things with his fingers at the same time.

Sweet Jesus, thought Juliet, thundering towards the quickest and most powerful orgasm she'd ever had. As far as 'just sex' went, this was divine.

Chapter 32

Floz awoke from the best night's sleep she'd had in a long time. She couldn't remember dreaming at all about Nick and she didn't stir in the middle of the night and get up to check for emails. The wine had blotted out her pain for a little while and given her some respite.

There were no emails waiting for her when she switched on her monitor. She quickly dressed and went to make herself a cup of coffee, and gasped as she entered the kitchen because there was a man in it – a huge man with platinum-blond hair, meaty legs and a pink satin frilly dressing-gown, and he was standing by the kettle waiting for it to boil. Had he slept on the sofa? If so, why was he wearing Juliet's robe – or trying to wear it. Commonsense told Floz that Steve and Juliet would *never* share a bed under any circumstances. So, what was going on?

'Morning,' said Floz.

Steve whizzed around, the satin gown parting enough for Floz to see that underneath the robe he was naked. She averted her eyes quickly and Steve fastened up the robe.

'Sorry, Floz. I expect that's put you off sausages for life.'

Despite the pocket of embarrassment, Floz laughed.

'Suits you,' she said, as he firmly knotted the belt around him. 'It's Juliet's.'

'No!' said Floz with a grin.

Steve wiped off beads of sweat which had just formed at the back of his neck.

'So . . . er . . . how come you've got it on?' Floz persisted.

'Can't . . . er . . .' began Steve. More sweat. 'Can't find my pants.'

'Oh,' smirked Floz.

'She's . . . er . . . sent me out to make a bacon sandwich and bring tea.'

'Sent you out?' gasped Floz. 'You mean you *slept together*?'

'Didn't get much sleeping done.' Steve clamped his hand over his mouth, realizing that was a tad indiscreet. 'Kettle's boiled. Cuppa?'

'Coffee, please,' said Floz. *Well, well, well.* Boy, she couldn't wait to hear the details about this one.

So there they both were, standing in the kitchen in their dressing-gowns, drinking tea and coffee, Steve cooking bacon on the George Foreman griddle, when there was a crunch in the lock and in walked Guy with the can of paint that he had promised to bob in and drop off. Except that his senses were alerted to the tinkly sound of Floz's laughter mingling with Steve's deep tones.

'Hello,' he called, striding into the room. 'I've brought the pai—'

Then he saw them. His best mate and the object of his affections cosy and half-undressed in the kitchen sharing pleasantries. Juliet's words came back to him: *Floz and Steve seem to be getting on very well. I reckon there's a spark there.*

The fact that Steve looked horrified and Floz instinctively pulled her dressing-gown around her told Guy everything he needed to know. *The rat.* He would never have believed that his best friend would have moved in on Floz when he knew that Guy carried a torch for her. But Steve sure as hell wasn't there because he'd spent the night with Juliet – that much Guy did know.

'Paint!' roared Guy, exiting the flat so fiercely that when he slammed the door shut, the whole building seemed to rattle.

'Oh shit!' said Steve. He hadn't thought that Guy would have reacted so badly to him and his sister getting it together. 'Here, quick, take over the cooking, Floz.' Steve thrust a spatula at her and sprinted across the room and out of the flat, taking the steps like a Hollywood stuntman. He was just in time to throw himself over the bonnet of Guy's car as it started to accelerate away.

'You wanker!' said Guy. 'One: I could have just killed you and two: I want to kill you.'

'Get out of the car,' said Steve. 'Look, I really like her and it just happened.'

'Bollocks. Get off the bonnet and get back to your shagging.'

'I'm not getting off this bonnet until you turn off the engine.'

'I'll drive down the road with you in a minute.'

'Go on then, you thick arse!'

The car jerked forward and threw Steve off; he landed on something very prickly in a herbaceous border. By the time Steve had managed to extricate himself from the thorns of an old rosebush, Guy was long gone. His fast accelerating car threw back a cloud of dust – the kind usually associated with the Batmobile. Tim Onions from the flat downstairs came out of the building dressed in a very badly fitting faded black suit and carrying a battered old briefcase to find a transvestite in a pink satin garment that left nothing to the imagination standing in the drift of fallen leaves. He scuttled off to his pristine Austin Maxi before he could be raped. It was bad enough that there were druggies in the town, but now the flashers were moving in as well.

Juliet was waiting for Steve upstairs, cross-armed and annoyed that her post-coital breakfast in bed ideal had been so rudely interrupted. She looked at her best dressing-gown covered in soil and small stones and a bewildered slug.

'What the bloody hell . . . ?' Then her tone flipped to one of concern when she spotted his knee bleeding. 'Steve, are you all right?'

'It's okay,' puffed Steve. 'I'm fine.'

'What's up with our Guy?'

Steve picked up his mobile and dialled Guy's number. It went straight onto voicemail. Steve left a brief message for Guy to ring him, but guessed he wouldn't.

'He was defending your honour,' said Steve. 'He's obviously really pissed that I've seduced you.'

'You seduced me? Yeah, right. Anyway, he can mind his own goddamn business,' said Juliet, grabbing him by the satin belt. 'I'm thirty-four, not four. Now, sod the bacon sarnie, where were we?'

Steve, however, could not perform. Not with the spectre of Guy's face hanging in his brain. He didn't want Guy thinking he'd hurt his sister or use and abuse her. But try as he might, he couldn't get in touch with him at all that day to tell him as much.

Chapter 33

That evening, Juliet and Floz got a cab to the Centennial Rooms early enough to get a good ringside seat. The Centennial Rooms were in a once-beautiful theatre hall with elaborate stonework. Sadly it had been allowed to grow grubby, and no one cleaned off the pigeon shit from the facade any more. Only the patronage of an ex-factory-owner's very old widow kept it from being shut up and abandoned.

Juliet and Floz hardly had to fight anyone for the front seats – flip-down brown velvet, way past their best days but comfortable enough.

'Quite exciting, isn't it?' enthused Juliet. 'I'm looking forward to seeing some muscly flesh.'

'Yes,' agreed Floz, who had seen enough male flesh in their kitchen that morning to last her a couple of lifetimes.

Behind them, people were really filtering in now and a busload of pensioners, many in wheelchairs, arranged themselves in the wider, accommodating Disabled spaces. Soon, there didn't seem to be a lot of empty seats. The hall took on a different character when it was full of people – it felt less drab with a little crack of electricity in the air, as if it had been injected with life.

'I hope they do ice creams,' said Juliet. 'They do at some places, you know. You can get popcorn at Wakefield Hall.'

'Ice cream, sweat and groins. Sounds delightful,' smiled Floz.

'It's actually much better fun to watch if you get a big crowd in,' said Juliet. 'The atmosphere is brilliant. The crowds have got smaller and smaller over the years, alas, but it's still a laugh. Makes a change from watching soaps anyway.'

'So Steve's playing the baddie tonight then?'

'Yes, Steve is the bad guy tonight,' echoed Juliet, quite surprised by the fact that not only was she saying his name without her customary annoyance, but her voice actually went soft as it came out of her mouth. 'Guy's the goodie, but he's down to lose for a change.'

'Looking forward to seeing *Steeeeve* in his costume?' teased Floz as Little Eric bounced into the ring followed by two busty women with goddess bodies but faces of Staffordshire bull terriers.

Juliet sniffed. 'Floz, I've seen *Steeeeve* loads of times before in his costume. We aren't having a relationship, you know. It's just sex.'

As expected, Guy didn't call to pick him up for their bout at the Centennial Rooms, so Steve had to drive there himself. Guy, who was always on time, wasn't in the dressing-room. Little Derek was pacing about in there and not in the best of moods.

'What am I supposed to do? They'll all want their bloody money back. Where the bloody hell is your mate?'

His mood wasn't helped by the fact that Jeff Leppard should have won in the sixth round but twisted his ankle running away from Klondyke Kevin in the second and had to be carted off. And the new lad 'The Barnsley Chopper' had nearly knocked out the Grim Reaper by tripping over his own foot and nutting him before they'd even started round one, the stupid big Jessie. And Guy hadn't even turned up and he was due on in a minute.

'You'll have to go on with Alberto.' Derek got his cigarettes out of his pocket. He didn't care that he couldn't smoke in here; if he didn't light up and get some calming nicotine inside him he would blow up.

'Not a fecking chance, Derek.' Steve started to back up. 'He's a maniac.'

Then the dressing-room door opened and Little Derek breathed a sigh of relief that could have put out a forest fire as Guy walked in ready to fight with his plain blue costume and white boots.

'Finally! Where the fuck have you been? Are you all trying to give me a fucking heart attack tonight?' Derek puffed on his cigarette and wafted wildly at the smoke so it didn't set off any fire alarm sensors.

Guy didn't answer. He threw his bag down on the bench and cast Derek and Steve a look so black it should have been on a paint chart listed as 'hell'.

'Guy, before we go on . . .' said Steve.

'Save it,' said Guy, half-Heathcliff face, half-Rottweiler.

'Get on that stage, you pair of—' Little Derek was cut short as Tarzan and the Apeman and the Pogmoor Brothers burst in and nearly knocked him flying.

'Guy . . .'

But Guy wasn't in the mood for talking. He was, however, in the mood for fighting.

Juliet was 'whow-whowing' as Steve made his entrance, loud enough to make herself heard above all the rest of the boo-ing. Then Guy followed and the hall erupted into cheering.

'So what do you think?' said Juliet.

'Er . . . Steve looks nice,' replied Floz.

He did actually, thought Juliet. Very attractive in his black trunks and his long white hair flowing behind him. She remembered her legs wrapping around his thighs last night and felt decidedly quivery. God, what was happening to her? Why was she suddenly seeing a different Steve Feast to the one she had been looking at for thirty years?

'He doesn't look bad,' Juliet conceded casually. Then she caught Floz grinning at her. 'I know what you're thinking but it really is just sex. A mutually beneficial arrangement until Piers Winstanley-Black is mine and Steve can pull Little Derek's daughter Lambrusco, or whatever she calls herself.'

Floz too was focusing on Steve, for no other reason than she was trying not to look at Guy. Especially as that blue costume was very clingy and her eyes kept dragging over to him against her will. To make it worse, Guy caught her staring and the scowl that he gave her in return made her feel as if she had done something wrong. Probably breathe.

'I want a good clean fight, boys,' said Little Eric. 'Down in the fourth, lad,' he whispered to Guy.

'Not a chance,' said Guy in the same flat voice as the Terminator. He could see Floz in the front row. She'd obviously come to see her new boyfriend. Shame he was going to be steamrollered.

Ding ding!

Guy grabbed Steve with undue force and slammed him into the corner, cracking his back.

'Bloody hell,' laughed Steve. He bounced back and grabbed Guy around the head speaking into his ear. 'I know what you're thinking . . .'

'Do you?' said Guy, twisting expertly out of the hold and knocking his duplicitous opponent to the ground.

Little Eric groaned. He couldn't afford for this bout to end in less than four rounds. The crowd already felt short-changed by wimpy Leppard hobbling off like a big girl's blouse.

Steve rolled over, just avoiding Guy's powerslam which would have broken his ribs – and the stage – had it landed.

'I won't use her, you know!' said Steve. 'I've liked her since I first laid eyes on her. I care a lot about her.'

Guy made a snatch for Steve but missed.

'How could you?' Guy growled.

'Bloody hell, Guy. I never knew you were that possessive. What's up with ya?'

Guy lunged at Steve using his head as a battering ram against Steve's stomach. Severely winded now, Steve was grateful for the bell. *Ding ding!*

Steve pulled back, avoiding the giant hammer-like hand swinging in his direction. Little Eric pushed Guy none too gently into his corner.

'Steady, you. You've got to last four rounds,' said Little Eric. He stopped short of reminding Guy that he was supposed to be the good guy because he appeared to be winning some brownie points from the crowd. At last a fight that actually looked like a proper bout, and not like two ballet dancers arguing over a handbag.

Ding ding!

Steve and Guy circled each other like warring crabs.

'I'm going to batter you to a pulp,' snarled Guy.

'You think you are,' said Steve, 'but you're not. You don't own her, you know. Bloody hell, I don't think anyone would *dare* try and own her! What do you want me to do – apologize?'

'Yes, for starters.'

'I would if I thought I had anything to apologize for!'

'Yeah, 'cos you didn't look at all guilty half-naked in the kitchen together this morning, did you?'

Grappling ensued. Guy grabbed Steve in a very tight chin-lock that Steve couldn't get out of. As Guy piled on the pressure, Steve thought that he might have had an easier time if his friend hadn't turned up and he'd had to fight Alberto Masserati instead. Then Guy slipped, and in the split second when he released his arm pressure, Steve twisted up and out. Guy made a sweep for Steve, missed and instead Steve grabbed his arm and sent him flying into the ropes, winding him. He followed it up with a side headlock. *Gottim*. Then Guy's words came back to him.

'Hang on, what do you mean you caught me half-naked in the kitchen with her this morning? You don't think . . . ?' *Ding ding!* 'Bloody hell,' said Steve as Little Eric ripped them apart.

'There's another two rounds to go. Pace yourselves.'

'You'll get your four rounds, don't you worry,' said Guy, and thumped Steve on the back as he retreated to his corner. The crowd went nuts. Someone threw a shoe into the ring, hitting Guy on the chest.

'Is it always this aggressive?' asked Floz.

'Well, it's slightly different to usual. Probably a change of tack to attract punters. After all, they *are* sworn enemies on stage,' said Juliet, who was loving it. In a past life she would probably have been knitting by a guillotine.

'It's very good acting,' said Floz, not quite convinced that Guy was putting on his aggression, which looked very real. 'I thought Guy was supposed to be the goodie.'

'He was,' said Juliet, not taking her eyes off the ring in case she missed anything. 'Don't know why they've changed it.'

The two men glowered at each other across the diagonal space between them. Steve was really pissed off, now he realized that Guy wasn't being ultra-possessive over Juliet but thought he had spent the night with Floz. It wasn't much of an indication of their friendship if Guy really believed Steve would steal away the woman he had a hell of a mighty crush on. Even if she wasn't actually *his* yet.

Ding ding!

'You're an arsehole, do you know that?' said Steve, slowly coming towards him. 'I've just realized that you thought I'd spent the night with Floz.'

'Well, you didn't sleep with Juliet, did you?' Guy laughed humourlessly.

'Actually I did,' said Steve.

'You sodding liar,' said Guy, and with a spurt of fury he threw himself at Steve, who tottered, allowing Guy to over-power him and twist him into a Full Nelson, bending his arms back, forcing his neck forward.

'*Aaarrghghh!*'

'Hurt, does it?' spat Guy. 'You haven't felt anything yet.' He propelled Steve forward, then he followed him, twisting his body over and through the ropes. They both tumbled out of the ring, narrowly avoiding a bloke with his leg in a plaster cast.

'*War-ning, war-ning . . .*' came the chant from a highly charged audience. Juliet was leading the mantra at her side of the hall.

'You are dead, mate!' promised Steve, climbing back into the ring, helped by a couple of little old grannies, grateful for a feel of his muscly leg.

'Yeah, course I am!' returned Guy, yelping as a lumpy woman ran at him and started battering him on the back with her hand-bag. He quickly sprang into the ring to avoid her.

Little Eric made a meal of giving Guy a warning, much to the pleasure of the crowd. They were baying as loudly as if they were in the Coliseum watching Christians take on lions. *Ding ding!*

Right, this is war, thought Steve to himself. If Guy wanted to fight properly, then he'd give him exactly what he wanted. He was going to make sure that Guy flaming Miller had a fourth and final round that he'd never forget.

Ding ding!

The two men came at each other like mad bulls clashing in the epicentre of the ring. Equally matched in anger-fuelled strength, neither managing to push the other off or down or get purchase on a head, an arm, a neck.

'I'll make you listen to me if it's the last thing I do, you stupid, thick knobhead!' yelled Steve.

'What are you going to tell me? That you couldn't help yourselves?' Guy hurt inside. He wanted to go on fighting forever, because at least he could hold himself together when he was doing so. He thought he just might crumble into pieces if he stopped.

'Bloody hell! What's he playing at?' winced Juliet, realizing this fight *was* real.

'That's for not even having the guts to admit it,' stormed Guy, hooking his leg around Steve's and seeing him stumble to the canvas. ' "Slept with Juliet"! Yeah, like I'm going to believe *that*!'

'What's he saying?' asked Juliet, catching wind of the word 'guts'.

'I don't know.' Floz bit her lip. 'But they're arguing about something.'

'I've never seen Guy act like this before, on-stage – or off,' said Juliet, thinking, What on earth is up with him? In the past couple of weeks her brother had changed from being a quiet, gentle man in the shadows to Mr Mean and Moody with cooking skills sinking to the level of their mother's. She only hoped he wasn't heading for another breakdown.

'That's not acting,' croaked Floz, seeing the black look in Guy's eyes. Not even Laurence Olivier could fake fury like that.

'Surely he can't be that annoyed that Steve and I spent the night together?'

Floz shook her head. Lord. Guy really *was* possessive over his sister then. No wonder he didn't think much to Floz, usurping his place as best friend. It explained a few things.

Guy draped his arms over the ropes, waiting for Steve to get up so he could clothesline him – ram him with his arms open and knock him to the deck. Then he could climb out of the ring and go home.

'*Up, up, up, up,*' the crowd chanted, as Little Derek counted. '*Five, six, seven . . .*'

Steve stumbled to his feet. Guy launched himself forward, but Steve deftly leaped out of his path and stuck out his leg. Guy tripped but didn't go down. As he righted himself, Steve locked his arm around Guy's neck, pulling his head down into his ribcage in a Grovit lock. It hurt like a bastard.

'Gotcha. Now this, Guy Miller, is for thinking that I'd done the dirty on you.' Steve rolled his hips, turning his wrist until Guy's neck felt as if it was about to snap and he yelped. 'And the reason I couldn't look you in the face in the kitchen this morning was because I'd just got out of your sister's bed. Really and truly. Are you listening to me, you arsehole? *Juliet's* – not Floz's – bed!'

'Bollocks! Arrghghh! Ju hates yooouuu!'

'Not any more she doesn't. Ask her yourself.'

'You expect me to believe that?'

'Bloody hell, how many more times? YES.'

'Not you and—'

'NO.'

'*Arrghghh!*'

'Submit, you thick bastard, and let's go and have a pint.'

Guy submitted. Little Eric bent to hear the words and declared the match over. The crowd stood to cheer. Steve did a lap of honour whilst Guy lay limp in the ring.

'*Easy easy easy . . .*' yelled the applauding crowd.

Steve and Guy had never fought in their lives before that night. Not even when Guy was out of it a few years ago and would have fought a brick wall if it meant losing some of the pain that had built up inside him. Steve's meaty paw came out to help him up and Guy took it, and together they clambered out of the ring and went back to the changing rooms, signing some programmes on the way.

'I'm sorry,' said Guy, when they were stripping off. 'I thought . . .'

'Yes, you told me what you thought.'

'I just presumed . . . you get on so well with Floz and—'

'And Juliet and I don't – or rather didn't,' Steve finished for him. 'Well, no one is more surprised by the change of events than me, you can trust me on that one. Oh sorry, I forgot – you *don't* trust me, do you?'

'Don't,' cringed Guy, burying his head in his towel. 'It's just that you and Floz are actually quite well suited,' he mumbled.

'I wouldn't do that to you, mate. Not even if I fancied the arse off her. Which I don't,' Steve added quickly for clarification purposes. 'She's lovely, but, well . . . Juliet and I want the same things, I suppose.'

'What?'

'Some warmth, some fun. Somebody to wake up with, no promises, no regrets at the end. I'm not disrespecting her, Guy,' Steve said quietly. 'I like her a lot. I always have.'

'You never told me that.'

'I never told anyone,' said Steve. 'I didn't think I had a cat in hell's chance with her.'

Juliet and Floz were waiting for them at the stage door.

'Were you arguing for real out there?' asked Juliet.

'Don't be daft,' laughed Steve.

'You know it's all staged,' said Guy, mirroring Steve's amusement. 'Little Derek told us to put it on a bit. Are you coming for a pint with us?'

As Juliet said yes, Floz declined. 'I've got a bit of work to do,' she explained.

Guy's heart sank.

'Oh, come on,' said Steve – for Guy's benefit. 'Just one. It's too late to write jokes.'

'No really, I can't. It's a busy time for me and I have deadlines to meet.'

'You take my car, I'll get a lift home with Steve then,' said Juliet, handing Floz her keys. She would have bet her life that

Floz wasn't going to work. So what was she rushing off for? Something to do with that 'old flame', she bet.

Floz was glad to escape from Guy. He unsettled her. Those looks he had cast her from the stage during the bout were scary. She wondered again what it was in Guy's past that had made him need the staunch friendship of Steve – something which both Juliet and Coco had nearly let slip. She wouldn't have put a mental illness past him.

None of them noticed the old man in the suit at the back of the hall. He had taken a few photographs on his phone and was sending them over to his son now. What a very interesting night, he thought.

Chapter 34

When Floz got home to the flat, she went straight to her PC, but there was no mail. A lump of heavy disappointment settled inside her. She made herself a coffee and warmed her hands on the mug, but it couldn't defrost the chill in her bones.

She sat at her keyboard and began to type.

Dearest Nick

Just a wee email to wish you well and hope that things are easy for you. You're on my mind so much. I ache to give you some comfort and feel so helpless that I can do nothing from this distance except pray for you.

I am hurting so much – I just wish we had met and that I had held your hand so I could recall it rather than imagine it. Life feels so very cold at the moment.

Wishing you gentle days and nights, my love.

Cherrylips xxx

By the time Floz had changed into her nightie and brushed her teeth there was a reply.

Cherrylips

Then I think its time to say goodbye.Its not easy this end
either,too many what ifs and all the rest.This will be my last
message,we each have things to do and so its time that we
do them.Take care and live out a million dreams.

Nick

Floz screamed at the PC, 'No, no, please don't leave me!' She
didn't want him to go. She didn't want to be left in the wilder-
ness again, hunting in the dark for information. But he must
tire so easily and it wasn't fair of her to make him feel obliged
to write. She had to let go – she knew it, but did not feel it.

She tossed and turned in bed and was still awake long after
Steve and Juliet stole into the flat, stifling their giggles as they
retired to her bedroom to make each other feel warm and wanted.

September

September is the month of fruits fattening and crop gathering
Of blush-sky evenings and golden afternoons
Of leaves toasting and fires burning
Of mists curling and large wine moons

'September' by Linda Flowers

Chapter 35

Steve awoke the next morning and immediately smiled at the sight of Juliet, fast asleep beside him and snoring ever so slightly. He'd never realized before how thick and dark her eyelashes were or what a lovely shape her mouth was. Her eyelids were fluttering as if she was dreaming. He shifted across the bed and snuggled into her and, in sleep, she nestled against him.

It was a delicious feeling and one which he savoured. He had slept with a lot of women in his time, hoping to find this sort of connection that would make him want to hang around the next morning and share breakfast and conversation and plan future dates. He never had. He thought about the events of the previous night and how Guy had thought he had moved in on Floz. He loved Guy like a brother and wished he could find some way to convince Floz that he was a great bloke. They could bring each other a lot of happiness if they got it together, he was convinced of that – and the elder Millers thought she was lovely. The Millers had been the family he'd always craved, the sort of family he wanted for his own children one day. He knew he had a reputation as a dog, but in his heart of hearts, more than anything Steve wanted a wife, children and a warm, safe home. And he wished the same for Guy – that he would settle down with someone who would bring his heart peace at least. His friend had lost a big chunk of his life, but hopefully the opening of his new restaurant was the kick-start he needed to go for it and make up for all the time he had lost after Lacey Robinson's suicide.

Talking of which, he remembered that he had something to tell Guy that would really make his day. He had seen it whilst driving from his mum's yesterday. He reached for his mobile, but his fingers fell short of it and he didn't want to dislodge Juliet from his embrace to get it.

He knew he would have to be careful because this was just sex to her and he'd lied and said it was just sex for him too. He'd get mashed one day because as soon as Juliet met someone who would satisfy her emotional needs as well as her sexual ones, he would be toast. But for the moment, Steve Feast was happy existing in the here and now, pretending to himself that this was forever.

He lay close to Juliet for the next twenty minutes until her alarm went off and totally forgot to ring Guy.

Chapter 36

Floz knew there would not be another email waiting for her when she woke up, but she checked all the same. She had to trust that one of Nick's sisters would let her know 'when'. But a letter was bursting out of her and she wrote to him again.

Dearest Nick

This is written without any hope whatsoever of a reply. Feel free to ignore it or read it – that is your prerogative.

I feel so privileged that you came into my life at all. You were always special – and this is coming from a total scep-tic because you, alone, know my history.

I used to envy the way my parents looked at each other. I always wanted someone who adored me like that. I know I was an accident. I know there was no true space for me in their lives then – and now. They were all the other ever needed – or wanted. You were the only person I knew would love me as much as I loved in return. I will never find the equivalent of you. You were unique – damn you.

I can only guess that you are surrounded by your family's warmth. They always sounded so wonderful.

All my love

Cherrylips xxx

She pressed send and knew that now she really had to let go. She had said everything she needed to. She gulped back the tears, dressed and prepared to write jokes for the greetings-cards industry. But she waited until the giggling Juliet and Steve had left before emerging for her breakfast.

Guy rose and dressed and put some fresh coffee through the percolator. He hadn't slept well. He was due at the bank this morning to dot the 'i's and cross the 't's on a loan agreement. Whereas he had merely existed for a few years, breathed and eaten and worked, now he felt as if he was about to leave the plodding slip-road in life and rejoin the motorway. A thought that both thrilled and terrified him.

Over the years he had spent little, saved his wages and invested wisely, and he had enough money to buy the restaurant almost outright. Kenny might have thought he was giving Guy a bargain, but he had failed to take into account the massive refurbishing costs if Burgerov were to shed its cheap bistro image and become a centre of serious cuisine. Guy was a good, steady customer of his bank and they had readily agreed to lend him the money he asked for after submitting estimates from reliable local builders.

Guy seriously needed to find somewhere else to live, a place big enough to spread out in, unlike this bolt-hole which had put him up for too long and for which he felt no affection. He wanted a home, he wanted somewhere he could bring a woman back to and a kitchen where he could be creative. His mind strayed to buying somewhere like Hallow's Cottage and living there – with Gina – but that thought was quickly expelled. She might have been available to him, but she wasn't the one he wanted. He dared to think of Floz snuggled next to him on a big sofa in a refurbished Hallow's Cottage, beams above their head, a baby in a bouncy chair at their side. It was so perfect a picture that it hurt, because Floz Cherrydale obviously didn't feel the same and so that was sure never to happen.

Anyway, buying the restaurant would put paid to all of his savings. A house would have to wait. That was the trouble, he had a picture in his mind of him and Floz and Hallow's Cottage and really everything else would be second-best. And he'd had enough of second-best to last him a lifetime.

Chapter 37

Steve arrived at the flat that evening with a Chinese takeaway banquet for three.

'Thought I'd surprise you,' he said, then noticed the smell of garlic in the air. 'Oh, have you eaten?'

'I was just about to dish up a spag bol,' said Juliet. 'It's okay though, it'll do for tomorrow. That all right with you, Floz? Fancy a Chinese with us?'

'Yes, that's fine by me,' nodded Floz, closing her notepad and going into the kitchen for plates.

The three of them watched a film about Jack the Ripper afterwards. Then Floz went to bed, leaving Steve and Juliet leaning on each other on the sofa.

'Are you staying?' she asked.

'Well, I will,' he said, 'but I'm too knackered for sex. I've been plastering a ceiling and my back is killing me.'

'I'm tired myself,' said Juliet through a yawn. 'Let's just sleep then, shall we? I'll relax you with a massage.'

'That sounds bliss,' said Steve – and meant it.

Surprisingly, there was an email from Nick in Floz's inbox which she checked as a matter of course before she went to bed.

Cherrylips

I have a cousin who lives alone.He lost his wife in a car accident 12 years ago and has no children.He is trapped in his
greif.So,he makes no new friends.He could start a new book
but prefers to be stuck on the last chapter of an old book
forever.I'm proud and sad that I will be missed,makes it easier
somehow than doing the down the toilet dead goldfish route.

My point is that there are countless unique guys out
there just waiting to meet a girl like you and the only barrier
stopping them is you.

I wish you life,love and great (moderately safe)adven-
tures and maybe the ability to worm hooks,especially if one
day you adopt a son and teach him to fish.

Nick

Floz burst into tears. All day she had been getting to grips with
letting go, felt she was mastering it, and now she was all ripped
open again. She sat at her PC and wrote the one question she
now had to ask.

Dearest Nick

I'm sorry, I am writing too much and tiring you. Just one
more question that will not require any detail in the answer.
Please tell me definitively, without elaboration – truthfully
because I can take it – did I have any place in your heart
these past eighteen months?

Cherrylips

Floz tried to sleep, and managed it but not well. She awoke in
the wee small hours knowing without any doubt that a new

email had arrived for her. She was right. That she was so in tune with Nick strengthened her belief that they would have been so right for each other, had fate been on their side.

Dearest Cherrylips

you are not writing too much.i read much better than i write nowadays.my spellcheck is in therapy and not expected to return to normalcy.gave up on capitals but still punctuate. don't know if you have Boost over there but don't drink it if you don't have to.it tastes like its good for you,has three colours,white,brown and pink.has the flavour of dirt with sweetner added.Snowed on the mountains last night,guess global warming is over.

make sure you keep writing those jokes and smiling. There is too much sadness out there.And to answer your question,you are the only woman I think I ever knew.You are and will always be my constant if only.

Nick

Chapter 38

On the following Monday morning, Floz sat at the window enjoying her first coffee of the day and a slice of toast. The school was open again after the long summer break. Children were walking up the road towards it in their pristine uniforms, shiny shoes and new coats with mittens on strings poking out of their sleeves. Some of them looked little older than babies as they gripped their mothers' hands and skipped along. It was an achingly sweet sight.

Tim, from downstairs, was raking up leaves, but as soon as he gathered a pile, the breeze blew on them and sent them whirling up into the air before he could scoop them up into the green bin. The autumn wind was a minx, Floz decided with a grin as she watched him.

This week's work brief was Christmas, but there was nothing odd about that. She often had to write copy about Easter in December, and 'Happy Hallowe'en' cards in March. Many a time she would be writing about Santa when the newspaper headlines were, PHEW, WHAT A SCORCHER. Such a shame no one sent 'Happy Autumn' cards. It was such a bonny time of year.

Yet people scurried through leaves, seeing only nature's nuisance litter and paying no heed to the glorious mix of colours: scarlet, gold, rust, bronze, spice, claret, amber, crimson, copper. They gave a cursory glance upwards to the big blushing Harvest Moon, once so important in helping farmers work extra hours on their crops at night. They failed to notice the raspberries and blackberries fruiting fat and sweet on the brambles or the sweeping bleed of poppies in the fields.

Floz always loved that autumn brimmed with activity. At Harvest Festival, people sang rousing hymns in church of 'swelling grains' and 'sweet refreshing rain', children collected groceries in baskets to give as gifts to pensioners. At Hallowe'en, families scooped out pumpkin heads and placed them outside their doors to tell little skeletons and witches there just might be 'treats' available here, if they knocked and promised not to 'trick'. Then, when November came, the night air was filled with crackles and smoke and sizzling barbecues, fizzing fireworks and booms, bangs and merriment. Yet most people instinctively thought of autumn as a 'non-season' – a mere fill-in between beloved summer and sparkly winter.

Floz had more reason than most to hate autumn, but she could never quite manage to believe that God would paint the season with such a beautiful palette if He were not imparting a message of hope: that the earth was not dying, but preparing to rest and renew itself and would survive to flower again. And she *so* needed to keep her faith that there was a God – and a heaven.

She took herself out for a walk around the shops and ended up in Morrisons, wandering idly down the aisles but not seeing anything that might tempt her appetite. Food didn't interest her much at the moment but she forced herself to eat when she felt weak and shaky. She looked down at her shopping trolley. She could have sworn she had put some potatoes in there, but there were none. There was, however, a huge bag of onions which she didn't need. She was tired out: physically from not sleeping too well, and mentally from thinking about Nick and filling in the gaps as to what could be happening to him, what his family were going through, his niece and nephew, even his dogs. He had two beautiful huskies – Amak and Pilitak. They were Inuit names, she remembered him telling her. Amak, the female, meant 'playful'; Pilitak, the male, meant 'useful'. She had a feeling there would be a lot of people pining for the demise of this strong, lovely man. And animals.

She had not heard from him in nearly a week now and suspected the worst. The not knowing was tearing her apart.

The woman on the till asked Floz if she was all right because the tears were rolling down her cheeks as she put her shopping into the carrier bags.

'Yes, fine.' Floz attempted cheerfulness. 'I think I'm allergic to this eyeliner.'

It was a crap lie, but the till operator kindly played along.

'I once had one of those,' she said, standing to help Floz pack. 'Made my eyes look like pissholes in the snow. And it wasn't a cheap one either.'

Floz chuckled, grateful to her. There were some lovely people on this planet, making life run a little more smoothly with just a gentle word or two.

In the car park, Floz noticed a man fiddling underneath the bonnet of his car.

'Turn the engine, Gron,' he was calling to someone in the driver's seat. The voice was instantly familiar.

'Mr Miller? Are you all right?'

Perry Miller straightened up.

'Oh hello, dear Floz.' He leaned over and gave her a kiss on the cheek. 'Spot of car trouble. Can't work out what's wrong with it at all. It's just had a damned service.'

Grainne emerged from the car and waved. 'Hello, Floz,' she said brightly. 'We're having some car trouble. It's just had a service . . .'

'I've told her, Gron,' cut in Perry with a rare snap in his voice. Floz noticed that he looked weary. He was a seventy-year-old man, still under the impression that he had the energy levels of a twenty-year-old. He was used to doing the rescuing in his family; the role of 'rescuee' obviously jarred with his pride.

'Look, why don't I run you both home?' suggested Floz.

'No, no, we can get a taxi,' said Perry. 'You're a busy girl.'

'I didn't hear that,' said Floz. 'Let me put my shopping away and I'll bring my car round.'

'Thank you so much,' smiled Grainne, who looked relieved. 'My ice cream must be nearly defrosted.'

A few minutes later and Floz was driving towards them. Just for a moment, she imagined it was her own parents she was helping because they needed her. They would never be in that position, though. She had no doubt that when anything happened to one of them, the other would follow soon after. They would never want anyone but each other – it had always been that way, and always would be. She coughed away the emotion rising within her again. She would never grow out of the feeling of being surplus to her own mother and father's requirements.

'I've told the customer service desk that you've broken down and they gave me this to put in your windscreen,' said Floz, handing Perry a piece of card saying *Authorized vehicle parking*. Then you won't get fined for being here over two hours.'

'Oh, that's very kind of you, dear Floz,' gushed Grainne.

They loaded the Millers' shopping into her boot and then Floz set off for Maltstone.

'Sorry to put you to all this trouble,' said Grainne, all snug in the back.

'Really, it isn't any trouble at all,' replied Floz and meant it.

'I can't understand what's wrong with it.' Perry was still mulling over the problem.

'Perry has always been very good with cars,' Grainne said. 'It must be an odd one if he can't work it out. Never mind. Guy and Steve will sort it for us later. And if they can't, they'll know a man who can. One of their wrestling friends will be a mechanic, I'm sure of it.'

When they got to the house, Perry was insistent on giving Floz a fiver for her petrol. Floz was equally insistent on not taking it.

'Floz, I don't want you to be out of pocket,' Perry said sternly.

'Perry, I am not taking that money,' Floz told him, as she carried in the shopping for them. 'And there's an end to it.' Then she drove off before the pair of them held her at ransom until she had put the money into her purse.

'What a sweet girl,' smiled Grainne, waving until Floz's car was out of sight.

'Isn't she just?' nodded Perry.

'I wonder what's troubling her, though. She looked so awfully sad in her eyes. Did you notice how red they were?'

'I thought the very same,' agreed Perry, taking his pipe out of his pocket. 'Lovely girl, but sad.'

'How could you not want to see a daughter like that very often?' Grainne's smile dropped. 'Some woman is either very stupid or very selfish.'

'I stopped judging others by my own standards many years ago, my darling,' said Perry, putting his arm around his wife and leading her inside. 'There are a lot of people in this world who can't love, and I'm just glad that we aren't them.'

Juliet flew into the flat that evening and strode right over to Floz looking murderous.

'Thanks to you and your damned kindness to my parents, we've been invited for Sunday lunch,' she bellowed. 'And the worst of it is, my mother's doing the cooking. Thanks a lot, Floz. Next time, leave them in the bloody car park.'

Floz burst into laughter.

'You think it's funny, Floz Cherrydale,' said Juliet. 'Just you wait until you're in A and E getting unpoisoned.'

Chapter 39

Despite Juliet's exaggerated and pretend dread of the Sunday dinner to come, Floz was really looking forward to it. It would take her mind away from Nick and how he was. Eleven days since his last email. But her daydreams had been full of him and so easy to slip into. In them they lived together in a log cabin at the side of a lake. She was tapping on a laptop, he was fishing and they would eat the catch on a table outside on a porch on nights lit by a large bone-white moon. She thought about him pulling her onto the bed and kissing her till her nerve-endings were on fire. And he would say, 'I love you,' and she would feel that he meant it. *His constant 'if only', as he was hers.*

Juliet crossed herself with her right hand before she pushed open the front door to 1, Rosehip Gardens.

'If I die because of my mother's cooking, Floz, I'll come back and haunt you,' she said.

'Don't be daft,' laughed Floz, as she followed Juliet inside. A pleasant smell of a roast dinner in progress greeted them.

'Hellooo,' said Perry, greeting them both with a kiss. 'You're the first here. I've just seen Steve's car pass, so he'll have gone for Guy.'

Floz's heart jumped in her chest. So Guy was coming too then? What was it about that man that did funny things to the rhythm of her heartbeat?

'What was up with the car in the end, Dad?' asked Juliet.

'Alternator,' replied Perry. 'Guy and Steve got it sorted for me.'

'Does your mum know about you and Steve?' whispered Floz.

'What, that we're not in a relationship but just having wild sex? Er, no, Floz,' Juliet whispered back with an Elvis lip.

'Ah, fair point,' said Floz, who wanted to add, 'Just sex, my eye.' There was genuine affection between Steve and Juliet. Any idiot could see that.

'That chicken smells very respectable,' Juliet said. 'Have you bought an oven-ready one from Morrisons and are just browning it off?'

'No, I have not. And it's turkey,' said Grainne, turning to Floz. 'Honestly, to listen to my family you'd think I'd burn water. I could always make a very respectable Sunday lunch.'

The front door opened and Guy and Steve came in.

'Hi, girls,' waved Steve, trying to act cool and unboyfriend-like. Guy nodded at them. Floz nodded back, but smiled at Steve.

'Floz, are you losing weight?' said Steve, noticing that her cheeks seemed a little more hollowed than usual. 'Doesn't she look as if she's lost weight, Guy?' He set that up for his friend. Women always liked to be given a compliment like that.

Guy felt that, despite Steve's well-meant remark, Floz might be uncomfortable with everyone assessing her figure, and wanted to help her out. And his instinct told him that the best way to do that would be to say, 'Hadn't really noticed.'

'Charming.' Juliet clicked her tongue. 'You always did have the gift of the gab, Guy.'

'I didn't mean that she hadn't,' Guy jumped in defensively. 'I just meant that I hadn't been looking at her . . . at all . . . in that way . . . in any way, actually . . .'

Steve groaned. A picture of a man digging himself further into an enormous hole flashed into his brain. He saw Floz's cheeks growing pink and heading towards scarlet so he stepped in, clapped his hands and started to open the bottle of rosé fizzy wine which he'd bought for the girls.

'I thought you might have brought Raymond along,' said Grainne.

'He's away at some perfume convention this weekend,' returned Juliet. 'Good timing on his part, that's what I say.'

'I can't get this damned thing open,' Steve snarled, then yelped as he cut his finger on the wire clutching the cork.

'Give it here,' said Guy. He took the bottle, twisted the cork and it shot out like a bullet, narrowly missing Floz. Guy slammed his hand on top of the bottle as froth raced up the neck, with the result that it jetted out sideways and all over Floz's top half.

'Goodness me!' said Grainne, running off for a towel. 'Your lovely white shirt as well.'

'It's fine,' said Floz, wanting to throw herself through the picture window, leap over the garden fence and run as far away from Guy Miller as possible.

'I'm so sorry,' said Guy, holding fingertips of despair to his forehead.

'It's okay,' said Floz, wiping herself down with the back of her hand until the towel arrived and realizing with horror that her shirt was now see-through and one lacy bra-cup with a pink trim could clearly be seen. Rosé wine dripped off her fringe. She didn't have enough hands to try and blot the wet patches, dry off her hair and cover her boob.

'It's probably because it's not chilled and has been rolling about in the car,' explained Steve. 'Sorry, I should have bought it last night and kept it in the fridge.'

'It's all part of the general parcel of doom,' sighed Juliet. 'Doomed, we're all doomed.'

The timer on the cooker went off.

'Ooh, everyone to the table, please!' Grainne clapped her hands excitedly. Steve dived onto the seat that Guy was heading for and so forced him to sit opposite Floz. He tried to look anywhere but at her bra through her shirt, and failed for the split second when she caught him. She had a good mind to point upwards and say in a tight voice, 'This way to my eyes.'

'Wine, anyone?' asked Guy, picking up what was left in the first bottle of rosé. He nearly dropped it because it was wet and slipped through his fingers.

'I'll do it, shall I?' said Steve. He poured three expert flutes of it for the ladies, then some white for himself, Perry and Guy.

Grainne ferried in plates loaded with slices of turkey breast, sprouts, colcannon potatoes, uniform-looking Yorkshire puddings, roasted parsnips and crushed carrot and swede.

'Mum, these are Aunt Bessie's Puddings, aren't they? You cheat,' said Juliet, although it had to be said she was impressed with how normal the meal looked.

'I could never do the puddings,' said Grainne. 'And thanks to Aunt Bessie I don't have to struggle with them.'

'This looks grand,' nodded Perry.

Steve tucked in. He'd always loved eating at this table with the Miller family. Grainne could make a mess of beans on toast, but it was never the food that was the most important factor of the enjoyment for him. He couldn't remember eating with his mother at a table and there was never any of the chat and the laughter that he found here in Rosehip Gardens.

'So, how's the wrestling going, Steven?' asked Perry, pouring some gravy on his potatoes then attempting to fish out all the lumps. It had the texture of frogspawn.

'Limping along,' said Steve. 'It's nice to get together with the lads, but one by one they're all packing it in.'

'That's a shame,' said Grainne. 'I suppose it's only the American stuff that the kids are interested in.'

'More or less,' sighed Steve. 'That's where all the action is. Plus the British stuff isn't on the telly any more.'

'Can you not get a job over there with them, Steven?' Perry was now squashing the lumps with the back of his fork.

'I wish,' said Steve, taking the tip from Perry and turning his own fork over to flatten the gravy.

'Who's the man in charge over there? I'll have a word with him for you,' smiled Grainne.

'His name is Will Milburn,' said Steve, taking an emergency swig of wine. How much salt had Grainne put in the carrot and swede?

'Is he a big wrestler himself?' asked Perry.

Guy stepped in to answer for Steve, who was coughing hard.

'No, he's a short little midget.' *Whoops.* He turned quickly to Floz. 'No offence, Floz.'

WHOOPS.

'None taken, I'm sure,' huffed Floz.

'How tall are you, Floz?' asked Perry. 'I'd say five foot one.'

'Five foot two,' replied Floz, waiting to hear what Guy would come out with next.

'And what do you weigh?'

'Dad.' Juliet was the first to raise her hands up in frustration.

'She's only wee,' said Perry. 'I'm sorry if that embarrassed you, Floz. I only meant that you're a little . . . what're those fairy-things called?'

'Gnome?' said Guy. *Shit.* '*NYMPH.* I meant nymph!'

'Yes, a wee nymph,' said Perry.

'Not a nymphomaniac then?' Steve roared with laughter.

'You see what I mean?' Juliet turned to Floz. 'Next time call the RAC out for them and hide behind the nearest bush. Never let them owe you a favour again.'

Thankfully the conversation around the table turned to Perry's plans for his garden and sog-wet-through, shortarse, gnome-like Floz was allowed to sit back in the shadows away from confidence-stripping spotlights.

Grainne presented a rather dodgy-looking Black Forest gâteau for dessert.

'You're supposed to take the stones out of the cherries, Mum,' said Juliet, nearly breaking her back tooth.

'Did I just taste pistachio nuts?' mused Perry.

'Yes, I had some left over. I thought it would add a bit of interest.'

'I think in future we'll leave the party food to Guy,' Perry said, winking at his son.

'Mum made a better lunch than I did last time I cooked here,' Guy said, pulling a cherry stone out of his mouth. 'I had a real blip that day.' At last, the chance to hammer the point home to Floz, in case she thought that was his usual standard of cuisine.

'You were doing fine, Grainne, until the cake,' Perry said, rising from his seat to replenish everyone's glass with wine.

'I've done some home-made mints to have with the coffee,' announced Grainne proudly. She wondered why that was greeted with a heavy silence and not a resounding cheer.

There was no getting away from the goodbye kiss after the coffee and the home-made fondant mints – with raisins soaked in crème de menthe – had been attempted. The Millers were an affectionately demonstrative family. Floz found herself getting a bit nervous that Guy would stab her eye with his nose or nut her again. She hid behind Juliet, hoping that she could get away with just waving at him.

'Have you said goodbye to Floz, now Guy?' Perry Miller pushed his son forwards.

God, thought Guy.

God, thought Floz.

Floz raised her head expecting concussion to follow shortly. Guy bent his head, expecting his body to do something random and mortally injure her. He made his finest effort to kiss her squarely on the cheek, Floz made her finest effort to squarely present her cheek to him. Guy moved in too soon, Floz moved too late with the result that Guy's lips landed with perfect precision onto her own.

The kiss seemed both fleeting and everlasting at the same time. Guy noticed how soft her lips were and again detected the faint hint of strawberries on her skin. Floz noticed how firm his lips were, the hint of coffee and whisky on his breath and, as he drew away, she caught the last notes of Guy's after-shave: the scent of cedar and fresh air. He smelled like an autumn walk in a wood, after the rain.

For a split second there was just the two of them in the room and no thoughts of anything else but the sensation of lips upon lips. No Nick, no Lacey, no past, no future, just that moment existed.

Both of them would secretly replay that kiss – Floz almost as many times as Guy, despite all her inner protestations that he was a man to be avoided at all costs.

Chapter 40

'I'm worried about Floz,' said Juliet that evening. She was cuddled up to Steve on the sofa and Floz was having yet another early night.

'Have you ever considered that she might be tired and that's why she's having early nights?' said Steve, weaving a hank of her black hair around his fingers.

'Well, considering she's having so many early nights, she looks shit for them. Her eyes tell me she isn't sleeping well. And you're right – she's losing weight.'

And that wasn't all. Juliet didn't say it aloud because it would have felt the wrong side of gossipy to say that Floz no longer waited to have her first glass of wine with Juliet in the evening. She had usually had one – or maybe two – by the time Juliet got in.

'Have you asked her if anything's wrong?'

'Course I have. She said there isn't, but there quite obviously is.'

'She's just much more of a private person than you,' said Steve, taking a chocolate and putting it between Juliet's lips because he knew it was her favourite flavour. 'Not everyone wants to talk if something is wrong.'

'Something *is* wrong – I know it and I will get to the bottom of it,' said Juliet. 'One way or another. Anyway, are we having sex tonight?'

'If you like,' said Steve.

'Don't be too enthusiastic, will you?' tutted Juliet, pulling away from him, but his arm looped around her and reeled her towards him.

'I'd love to have sex with you. But I'm equally as happy lying here like this,' he clarified.

'Good, that's settled. We'll lie here for a bit and then have sex. Then we'll both be happy.'

It was an added bonus to be having sex that night because Juliet's regular-as-clockwork period hadn't happened today as it should have. She wasn't that worried – it was only a day late. So far.

Chapter 41

Steve walked around the brand new Mercedes two-seater sports car. He could barely stop the purr that was rising in his throat as the salesman pointed out all the features, knowing that this sale was in the bag. It was the sort of car that would draw Chianti Parkin to him like a sex magnet. Except for some inexplicable reason, she wasn't even on his mind as he studied its features. He was thinking of Juliet sitting in the passenger seat, hair streaming behind her as they tore along a beach road in the sunshine.

'Will you be wanting finance?' the salesman asked.

'Nope,' replied Steve. 'I'll pay for it by Switch.' Steve had been saving up for a long time towards this moment – sailing out of here with a swanky car that he could truly call his. But the salesman was too cockily confident that he'd sealed the deal, so Steve tagged on a very casual: 'That is, if I take it.'

'How can you not?' laughed Mr Smug the Salesman.

'Because I'm weighing it up against a Porsche and a Jag that I've test driven, that's why,' fibbed Steve convincingly.

'No comparison with this baby,' said Mr Smug.

'Oh, I beg to differ,' said Steve. 'The Jag was a very comfortable drive in particular. Smooth as silk. And it clung to the road around corners.'

'Ah, but how much do you really know about these top of the range—?'

'Quite a lot,' interrupted Steve. 'I've been repairing and souping up cars since I was eleven.' A fact that was quite true. He had had a Saturday job with a rough-arse of a man on their estate who owned a car workshop. He didn't mention that a lot of the top-of-the-range cars which came through the doors were ringed, resprayed and sold on in the dead of night or souped up for robberies.

The young salesman's oily smile trembled on his lips as he began to realize that he might be out of his depth slightly here if they started trading car facts.

'Perhaps you'd like to take our model for a spin,' he said. 'Or we have a scheme where you can hire a similar model – at a very reasonable rate – for up to a week in order to fully appreciate the effect a car of this quality will have on your life.'

'That sounds great. I'll be in touch,' said Steve, holding his hand out to shake and signify that he was leaving Mr Smug for now.

He swaggered out of the car showroom and went back to his vehicle outside the empty building next door that had a huge flapping *For Sale* notice nailed to the wall. Then he remembered what he had to tell Guy and rang him straight away.

Chapter 42

Juliet was staring into space with a quizzical look on her face. There were several things on her mind at the moment that she didn't like. Firstly: she was actually planning to cook Steve a meal tonight. That lifted their 'just sex' relationship into the dangerous territory of dating. She couldn't date Steve Feast – he was a knob. She'd thought he was a knob for nearly thirty years. But her mind kept taking her back to bed with him and how tender he was with her there, how selfless, and she had to admit he had a point thinking he was God's gift to women. She hadn't come as hard or fast with any other lover, not even Roger.

Secondly: she was turning into Coco, checking her phone regularly to see if there were any texts from Steve and when there weren't, testing that her phone was working properly. When he did text or ring, she perked up like a stick of celery placed in a tumbler of water. Steve Feast was now her number one on speed-dial as well. She felt ever so slightly vulnerable. Her heart was opening up *for Steve Feast* of all people – and when that happened, there was always the danger of getting hurt.

And thirdly: where the hell was her bloody period? She couldn't possibly be pregnant because they'd used condoms. Except for the very first time, when they'd got carried away and started having sex bareback, before Steve had stopped, pulled out, been sensible and put a Durex on. She knew it was highly unlikely that her period hadn't come because she was pregnant, but she still wanted to see some physical evidence of that so she could 'eliminate it from her enquiries'.

She was so caught up in her thoughts that she didn't even notice Piers Winstanley-Black stick his head into the office and wait for her to do her customary swoon. When she didn't, he felt most aggrieved and – as is the contrary nature of men – his interest in this buxom creature who had suddenly become indifferent to him cranked up by several degrees.

Chapter 43

The car squealed to a stop at the side of the house. Seconds after Guy had got the phone call from Steve he was up and dressed, and trying not to drive too fast to Hallow's Cottage, which was set well back from the road between Maltstone and Higher Hoppleton. He was almost shaking as he pulled up sharp by the *For Sale* notice. It was being sold by Stanby's Estate Agency, apparently. He was just keying their number into the phone when he noticed the cottage doorway open and a rather round man with a bald head and thick glasses bring out a black binliner.

Guy sprang out of the car and called over to him, 'Excuse me, do you live here? Can you give me a few details about the house? If it's no bother.'

The man jumped, recovered and then said, 'I'll show you round if you like whilst I'm here. You'd best pull into the drive though.'

'Thank you, that's brilliant,' Guy called over his shoulder as he hurried back into the car. He parked and got out again. 'Sorry to land on you like this, but I've just found out this morning that the cottage is for sale.'

'It's not been on the market long,' said the man, holding out his hand and making his introductions. 'Grant Taylor. I'm the owner's nephew. Well, the late owner. My aunt died in July, and we live in Norfolk now so it's a bit of a trek up here and everything has got a bit overgrown, as you can see.' He gestured towards the wild garden. 'Anyway, come in. Sorry, I can't offer you a cup of tea because I've had the electricity cut off until it's been sold.'

'Oh, no worries,' said Guy, following him into the cottage. 'I'm just glad I caught you. I was about to make an appointment with the estate agent to do a viewing when I spotted you. I came here with my granny once when I was a little boy. I thought it was beautiful.'

He told himself off for sounding too keen, but he couldn't help himself.

'Not so lovely now,' said Grant. 'She hadn't decorated for at least thirty years. It's like being in a bloody time-warp. And it's a rotten financial climate to sell a house in, never mind one like this. Feel free to have a look around.'

'Don't you want to accompany me?'

'No, you're fine. There's nowt to nick, lad,' laughed Grant.

Guy started with the room he was in. It had surprisingly high ceilings for such an old, heavily beamed cottage. It was a huge square room: Guy pictured it with new windows and a big fire blazing in the wide inglenook fireplace. Then he went into the kitchen area and saw it in his mind's eye with gleaming worksurfaces and a centre island – and Floz, heavily pregnant, sitting at a wooden dining-table tapping away at her laptop. He thought of leaning over her, kissing her on the lips as he had done at his parents' house – but intentionally. He could imagine her strawberry scent in the air.

There was a cloakroom which he saw full of children's boots and dainty ladies' stilettos. And another room off, a second sitting room that would have served as an office or a games room where he and his children would try and outdo each other on Wii Tennis.

Up the stairs was a generous bathroom with two windows, but he didn't see the horrible green suite, he saw Floz and

himself soaping each other in a shower. And in the largest of
the three bedrooms, he visualized rolling around on a large
four-poster, tangling Floz up in the sheets. He had to severely
adjust his trousers before he went back downstairs.

There was plenty of land around to extend if needs be, a
rickety old garage that needed pulling down and rebuilding,
and what looked like a stable big enough for two horses. In
short, there was a lot of work to be done to make Hallow's
Cottage half-decent. It would cost quite a bit – but boy, would
it be worth it. Visions were dancing loudly and colourfully in
Guy's head.

'How much are you selling it for?' he asked.

'The estate agent said it's worth £200,000,' said Grant.
Guy's heart sank. 'But what with this climate and all that needs
doing to it, I've put it on for £160,000 – or thereabouts. I
want a quick sale. Are you interested?'

Guy's breathing was shallow and fast. 'Yes, I'm very interested,' he said. Commonsense told him to shut up. He didn't
have the funds if he was buying the restaurant, or the time to
do all the work required. But Guy Miller's heart was thumping
with excitement and he wasn't going to acknowledge any
voice talking sense. He had been too quiet and played it safe
for too long. And faint hearts didn't win fair ladies.

Chapter 44

In the staff toilet Juliet weed on the pregnancy test wand and waited. She couldn't be pregnant. Steve's unsheathed willy was only in her for a few seconds. *But what if you are?* In her waiting time she thought what it would mean if the test came up positive. It felt as if she were back in Orchards opposite that anti-abortion creep. *What would you do? I don't honestly know! You don't know? You don't know if you'd murder your own flesh and blood or not?* Well, now she was facing the very real possibility that she *was* in that situation, she knew that NO WAY would she have an abortion. It was mad though. Her – Juliet Miller – pregnant? She hadn't ever seriously entertained the idea of having children. Roger had been about as paternal as Herod and Juliet enjoyed her independence and freedom far too much to be hampered by rugrats.

She had the sneaking suspicion that if she told Steve she was pregnant, he would be pathetically happy about it. He was like a big kid himself. She could easily visualize him zooming around the room with a son playing Superman and teaching him wrestling moves.

For the first time, Juliet let herself think about being married again, having a husband and watching her mum and dad coo over a baby. Carrying a little boy around on her hip or holding the hand of a little girl. And then projecting herself forward to bash the spotty teenager who broke her daughter's heart.

Juliet's watch beeped: the allotted waiting time was over. She looked down at the stick. It was negative. She had thought she would have felt more relieved than she did.

Chapter 45

Cherrylips

less druggy this morning and less babbly.tell me you feel good,that life is beautiful and the future holds promise and adventure.that you have hope and dreams,that the sun rising brings you joy and the sound of laughter warms you up.that is what i would love to hear from you.that when you count your blessings they outnumber everything else,that your loved ones light up your life.the important things that make life a pleasure and eternal.your existence is a gift to me and your long,happy future a wish of mine.

Nick

Floz received the email after thirteen days of no contact and her joy level rose like the puck on a Strong Man Striker machine after Andre the Giant had hammered the lever.

She had tried so hard not to look glum around Juliet, especially after Juliet had asked her outright if she was upset about Steve staying over so much.

'You've been so down recently, we wondered if that was the reason,' she had said.

'Oh no, please don't think that,' said Floz, horrified that she'd been seen as a mope. The last thing she wanted to do was put a dampener on Juliet and Steve's lovely romance.

'What about your old flame, Floz?' Juliet dared. 'Are you still in touch?'

'Yes, we are,' Floz replied quietly with a fond smile but she pushed the subject firmly back onto Juliet. She was obviously not open to questions about *him*. 'It's great that you're a couple. Steve is so nice.'

'We aren't a couple.' Juliet made the point clear. 'It is just sex. That's all.'

'Okay, I believe you,' smiled Floz. 'But whatever it is, you both seem happy and I am happy for you. Of course I don't mind that he stays over.'

And she didn't, that was true. She wished she could have what they had. Writing to Nick again had opened up a portal in her heart that made her ache for a man's arms around her – the way Steve's wrapped around Juliet. Steve looked at her with such big wide eyes, she was surprised his pupils didn't dilate to bursting point. And he had a permanent sloppy grin on his face. And however much they protested otherwise, it was quite obvious that neither of them were in their 'non-relationship' for the 'just sex'.

As Floz re-read her mail from Nick, that initial flare of joy crashed to earth. Nothing had changed, he was still dying. She felt that a massive sore inside her had been picked open and was bleeding. She didn't want him to suffer, she wanted him to be at peace, but she didn't want him to die. It made no sense. Nor did the fact that the biggest love of her life was a man she had never met. She had always been a sensible, practical woman and yet this had happened to her. And when the disease finally crushed the last breath from him, would she feel she was being disloyal if she grew close to another man in the future? Would Nick then be watching her from heaven and hurting that her heart had moved on? She ached so much for someone real and *there* to touch her, kiss her, love her. She felt scooped out inside, as hollow as a Hallowe'en pumpkin head.

Chapter 46

In the wee small hours of the following Sunday, after a hellish shift at Burgerov, Guy was sitting at the tiny table in his flat with a pad and pen and a calculator. Whatever way he did his sums, he would never be able to afford Hallow's Cottage. It was either the restaurant or the cottage: he *needed* the restaurant and *wanted* the cottage. It was really no contest, but his head and heart were at war with each other.

Floz Cherrydale had awoken a dragon in him that made him want to brush off the dust that had fallen over him in the past years, take on the world, impress her, woo her, win her from the 'old flame' who Juliet said had come back into her life. He felt full of fire and lust for life. There were just a few obstacles to overcome – like finding nearly a couple of hundred thousand pounds and convincing the woman of his dreams that she didn't hate him, after all – and that she should abandon any plans to get back with whoever this mystery man was.

Floz awoke in the middle of the night after dreaming that Nick was stretched beside her. It was such a potent and vivid dream that in it she could feel his hand on her thigh, smell his skin which was like an autumn walk after the rain. It was Guy's scent. She had no idea what Nick would smell like: she thought salt and pine, but she would never know, never brush her fingers against his face. Tears began to gush down her cheeks when she realized she was alone in her bed and the only scent on the pillows was her own.

She got up to get some tissues. She was so tired, but she had lost the ability to find deep refreshing sleep. Padding softly into the kitchen, she made herself a decaff coffee and put an enormous slug of brandy in it as well. Then, when that was finished, she made herself another.

Chapter 47

'How's the just sex going?' asked Coco, ringing Juliet first thing the next morning.

'Fine,' said Juliet with a diffident sniff. 'We're having a laugh, that's all.' She didn't mention that sometimes when Steve stayed over, they didn't actually have any sex at all, just cuddled up in bed and snogged and talked. 'How's Gideon? He's keeping you away from me. I've forgotten what you look like. Are you that fat, blond bloke with the pierced lip?'

'Oh, give over. Anyway, you're always with Steve these days, lady, so three words: pot, kettle and black. Now, back to Gideon – he's fabulous.' Coco sighed like Judy Garland about to sing 'Somewhere Over the Rainbow'. 'I really like him, Ju. And I think he really likes me. At least he said so. But we all know that words are cheap.'

'Don't tar all men with the same brush,' warned Juliet. 'Gideon just might be the one who doesn't let you down.'

'I hope so,' said Coco, with a smile in his voice. 'The sex is perfect.'

'Spare me the lurid details,' said Juliet hurriedly.

'I will if you will.' Coco shuddered at the thought of a man and woman having sex together. 'And how's lovely Floz?'

'Hmm, lovely Floz. There's a mystery.'

'Ooh,' said Coco, who loved a gossip. 'What do you mean?'

'She's awfully quiet at the moment and I know she hasn't been sleeping well because I've heard her getting up at stupid hours to make a drink. Quite honestly, Coco, she looks ill.'

'Have you asked her what's the matter?'

'Of course I have, and she says nothing is.'

'What about the mysterious old flame?'

'Well,' Juliet checked that she wasn't being overheard, 'when I asked her about him, she changed the subject.'

Through the window Juliet saw Piers pulling up outside in his big black BMW. The least posh car in his mini-fleet. 'Know what I think? That he's not an old flame but she's talking to someone on the internet. That would explain why she goes to bed so early. Well, goes into her room early anyway. Then I think she types to this mystery man for so many hours that she's knackered in the morning.' It was the only viable answer. Juliet was incredibly proud of herself for having worked it all out.

'That doesn't make sense,' sniffed Coco. 'She was the one who said that you should move relationships from cyberspace into the real world as soon as possible. So how come she never goes out to meet him? And that doesn't explain why she's so obviously depressed, does it?'

'Hmm,' mused Juliet. Well, that totally cocked up her theory. Then she suddenly thought of another angle. 'Ah, what about this then? You're right, Floz was adamant that she didn't want to join up to Singlebods with us, but she seemed to know an awful lot about online dating. Maybe she's a bit embarrassed about admitting she's on a site after being so negative about it to us. Maybe she's doing everything she told us not to do, because we all know how hard it is to follow your own advice.'

'Maybe,' agreed Coco. 'And maybe she's down because she's feeling a bit lonely with you and Steve getting it together and seeing Gideon and myself getting on so well after meeting on the net that she's giving it a go but keeping it secret. Oh, I do hope she's found someone nice.'

'Oh God no. I hope I'm not making her feel pushed out. I've asked her if I am, and she said no. What if she's not telling the truth to spare my feelings? I have to find out what's going on, Coco. What do I do?'

'I've got to go, Ju. I'll have a think and get back to you. The wholesale rep has just arrived. He's very handsome.'

'Oy, eyes down, you! You're taken.'

'I know,' chuckled Coco. '*Ciao bella.*'

Juliet hit disconnect and pondered on the mysteries that were filling her life at the moment. Number one mystery still being: where the bloody hell was her period?

Chapter 48

CL

Back home today.scared homecare sat.morning.slept through massive nosebleed and she panic moded when she went to wake me up.have a torched nose and a liter of red cells for my reward.I hate hospitals.told them I was going home but had to wait till today to get out

N

Floz read the email and again imagined the big hunter-gatherer man in his photos reduced to the indignities he was now suffering whilst clawing at his last reserves of dignity and independence which were slipping away from him with every hour that passed. He couldn't even manage to write their full names on the email.

Floz got up from her office chair and reached for the tissues on the windowsill. Outside, a crocodile of paired-up children carrying baskets was winding down the road from the school. It must be Harvest Festival, thought Floz, and they were heading to church with their gifts of groceries and fruit collected for local pensioners. They were all wrapped up warm against the biting wind which was tugging at the remaining leaves on the trees and whirling them into drifts against walls.

'*Conkers, I'm collecting conkers, I'm trying hard to find the biggest and the best,*' they were trilling.

The sight of them brought a desperately needed lightness to her heart.

Then Lee Status, bless him, rang her up and dragged her fully into the here and now by asking her if she could get him ten jokes about boobs written by the end of the day.

Chapter 49

Piers Winstanley-Black studied Juliet as she looked for a file in the cabinet. She had worked with him for over four years but he was only really *seeing* her recently. He wouldn't have said she was his regular physical type, which was stick-thin, blonde, big jugs and personality way down on the list of importance. He was getting bored rigid by his regular type. There was little thrill in the chase, because they took one look at his Rolex or one of his elite cars and instantly dropped their knickers. And any pride he found in the beautiful trophies he escorted to restaurants was equally short-lived. Going out to dinner with a woman who thought that Puccini was a sort of pasta was no longer even vaguely amusing.

He couldn't understand why he hadn't considered Juliet as a potential mate before. She was the full package really – body like an earth mother, fab knockers and long shapely legs, a thick sheen of black hair, full red lips, sparkling slate-grey eyes. She dressed beautifully, oozed sexual confidence and had the cheekiest smile, thanks to that gap in her front teeth. And she was bright, intelligent, professional. And, these days, she was giving him those disinterested looks that made him want to win her over and see once again that adoration that had been there since he first introduced himself as her new boss.

They were alone in the office. He had deliberately waited

until Daphne and Amanda were at lunch before calling into the office on the pretext of looking for a file which he knew was sitting on his desk upstairs.

'Er, Juliet,' he called. She didn't respond, and even that excited him a little. 'Juliet!'

'Oh yes, sorry, Piers,' she said, smiling at him. An employee smile though, not the usual 'proper' one.

'I've been thinking. Are you doing anything on Thursday night?'

'Thursday?' Oh God, she hoped he wasn't going to ask her to work late. She was thinking about asking Steve if he wanted to go to the pics to see that new action film he'd been raving about. 'I'm not sure.'

Hard to get. Wow. He had to win her.

'I was wondering if you'd like to go out to dinner with me.'

Bloody hell. Juliet really hadn't seen that one coming. Dinner. With Piers Winstanley-Black! She'd waited longer for him than Sleeping Beauty had for her prince.

'That would be wonderful,' she said, sounding cool and calm and collected with no desire to run around the room screaming '*Yesss*,' as she had imagined she would do if she were ever in this position.

'I thought we might try out that new restaurant near Huddersfield. Four Trees.'

'Four Trees!' Juliet tried to keep the stammer out of her voice. Four Trees was very expensive and swanky, and the waiting-list for a table was weeks – if not months – for anyone who didn't know someone there who could pull a few strings. The chef had been trained by Raul Cruz, the Spanish super-chef who made Gordon Ramsay look like a dinner-lady. 'Lovely.'

'My driver will pick you up, then we can both have a glass of wine,' said Piers. 'I think I'll enjoy having dinner with you, Juliet.'

'Yes, that will be very nice,' said Juliet, returning her attention to the file and wondering why, after the initial explosion in her head and pants, the prospect of a date with her dream man wasn't half as exciting as the long anticipation of it had always been.

'You're in shock, that's why,' said Coco on the office phone later. 'You didn't think it would ever happen and your brain can't process that it has.'

'Me – going out to dinner with Piers Winstanley-Black! Juliet Winstanley-Black. Mrs Juliet Winstanley-Black.'

'And you think *I* jump the gun,' said Coco. 'Anyway, listen, I rang *you* to tell you some information. Guess who has just texted me?'

'The Pope? Deirdre from *Coronation Street*? I don't know – thrill me.'

'Darren,' said Coco with delight.

'Darren? As in Disappearing Darren?'

'Yep!'

'What did he say?'

' "Hello, how are you? I've missed you".'

'Didn't miss you that much that he couldn't pick up the pissing phone,' huffed Juliet. 'I hope you told him to go fuck himself.'

'Nope,' said Coco with a very self-satisfied grin. 'I'm returning the silent treatment and ignoring him.'

'Good for you,' said Juliet, impressed. 'Take back the power and don't give the bastard head-space.'

'Which is surprisingly easy with Gideon in my life,' said Coco with a contented sigh. 'He brought me chocolates and champagne last night and a DVD of *An Affair to Remember* which we watched from start to finish. It was such a lovely evening. Anyway, less of me and more of you – what are you going to wear for your big date? Something black and sophisticated? Shall I come dress-hunting with you tomorrow?'

'Yes, please,' begged Juliet. She shifted in her chair and, because her mobile phone was in her back trouser pocket, she did the customary trick of making it ring '1' on speed-dial, something which used to drive Coco mad until he made her remove his number from the list. Steve was now number '1' and when his phone rumbled in his pocket, he picked up and quickly realized that Juliet had rung him by mistake. She was on a landline phone to someone, judging from the half of the conversation that he could hear.

'Have you told Steve?' asked Coco.

'I haven't told him yet. Anyway, the deal was that we'd only be together until I pulled Piers or he pulled Lambrini. Obviously I'll have to tell him before I go out with Piers on Thursday.'

'Yes,' replied Coco. 'I suppose it'll have to end if you're going out with the boss.'

'I was never "going out" with Steve anyway, it was just sex. He knows that and I know that,' said Juliet. 'I couldn't seriously look at someone like Steve Feast, for God's sake. He's a knob.'

'Bit harsh,' said Coco. 'I've always thought he wasn't half as bad as you painted him. And just remember what he did for your brother when he needed a friend.'

Juliet didn't admit it to Coco, but she knew it was a bit harsh too. She was protesting too much and she didn't really know why.

Steve hung up on his mobile. He had a sharp ache in his chest that spread through him until he was filled with it. He didn't know why he was so cut up about what he had just heard. He knew that Juliet had always thought of him as a knob and the rules had been very clear from day one that their arrangement was 'just sex', and a temporary one. He hadn't learned anything new from hearing her talking on the phone then.

Maybe it was time to test-drive that Merc and seriously go for Chianti Parkin with a full charm – and expensive car – offensive. And forget once and for all about Juliet Bloody Miller.

Chapter 50

When Juliet received the curt text message from Steve to say that he wouldn't be over that evening as he was too busy, she tried not to admit to herself that she felt a stab of disappointment. In the three weeks since their 'just sex' pact, she had seen him every day and taken it for granted that this would continue. But it seemed he had blown cold on her now, so that gave her all the excuse she needed to forget about him and concentrate on the big prize. She wondered why Piers Winstanley-Black had suddenly turned the spotlight of his attention onto her and whether it was because she had turned her spotlight away from him. Once Darren realized that Coco wasn't pining for him, he had come running back with his tail between his legs. There was a lot to be said for the old adage 'Treat them mean, keep them keen.' Games, though. Oh, to be happily settled and past all the head-fuckery that relationships inevitably brought with them.

Piers had even brought her over a coffee that afternoon, much to the delight of Daphne and Amanda, who were making kissy faces behind him. And he seemed to be hanging around her office today, passing little verbal niceties and making up for years of ignoring her. It was all incredibly flattering.

She rang Floz and asked if she fancied sharing a Chinese with Coco as she wanted to celebrate the news of her

impending date. It was four meals for a tenner at the Great
Wall – including delivery. Then she almost rang Steve. She
stopped herself just in time whilst wondering what he was
doing that evening that was so damned important.

'We're going to be *sooo* full, having four meals between the
three of us,' said Coco, stretching out on Juliet's sofa later and
looking like a slim Siamese cat, albeit one who wore drop-
crotch jeans and very expensive shirts.

'No, we won't. I've invited Guy to make up the numbers,'
said Juliet.

'Guy?' echoed Floz. *Great.* She wondered if he would
attempt to kiss her hello and if so, where his lips would land on
her face. Then she wondered why she was wondering that and
tried to shake the thought from her head.

'Here's to my date with the gorgeous Piers Winstanley-
Black,' announced Juliet, toasting herself with a glass of white
Zinfandel.

'Have you told Steve yet?' Floz asked.

'Nope,' said Juliet, unable to keep the annoyance out of her
voice. 'I was going to tell him when he came around tonight,
but he texted and said he's busy.'

Steve had parked outside Little Derek's gym in the nearly new
Mercedes sports car that he'd hired for a week at a cut-price rate
to entice him to buy. He had felt the need to drive thoughts of
Juliet and Piers Baldy-Black out of his brain by pressing on some
punishing weights. It hadn't worked that well because they were
still in there, smiling at each other over a posh dinner-table.

However, something was obviously on his side because just
as he zapped open the door lock, Chianti's natty little Spitfire
pulled around the corner and parked behind his bumper. He
saw her mouth round in a wow through the windscreen.
Bloody hell. Talk about perfect timing.

'Hello, Chianti,' said Steve, watching her long slim legs unfolding from her car. 'How are you?'

'Hello, Steve,' said Chianti. For once she said his name with a trace of interest. 'This your new car?'

'Oh yeah,' said Steve, with a casualness that he had often practised in the mirror in case this day ever came. 'Just picked it up.'

Chianti looked at Steve in context. He was good-looking with a great body, she had always thought so, but not judged him rich enough to afford a car like that. Steve Feast suddenly became significant. And there was no one else on the horizon at the moment.

'Is it comfortable?' she asked, touching the car bonnet with her long, manicured fingers.

'Very,' said Steve.

'So where are you taking me out in it on Friday?' said Chianti, flicking her long blonde hair flirtatiously and biting on her lip.

'Taking you out F . . . Friday?' Blimey, thought Steve. That was easier than he had imagined. 'Erm. What about we go for a Thai meal at the Setting Sun? It's nice there.'

'Okay. I'll meet you here at seven p.m.'

'Yeah, no worries,' said Steve, his outward coolness belying the chaos that was going on in his head. Jesus!

'Are you coming into the gym?' said Chianti.

'I've just been,' said Steve. 'I've done my weights for today.' He flexed a giant bicep in her direction and Chianti's eyes rounded again. She appeared to be seeing Steve for the first time. And her pupils were large and black and liking what they saw. 'So, I'll see you Friday.'

'Bye, Steve,' smiled Chianti, fluttering her big false eyelashes like bat wings. She swanned into the gym then and Steve clenched his fists in victory when the door closed behind her. The prospect of Chianti Parkin in his car and on his arm would chase away any thoughts of Juliet. And he would ring Juliet and tell her he was ending their 'just sex' relationship before she had the chance to tell him about her Thursday date with Winstanley-Black. He hoped the satisfaction that gave him would salve the dull heavy pain that was lodged in his chest.

Juliet was looking at the Chinese menu and wondering why her stomach was both growling with hunger and feeling hellish queasy. Even the thought of her usual favourite 'crispy chilli spicy beef' wasn't making her mouth water at all.

'You're probably suffering from nerves about Thursday,' said Coco.

'I don't get nerves,' said Juliet. 'As you well know.' She swished her wine around in her glass. She didn't feel like that either.

'Why didn't you bring Gideon with you?' asked Floz. 'I'm so looking forward to meeting him. He sounds charming.'

'He doesn't exist,' laughed Juliet. 'He's a figment of Coco's sexually frustrated imagination.'

'He so does exist,' was Coco's haughty comeback. 'He's pulling an all-nighter trying to get a computer system mended in an office so it doesn't disrupt the day work. He is such a hard-working boy. Another first for me. I usually end up with lazy bleeders.'

'And you believe he's working all night?' teased Juliet.

'Yes I do, naughty!' Coco slapped her arm. 'He knows I've been mashed in the past and so he rings me a lot to reassure me. He's so patient and kind.'

'I think I'm going to like this Gideon when we eventually see him,' winked Juliet.

'See? They're not all nutters on the net.' Coco stole a glance at Floz to see if she reacted to that. Floz didn't react at all. Or did she? The way her eyes stayed glued to the takeaway menu – her non-acknowledgement – could have been seen very much as a reaction.

The door entryphone sounded and Floz twitched. Guy had arrived and she instantly felt unsettled. Juliet buzzed him up and he must have taken the stairs ten at a time considering how quickly he arrived. Obviously not racing up them for me though, thought Floz.

He was wearing jeans and a smart pink shirt in which his shoulders looked huge. Floz wished she'd had more warning that he was coming. She felt slobby in her comfy leggings and long grey T-shirt with the silly red strawberries all over it, but Juliet might have questioned her if she'd changed into something else. Juliet made Hercule Poirot look like Trigger from *Only Fools and Horses*.

'Hello, darling,' called Coco and blew him a 'mwah mwah'.

'Hi, Coco, Floz.' Guy waved shyly. Good, thought Floz. He wasn't going for the hello kiss then. Her eyes were drawn to his mouth as he said something to Juliet. It looked as soft as it had felt when he inadvertently kissed her on the lips, a hint of coffee and whisky on his breath. *God Almighty – get a grip, Floz*. She really was mixed-up. She blamed that dream in which Nick and Guy fused into one. Her brain needed to work on separating them – and fast.

'I think I'm coming down with something,' Juliet grimaced, wiping her perspiring forehead.

'Have you been near any schools?' asked Coco. 'You might have caught one of those bugs that's always going around them.'

'Yeah, I hang around a lot of schools, Coco. It's a habit I so must break.'

Coco thought for a moment then laughed heartily. 'Yes, fair point. I can't see you anywhere near a school.'

'Talking of schools, you might laugh, but I did a pregnancy test this week,' said Juliet, making Coco, Guy and Floz do a synchronized sharp intake of breath. She held up her hands to stem the questions before they came. 'Don't worry – it was negative so no one needs to say anything to Steve. But my period is late.'

'Menopause?' suggested Coco.

'Cheeky sod,' said Juliet. 'I'm not worried. I must be due to start though because my boobs are really sore.'

Floz felt a blush creep across her face. Talking about boobs and periods with Guy in the room felt wrong. Not that he seemed to mind; he was obviously used to it. A Heathcliff who was in touch with his feminine side? Surely not.

Coco wasn't comfortable with it though. 'Oh purr-lease.' He covered up his ears. 'Just pick from the menu, will you, and let's order. Starving as I am, you're in danger of putting me off with your filthy period talk.'

'You ever missed a period, Floz?' asked Juliet, ignoring him.

Floz gulped. 'It could be just excitement or stress,' she said, staring hard at her takeaway menu. 'Maybe if you stop thinking about it, it will . . . arrive.'

'Okay,' conceded Juliet. 'I'll try. Everyone got a menu? Good, then let's order.'

The food arrived twenty minutes later, just as Coco had finished his monologue about Darren, who had now texted quite a few times hoping to be forgiven and allowed another chance. It was a tragic tale but he told it with such exaggerated gesturing that it made them all laugh. Plus Coco was happy with Gideon now and out of the dark place in which Darren had consigned him for a while. Guy was happy to sit back and let him take centre-stage. At least then he could enjoy just being in Floz's gentle presence without opening his mouth and upsetting her. He knew he risked being thought of as dull for staying silent, but rather that than alienate her any more.

Juliet didn't want to appear a party-pooper and forced some of the food down when it arrived but it didn't sit well in her stomach.

'What's wrong with you two girls?' noted Coco. 'There's nearly as much food on your plate as when you started. Your cheeks look well hollow, Floz. You're losing even more weight, aren't you? My bloody left eye weighs more than you at the moment, girl. Get some of that fried rice down you. That's an order.'

'Honestly, I'm stuffed,' said Floz, aware that Guy's attention was on her also.

'Everything all right with you, lovely?' Coco prodded, hoping that Floz would give up her secrets with a bit of light coaxing.

'I'm fine, Coco.'

'Not working too hard? You look a little tired. Doesn't she, Guy?' and he looked at Guy for affirmation.

Guy was scared to comment because his mouth did not behave in Floz's presence. He nodded instead, which was equally as damning.

'Oh, do I?' Floz gulped. She thought she had done a good make-up job on the dark circles under her eyes. Obviously not.

'You need a good massage. That's what I always have when I'm stressed,' said Coco.

'Guy did a massage course once,' put in Juliet.

'A crash course in sports physiotherapy,' Guy corrected her, worried where this was going.

'Yes, but you did massage as part of it,' Juliet corrected his correction. 'Why don't you—'

'I'm fine!' Floz jumped in. She didn't want to imagine Guy Miller's hands around her neck. He was more likely to strangle her than massage her.

'Have you been sleeping okay?' Coco pressed on.

Talk about laying it on with a trowel, thought Juliet, giving him a warning glance. He managed to make *her* look subtle.

'Fine,' nodded Floz. 'I'm sleeping fine.' She felt hot under the glare of everyone's attention.

'All night?' said Coco.

'For goodness sake,' snapped Juliet. 'Have you been recruited by MI5?'

'I'm just concerned for my friend,' said Coco. 'Not man trouble, is it? Juliet said an old flame recently came back into your life.'

Juliet kicked Coco's leg under the table.

'We weren't gossiping about you,' Coco quickly added. 'Ju just mentioned it to me, because . . . well, she tells me everything.'

Floz's cheeks had gone through all the pink paint charts and were now in the neon reds. She stood up so quickly that she felt faint for a second. 'Anyone fancy a coffee?' she said breathlessly.

'Shall I give you a hand?' Guy asked.

'No, thanks,' Floz said, her tone clipped and self-defensive. 'I think I can manage to put a kettle on.'

'Well done, Coco,' whispered Juliet when Floz was safely out of the way. 'Talk about using a sledgehammer to crack a nut.'

'I handled that all wrong, didn't I?' sighed Coco, flapping at his face with his hand. 'Will she hate me?'

'I don't think she's capable,' said Guy, a little too loudly. Floz heard him and wondered what she was not capable of. Getting a good sleep? Eating a full portion of rice? Finding someone to love her? She bet it was the last one. She wished she hadn't mentioned anything about 'the old flame' because it was obvious that Juliet had blabbed her business. They had all clearly been gossiping together, wondering what was happening in her love-life, possibly why she never met up with 'the old flame', maybe even discussed if he existed – as they had joked about Gideon.

She pasted on a bright, brave smile and took the coffees through to find that the atmosphere at the table was thicker than Grainne's gravy. Coco was worried he'd upset Floz, Guy just hoped the ground would rise up and swallow him, knowing that another chance to shine in Floz's eyes had been totally bollocksed up, and Juliet just wanted to get to bed.

Juliet was awoken by a wave of nausea in the early hours of the morning. As she went to the bathroom, she noticed once again a sliver of light coming from the gap under the door of Floz's room. She tiptoed over and pressed her ear to the door. Floz was definitely awake and typing on her laptop.

'Floz, are you up?' she called and tapped lightly on the door.

'I'm just doing a bit of work,' called Floz, with a sniffle in her voice that she tried to cover up by then coughing.

'Want a coffee?'

'No, I'm fine, thanks. I was just turning my PC off because I'm tired now. Goodnight, Ju.'

Juliet's hand fell on the handle. She knew if she opened the door she would find that Floz had been crying. But it would have been mean to put her on the spot like that, especially as she obviously wanted to be left alone. And Juliet was feeling too delicate and tired to storm in like the SAS and blow apart whatever was going on.

'Night then, Floz. Sleep well.'

Behind the door Floz turned off her printer. She had been cutting and pasting all her emails to and from Nick, changing the fonts to a nice script, so she could run them off onto ivory hammered paper, fold them and preserve them like proper letters rather than emails. They belonged in a keepsake box wrapped in ribbon, not on a memory stick.

She was dog-tired but knew she wouldn't sleep without assistance. She took a half-bottle of brandy out of her desk drawer and drank a throatful directly from the neck.

Chapter 51

Juliet did feel better in the morning, though that quickly subsided when the text from Steve arrived.

Guess what? Going out with Chianti on Friday. Sorry can't see you at the moment, working in the evenings.

A sudden fury reared and coursed wildly through Juliet. She opened up a reply note and stabbed in her own text.

No worries, v busy too so couldn't see you anyway. I'm out to dinner with Piers WB on Thursday at Four Trees. Worked out well then. Good luck on your date. She didn't put kisses on the end either.

She couldn't believe there were hot tears in her eyes when she hit send. She felt stupidly all mixed-up and emotional.

'Steve can't see me this week,' Juliet said, as matter-of-factly as she could to Coco when they were dress-hunting in Next. 'He says he's working *and* he's going out with Chianti on Friday.'

'Well, that's a coincidence, isn't it?' oohed Coco, holding both a sober black dress and a bright red dress up against Juliet. 'You both pulling your dream partners in the same week.'

'I can't see what he sees in Chianti Parkin,' said Juliet, snatching the red dress from Coco and heading off to the changing rooms. 'She's a vacuous, plastic Barbie.'

'Not jealous, are you?' smirked Coco.

'About Chianti?'

'About Steve pulling Chianti, I meant.'

'Do me a favour,' laughed Juliet, disappearing into the cubicle with the brave, scarlet frock. 'Steve Feast is a knob. Haven't I always said so?'

Chapter 52

Guy barged into his office and closed the door on the kitchen before he killed either Igor or Stanislav. They were both hungover and fit for nothing. And if that wasn't enough, they had obviously been fighting someone else or each other from the evidence of the bruises and cuts on their faces. Just what he needed for front-of-house men when there was a corporate lunch of twenty-five people to serve.

He slumped at his desk and rested his head in his hands. What the frig had he taken on here? A run-down restaurant with idiot staff. He wasn't sure he had the energy to make this dump into anything special. Another dream to add to those other two which were out of his reach: Hallow's Cottage and Floz.

There was a timid knock at the door.

'Come in,' he barked, hoping it wasn't anyone with a black eye, because they just might go away with another one.

'Hi,' said a cheery voice. Gina pushed open the door with her trim bottom because she had a mug in one hand and a handful of letters in the other.

'I thought you might need this,' she said with a big blue-eyed smile, putting a steaming strong coffee down in front of him.

'Thanks, Gina,' replied Guy. At least he could rely on someone in here.

'I've rung the agency and they're sending a couple of waitresses. Igor can work in the back with us. I'll have to send Stanislav home. He's just vomited on the back step.'

'Thanks, Gina,' Guy said wearily. He hadn't the strength to think of anything more innovative.

'Drink that coffee and have a break.' Gina handed him the post. 'You never know, there might be a big fat Premium Bond winner in there,' she laughed.

'I wish,' said Guy. He smiled at her, genuinely grateful for her kind efficiency. 'What would I do without you?'

Gina didn't answer. She just went back into the hell of the kitchen and sighed. The first chance she got an 'in' with Guy Miller, she would make sure he never wanted to do without her again. Underneath her lake-calm exterior were deep whirling waters ready to suck him down. She'd make him hers and keep him hers if it was the last thing she ever did.

Guy opened the first letter. It was the solicitor advising that completion on the sale of the restaurant would be sooner than initially thought. Great, thought Guy. That was all he needed to know – that he would be wearing Kenny's cast-off millstone around his neck in the very near future. The second was a large envelope containing a clutch of bound papers from an interior design company pitching for the job of transforming Burgerov from shit-hole to palace. They had obviously done their homework, taken secret photos at some point inside the restaurant and drawn up their vision of what they could do to it.

Guy's jaw dropped open. If was as if they had peered into his brain and seen his ideal of that beautiful Florentine restaurant. Thick drapes at the windows, creams and tranquil greens, stucco walls, tall flowers in the centre of the tables – it was the Burgerov he had envisaged so many times. Their pictures were stunning. Especially as the waiters they had sketched into them were cleanshaven, scar-free and smiling.

Thanks to that coffee and those drawings, Guy was once again fortified. The Burgerov experience would soon be consigned to that part of his brain which imprisoned all his worst memories. One dream, at least, was within touching distance. Guy Miller was back in the game.

Chapter 53

That Thursday, Steve woke up early, having had a really rough night's sleep. And doing easy plastering on a pub wall gave him too much time and opportunity to think about it being Juliet and Piers's big day. It was lucky that he had an early finish because he was wrestling that night. He called in at Burgerov on his way home. He needed to let off steam before he went mad with all the possible outcomes of that date crashing around in his head.

'I just don't know what she sees in him,' said Steve, sitting on a stool in the kitchen, as Guy magicked up some of his fabulous made-from-scratch mayonnaise with effortless turns of his whisk. 'Well, apart from the big car, big house, brilliant job, Coutts chequebook and designer clothes. And I suppose good looks. And the fact that he's taking her out to Four Trees. I mean, he would have to take her to the poshest sodding restaurant in the county.'

'. . . Until very soon,' amended Guy. 'Then that place will be here.' He sighed as he looked to the side and caught Varto making a right cock of a prawn cocktail.

'Obviously I meant that,' said Steve, who was looking very glum considering he had pulled the ultimate in leggy blondes – Chianti Parkin.

'How did Juliet take the news about you and Chianti?' asked Guy.

'She wished me luck. She actually wished me luck!' said Steve, throwing up his hands with an air of incredulity.

'Well, that's good, isn't it? You've both moved on at the same time. I mean, how long have you been trying to get Chianti to notice you? And now she has. So why are obsessing about Juliet and her boss?'

'I'm not!' protested Steve. 'I just can't understand how she can fancy him. She loves him and thinks I'm a cretin.'

'Steve, stop thinking about Juliet and go out with Chianti Parkin. How many litres of saliva have you dribbled over her? And now she's interested.'

'Yeah,' said Steve, in a voice that suggested he'd just signed his own death warrant rather than witnessed six lottery numbers and the bonus ball coming up. 'You're right.'

'I wish I had as much luck with women,' Guy chuckled.

'One woman, you mean,' Steve amended.

'One Floz equals all of my back catalogue and yours put together.'

'Excuse me.' Behind Guy, Gina coughed to alert him to her presence. He turned and she asked him if the fish order had arrived.

'She fancies you,' whispered Steve, when she went into the larder. 'Something rotten as well.'

Guy changed the subject. 'I went to see the cottage.'

'And?' said Steve, watching Gina leave the larder and cast her eyes over to Guy. She really did have it bad for him. He was no expert at body language, but blimey – even Tim Nice But Dim could have spotted her infatuation.

'It's a total wreck. And I'm going to have to forget it because I couldn't nearly afford it.'

'Have you tried asking the bank?'

'No point,' replied Guy.

'I know a bank you could go to,' said Steve.

'Which? Bank of Toytown?'

'Bank of Mum and Dad.'

Guy stopped whisking for a moment. 'I wouldn't ask them.'

'They wanted to give you the money for the restaurant. If my son needed money and I had it . . .'

'I don't *need* it – the cottage is just something I want.'

'You *do* need it,' corrected Steve. 'You need it to give you a kick up the arse to start living again. You need to start snogging women and dating and waking up with them again,' he said, swinging his bag over his shoulder. 'And if Floz really has got an old flame back in her life, you'd do far worse than asking out that Gina bird. It's time to move on, Guy. Onwards and upwards.'

Chapter 54

'Will I do?' asked Juliet, twirling in her new harlot-red dress which made the best of her full figure and neat waist.

'You look lovely,' smiled Floz. 'How do you feel?'

'Great,' said Juliet, feigning ecstasy, although if truth be told she didn't feel half as excited as she should. And even though she had starved herself all day, she didn't feel in the slightest bit hungry.

Her head should have been full of thoughts of Piers Winstanley-Black snogging her, but it wasn't. It was full of jealous feelings about Steve going out with Chianti the next night, and she hated that such negative vibes were eclipsing the excitement she'd anticipated. She knew it was unreasonable to feel like that. Nor was it logical. She was obviously in the grip of some bug and not well.

A car drew up outside – a Bentley. Floz looked out of the window and put a thumbs-up at Juliet.

'He's here,' she said. 'Have a lovely time, won't you?'

'Of course I will,' said Juliet, sticking out her boobs and her chin. 'How can I not?'

Piers Winstanley-Black's eyes were on stalks when Juliet got into the back of the car with him. But despite the sharp-cut suit, the hand-made shoes, the big handsome smile, Juliet's pupils refused to dilate.

Chapter 55

When Steve had finished his wrestling bout that evening, he noticed the old man messing about with his mobile in the reception area. He also noticed the bulky teenager knock into him accidentally and send him toppling over a stack of chairs. Steve rushed over to stop him hitting the ground.

'You all right there, old lad?' he said, giving the elderly gent his arm as support.

'I'm fine,' said the man, who had a very weird accent. Half-Arthur Scargill, half-John Wayne.

'Can I get you anything? Glass of water or something?'

'What's your name, son?' drawled the man.

'Steve. Steve Feast.'

The man leaned on Steve's arm as he stood.

'I enjoyed watching you very much tonight. I was also here three weeks ago when you were the bad guy in that four-rounder. Impressive stuff.'

'Oh, that night,' chuckled Steve, remembering that was the night when Guy thought he had slept with Floz.

'You're a good wrestler.'

'Aye, I am,' said Steve. 'But I should have been grappling in the fifties when it was big-time over here.'

'Or wrestling now in America where it still is,' said the old man.

'I wish,' said Steve, waving goodbye to the old fellow now that he could see he was all right. 'Don't I bloody wish.'

It was fairly quiet in Burgerov that evening, although a party of eleven were booked in at the stupid hour of 10 p.m. They were travelling up from Southampton en route to Glasgow and had paid Kenny Moulding over the odds to feed them. Kenny didn't pass on any of the profits to the staff who would have to work so late to accommodate them – obviously.

Steve's words had been going around in Guy's head since he left. He was right, he did both need and want to rejoin the human race and feel close to a woman again. The trouble was, he didn't just want any woman, he wanted Floz Cherrydale. He had to get on the right foot with her, talk to her, get her to know the real him, and get to know the real her, give it every chance before he walked away and moved on. It defied reason why he had fallen so deeply and quickly for someone he had hardly spoken to – and who couldn't stand the sight of him. All he knew was that it wasn't infatuation: this was love – indefatigably and absolutely. And he wanted to impress her so much that all thoughts of mysterious old flames were extinguished.

Guy checked his watch. Juliet would be on her date now, leaving Floz on her own in the flat. He had an hour and a half until the Southampton party arrived. A surge of adrenalin spiralled upwards through him. *Yes, do it.* It was now or never.

He ripped off his apron and called to Gina: 'I'll be back in an hour. You're in charge.'

He grabbed his car keys and strode out into the balmy autumn evening. The moon was huge and low and pink as rosé champagne. A *Wine Moon*, or a *Harvest Moon* as it was more commonly known. He hoped that was a sign that tonight he was going to harvest the affections of Floz Cherrydale. Tonight he was going to make her take her previous opinion of him and rip it up into shreds. Tonight they were going to start everything again.

Chapter 56

Guy pressed the entryphone button outside his sister's flat. He was so full of gung-ho natural chemicals, he felt he was either going to throw up or start ripping up cars.

'Hello?' came Floz's gentle voice.

'It's Guy,' he said. 'Can I come up?'

'Yes, of course,' Floz replied, her voice stiffening by ten degrees. She instantly predicted what would happen next: he would walk in, ask for Juliet, find out Juliet wasn't there and then use that as an excuse to do some saturnine Heathcliff-type frowning, as if his sister's absence was Floz's fault.

Guy bounced up the stairs and pushed open the flat door.

'Hi, Floz . . . er . . . where's Juliet?'

Yep, thought Floz. Correct so far.

'She's out. With Piers. Didn't you know?' replied Floz, getting ready for a sulky mask to drop over his face.

'Ah yes, she did tell me.' Guy slapped his forehead with his hand and it looked like the rubbish acting it was.

'Can I help?' she asked, wondering what the heck he was up to.

She looked so tiny, he wanted to fold his arms around her, lift her up and kiss her soft lips again until her pale cheeks were as flush-pink as the *Wine Moon* outside.

'Guy? Can I help?' repeated Floz.

Guy shook himself out of his reverie. 'Sorry. I . . . er . . .

wondered . . .' His phone went off in his pocket. 'I'm a
Barbie Girl', at a thousand decibels. 'Oh God!' Once again
he'd failed to make the phone behave. He pulled it out of his
pocket and saw it was Kenny Moulding who was ringing.
Well, stuff him – for once he would have to wait. Guy tried
to switch off the phone but his big finger wouldn't depress
the switch properly. *Let's go, Barbie.* He was so flustered he
dropped the phone and it bounced under the sofa. He fell to
the floor, scrabbling around for it. He had the feeling that if
he stamped on it and threw it from the window into a lake,
the damned tune would still be playing. He couldn't lever the
back off to remove the battery. He banged it on the coffee-
table to kill it, all the while aware that Floz was frozen to the
spot, watching him make an even bigger arse of himself than
all the previous times put together.

'Sorry about that,' said Guy. 'I bought the phone from eBay.
I can't get rid of the last owner's tunes from the memory, and
however much I try and alter the ringtone . . . anyway, all
that's very boring, sorry. Erm, Floz, I came to ask—'

Then the entryphone buzzed hard and impatiently as if
someone was stabbing it.

'Excuse me,' said Floz, going to pick it up. Guy could
hear the sobbing coming from the receiver at the other side
of the room.

'Come up, Coco,' said Floz into the phone. 'I'll put the
kettle on.'

'Oh shit.' Guy meant to say this under his breath, but it
came out loud.

Quick – there's still time!

'Floz, the thing is . . .'

Then Coco fell through the doorway and threw himself
onto Floz.

'Gideon and I are finished!' he said. 'He's been seeing a
florist behind my back. I looked at his mobile and he's been

making loads of calls to him. Oh, why are men such bastards? Why, why?' Then he spotted Guy and temporarily broke off his dramatic wailing. 'Oh hi, Guy. How are you?'

'I'm fine, thanks, Coco,' said Guy, his mouth a grim line. 'Never better, in fact.'

'What was it that you came for, Guy?' asked Floz, holding Coco as he collapsed again onto her shoulder.

'Why? Why me?' cried Coco.

'Nothing. It doesn't matter,' said Guy tightly. He was so angry that he had got so close to setting the record straight with Floz. Angry that fate – in the guise of an hysterical gay perfume shop owner – had stopped him from asking Floz out. Angry that he'd lost so much time. Angry that Hallow's Cottage was out of his reach after so many years of coveting it. Angry that even his bloody phone was against him.

Then Juliet walked into the flat and announced that she had just thrown up all over Piers Winstanley-Black's Savile Row suit.

Chapter 57

Juliet sat on the sofa in her plum-purple flannelette pyjamas sipping on a glass of lemonade. Order had been restored. Whilst Floz was making tea, Coco had listened to the twenty voicemail messages that Gideon had left on his mobile. It appeared that he wasn't 'knocking off a florist' as accused. And if Coco went home to his house he would find that Gideon had actually conspired with the said florist to fill his bedroom with bouquets as a surprise.

'You should trust him or you'll lose him,' warned Juliet. 'If you start hunting around for evidence, you'll find something to twist and make it fit what you want to believe of him. Don't be such an arse again.'

'I won't,' said Coco, who more or less flew home on a current of glee.

After being assured that his sister was just suffering from a tummy bug, Guy exited the flat quietly and returned to work without actually saying why he had called round. His expression was now so dark, he made Heathcliff look like Frank Carson.

At last peace reigned in Blackberry Court and Juliet cracked open some Jaffa Cakes for which she had a sudden ravenous craving. She hadn't eaten all day – give or take the cheese tarte that had been in her stomach temporarily in the Four Trees restaurant.

'All those years waiting for a date with Piers Winstanley-Black and I end up throwing up on him,' chuckled Juliet. 'Can you believe it? You'd think dating would get less dramatic the older you get, wouldn't you? Obviously not.'

'No, it gets worse,' nodded Floz with a telling sigh that she didn't mean to make but which Juliet noticed and stored as further evidence of a mystery man in Floz's life.

The house phone rang; It was Coco, brimming over about how his flat was like Kew Gardens and there were rose petals all over his bed.

'What was Guy doing here, by the way?' asked Juliet, after that call had ended.

'I never did get to find out,' said Floz. There were a few moments of quiet before Floz braved what she was dying to air. 'He doesn't like me very much.'

Juliet shook her head. 'Don't be daft. I just wonder . . .' Then she stopped.

'Wonder what?'

'I just wonder,' Juliet began cautiously, 'if you might remind him of an ex-girlfriend. It's just a wild guess but she was your height and build. Sour-faced cow.'

'Great, thanks.' Floz puffed out her cheeks. Juliet obviously attended the same charm school as her brother.

'Sorry, I didn't mean that you're a sour-faced cow,' Juliet stressed. 'You don't actually look anything like her in your face. But he is a bit shy with you, I've noticed. It did cross my mind it might be because of Lacey.'

'Oh,' said Floz. 'I'm presuming it wasn't someone he split amicably from then.'

'Actually, they did split amicably and stayed friends,' said Juliet. 'That was the problem, he was too good a friend to her, to be honest. She used him. She was a nutter. I hated her. We all did.'

'Ah!' said Floz. So, Guy thought she looked like a nutter-ex of his. Someone that everyone hated. It was getting better and better.

'Anyway, I shouldn't really speak ill of— her.' Infuriatingly for Floz, Juliet stopped herself from finishing off the sentence and picked up an earlier thread of the conversation. 'About Piers – I exaggerated slightly when I said I threw up all over his suit. He only got a splash on his sleeve. The floor got the rest. It was tiled so I imagine it was quickly cleaned away. How bloody embarrassing.'

'Well, it couldn't be helped.' Floz topped up Juliet's glass of lemonade for her.

'I had absolutely no warning my starter was going to come back up or I'd have rushed out to the loo. That was the scary thing.'

'What did Piers say?'

'Not a lot at first,' cringed Juliet. 'I think he was in shock. I don't imagine anyone's ever thrown up on him before in an exclusive setting or otherwise. I have to give him his due though; he drove me straight home and saw me to the door. He was a perfect gentleman all evening – just like I imagined he would be, courteous, handsome, attentive . . .' then Juliet fell silent.

'But?' Floz was forced to supply.

'You'll laugh,' said Juliet. 'I'd laugh myself if I didn't feel so confused.'

'Try me,' said Floz, nudging her arm with her own.

'Bloody sodding swining Steve Feast, that's what's up.'

'What do you mean?'

Juliet dropped her head into her hands. 'It's mad. There I am, sitting opposite Piers Winstanley-Black – my dream man who I have been slavering over for years. He's just poured me some wine which is fifteen quid a glass, I'm choosing from a menu created by an award-winning chef and all I can think is, "Steve will be wrestling tonight. Which costume will he be in? Will Chianti be there watching? Have I crossed his mind at all since he pulled the plastic cow?" '

Then she burst into tears. 'Oh, Floz, I can't believe I'm saying this but I think I've managed to fall in love with him. How the fuck did that happen?'

'Oh, love.' Floz put her arms round Juliet; her shoulder was still damp from Coco's sobs. 'I don't know how these things happen, they just do and we have no control over the way our hearts work. You should tell Steve how you feel, because I think he'd be thrilled.'

'How could he be?' said Juliet, wishing she could stop crying. She never did a soft thing like girly crying. And never over a man. 'He's going out with his dream woman tomorrow. We had a "just sex" arrangement and it was me that kept hammering the point home that that's all it was. Look at me, I'm a bloody wreck. My periods have stopped, I'm crying, throwing up and everything I eat tastes funny. What the buggering hell is up with me?'

Floz pushed Juliet back and looked at her square in the face.

'Ju, you're not going to like this,' she said.

'What? What?' cried Juliet.

'Juliet, I think you need to do another pregnancy test.'

Asda was open all night. Floz drove down to get one whilst Juliet stayed at home within striding distance of the loo. After Juliet had weed on the stick again, they both sat on the sofa and watched it. Two faint blue lines appeared in the boxes and got darker and more defined.

'But I *did* a pregnancy test and it was negative,' said Juliet, too shocked for tears.

'Maybe you did it too early for the test to pick up,' said Floz, who felt a bit light-headed herself.

'What am I going to do?' said Juliet. It was too enormous to take in. Pregnant? By Steve Feast, whom she had hated since school and yet now she couldn't get him out of her brain – something she had only discovered when he left her life.

'You're going to go to sleep, that's what you're going to do,' said Floz. 'Because we can't do anything now, it's far too late. And you need to rest your brain and your body.'

'I won't sleep,' said Juliet.

They put on *Bridget Jones* and watched it sitting together on the sofa, until the pair of them nodded off like two brain-weary bookends.

Chapter 58

Juliet awoke first the next morning and stretched out her arms. She felt hungover, rough, adrift and hurting, because the predominant thought in her head, eclipsing everything else – even her apparent pregnancy – was that Steve was seeing Chianti that evening. Beautiful, leggy, slim (if chavvy), designer-dressed, unpregnant Chianti, who he had been in lust with for aeons.

She sobbed into the furry throw which she must have reached for in the middle of the night to cover herself. She did so silently, so she wouldn't wake Floz. What a bloody fine mess she'd managed to get herself into.

Floz awoke to the smell and sizzle of bacon. She went into the kitchen to find it on a low heat unsupervised because Juliet was in the loo throwing up. She looked green in the gills when she emerged, wiping her mouth. Floz couldn't have imagined that someone as strong as Juliet could look so sad, so bewildered.

'I rang in sick,' she said.

'Too right you did,' said Floz. 'Shall I take over the cooking?'

'I don't know why I started cooking bacon. I don't want any. I think I just wanted something to do.'

'I'll make some tea and toast,' said Floz, pushing Juliet back down onto the sofa. 'I'll take the day off, we'll sit and watch the breakfast TV news and *Jeremy Kyle* . . .'

'I feel like someone off *Jeremy Kyle*,' Juliet huffed, catching sight of herself in the wall mirror. She was the colour of an anaemic snowman.

Halfway through the DNA results on a 'who was the father' story, Juliet nodded off. Floz crept off to check her emails whilst she could. There were a couple of briefs from greetings-card firms but nothing from Nick. She sat on the sofa next to the sleeping Juliet and wrote some jolly birthday jokes because her own head was full of stuff she wished she could lose too.

Chapter 59

She was absolutely beautiful. A body to die for, thought Steve, as he ran his hands all over her. He wanted to shag her there and then, but she was a car and there were rules about that sort of thing. He inserted the key into the ignition, and fired her up. She purred as he slipped out of his drive and smoothed out into the road. He was going to buy a Merc from the slimy sales-man. And the one he had in mind was two luxury grades up from this available-for-hire model. He couldn't wait to climb in and pull the scent of her into his lungs. There was no perfume like that of a brand new car.

Steve took her for a burn-up on the motorway and felt like a king as she eased past everything to the left of him whilst he listened to 'Silver Dream Machine' on a continuous loop on the surround-sound CD player. Who needed women when there were machines like this? He held onto that thought hard, because it kept wanting to slip away.

Juliet's day had been the worst she could ever remember. The best bit was falling to sleep and finding oblivion. She woke up to Alan Titchmarsh's smiling face on the television, and it was no reflection on him that five minutes later she was retching again. But there were things inside her that ached far more than her strained stomach muscles ever could. She couldn't think straight. The one thing she never wanted to be in life was a single mother.

Dear Floz was fussing around her like a red-haired hen, tucking the big snuggly throw around her and feeding her lemonade and the ginger biscuits she had been out to the corner shop to buy because apparently ginger was a vomit-suppressant, so she said.

The clock hands had crawled around the face more slowly than was legal in the laws of time and physics, Juliet was sure. Somehow it had gotten to *EastEnders* time and she tried to concentrate on what was happening, but her brain wasn't strong enough to bat away the images of Steve in a suit, Chianti in a slinky size zero strapless, backless, frontless, sideless frock and Empire-State-Building heels. Chianti would probably be in Steve's arms now, and his brain would be full of nothing but savouring the moment. And her body.

The sound of the entryphone buzzer thankfully interrupted those torturing thoughts.

'I'll get it,' said Floz. 'You sit there and rest.'

'Please tell me it's not Coco and more wailing,' said Juliet. 'I can't handle him tonight if it is.'

'Er no,' coughed Floz, a few seconds later as she buzzed the visitor up.

'Who is it then? Guy? Not Mum and Dad. Please, Floz, don't let them in if it is,' Juliet called as Floz opened the door, and in sauntered Steve.

'All right then?' he said, casual-as-you-like. He was in black trousers and a white shirt, and a loosened blue tie, the same shade as his Swedish eyes.

'I'm fine,' Juliet gasped, acutely aware of the dress imbalance. He was all smart and she was in baggy pyjamas that she had been wearing for nearly twenty-four hours. And she felt even more of a slattern for not having any make-up on.

Steve threw himself down on the sofa next to her. Floz

made a discreet exit and left them to it. She had her fingers crossed and was willing Juliet all the luck in the world.

'What are you doing here?' Juliet said, modestly pulling the neck of her pyjamas closed.

'Well, I wanted to come here and see you. Are you okay?'

'I've got a bit of a tummy . . .' – *passenger* – Juliet cleared her throat, 'upset.'

'Oh.' Silence.

Juliet daren't breathe. This was a dream and one as delicate as a bubble. If she moved it would break and she would be back on the sofa alone with that furry throw and watching Phil Mitchell trying not to murder someone.

'How was your date?' she whispered eventually.

'Not that great,' said Steve. 'Which is why I'm here.'

'Why was that?'

Steve turned to Juliet, his bright eyes locking onto hers.

'Because I didn't want to be there with her. I wanted to be here with you.'

'Did you?' Juliet squeaked.

'Yes.'

'It's only just after eight o'clock now though. What did you tell Chianti?'

Steve cleared his throat. 'That I'd made a mistake and we should forget about carrying on with the date.'

'God, Steve, you really do have the gift of the gab.'

'That's what she said before she belted me.' He rubbed his jaw.

'That all she said?'

'Yep, pretty much.' He left out the bit about her screaming at him like a harpy and insisting on getting a taxi home rather than letting some obviously deranged 'fucking bastard' drive her.

'Oh. Right then,' said Juliet, not quite believing this was happening. It was a joke, of course. Any minute he would say, 'Naw, she stood me up.' But he didn't. Both sat like frozen statues on the sofa, not knowing what was going to happen next.

'Juliet,' said Steve eventually. 'I know you think I'm a knob—'

'Steve, I know I said—' she interrupted him, and he interrupted her right back.

'. . . but I love you. And I know that you probably had a great time with that bloke you work for yesterday and are going to tell me to fuck off because you're going to get married to him, but I just wanted you to know that I love you. All right?'

She didn't answer and he took that as a sign she daren't tell him he was right and that she did have a great time with Piers Rumpole-Kavanagh. He sighed heavily and stood.

'I'll go. I've made a cock of myself. Or rather "a knob". Yet again.'

'I love you as well,' Juliet blurted out in a very wobbly voice. 'I don't know how or when it happened but it did and I've been miserable as sin since you told me that you and Chianti were going out.'

'You are fucking joking,' said Steve, raking his hand through his hair. 'I'm sorry for swearing. I'm in shock. Bloody hell.' He sat back down on the sofa again before he fell, because his legs suddenly felt as shaky as Juliet's voice.

'No, I'm not joking. And you are the least knobbish person I know,' said Juliet, loving it as Steve reached out for her hand and held it tenderly, then raised it to his lips and kissed it. He made her feel delicate. No one had ever made her feel like that before.

'I can't take this in,' said Steve. His eyes were filling up with tears. 'What a barmy bastard week this has been. What next?'

'Steve.' Juliet took a deep breath. *In for a penny* . . . She might as well tell him everything. 'Steve, I'm pregnant. By you.'

He was now gripping onto her fingers as if they were the only thing keeping him from falling off a cliff.

'A little baby us,' was all he said, before his tears broke out, making a large, wet and joyous exit from his blue, blue eyes.

In her room Floz was crying too, softly. It was over, finally. An email had appeared on her screen from a man she didn't know – a Chas Hanson. The name was vaguely familiar, but she couldn't remember why. She had opened it to read:

Dear Floz

I am sorry to inform you that Nick passed away on Sept 22nd.He spoke of you often and with great fondness.He passed away among friends and family and we shall all miss him.His ashes were spread on Mount Robson.

Sincerely

Chas Hanson

Then she recalled that Chas was the name of the man who Nick had once told her was his oldest friend – the brother he had never had. That's why the name was familiar.

Chapter 60

The next day Steve parked the hired Merc outside his mother's semi and wondered if it would have any wheels on it when he saw it again. Even the fact that Steve was as big as a brick shithouse wouldn't have stopped a druggie having a go at breaking in to see if there was anything worth nicking and trading for a five-quid fix. It had been a tough enough estate when he was growing up in it, but it did have a lot of decent – if poor – families living in it. Now it looked more like a landfill-site than a housing estate. Every time he came here he felt claustrophobic from the weight of bad memories.

But today, nothing could dampen his spirits. Juliet Miller loved him and he was going to be a daddy. He felt the uplift of joy so strongly, he was convinced he could fly if he raised his arms. His child would never have to go out in unwashed clothes with an empty stomach, and he or she would know what it was to be loved and protected.

Juliet had wanted to come with him that morning and see his mum. She wanted them to announce together that they were having a baby. Juliet thought she knew what to expect, but she didn't. In all the years they'd known each other, Steve hadn't even let Guy over the threshold of his home. He loved his mother but he was ashamed of her and the state of the house. The 'scruffy' names he was called at school by some rotten kids still rang in his ears.

Despite spending so much time with Juliet recently, Steve hadn't done it at the expense of neglecting his duties to his mum. But recently she seemed to have totally given up. He suspected she didn't even try to make it to the toilet any more or feed herself if he wasn't there, but yet she always had access to booze.

'Hello Steve,' called Sarah Burrows, emerging from behind her scrubbed front door.

'Hello, darlin',' returned Steve. 'You and Denny all right?'

'Yes, fine,' said Sarah with a smile, too bright to be truly convincing. 'I checked on your mum last night and took her some soup, but she didn't eat much. I had to feed it to her, Steve. But not much of it went in. I tried to clean her up . . .'

'Oh, Sarah. You shouldn't feel that you have to babysit her. I might have to move back in for a bit again.'

The thought of it filled him with dread, but over the years he'd had to do it occasionally. This time, he suspected that she wouldn't have the strength to protest as she usually did. Juliet would understand, of that he had no doubt.

'I've seen Artie Paget's lad delivering booze for her,' said Sarah. 'I hate to tell tales but I . . .'

Paget, Paget, Paget. That damned name again. Another generation of Pagets intent on fucking up their lives.

'Thanks for telling me, love. Give young Denny my best – and thanks, Sarah. Thank you for caring.'

The shrill *dring* of a cooker timer went off in the kitchen behind her. Probably to tell her that a thick, bubbling stew was ready for Denny's lunch, thought Steve. Something to fill her boy's stomach, made with love. His eyes filled with water as soon as Sarah's door closed.

His mother was wrecked on the sofa again.

'Hiya, Mum,' Steve said softly. He touched her hand and she pulled it away.

'What do you want?' she mumbled. 'I haven't got anything for you.'

'It's me, Mum – Steve. I've got some great news.'

'Oh, it's you.' Christine Feast's head nodded on her thin neck. He looked at her lolling back against the tatty orange sofa and the tears rolled from his eyes. That's the sight he remembered from every Christmas Day, his mum pissed and incapable, either with or without one of his transient stepdads in the same state. He lived on fish fingers that he'd learned to fry for himself, in between the meals he got at the Millers' table. He swore one day he'd have kids of his own and share in the childhood he'd never had. So many times now, he'd imagined him and Juliet having those babies – and now they were. How he wanted his mum to share in his joy. She wasn't that old. There was still time for her to get better.

'Mum, you're going to be a grandma,' he said. 'My girlfriend's having a baby.'

Mrs Feast opened her eyes but there was nothing behind them that told him she'd understood. Then she was seized by a cough that racked her emaciated body. Steve went into the scruffy kitchen to get her a glass of water. He wondered how it could have got so messy so quickly. He'd scrubbed it the last time he'd been here, even wire-wooled all the muck out of the tile grout. But he could never get rid of that rotting smell, however much bleach he used.

Mrs Feast leaned forward and started retching.

'Here, Mum, there's some water.'

She let him lift the glass to her lips. Her fingers closed around his as she drank; they were so cold despite the furnace of heat in the room. Then she started gasping for breath and clawing at Steve's shirt and desperately attempting to pull air into her lungs. And Steve didn't even hesitate to ring an ambulance. At last the authorities might be able to do something for her where he had failed.

Chapter 61

There was a big difference in the Juliet Miller of Friday night, pre-Steve visit, and Saturday morning post-Steve leaving. In between her bouts of queasiness, Juliet was wrapped up in a light and airy bubble of *luuurve*. She emerged from her bedroom stretching and floating like someone out of a Rock Hudson and Doris Day film.

'Good morning, Floz. You can stop worrying about me now for I am in seventh heaven,' said Juliet, seeing her flat-mate unloading the dishwasher in the kitchen.

'Morning,' replied Floz, busily flitting around the kitchen making coffee and slotting bread in the toaster so Juliet wouldn't see how rough she looked. Her head was banging as well. Brandy might have knocked her out, but it charged a price for the privilege. 'Are you both okay?'

'Steve's gone to his mum's to check on her. He wouldn't let me go with him. I know she's an alcoholic and I can imagine the state she's in, but still . . . she'll be my baby's grandma. I should meet her after all these years.'

'Have you never seen her?' asked Floz.

'Never,' replied Juliet.

'Poor Steve,' said Floz. 'What made his mum end up like that?'

'He never talked about it,' said Juliet, appreciating then that Steve had never played the 'poor me' card, which he could have if he'd been a true attention-seeker. 'Guy once told me that she came from a family of alcoholics herself. I expect she just followed what she knew. Some people don't fight hard enough, do they? They just accept the path of least resistance.'

Floz nodded. A picture of her ex-husband Chris crossed the front of her mind. They had so much pressure on them when they were married. Did he sleep better in a police cell with his stomach full of strong lager than he ever had sober with responsibilities? Was alcohol really a maligned saviour?

'When he gets back, we're breaking the news to my mum and dad. I can't imagine what they'll think. There's quite a lot for them to take in.' Juliet reached for her bottle of Gaviscon and gulped it from the bottle-neck. She'd never had heartburn before. What a bloody awful side-effect of pregnancy that was.

'They'll be thrilled,' said Floz, turning to the fridge, giving Juliet little chance to see the heavy puffiness around her eyes.

Juliet dissolved into giggles. 'Me and Steve Feast! Having a baby? Jesus, I didn't see that one coming. I'm meeting Coco for lunch to tell him the good news. Fancy coming?'

'Thanks, but no. I'm spending the day writing Father's Day cards,' replied Floz.

'That's appropriate,' laughed Juliet and disappeared into the bathroom.

Chapter 62

Steve sat by his mam's bed. In a hospital nightie, she looked cleaner than he could ever remember seeing her. She was unconscious and because of that he could take her hand without her moving it away.

He thought she'd never liked him. He couldn't ever remember her saying she loved him or giving him a kiss. Or holding his hand, and he'd so wanted her to take him by the hand and lead him to school like all the other kids' mams did.

He stroked her rough knuckles and curled her fingers round his own, pretending that she was holding him back. He knew it was pathetic to try and draw some love from her, as if she had any within her to give him.

'Mam, I'm going to be a dad,' said Steve again, hoping she could hear him this time. 'You're going to be a nana. I bet you'll like that, won't you? I bet that makes you well again and gives you something to want to live for.'

He knew when the baby arrived that he would shower it with cuddles and take it to school and give it memories of a parent with big loving hands who held it tightly because it was important. They say you didn't miss what you never had, but Steve Feast would have argued against that, because he had a gnawing ache in him for the warmth he had missed. He'd slept with loads of women hoping to find affection, even for a little while. And he had – but it wouldn't have compared to having his mam walk him to school one morning with his hand inside hers.

But Juliet Miller was different. With her he could almost forget the coldness of his past. Her feelings for him were honest and he loved the way her arms were possessive of him, even in sleep. He wanted to spend the rest of his life with her, make her his wife, give his baby a name and a home.

Steve held his mum's limp hand, then with a sudden burst of consciousness she pulled it away. Then her chest buckled and machines started bleeping and nurses flooded in from all directions and he was once again pushed away from her.

Steve phoned Guy at four. He didn't ring Juliet because he didn't want her in a hospital in her condition, around death. He wanted to look after Juliet, not for her to have to look after him.

By the time Guy arrived at the hospital, Mrs Feast had gone. She would never see her grandchildren, she would never get well again. Steve sobbed on his shoulder, as Guy had sobbed on his once, wanting to turn the clock back and take someone's pain away, heal them, make them happy when they had no inclination to do it for themselves.

Chapter 63

Dear Chas

I'm awfully sorry to trouble you. When I was emailing Nick he said he would arrange for his sister to send me a photo of him. I have some of him as a little boy but, long story, I didn't keep the ones of him as a man. Do you think, when it's sensitive to do so, that you could ask her for me? I think so much about him, it would help me grieve and I do need to grieve.

Very kindest regards

Floz Cherrydale

Floz

I will see what I can do for you.I live in Calgary but I'm going over to Okanagan at the start of the New Year and will bring it up.I will do my best to get some sent to you.Not to worry about troubling me.

I'm taking my boat out the first weekend in October and

spending the day trolling and remembering Nick.He showed me how to fish for salmon a couple of years back.I'll go catch some for him.

Chas

Chapter 64

Perry and Grainne were absolutely delighted about the baby news, though a little shocked to hear that Steve was the father and that he and their daughter had been conducting a 'secret romance', which Juliet had decided to call it instead of a 'shag-fest'. It was a confusing time though, with such lovely news to celebrate in the middle of such sadness for Steve.

On the Monday night, Juliet awoke to find Steve sitting on the corner of her bed looking at an old picture of his mum as a much younger woman. She was posing for the camera in an overgrown garden with her boy. Steve was holding his hand up to be taken; Mrs Feast's hands were clasped in front of her.

'Hey,' said Juliet, her arms closing around him from the back. 'Get some sleep.'

'I should have done more to help her,' sniffed Steve. 'I should have forced her into a rehab place.'

'She wouldn't have gone, love. If you couldn't make her, no one could.'

'Please don't come to the funeral with me tomorrow,' whispered Steve. 'I've told Guy I just want to say goodbye to her by myself.'

'I bloody am coming,' said Juliet. 'As if I'd let you go through that on your own.'

'It'll be miserable.'

'It's a funeral. I'm not expecting clowns.'

An unexpected well of laughter bubbled up inside Steve and he gave up the fight. 'Thank you,' he said.

'You don't have to thank me,' tutted Juliet, kissing his stubbly cheek.

'You've given me hope,' said Steve tenderly. 'You're giving me everything I wanted in life. I just wish Guy could be as lucky.'

Juliet nodded into his shoulder. If only her brother – and lovely Floz – could find what she and Steve had with someone too, she really would be the happiest woman in the world.

Chapter 65

After the funeral Steve drove around to his mother's house. He didn't want to go in, he just wanted to look at it for one last time. He didn't know why – only that it felt right now to show Juliet what he'd come from, what he'd escaped from and where she and their baby would never end up. As he parked his car, he could barely believe his eyes at the sight of Sarah's fence smashed in, bike tyre-grooves over her lawn. Her hanging baskets had been ripped off and upturned and Sarah was sweeping up the soil, pausing to wipe tears away with the heel of her hand.

'What the bloody hell?' said Steve, leaping out of the car.

'Oh hello, Steve. Did it go all right, love? I'm sorry I couldn't make it. I daren't leave the house in case *they* came back.'

Steve didn't answer the question, but rather posed one of his own. 'In case who came back, Sarah? What happened to you?'

Then young Dennis appeared in the background with a swollen bottom lip and a closed black eye.

'Is this down to Artie Paget's lad again?'

Strong, quiet Sarah looked broken as her shoulders dropped.

'Right,' Steve said with a grim intake of breath.

Juliet was just getting out of the car.

'Stay in, love,' said Steve through gritted teeth, marching back to the driver's side.

'Whatever you're thinking, don't do owt,' begged Sarah.

'I'm sorting it. Don't you worry. Once and for all, this ends today,' said Steve. He remembered the address Sarah had given him last time he was here. Anyway, it would have been easy to spot where Artie Paget lived. His house had a massive satellite dish perched on the wall and a vintage Jag parked outside it. And through the front window Steve could see the biggest TV in the world in the lounge.

'Juliet, don't get out of the car, sweetheart. Promise me you'll just sit there. Remember you're carrying a bairn,' Steve said. And for once, Juliet Miller did as she was told.

Steve hammered on Artie Paget's door with his mighty fist. And he hammered again when there was no answer, though he knew someone was in the house.

A cocky little kid with longish hair, and trainers that cost more than the entire contents of Steve's mum's house, came to the door. He looked about ten years old in stature, but had the hard eyes of a street-wise adult.

'All right, all right,' he said. 'Who are you?'

'You must be Tommy,' said Steve, keeping a tight rein on his anger – for now.

'Who wants to know?'

'I want to talk to your dad.'

'What for?'

'Never mind what for, just ask him if he'll please get out here now.'

A couple of neighbours had appeared on doorsteps and a few curtains were twitching as Steve watched Tommy Paget move slowly back into the house and shut the door calmly behind him. Steve wasn't in his most patient mood and when Artie Paget didn't materialize straight away, his mallet fist and the door met again, even harder this time.

Steve was just about to hammer on the door again when it opened and there, with his tan, banana-blond dyed hair and gold front teeth stood the wide and nasty Artie Paget. Steve knew his reputation as a big hard man because he lifted a few weights at the gym, smoked a fat cigar and swaggered around wearing a Crombie. Steve also knew that he was a joke to the real gangsters to whom he aspired. Artie Paget: father of the little scrote who no doubt had a lucrative sideline supplying poison to Christine Feast. Artie Paget: ringleader of the gang at school who had led the cheers of 'Scruffy Steve'.

'Who the fuck are you?' snarled Artie.

'I'm here about your lad, Tommy,' said Steve, dispensing with formal introductions. 'He's upsetting some friends of mine with his "boyish antics".'

'Well, if it isn't Scruffy Steve.' Artie's lips stretched into an unpleasant smile before withering back to a puckered moue. 'Fuck off,' he sneered and attempted to close the door, not expecting that the door would be kicked back open.

'Like I said, it's about your Tommy.'

Tommy stood behind his dad, arms folded, head at a bolshie angle and an assured smirk playing on his boy-handsome face.

'Fucking hell – Scruffy Steve trying to tell me what to do. How fucking funny is that? How's your piss-head mum these days? Has she learned how to turn on a fucking bath tap yet?' laughed Artie, as a tasty flood of childhood memories rushed back at him.

'You'd better tell your lad to lay off bullying kids at school and smashing property which isn't his,' said Steve, his jaw tightening at the mention of his mother. But he kept the lid on his anger, for Sarah's sake.

'Or what? You going to kick his ass, *Scruffy*?' mocked Artie.

'Nope, I'm going to kick yours,' said Steve, casually inspecting his fingernails.

Artie Paget, aware that there were a lot of eyes on him, gave a cocksure little chuckle, put his hand in his trouser pocket and made to go back inside. Then, without warning, he twisted round and aimed his fist at Steve's nose. His hand was dressed with a vicious line of brass knuckles that would have smashed Steve's nose flat to his face had it made contact. But Steve had done a lot of boxing training in his time, as well as wrestling, and he could 'move like a butterfly' along with the best of them.

As Artie Paget fell forward, Steve's own fist came from below in an expertly executed uppercut. That punch had years of hurt and longing, frustration, pain and tears in it. They could hear Artie's jawbone crack in Wakefield.

Artie Paget lay on the floor, whimpering like a kid. He couldn't come back from a punch like that, nor did he want to because he knew there would have been a lot more to come. Steve hadn't even skipped a breath.

'You . . . bastard!' was all he managed, trying to claw back some dignity and with a series of snarling noises, but also not wanting to give Steve any more reason to hit him again. Blood oozed through his fingers.

'And, do you know what, Paget, every time your Tommy even looks at Denny or his mam's house, I'll come back and bray you. Have you got that? Has it sunk in to your tiny brain? Because what I'm telling you is really simple. Sort your lad out, or I'll sort *you* out. And I'll keep on doing it until he stops.'

Artie gave a reticent nod.

'Is that a yes?' pressed Steve.

'I said yes, all right,' growled Artie, spitting blood as he answered.

'Good,' said Steve, and smoothed down his black suit. 'Thank you.'

From the smattering of applause he got from a few neighbouring houses, he reckoned that Artie Paget wasn't the most popular man on the estate. Steve pulled open the car door, threw himself in and clunked in the seat belt, all the time aware that Juliet was looking intensely at him.

'What?' he demanded.

'You're not all mouth at all, are you?' she said, totally flab-bergasted. 'You really can handle yourself.'

'Of course I can handle myself, woman. I'm a bloody wrestler.'

'But I thought it was all fake fighting. I thought you were all softies really.'

'Well, you thought wrong then, didn't you?' huffed Steve.

He was one big ball of testosterone in a very smart black suit and he was going to use it to drive straight to the council Housing Offices right now and not leave them until someone made him a promise that Sarah and Denny would be shifted out of Ketherwood before autumn was out. Santa would be coming early for them this year.

Chapter 66

Dear Chas

I am so sorry to be troubling you again, this really is the last time, but I wondered if you could tell me when Nick's birthday was, so I can remember him. Hope you are well. I miss speaking to him so much.

Floz

Floz

Nick's birthday was April 14th.

Chas

When Floz got the mail from Chas she was confused. She was sure from past conversations she'd had with Nick that his birthday was 'in the fall'. She recalled him sharing memories of a birthday in some beautiful gardens. She still had it tagged on to her bookmarks – Butchart Gardens in Victoria. It was about three hundred miles and a two-hour ferry trip from where he lived as a child. He said he hadn't been allowed to chase squirrels, pick flowers or play in the dirt. 'Not a paradise for a six-year-old expecting a cake and a party.' She knew he had said that. And so she was almost certain that his birthday was in early October.

Was it likely that Chas had got it wrong? Not very, if they had been best friends from childhood. She Googled Nick Vermeer, his death date, his birth date and Mount Robson, but could find no mention of him at all. There was neither an online obituary, which she might have expected, nor an RIP page set up on Facebook for him by friends and family, or his ex-military buddies. She knew, by profession, he was a prominent engineer on oil rigs which might have brought up an entry – but nothing. There was not one word on the whole worldwide web about a man called Nick Vermeer.

Chapter 67

When the proposal came it was not at the top of the Eiffel Tower as Juliet had long fantasized about, but in the chip shop down the road, the day after Mrs Feast's funeral.

Juliet had suggested she and Steve walk into town and go to the pictures. She knew he loved the cinema and thought it might cheer him up. After the film they called in at a nearby pub for a couple of drinks – lemonade in Juliet's case, a couple of double vodkas for Steve. They walked back too because it was a lovely crisp evening with a sky full of stars. Dried brown leaves were scuttling across the road, impatiently not waiting for the green man to signal that it was safe to do so. Opposite to the chip shop was a playing area, and some kids – out too late – were throwing sticks up at the chestnut trees there, trying to knock the conkers down. Steve's arm came around Juliet and she savoured the feeling. They decided to call in at Cod Almighty, which was just around the corner from Blackberry Court.

'Fish and chips twice, two cartons of peas and two teacakes,' said Juliet, who was properly hungry for the first time in ages.

Steve inhaled and his stomach groaned appreciatively. He hadn't eaten properly in days either, and so the vodkas he'd had in the pub had gone to his head, making him feel a bit spaced. That's when he knew he'd had enough.

He looked at Juliet and could hardly believe she was his.

What a formidable force she was, even at school. His whole insides warmed up when he thought of her. God, she turned him on something rotten. His stamina with her was better than with others in his twenties. And when the sexual part had been satisfied, the cuddling up and falling asleep bit was just as wonderful. And the waking up and seeing her smile light up when he brought her a cup of tea. And the splashing about in the bath together, despite it being a bit of a squash – his legs wrapped around her, nuzzling into her neck. Talking to her, laughing with her, verbally sparring with her, physically sparring with her. He grinned and felt the time was right to say the words.

'Juliet Miller, will you marry me?'

At the same time, the shop assistant asked, 'Do you want salt and vinegar on these?'

Juliet froze, in fact everything seemed to freeze. Apart from Steve swaying slightly from the effect of the vodkas, the chip shop looked like a still-life. All that was missing was a bunch of grapes and a vase in the background. She was in such shock that she gave him the answer meant for the gob-smacked chip lady.

'Er . . . no thanks,' she said.

'All right then,' said Steve.

'I meant to the salt and vinegar. What did you say just then, Steve?' said Juliet. Had she really just heard what she thought she had? She felt a bit woozy.

'I said, "Will you marry me?" '

'Oh,' said Juliet. 'I thought you did.'

'Well?' He stumbled against the counter.

'How about asking me in the morning when you're sober?' said Juliet, gasping. It was too big a question to ask when she knew his head wasn't totally clear.

'Okay,' he said.

Steve paid for the take-out and they walked home in silence.

The rest of the evening was a strange blur. Neither of them mentioned the proposal again, though Juliet's head was playing it on a continuous loop. Neither of them could eat much of their fish and chips in the flat. Neither of them could talk much sense either. It was as if they were strangers on a first date. Steve even mentioned the weather at one point. When they went to bed, they kissed each other goodnight and both stared ahead into the dark, wondering what the morning would bring, not realizing the other was doing the same.

Chapter 68

When Juliet awoke, Steve had been awake for almost an hour, lying there, his arm around her head on the pillow. She opened her eyes, instantly remembered the proposal and gulped hard.

'Morning,' she yawned, not daring to look at him. Her nerves were already in shreds.

'Morning,' he answered.

To say the silence that ensued was a bit awkward was akin to saying the sun was a bit hot. Both of them lying on their backs, staring at the lightbulb, hearts racing like whippets chasing a hare.

'Do you remember what I said last night?' Steve asked eventually.

'Yes,' said Juliet, the word more a breath than a voice.

'Oh hell, I wish you hadn't said that,' groaned Steve.

Floz was awoken by crashes in the lounge. She flew out of her room expecting to see the world's most unsubtle burglar, but instead she found Steve cowering behind the sofa and Juliet missiling shoes at him.

'Bastard!' she was screaming.

'Juliet, will you listen to me!' Steve was bobbing his head up to try and explain and then escaping down to a position of safety as Juliet lobbed a court shoe in his direction.

'What the heck is going on?' cried Floz.

'I'm so sorry for waking you, Floz, but this . . . this *swine* proposed to me and then took it back.'

'Ow,' said Steve as a large red Croc scored a bull's-eye on his crown. 'Floz, stop her. Just let me talk to you, Ju. I *didn't* take it back. Juliet, give me ten seconds of ceasefire!'

But Juliet was in no mood to listen and launched a boot grenade at him. 'You're not husband material anyway. I wouldn't marry you if you were the last—'

Floz threw herself at Juliet as she picked up a five-inch stiletto. 'Whoa!' she screamed. 'You'll kill him!'

'Good,' snapped Juliet.

'Ju, please, listen,' said Steve, holding up a white tissue of surrender.

'Stop before you hurt the baby,' Floz insisted, not letting Juliet's arms go. Juliet was huffing from her exertions but Floz's words sank in. Yes, her baby was hearing this; she needed to calm down.

'You've got ten seconds, knobhead,' said Juliet, mouthing the last word so that her baby didn't hear it.

Steve's head and shoulders dared to pop up.

'I didn't want you to remember that I'd proposed . . .' He saw Juliet's lip curl back over her teeth again so he continued quickly, 'Because I shouldn't have done it in a bloody fish and chip shop. I hoped you'd have forgotten ONLY so I could have taken you out somewhere nice today and done it properly, by a river or over a glass of champagne, on bended knee and holding a ring out – not in front of a woman asking us if we wanted salt and vinegar on our frigging cod!'

Juliet swallowed. 'Oh,' was all she managed to answer.

'That's what I meant,' said Steve. He stood up as Juliet's grip on the shoe loosened and it fell from her hand.

'Well?' said Floz, arms folded. 'The man deserves an apology.'

'I'm sorry,' said Juliet. She felt her insides turn to mush.

She'd read about men who exhibited this level of tenderness in works of fiction, but never thought she would have been the recipient of it herself. She felt humbled yet again by Steve's respectful and loving ways.

'Juliet, I know we've only just started going out together but we've known each other all our lives. I want the baby to be born to Mr and Mrs Feast . . .'

'Oh, Steve.'

'And if it doesn't work out, divorce is easy enough these—'

Floz held up her hand. 'Shhh! Quit whilst you're ahead, Steven.'

Steve took Floz's advice and didn't finish his sentence but started a fresh one. 'I just want to marry you, Ju. And I want to marry you soon.'

'I don't need champagne or fancy settings, Steve. This will do very nicely, thank you,' said Juliet, who couldn't imagine that the addition of a bottle of fizz or a big moon outside the window could make her feel any more gooey and melted inside than she did at that moment.

Steve held his arms out and Juliet drifted into them.

'We'll go ring picking after work, okay with you?'

Floz grabbed her coat and brolly and left the flat to give them some privacy. Her brain felt crowded and at bursting-point. The clouds were heavy and grey but the breeze was too high to raise her umbrella. It didn't matter. She wanted the rising wind to blow through her and drag away all her thoughts – every single one of them. A brisk autumn walk in the rain was exactly what she needed.

October

'Youth is like spring, an over-praised season more remarkable for biting winds than genial breezes. Autumn is the mellower season, and what we lose in flowers we more than gain in fruits.'

Samuel Butler

Chapter 69

Guy was determined to get it right this time. This celebratory feast the night after the official engagement – i.e. not the one in the chip shop – was going to knock everyone's socks off, especially Floz's. His mum and dad's kitchen floor almost needed reinforcing from the amount of food he was going to cook that evening. He would make the Queen's Christmas dinner look like a McDonald's Happy Meal.

Perry and Grainne were still in a state of rapture with a grand-child on the way *and* the news that morning that Juliet and Steve were getting married on her birthday – 5 November. They did worry that it was all a bit fast, but then reminded themselves that they had met and married within four months. The local vicar at Maltstone, the Reverend Glossop – otherwise known as the Reverend Gossip for his propensity to chatter quite a lot – had a cancellation on that day. It was either that or 4 March, and seeing that was the anniversary of Juliet's first wedding – well, that was a bit of a no-no. Everyone agreed that as a wedding date, as well as a birth date, Bonfire Night seemed to suit Juliet down to the ground.

Guy had rung Juliet to ascertain whether Floz had any food allergies other than strawberries, because he wasn't going to take any chances. Luckily, she hadn't. He was doing his speci-ality sea-bass for starter, a feast of various meats for mains and a

trio of chocolate desserts for pudding. He was going to tickle
every one of her senses with this menu. He would seduce her
with food: she would be putty in his hands.

Floz sat alone in the flat, finding it hard to concentrate on that
day's brief – 'Congratulations On Your Pregnancy' verse. She
looked at the visual images that Lee Status had emailed over for
her to match with the copy. The graphic designer had created
some stunning pictures of beatific women with big rounded
tums. Floz thought of Juliet growing bigger by the day, how
her stomach would push proudly against her clothes, how her
walk would alter, how she would rest her hand on her abdo-
men and feel the baby flutter inside her. She pictured Juliet and
Steve lying on the bed, and being fascinated as they watched
her tummy shift as the baby rolled within, wriggling to get
comfortable. She thought of Juliet asleep in a rocking chair,
lulling the baby to sleep with her calm, soft breathing. She
would look beautiful.

But Floz sent an email to Lee Status and lied that she had a
stomach bug and wouldn't be able to do the brief. Then she
curled up on her bed and tried to make her mind go blank so
she could sleep, but gave it up after nearly an hour.

She got up hearing the alert that she had email. Chas Hanson
had sent her a message. Had it been in an envelope, she would
have ripped it open.

Floz

Just checking all is okay with you.Remember that greif
loses its hard edge after a time and the wonderful residue
is a collection of warm memories.I just thought that might
give you comfort.

Chas

Floz read the mail over and over again. She didn't know if that was true; some grief lodged in your heart and never lost its hard edge – you just learned to co-exist. Still, it was a kind thought to send, to try and comfort her. It was like something Nick would have said.

Steve was first to arrive at the Millers' house. He had just picked up his new car. In light of the circumstances, he had traded in his Volvo for a seven-seater people-carrier with a massive boot, comfy seats and a zillion safety features: the perfect family car. He drove it off the forecourt imagining baby car seats in the back and Juliet with a ring on her finger sitting next to him, and probably instructing him how to drive properly. It was a much bigger turbo thrill than he could ever have got from a four-litre fuel-injected engine.

Coco arrived next, by taxi, making an extravagant and kissy entrance and marvelling over Juliet's solitaire diamond engagement ring. He was alone because apparently Gideon was far too shy to meet everyone at once in a big gathering.

'Are you sure he even exists?' Steve teased him. 'No one has seen him yet.'

'Look.' Coco fumbled with his mobile phone for a moment then thrust it under Steve's nose. 'Here is a picture of us taken together.' The image was blurred and dark though. All Steve could tell was that it was two male heads together.

'That could be anyone,' he objected.

'Well, it isn't. It's Gideon and me, so there,' said Coco huffily.

'Champagne, Raymond?' asked Grainne, proffering a long flute of pink fizz.

'If I must.' Coco sighed dramatically. There were only three people whom he still allowed to call him Raymond to his face: the Millers and his grandma. Mind you, his granny was a bit senile now and more often than not called him Brenda.

'SHIT!' The exclamation from the kitchen accompanied a clatter of pans falling on the floor.

'Everything all right in the galley?' called Perry, shivering with delight as the champagne made a glacial trail down the inside of his throat.

'Fine, Dad,' replied Guy, convincing no one.

'Want me to help you, dear?' asked Grainne.

'No, no, no,' everyone cried in protest.

Someone rang the doorbell and Guy's heart leaped up into his mouth. It had to be Floz and Juliet arriving. Guy made a quick check of himself in the small mirror that hung on the kitchen wall. Then he went out to say, 'Hi' – except there was no Floz, just his sister.

'Isn't Floz coming?' he barked nervously.

'She's parking the car,' said Juliet. 'We're going to leave it here and pick it up tomorrow. Oh hello, Juliet, nice to see you, Juliet!' she added sarcastically.

'Nice to see you, Juliet,' said Guy on a great big exhalation of breath before going back into the kitchen.

'What's up with him?' Juliet asked Steve, thumbing at her brother's disappearing back.

'You know what he's like when he's cooking – a perfectionist.'

'Why did he say Floz's name so aggressively? Doesn't he want her here?'

'Don't be daft.' Steve laughed a little nervously because he didn't want to spill Guy's secret. Especially not to Juliet with her big gob.

But Juliet picked up from that tinny laugh that Steve knew a little more than he was letting on. Maybe Floz was right, after all, and her brother didn't like her that much. How odd.

Floz parked the car almost absently. Chas's last mail was circling her brain like a hungry buzzard. *Grief loses its hard edge after a time . . .* She didn't know why she was mentally chewing on his words. She just hoped her brain would work out what it was doing and spit out the answer to her.

She straightened her dress, a jade-green one with a belted waist. It picked out the green in her eyes and made the colour of her hair like bonfire flames by comparison. She rang the doorbell, the words of that last email from Chas still playing like a stuck record.

Guy heard Floz arrive. He bobbed his head out of the kitchen to see her there dressed in green, her hair in soft curls around her shoulders. He raised a giant arm, said, 'Hi,' and retreated back into the kitchen before Floz could return the gesture.

Now Juliet could see exactly what Floz meant. He couldn't have given Floz a shorter greeting if he'd tried. Well, that wouldn't do. She would mend that bridge if it killed her. She couldn't have her friend and her brother out of sorts with each other.

Coco made up for Guy's coldness. He bounced over to give Floz a big hug and passed her on for hello kisses to the rest of the Miller family and Steve.

'Wonder how Piers is going to take the news of your impending change of circumstance?' said Steve, nudging his champagne flute into Juliet's glass of Eisberg.

'I wonder,' she said. She did not add that Piers, presently in London, had sent her a flurry of texts begging her to go out on a second date with him, and that she had replied that she had been swept off her feet and proposed to – quite unexpectedly – by 'an old flame relighted' as she put it. She didn't mention the pregnancy, that was perhaps one detail too cruel to give to a man so obviously enamoured. And, also, best mentioned later on, formally, when discussing her maternity leave.

She giggled to herself, thinking that she had turned down Piers Winstanley-Black for Steve. She took a sly look at him whilst he was laughing with her dad and Coco. *How could I ever have thought he was a knob?* He was so tall and big and solid and handsome, and his hand kept brushing her arm as if he liked the feeling of being constantly in touch with her. It was knicker-meltingly romantic. She hadn't felt as runny inside for any man – ever. Not even Roger in the beginning, when he made her sigh a lot with his corny lines snatched straight from crap B films – though at the time they sounded macho and fabulous.

'How's the . . . er . . . courting going, Raymond?' asked Perry, who was trying to be part of the twenty-first century but still found it a little odd to ask one man how he was romancing another one.

'Oh, Perry, I've found my soul-mate. We'll be like you and Grainne one day.'

'What about you, Floz?' asked Grainne. 'Have you found yourself a nice young man to settle down with?'

All eyes turned to Floz. Even in the kitchen Guy downed tools to cock his ear.

I did and I lost him and he came back and he died.

Floz swallowed hard and a glassy cast swelled in her eyes. Her discomfort was evident to all. Juliet leaped in to rescue her.

'God, how embarrassing are parents? Let's all sit at the table and await the food,' she said, giving her mum a disapproving look.

Steve and Coco and Juliet exchanged knowing glances. Juliet was now 100 per cent convinced that Floz was having some secret man trouble. And she made up her mind to find out once and for all what was going on in Floz's life that was making her so depressed. Guy returned to plating up the sea-bass, wondering why Floz hadn't answered the question and why everyone had hurried to sit down. It would have been easy enough to say, 'No, not yet.' So why hadn't she?

'Dinner is served,' he said, appearing with the first five plates balanced on his arms. He served the ladies first, something Kenny's idiot waiters never did, however much Guy had bollocked them for it. He took his place at the end of the table,

next to Floz, because that's where Juliet had directed her to sit.
She was going to make sure they became friends.

The fish was beautifully cooked – a triumph. Everyone was
making noises of approval.

'How nice was that?' sighed Juliet, blotting her lips with her
serviette. 'Aren't you a catch for some lucky single woman?'

Steve raised his eyes heavenward. He hoped Juliet wasn't
going to try and do some match-making.

'Isn't he, Floz? Isn't he a catch?' Juliet nudged Floz hard.

Steve kicked Juliet under the table and when she swung her
eyes around to him, he gave her a warning look.

'Yes, of course,' said Floz, staring bashfully at her empty plate.

'Let me help you clear the plates,' said Steve, quickly standing and gathering them up, following Guy into the kitchen,
where his friend immediately turned on him.

'Tell me you haven't said anything to Juliet?'

'No, I haven't,' Steve protested in a strained whisper. 'Do
you honestly think I'd tell her that you fancy the arse off Floz?'

'What's she playing at then?' said Guy.

'Fuck knows,' said Steve. 'Just dish up the main course and
fill her gob so she can't talk.'

Conversation in the dining room turned to weddings as
Guy began to carve up the crown of turkey and Steve the
tender leg of lamb.

'I don't want a big frock,' said Juliet.

'You have to have the full meringue!' screamed Coco in
disgust. 'You can't have a crappy plain one. And what are you
doing about bridesmaids?'

'Floz, of course,' said Juliet. 'And you as the male equivalent. I want you to walk down the aisle behind me, though I
wouldn't expect you to wear a dress, obviously.'

'Thank goodness,' snorted Coco. 'I'm not a tranny!'

'Oh how lovely,' said Floz. 'I've never been a bridesmaid
before.'

'Me neither,' chirped Coco. 'What colour will we be in?'

'I'm thinking autumn colours,' mused Juliet, harking back to that conversation with Daphne about her own autumn wedding.

'Ooh, plush.' Coco gave a shriek of glee.

'You'll have to get started on the arrangements, Juliet.' Grainne took a sip of wine. 'By my reckoning you've only got about thirty-five days until November the fifth.'

'Chuffing hell,' said Juliet.

'Well, if you can't pull this off, no one can,' smiled Floz. 'You're a true tour de force.'

Steve and Guy started to ferry in bowls of vegetables and perfectly puffed-up Yorkshire puddings.

'Oh, by the way, we booked the Oak Leaf for the reception this morning,' announced Juliet, expecting rightly that everyone would look at her aghast. 'I know what you're going to say, but I didn't want you cooking on my big day, Guy. Plus Burgerov is a shit-hole.'

'I agree,' said Guy. 'It's a shame but it won't be refurbished in time for your wedding otherwise I wouldn't have taken no for an answer. I could do the catering for you somewhere else if you—'

'No way do I want you doing anything on that day but joining in the festivities and being best man. It's decided. So don't give me any grief about it.'

Grief loses its hard edge after a time . . .

'So, what are you going to do with the flat?' asked Perry, spearing a large crunchy roast potato.

'What do you mean?' Juliet replied, through a mouthful of caramelized carrot.

'Well, I presume you'll be moving in with Steve. You can't get a pram up and down those stairs in Blackberry Court. There's no lift, is there?'

Juliet dropped her fork. Things had happened so fast she hadn't thought about any practicalities like that. Her dad was right, although Steve's place would be too tiny really for long-term plans – just having the one bedroom. *And if she did sell, where would Floz go?* She looked up at Floz and saw that she had just been hit by the same thunderbolt. And if she had looked to the side, she would have noticed that the thunderbolt had managed to floor Guy too.

'Floz,' said Juliet. 'I hadn't even thought about the flat.'

'Well, it's certainly something you *need* to think about,' said Floz in a calm voice that masked the inner turmoil that had just been unleashed in her. She had been living with Juliet for less than two months now, but it felt so much like a home. What were the chances of her finding a flat and flat-mate like this again? She had been too lucky living in lovely Blackberry Court with Juliet and being absorbed into this wonderful family. The prospect of leaving their warm world was a shivery cold one.

Juliet burst into tears.

'Hormones!' was Grainne's verdict as she quickly stood to put her arm around her daughter.

'Oh Floz, I'm so sorry,' sobbed Juliet. 'I honestly never thought about having to move out of the flat.'

'Don't be daft,' said Floz, her smile brave.

'I love my flat,' wept Juliet. 'I hate Steve's house.'

'I hate it myself,' said Steve. 'We'll have to get rid of both and buy something else. It's hardly big enough for me, never mind you and a baby as well.'

'Or *babies*,' Grainne threw into the mix.

'Oh my GOD I could be carrying twins!' Juliet couldn't bear any more thunderbolts. Her family was a twin factory. She and Guy were fifth-generation twins. 'How long will it take to sell up and move?' The enormity of having to sell two properties as well as have a baby and arrange a marriage fell on Juliet like a ton of rubble and made her tears flow faster.

'Oh God, what have I done?' said Perry, unable to remember

the last time he'd ever seen his daughter cry. 'Me and my big mouth.'

'Well, at least Floz could move into Guy's flat,' suggested Steve, trying to be helpful so the lovely meal wasn't spoiled.

'*What?*' said Guy.

'When you move out and buy Hallow's Cottage, I meant,' Steve said, seizing his moment to spill the beans for Guy and hopefully get him the help from his family which he refused to ask for.

'Hallow's Cottage?' asked Perry. 'That's never come up for sale, has it? After all these years?'

'You can forget Hallow's Cottage,' said Guy gruffly.

'I know, I know, you can't afford it, you already told me,' said Steve, planting a well-meaning seed quickly in the heart of the gathering.

Juliet had dried her eyes and Grainne returned to her seat, but the atmosphere around the table had changed just as surely as a stormcloud drifts across the face of the sun. Neither Juliet nor Grainne felt like eating any more food. Juliet was worrying about Floz. Grainne was worrying about Juliet worrying about Floz. Steve was worrying that he shouldn't have said anything about Hallow's Cottage. Perry was worrying that he had spoiled the atmosphere. Guy was annoyed that Steve had stirred up thoughts of Hallow's Cottage, which he would never own and never share with a woman like Floz. And if she had to leave the flat, bang went his chances of ever being able to call on his sister and see her by default. What if she moved away? Only Stripies, who rubbed against Guy's leg under the table hoping for some meat scraps, seemed carefree.

Hardly anyone ate the desserts. Guy cleared the plates and tipped the waste into the bin. His beautiful meal hadn't seduced Floz, after all; it had just been the backdrop to a much bigger story being played out with all the house-swapping news. Juliet felt tired and a bit headachey and so Steve drove her and Floz home in his new family car. Guy loaded the dishwasher, crashing the plates into the slots.

'Son, can I have a word?' Perry appeared in the kitchen door, puffing on his pipe.

Guy straightened up. 'Course, Dad, what's up?'

'Steve said you couldn't afford to buy Hallow's Cottage.'

'Steve's got a big mouth,' said Guy.

'I've just been looking at it on the internet.'

'Then you'll see why I wouldn't consider buying it. It's a dump.' Guy closed the dishwasher door and tried not to use the force that was stored up in his arm.

'Your mother and I have been talking.'

Guy held up his hand to stop his father. 'No. I know what you're going to say and the answer is no.'

'The answer is yes,' said Perry calmly. 'We are going to be giving Juliet a lump sum for her wedding and the baby, and we'll be giving the same amount to you. It's the right time to do this, son. The money is there for you both and there's no point in waiting until we die. Your mother and I would rather see you enjoy it and have it when you need it.'

He stretched out his hand in which he held a cheque.

Guy looked at the cheque. It was made out to him for £180,000.

'Dad, that's a hell of a lot of money!' said Guy, keeping his hands by his side.

'When your Uncle Stan and I sold the factory we made a big profit on the land at the side of it because we secured planning permission for it. Your mother and I are more than all right money-wise, and we'll enjoy seeing you buy that house rather than us having to die first so you can inherit what we want you to have, like with Stan and his son. God knows we've tried to make the pair of you have something from us for long enough – it's time for you to see sense now. Take the money, son, and buy the house. You've coveted it since you were a wee boy.'

Perry flapped the cheque at Guy and when he still didn't take it, he put it into his son's hand and closed his fingers around it.

'There, that wasn't so hard, now was it?'

'Dad, I don't know what to say.'

'Say, "Thank you, Daddy." That'll do.'

'Thanks, Dad.'

Guy threw his giant arms around his father and crushed him to his chest. He loved this man so much. And he felt love from him every day of his life.

When they finally drew apart, Perry lifted up his pipe again and puffed on it. Then he turned to go and tell Grainne the good news that Guy had taken the money. 'Go buy the house, son,' he said over his shoulder.

Floz pulled up pictures of Osoyoos on the internet. It looked as stunning as he had described it in past emails. She wanted to see it soon – in Nick's favourite season. Only then could she say a true goodbye. Although being anchored to grief seemed more desirable than cutting adrift and going in an uncertain direction.

Grief loses its hard edge after a time . . .

Chapter 70

Juliet was uncharacteristically down in the dumps. She'd spent hours over the weekend looking on the net for suitable houses for a family. Her mother and father were giving her and Steve a huge lump sum of money towards the wedding and a new home, which was exciting – but she was still feeling guilty about Floz.

At lunchtime on Monday she rang Steve almost in tears.

'Look, if the worst comes to the worst,' he said kindly, 'we can rent somewhere big enough so that Floz can stay with us until she gets a suitable place. How's that?'

Juliet smiled for the first time all morning. 'You don't mind?'

'No, course not,' said Steve. 'We'll have to put my place and yours up for a reasonable price so we've got a good chance of shifting them quickly. Then we'll buy somewhere. It's a bit messy but I'm sure it'll all sort itself out in the end.'

'I love you, Steve Feast.'

Steve smiled sloppily. He just hoped that the magic of their own fairytale ending would spread in Floz and Guy's direction.

That morning Guy was walking around Hallow's Cottage with Jeff Leppard, whose real name was Bob Sedgewick: Bob the builder extraordinaire.

'Well, Crusher,' mused Jeff, 'it's not as big a job for you as it might at first appear.' All the wrestlers tended to refer to each other by their aliases both in and out of the ring.

'Or for you. If you want the job.'

'Can we do it? Yes, we can,' laughed Jeff. 'It's quiet this winter, so I can set a gang on as soon as you complete the sale, if you give me a bit of notice when that will be.'

'I'll set things in motion straight away,' said Guy.

'Roof's sound as a pound,' Jeff went on, 'so you've not got that to worry about at least. Walls need a damp-proof course, obviously, and total replastering, but I presume you'll be getting Angel to do that bit for you. Floors all need sanding, but my God they'll be lovely. Look at the quality of those oak boards. Fucking smashing, they are.'

Jeff was smitten with the same vision as Guy as he imagined the cottage after his lads had gotten their hands on it. Except his vision didn't involve Floz in knickers, high heels and an apron frying bacon on the jewel of an old Aga that was in the kitchen.

When Juliet got in that night, there was a note waiting for her to say that Floz had gone shopping to Meadowhall and the answering machine was flashing.

'Message for Miss Cherrydale. I've emailed you the flight costs to Canada and accommodation choices as you requested. I'm just checking that you received them as you seemed in a bit of a hurry to organize it.'

Canada? Why the hell was Floz going to Canada – and quickly? And, more to the point, was it anything to do with that so-called mysterious 'old flame'?

Chapter 71

The answering-machine message had just finished playing when the entryphone sounded.

'It's me. Let me in. I have a surprise for you,' trilled Coco. Juliet buzzed him up and in he walked – and not alone.

The man with him was tall and well-built, had thick curly brown hair and trendy black glasses, and was everything that Coco's past partners had not been. There were no piercings or tattoos or pink streaks or weird trousers. Gideon was in a *geek-chic* suit. He was very handsome, Juliet decided, in a sexy businessman sort of way.

'This is Gideon,' said Coco, his face all smiles. 'We were just passing and Gideon said "Come on, let's call in and see your girlfriends." Where's lovely Floz?'

'Meadowhall, shopping,' explained Juliet, giving Gideon a nice friendly hello kiss. Fabulous aftershave.

'Fancy a coffee?' she asked, just as the entryphone rang again, causing her to mutter that it was like King's Cross in here sometimes. It was Steve and he had popped in to see if she was all right. He had Guy in tow. A Guy who was also very disappointed to learn that Floz was out.

Still, Coco was thrilled to be able to show off Gideon to more friends. And to prove to Steve that he really did exist.

'I'm worried about Floz,' said Juliet, pouring out four

mugs of coffee and a sparkling water for herself. 'She's going to Canada.'

'Canada? To visit? To live?' shrieked Guy, then leashed in his anguish. 'Why?'

'I only wish I knew.'

'We both feel something is very wrong with Floz,' said Coco, pressing his hand on his heart. 'It's not got a good vibe.'

'Go snooping on her PC then,' laughed Steve, not expecting Juliet to take him up on it.

'I could, couldn't I? Whilst she's out,' said Juliet, putting her glass of water down and heading for Floz's door.

'Whoa, whoa, you can't do that!' protested Guy.

'I can and I will,' said Juliet.

'I was only joking,' Steve said to her back.

'You can't interfere in someone's business like that!' Guy called after his sister.

'It's a good job sometimes that people do interfere,' said Juliet pointedly to her brother. He knew what she meant.

But Juliet was on a mission now and she was unstoppable.

'You, stand guard!' she said, directing her brother to the front door. 'Gideon, Coco said you're brilliant on computers. Help me.'

'I . . .' Poor Gideon didn't feel all that comfortable hacking into a complete stranger's computer, but Juliet had spoken and he felt her force immediately. He followed her into Floz's strawberry-scented room as meekly as a lamb.

'Okay, how do I bypass her password?' asked Juliet, switching on Floz's monitor.

'It's amazing how many people have "password" as password,' said Gideon, trying 'password' and seeing the proof of his statement as Floz's homescreen flashed up.

'Genius,' said Coco, mightily impressed.

'Go into her mailbox,' directed Juliet.

Gideon clicked on Floz's mailbox and Juliet looked down

the folders on the left: Lee Status, Finance, Canada, House of Cards . . . 'Click on Canada,' she said as excitedly as if she had just found the right combination on a safe.

A noise from the lounge made them all jump.

'Sorry, that was just me knocking into your lamp,' called Guy.

'Oh my God, read that!' Juliet suddenly exclaimed, patting her heart.

We really shouldn't . . .' said Gideon.

' "They say every story . . ." ' began Coco, and read to the bottom of the first email. 'Oh my, it's an email from a dying man!'

Steve appeared at the doorway. He too knew it was wrong, but he was drawn to look over Coco's shoulder and read along with them all. Then Guy appeared after being lured by all the 'oohs' and 'ahs'.

Guy read Floz's words to Nick, her heart pouring onto the page. He knew she had been crying as she typed this. He was jealous – jealous of a man who had this amount of pull with her. Jealous of a man riddled with a terminal disease.

They flicked from email to email contained in the Canada file, then opened up the first one from Chas announcing Nick's death and funeral. By this time the tears were rolling down both Juliet's and Coco's faces.

'Oh my, that's so sad,' sniffled Coco. 'Poor Floz. I never imagined—'

'That's funny,' said Gideon quietly.

'Funny? What do you mean, Gid? I don't see anything funny about it,' snapped Coco.

'No, love, not that sort of funny.' Gideon did some calculations on his fingers. 'According to this mail and when it was sent, Canadian-time, there could only have been two days for Nick to have died, been cremated and scattered and reported to Floz. That's a bit quick.'

His analytical brain was now tickled to 'engaged' status. He flicked backwards and forwards through the mails: he had a bloodhound nose and was on a trail. 'That's not right either,' he muttered to himself. 'I wonder . . . Pass me a pen, Coco.' Coco jumped to attention.

Then they heard a key in the flat door.

'Guy, quick, go!' yelled Juliet.

Guy lunged out of Floz's bedroom door and grabbed hold of the handle of the flat door, resisting Floz's attempt to enter.

'Hurry up!' Juliet hissed at Gideon, who was writing something on his hand. 'Oh and look, there's a mail from the travel agent. Delete that quick.'

'You can't—' began Steve, but it was gone. 'I suppose you've deleted that answering-machine message as well, haven't you? Oh Juliet.' He knew she had, he didn't need her to affirm it.

'Damn, the screen's frozen,' said Gideon, seeing an egg-timer appear. 'She needs this machine servicing. It's running so slowly.'

'Pull the plug or something,' Juliet panicked.

Outside, Floz was tugging on the door handle, aware that Guy was pulling it from the other side because she had just seen him – between the second when she managed to open it and when it snapped shut again.

'Guy, it's me!' said Floz, bemused as always with the antics of the man. What was he up to now?

'Yep,' said Guy, for want of something better to say. He knew that this wouldn't do his standing any good with her at all. And how the hell was he going to explain what he was doing? He mouthed 'Quick' at Juliet, who was holding out her hands in a gesture of helplessness.

'Let me in,' said Floz. 'What is going on?' She couldn't imagine in her wildest dreams why her flat-mate's brother would be holding the door shut so she couldn't get in.

Coco held up five fingers to Guy – five seconds then he could let go. Meanwhile, Juliet flung herself on the sofa, Steve flung himself next to her, Gideon and Coco assumed a tableau of innocent chit-chat with Juliet and Steve. Guy counted down and then released the handle.

Floz opened the door tentatively, and stepped into the flat the same way in case Guy had any more surprises in store.

'Sorry,' he said. He couldn't have sounded more pathetic if he'd tried. 'Just my little joke.'

'Guy Miller, you are not funny,' trilled Juliet, trying to help and doing anything but. 'He thought it would be funny to not let you in,' she said to Floz.

'Yeah, I gathered,' said Floz, sidling past Guy as quickly as she could and over to where Coco was standing with Gideon.

'Guess who this is?' said Coco, pointing to his boyfriend.

'You must be Floz,' said Gideon, leaning over and kissing Floz on her cheek. Floz nodded and said a quiet, 'Hi.' Her head was still trying to work out why a thirty-four-year-old *man* would play a game too puerile for a five-year-old.

'Just a flying visit. We have to go,' said Coco, twittering nervously. 'I need food. And I promised to cook.'

'I have to go too, I'm working in an hour,' said Guy, doubting that Floz would be in the least concerned about that. Steve also stood. A nervous mass exodus.

'Isn't Gideon nice?' said Juliet, after kissing Steve 'bye and closing the door. 'I'm so glad you caught him before he left.'

Floz nodded. But she wondered why Gideon had red writing all over his hand. And why everyone had acted so oddly when she came in.

The evening didn't end its peculiarity there. Juliet's mobile kept ringing, and each time she disappeared into the kitchen to answer it. There were at least five phone calls during the evening, and goodness knows how many texts.

'You okay?' said Floz.

'Fine,' said Juliet, who didn't look fine at all. 'I'm just going out for a while.'

'At this time?' It was half-past ten.

'Yes. I want to – to get some fresh air. I'll see you in a bit.'

'Juliet, are you really okay? Do you want me to come with you?'

'No!' she barked, then repeated the word quietly. 'Sorry, I mean no. I won't be long. Just a little nip out. Nothing for you to worry about. Honestly,' she lied.

Chapter 72

Juliet and Coco stood behind Gideon, who was operating Coco's pink laptop.

'Do you see the way "greif" is spelled?' said Gideon. On the screen in front of him he had the mail he had forwarded from Floz's PC sent to her by Nick.

'Wrongly,' said Juliet.

'Precisely. And do you see the way it's spelled here?' He opened up another forwarded email. This one from Chas Hanson.

'The same – wrongly,' said Juliet.

'Nick Vermeer and Chas Hanson make the same errors. And they both write *its* with no apostrophe when the meaning is *it is*.'

'So they went to the same school and Canadians are crap at grammar and spelling?' Juliet shrugged her shoulders. So far she wasn't seeing anything that incriminating, considering Coco had told her she must come over right NOW and see this.

'And they both use the same spacing after a full stop. Well, no space at all, actually,' Gideon went on.

Juliet tried not to say a sarcastic, 'Wow.'

'I could point out quite a few similarities of expression and syntax as well, but I'll skip it because here's my main point,' explained Gideon. He typed in an address and hit enter. A page came up full of gobbledegook writing. 'Not a program known to the masses, but luckily enough I have access to it.'

'What does all that mean?' asked Juliet.

'It means,' said Coco, 'that Nick and Chas Hanson both sent those emails to Floz from the same computer. From all the evidence I've seen so far, I think they might be one and the same man.'

Chapter 73

The next afternoon Juliet and Steve sat in Guy's tiny flat drinking coffee. Juliet had worked through her lunch-hour and left early. Steve had picked her up and driven her straight over there for a quick emergency pow-wow before Guy went to the restaurant to start his shift.

'I don't know how to handle this,' said Juliet, 'but I've got to say something. Floz is planning on heading out to Canada.'

'Why, though?' said Guy. 'Is she going out there to see where this Nick's ashes are supposed to be scattered? I can't work out what the scam is, if there is one.' It was a total mystery to him and he'd been thinking about it quite a bit since the previous night when Juliet called to tell him what Gideon had discovered.

'Is Gideon absolutely certain that this Nick and Chas are the same bloke?' Steve asked. Like the others, he hadn't a clue what could be going on.

Juliet's phone rang. It was Coco. Juliet put it on speakerphone.

'Where are you?' he asked.

'Guy's flat. We're just talking about what to do about Floz. How sure is Gideon that Chas and Nick are the same person?'

'Very sure. Is Guy's computer on? What's his address? I'm sending through an email now.'

Guy dictated his email address and opened up his laptop on

the table. A mail appeared in his box within seconds. Guy opened it to find a newspaper article.

HANSON, *Cody Campbell b. 14 April 1979, d. 22 September 2009. Born in Victoria, BC. Left to mourn him are wife Lysa Hanson, mother Mary Hanson, father Chas Hanson, sister Serena May Vermeer, brother-in-law Rocco Vermeer, niece and nephew Veronica and Vincente Vermeer, and cousins May Campbell Hanson and Constance Campbell Hanson. Memorial tba. In lieu of flowers, donations can be made to CDS Military Family Fund c/o CFPS, 379 Lafleur St, Ottawa, ON. Condolences may be offered to the family at www.cpfh@funeralhome.vic*

Published in the *Victoria Post*, 27 September 2009

'Are you still on the line?' asked Coco. 'Here's Gideon.'

'Hi, Gideon,' said Juliet, confused to say the least. 'Who the feck is Cody Campbell Hanson?'

'Someone who committed suicide last year,' said Gideon. 'I trawled the net and I found the obituary in the Canadian newspaper. Look at the name of his father.'

Juliet read: ' "Left to mourn him are wife Lysa Hanson, mother Mary Hanson, father Chas Hanson" . . . *Chas Hanson*?'

'Read on.'

'Okay: "father Chas Hanson, sister blah blah and brother-in-law Rocco *Vermeer*, niece and nephew Veronica and Vincente" et cetera. I don't get it.'

'Floz asked Chas when Nick's birthday was and he told her April the fourteenth. That's also Cody's birthday. And both Nick and Cody died on the twenty-second of September – although Cody died last year and Nick supposedly died in 2010. And note that Nick has the same surname as Chas's son-in-law – Vermeer?'

'But who the heck is this Cody bloke?'

'Sending email now. Found this in the *BC Times* archive; it's another Canadian newspaper.'

Guy opened the attachment.

MAN JUMPS TO DEATH FROM BUILDING

Police sealed off a large area in Fallon Square, Victoria, after a thirty-year-old male jumped twelve floors to his death from the residential building where he lived. Mr Cody Campbell Hanson was taken to Victoria General Hospital but was pronounced dead on arrival. It is believed that Mr Hanson's wife of two years moved out of the apartment that morning in order to reside with an unnamed man with whom she was allegedly having an affair.

'Bloody hell,' said Guy. 'Though I still don't get how all the pieces fit together.'

'No, but this fucker Chas Hanson knows,' said Juliet, incensed now. 'What do we do, boys?'

'We could tell Floz what we know so far, or . . .' Gideon stopped and sighed.

'Or what? Come on, Gideon. Help us,' pleaded Juliet.

'It's totally unethical and very wrong.'

'Just tell us, please.'

'Well,' Gideon said slowly, hating that he was even suggesting this, 'I could set up a false email address and someone could pretend to be her and write to this Chas bloke. But please don't let it be me.'

'Juliet, you'd be the best person,' said Coco.

'No, I wouldn't,' huffed Juliet. 'I could write a "Tell me what's going on, you sick bastard" letter though. And don't you think it's a bit dodgy with both of us in the same house? I'm bound to drop myself in it.'

'I don't want Juliet pressurized,' put in Steve. 'Guy – you do it.'

'What?' Guy looked at him in horror.

'Brownie points,' Steve muttered under his breath. 'You rescue her from this and you can be her hero, baby.'

'Yes, Guy, you do it,' said Juliet, without another thought. 'Gideon, send Guy the bogus email address. Guy, you'll have to tell this sicko that you i.e. Floz have changed email accounts. We don't want him corresponding with the real Floz any more by mistake, do we?'

'Well, that's a risk we'll have to take,' sighed Gideon.

'All right, I'll do it,' said Guy. They had to rescue Floz from whatever this was. No one could make any sense of it yet. However, they were united in thinking it weird beyond belief.

'What will you write?' asked Juliet.

'I don't know,' Guy told her. 'Let me have a think about it. I'll send an email to him before I go to work. I've got an hour and a half to concoct something.'

'Oh God,' said Juliet, reaching for her coat. 'I hope for Floz's sake this isn't some awful con. How sick do you have to be, to pretend to be a dying man?'

'Very,' said Steve. But as he'd grown up knowing, not everyone in life had other people's interests at heart. He was only glad his life was now full of people who did.

When Juliet and Steve left, Guy sat staring at the laptop screen. What the hell was he going to write to this Chas Hanson to make him confess he was a loony? He recalled Floz's soft words in her emails. She obviously had a great capacity to love, but he wondered if she had ever been truly loved herself. The section in the letter about her parents made him ache to put his arms around her and cuddle her. How awful to view yourself as an unwanted by-product.

He tried to think what a gentle person like Floz would write to make Chas Hanson confess to whatever sick game he was playing. He couldn't imagine her ever getting angry enough to threaten anyone, even someone sick like this man obviously was. He began to type.

Chas

I'm so sorry to contact you again. I was trawling the net and I found the attached obituary. I think there are too many coincidences to ignore. Please tell me what has been going on. I am beginning to think that Nick did not exist, but I need to know because I am suffering. Will you please reply to this email address? I've closed the other down as it is infected with a virus.

Kindest

Floz Cherrydale

He would give Chas Hanson twenty-four hours to respond, then he'd up the ante. And if Mr Chas Hanson, or whoever he was, didn't play ball, he was quite prepared to go out there and squeeze the story out of him first-hand.

Chapter 74

'Hiya, babes!' Lee Status's cheesy voice rang down the receiver. 'I need you to get cracking on this brief ASAP and I'm about to board a plane to Berlin. "Mother's Day" again, hon. Plenty of the old familiar: Mum doing everything, worrying, holding the lot together, multi-tasking, et cetera – you know the score.'

'Yep, okay, Lee. No problem.'

'Oh yeah, and loads of "New Mum" cards. The sort that a dad would buy for a baby to send to his wife. Can I have them a week today?'

'Okay.'

'Cheers, babe.'

Lee's timing was nothing short of perfect, thought Floz. Then Juliet breezed into the flat and asked her if she fancied going late-night shopping with her to Meadowhall to choose some baby stuff. She thought a cheery trip out to buy things for a new life might take her mind off the dead Canadian – who may or may not exist.

As usual, Juliet would take nothing less than yes for an answer. She applied her usual brand of well-meant emotional blackmail.

'Floz, I don't know where to start buying maternity things. Please help me. Steve is useless. All he wants to do is look at go-karts and big toys. I'm starting to have dreams that the baby has arrived and all I have ready for it is a set of boxing gloves. Plus I want to get Steve a bit extra for his birthday tomorrow. The big poof loves those bath balls from Lush.'

And Floz, being soft and obliging, grabbed her car keys and said, 'Okay, come on then and de-stress. I'll drive.'

In Debenhams, Juliet held up a tiny little romper suit in blue and a counterpart in pink.

'Do I risk buying a colour? Or do I buy both and keep the receipt?' she sighed.

'Why don't you plump for this,' advised Floz, and held up the tiniest little Babygro in white.

'Oh my GOD!' gasped Juliet. 'How beautiful is that?'

'I like to see little babies all in pure white.'

'You are so right, Floz.' Juliet looked at the green and lemon babygros in her basket and went to return them to the shelves and replace them with white ones.

Floz picked up another tiny white Babygro and held it up, under the arms, in front of her. She tried to imagine the weight of a little baby inside it. She rested it on her shoulder, imagined a baby mouth breathing warmly and softly on her neck, rooting for something to eat, the tiny fingers curling, the smell of baby powder.

She opened her eyes. No point in thinking like that. Not any more. Babies were always going to be for other people. Lovers were always going to be for other people. Her hope was fading fast that she was to be anything other than a woman destined to grow old, alone. Not even the glorious shades of autumn were working their magic on her. She gave herself a mental shake as Juliet called her to check out some darling little scratch mittens.

Floz went to bed that night and thought of Juliet and Steve as parents. Their child was going to be so lucky. It would not only be raised with love, but they would give it lots of their quality time. It wouldn't be foisted on au pairs and nannies whilst its parents lived the life of a childless couple. She could easily see Steve pretending to be a horse with a giggling toddler on his back, Juliet baking cornflake buns in a chocolate-smeared apron. She could see old Stripies sitting contentedly beside the baby, Grainne and Perry ringing up desperate to babysit. Even the child's eyes lighting up as 'Uncle Guy' swung him over his head like an aeroplane. Yes, Guy would be lovely with children. He obviously wasn't that brilliant at relating to women, but she bet he was very kind to children and old people.

Nick would have made a lovely father too. He never got the chance to hook a line for his son or show him bear-prints in the woods. And now he was gone.

Chapter 75

Guy got in from work in the wee small hours of the morning. He hated the place. Varto had sent out two fillet steaks with strands of hair in the peppercorn sauce. And Guy had seen a cockroach scuttle across the kitchen floor.

Kenny wouldn't let him sack Varto until he was safely out of the picture, because he was knocking off Varto's mother behind his wife's back, Guy had discovered that evening. Which explained why Varto thought he was untouchable. Guy couldn't wait to rid himself of the arrogant, lazy, unhygienic, thieving little git.

He went straight to his laptop but no email had arrived from Chas Hanson yet. Well, after the shift he'd had, there was no way Guy was going to give him the grace of twenty-four hours to respond. He wrote again to him, armed with some extra information he had found on the net, after doing a trawl on Chas Hanson's name at work during his break.

Dear Chas

Please help me. I need to know what is going on. If I don't hear from you, then I will contact the *Victoria Post* to try and find out the truth. I'm sure they would be interested in helping me solve this mystery. These days, with the aid of the net, it isn't that difficult to follow a trail and I must know what has been going on. You could save me a lot of time and heartache, and yourself the embarrassment, if you answer my email. I have found a Lysa Hanson on Facebook who is friends with Rocco Vermeer and May and Constance Campbell Hanson, the people mentioned in the obituary. If needs be, I will involve them as well in my investigation. I won't let this drop now until I have the whole story.

Floz

Then Guy dropped off to sleep. He awoke just before nine the next morning to find that Chas Hanson had responded to his threat and replied.

Chapter 76

Guy immediately rang Steve and read Chas Hanson's mail to him.

'Fuck,' said Steve.

'I can't tell her this,' said Guy.

'Oh mate, you have to.' Steve was speaking quietly as he was in Juliet's flat and Floz was in the kitchen getting her breakfast. 'And the sooner the better. Today, in fact.'

'It will sound much better coming from Juliet.'

'Yeah, you're probably right. I'll ask her when she gets up then.'

'Ask me what, Birthday Boy?' yawned Juliet, waking up at the sound of her name.

And then Steve passed her the phone so Guy could give her the final piece of the jigsaw.

Steve made a sneaky exit from the flat so that Juliet could be alone with Floz. He only hoped that Guy had got it right and Juliet *was* the best person to deliver the news. Juliet did tend to make bulls in china shops look like lambs in playpens.

'Where's Steve?' called Floz, as Juliet emerged from her bedroom. 'I've got a birthday card here for him. And a bottle of wine.'

'He's gone home to do something or other,' Juliet shrugged.

'You all right, Juliet? Morning sickness again?' asked Floz, studying her friend's troubled expression. 'You aren't allowed to be ill today, you know. Not if you're going to that very swanky hotel with Steve tonight.'

'No, I'm not feeling unwell,' replied Juliet. She had been so looking forward to the hotel, but there was no way she was going to go off for a night of nookie and leave Floz alone with her heart breaking all over the carpet.

'Can I get you anything to eat?' asked Floz. 'A bit of toast? Cereal? Yogurt?'

'No, Floz, I don't want anything to eat.' Juliet poured herself some juice and wondered how to begin. She was never lost for words. So how come everything she wanted to say was stuck in her throat like lumps of cement?

The phone rang just as Juliet opened her mouth to do the dirty deed. Floz picked it up.

'Yes, this is Ms Cherrydale . . . No, I can't remember seeing an email from you . . . That's odd, I didn't get an answerphone message either. If you send me the details again I'll ring you straight back and book this morning.'

'Book what?' asked Juliet.

'I'm going away for a few days,' said Floz, covering up the receiver.

'Where?'

'Canada.'

'Canada? Why are you going there, Floz?'

'Just because . . . I . . . it's a holiday.'

'Floz, tell them you'll ring them back. I need to talk to you. It's urgent. Please sit down.'

Whatever was on Juliet's mind looked serious; Floz did as she was asked.

'What's the matter? Is it you and Steve?' Floz asked with concern.

'There's no easy way to say this,' said Juliet with a fortifying breath. 'We hacked into your computer and read Nick's emails.'

Floz jerked in shock.

'You have to blame me for this one, no one else. I was worried about you, and you wouldn't say what was wrong, and something obviously was, so we look—'

'Who is "we"?' asked Floz slowly.

'Just me. And Steve. And . . . Guy.'

'Steve and Guy?'

'And Coco . . . and . . . Gideon.'

Floz wanted to get up but she was too horrified and embarrassed to move.

'Why would you do that?'

'Because we care about you.'

Floz closed her arms around herself, a tight, defensive gesture. 'That was so wrong of you, Juliet . . .'

'Please, Floz, there's a lot more to tell.'

'Like what?' rasped Floz, finding a rare fire in her voice.

'Guy wrote to Chas Hanson pretending to be you.'

'What . . . why?' Guy was now beyond the realms of weird in Floz's eyes. He was loop-the-loop.

'Because I asked him to. Gideon found out that – that Chas and Nick were writing from the same computer.'

'Don't be daft. They live hundreds of miles apart. *Lived.*'

Juliet reached into the papers she had hidden in a drawer. Gideon had printed out the incriminating emails and circled the evidence.

'They made the same spelling mistakes. Look – *greif.*'

Greif loses its hard edge after a time. That's what Floz had noticed – that incorrect transposition of e and i, not the sentiment.

'And their grammar mistakes are identical. Look – they both write "its" not "it's". There's other similarities too – see? They're all highlighted and colour-coded.'

'What are you saying?' said Floz.

'I'm saying that there *is* no Nick Vermeer, only Chas Hanson. He admitted it to Guy.'

The sort of flat, heavy silence that should have precluded a nuclear blast fell on the room.

'No, no. That's wrong,' said Floz, with a soft tremble in her voice.

'We dug around a bit and found out that Chas Hanson had a son who committed suicide last year.' Juliet found the copy of the newspaper article and passed it to Floz, then the obituary.

Floz noticed the names and dates. But none of it made sense. The names belonged to the wrong people, the dates belonged to the wrong events. Vincente was Nick's middle name. Rocco was the name of his first Malamute dog. He told her that one of his sisters was called Veronica . . .

'Then this arrived this morning in the fake email box.' Juliet handed over the final piece of the jigsaw and Floz read.

Dear Floz,

Nick never existed except in my own mind.Unfortunately I got in too deep with you and did not know how to end it.So I just quit writing.When my son died,I was totally lost.I thought then that I should write you again and somehow let my imaginary creation die but in a way that let you know that you had touched someone.My creation had abandoned you and hurt you, and in a totally strange way,I thought it would somehow allow you to move on.When you asked for my birthdate,I was thinking of my son and used his.In my own weird way,I was trying to bring him back ,even if it was only a fantasy.My depression and its consequences have screwed up lives and its time to make amends.In attempting to escape my own reality,I hurt others. The reason Nick so closely resembled my son is that I could not deal with his death.I am not asking for forgiveness because I do not deserve it.I am going to have to deal with my greif issue in the real world and not in a fantasy creation.

I owe you for dragging me back into reality and I know that must sound contrived,but even I know that my depression is deadly to myself and others.

CH

Floz's hand was trembling and the paper was fluttering.

'Nick never existed?' she whispered.

'No, love.'

'I fell in love with a man who never existed.'

'You fell in love with the creation of a sick mind.'

'I spoke to him. He sent me pictures of himself.'

'You spoke to Chas Hanson. I don't know what he looks like, we can't find a picture of him anywhere, but this is a photo of Cody, the son of Chas Hanson who died. Guy found it on Facebook. There's an RIP site set up for him.' Juliet handed over a picture of a smiling man at the side of a red car.

'That can't be.' Floz's heart-rate was thudding and she felt light-headed with shock. 'The pictures Nick sent me of himself look like this man, but older. He said he was forty.'

'He must be considerably older than that, Floz. His son was thirty when he died last year. We also found these pictures on the memorial site.'

Juliet handed over two pictures of Cody as a boy. One of him riding a toy horse, the other of him looking uncomfortable in a frilly shirt and suit.

Floz gasped. 'Nick said these pictures were of *him* as a young boy!'

'He lied. They're ones of Chas's son. I'm so sorry to have to tell you this, Floz. He's a conman.'

'But why would he lie? He never asked me for any money, he was never less than a gentleman . . .'

'That's one thing, I suppose. But he did leech off your emotions, Floz. Big time. The bastard.'

Floz's fists rolled and she began punching her thighs. The tears coursed down her cheeks.

'I can't believe I have been so stupid,' she wept. 'I trusted him. I told him everything about myself – even more than I told my ex-husband. I loved him. I loved a man who didn't exist.' And then she laughed, and it was a hollow, heartbroken sound that wounded Juliet to hear it.

'Oh, Floz, it's not that you're stupid, it's that they're clever. Very, very clever and manipulative.'

'How could anyone . . .'

'I don't know. All I do know is that you should walk away from this. Don't get embroiled in the sick mess of his games and his pain.'

'I was on the brink of going to Canada to walk in the footsteps of a man who never was. A man I grieved for. I was going to go to the place where I thought his ashes were scattered.'

'I know, love.'

And Steve and Coco and Gideon and Guy know what an idiot I am. Why does it embarrass me most that Guy Miller knows?

Then Floz suddenly leaped up and wiped her eyes. 'You know, you're right. I need to just walk away and forget this whole thing.'

'You have to, Floz,' said Juliet, her voice brimming with concern.

'Let's put *Jeremy Kyle* on and have lots of tea and toast,' said Floz, clapping her hands. 'Let me concentrate on someone else being told a load of lies. Sit right there, I'll put the kettle on.'

She disappeared into the kitchen. And Juliet believed the bright and breezy mask that Floz pinned on.

Chapter 77

'Are you sure you're okay?' said Juliet later, tugging her overnight bag to the door. Steve was on his way up the stairs to collect it.

'Yes,' Floz replied with a relaxed smile. 'Of course I'm okay. It's over, it's finished – so thank you for babysitting me today, but go and have a fab time tonight with your fiancé.'

'I'll worry about you.'

'Don't you dare,' said Floz, who had done her best all day to convince Juliet that she was fine. She just wanted Juliet to leave so she could drop the facade because it was exhausting. She wanted to crumble into a ball and shut out the world. She wanted total oblivion. She didn't want to wake up until the gnawing ache had gone. Tiny babies and young boys in photographs were swirling round in her head. Graves and funerals of people who had never lived . . .

She waved Juliet and Steve off, then reached for the whisky bottle on the cabinet behind the dining-table. It was vile and seared her throat. But she wanted to hurt herself, because she needed to hit out at something and the only target available was herself.

Floz was so blasted by nine o'clock that she would barely remember the phone ringing and breezily telling Guy that yes, she was perfectly fine. Of course she was.

After he put down the phone Guy attempted to start planning menus for the opening night of his new restaurant for the fourth time and failed. He couldn't concentrate. His thoughts were back in his sister's flat. He had this feeling that he couldn't quite shake off. Something about the way Floz had said she was 'fine' bothered him. She was laughing, and that 'fine' was too bright.

Juliet had slyly rung him earlier and told him that Floz was now up to speed with the whole story and that she had taken the news incredibly well. But would he mind just ringing her later, on some pretext, to make extra sure?

I'm fine. Honestly, I am fine. Why wouldn't I be fine? There had been a manufactured trill in her voice. Just like ten years ago when he had rung up Lacey and asked if she was okay. And he had believed her.

He shot out of his seat and grabbed his car keys in an almost seamless move, hurried on his coat and locked the flat door. On the way over, he was aware that his driving was too fast.

There was no reply on the entryphone when he rang upstairs, so he let himself in with his key.

The lights were on in the flat and the television was blaring out. On the sofa sat Floz, collapsed against the cushions. On the coffee-table there was a very depleted bottle of whisky and an empty bottle of Shiraz. There were two glasses on the table. One had fallen over and was dripping red wine on the table; the other was full of the Harveys Bristol Cream that Juliet had in the cupboard for when her mother called in. Guy was getting a headache even thinking about the state Floz would be in, the next morning. He did a quick check around and in the bin for evidence of empty blister-packs, but thankfully found nothing. It was the thought of her taking pills that had in fact weighted his foot down on the accelerator.

He pulled her up to a sitting position and gently tapped her face.

'Floz, can you hear me? Floz – wake up.'

'Guy,' said Floz, suddenly aware of a presence and squinting to focus on him. She gave him a big grin. 'Oh look, it's Guy who hates me.' Then she slid eel-like off the sofa and he dived to catch her with a 'Whoa'. *Is that what she thought? That he hated her?*

Floz laughed with her mouth but her eyes were red and there were lots of black rivulets down her cheek. She'd been crying hard.

'It's all right, I'm fine,' she said aggressively whilst attempting to brush him away.

Seconds later her whole body rhythmically started to convulse. Like Stripies did when he was about to part with a hairball.

'Oh bollocks,' said Guy, scooping her up under his arm and hurtling towards the toilet in the bathroom, but he got her in position too late and the first mouthful of projectile vomit tumbled colourfully down her shirt. The second hit the water in the loo. Floz groaned as her body tried violently to rid itself of the poisons she had put in it. Guy swept back her long flame of hair and held it with one hand; the other rubbed absently at her back whilst he said things like, 'Come on, get it up.' A lot of brightly coloured liquid came up, but no food. A whimper eventually indicated that she was spent and, with surprising daintiness, she wiped at her mouth with the pedestal mat.

Guy grabbed a cloth from the sink and dampened it dextrously with one hand, working the tap and squeezing the excess water out whilst holding onto her draped over his other arm. He wiped her face, took off the black lines down her cheeks. She responded to the coolness of the cloth with a sexily delicious, 'Aahhh,' that made him momentarily think about her making that sound in other scenarios. Ones that involved him hooking her legs over his shoulders. Her eyelashes were long and black, he'd never been level with her face before, never seen the little scar that crossed both her lips, the little dark beauty spot on her cheekbone.

Guy looked around for help. Her shirt was sodden and smelly, with vomit clinging to it. It needed to come off. He hoisted her to her feet, and when her legs buckled, he pulled her up again and then led her like a small child into her bedroom, pushing her gently down onto the bed whilst he looked in her wardrobe for a replacement top. When he turned around she was supine and snoring lightly.

'Oh no you don't, lady,' he said. 'You sleep now and you are going to have one hell of a head in the morning.'

He pulled her up into a sitting position; she was as floppy as a rag doll. She looked spent and exhausted. Guy wished that twisted Canadian was in the room. He would have forced him to look at the state Floz was in because of him. *See what you've done to her? See the damage you've caused? She could have choked on her own vomit and died because of you, you bastard.*

His fingers reached for the top button on Floz's shirt then snatched back as if she'd just slapped him. God, he couldn't do this. He felt like a perve. *What if she woke up and thought he was . . . ?*

In saying that, there was absolutely no way she was going to awaken suddenly and catch him undressing her. He looked around for assistance, as if he expected to find Juliet miraculously there, but she wasn't and wouldn't be until tomorrow, and there was no getting away from it. He couldn't leave her covered in her own sick. He rubbed his hands together as if to warm them up and then tackled the top button. It popped out of the buttonhole. Fine, so far so good. Second one – no worries. The third one was in between her breasts and he averted his eyes as the button slipped through the hole, and felt down for the next three. He'd undressed a few women in his time but this was different. They'd all been conscious, for a start, and reciprocating with his buttons. He'd fantasized about this moment lots, peeling the clothes off this woman with him now. Well – ripping, if the truth be told, with her making thrilled little squeaks in her throat and biting his earlobe. Enough of that. Here he was in the role of trusted knight in shining armour; it wasn't right thinking unvaliant stuff like that.

He slid the blouse off her shoulders, trying not to look at the rather lovely creamy lace bra cupping two rather lovely creamy breasts. There were three tiny tattooed hearts just visible on the top curve of her breast, two pink and one blue. God she was gorgeous, even here with a vomity shirt and big red eyes and hair roughed up like the bastard son of Don King and the Wildman from Borneo. Then he noticed the crucifix of an old scar across her stomach, the arms of it long and ragged. That must have been one hell of an operation she'd had. He got back to the job in hand and quickly threaded her resistant arms through the sleeves of another shirt and hurried the buttons onto all the wrong holes, breathing a sigh of relief when he'd finished.

'Come on, miss, water time.' He hoisted her up, despite the string of uncharacteristic abuse she gave him, and supporting her under the arms, led her over to the kitchen sink. With one arm keeping her from slithering to the floor, he filled a pint glass with water. He backed onto the sofa and sat her on his knee, forcing her to sip it like a nurse with a dehydrated baby whilst she grumpily protested and tried to bat it away. He pinned back both her hands with one of his and she wriggled in his lap. He gulped. His imagination was smoking with over-activity. He was in real danger of spontaneously combusting. *Concentrate, concentrate, man!*

He encouraged her to drink the water, gently and slowly so that it wouldn't come back up again. He needed to hydrate her properly. Then and only then did he cave in to her sobby request to let her sleep. She slumped gratefully against his chest and he let himself savour her body in his arms for a few minutes, his nose catching that strawberry scent on her skin. She felt so small and vulnerable and he hurt for her. Then he picked her up, carried her into her bedroom and slid her under the quilt, on her side. He left her fully dressed – he wasn't sure if his heart could stand unbuttoning anything again. He was already at the stage of needing beta blockers. 'BP 980 over 456,' they would have announced on *Casualty*. He slid off her shoes before he tucked the quilt neatly around her shape, and thought how dainty her toes were.

'Pull yourself together for fuck's sake, Guy,' said something angelic, yet foul-mouthed, on his shoulder. He gave himself a mental belt across the chops and plonked himself on the tub chair in the room. She was sleeping peacefully now, making snuffly noises like a contented baby. He'd just stay a bit to make sure she wasn't sick again before moving onto the sofa in the lounge. Just a little while.

Chapter 78

Floz's eyes flickered open and her brain spun into a frenetic attempt to assess the situation. She remembered opening up the bottle of whisky and the memory of the smell made her retch. She drank wine too. And she spoke to Guy on the phone, she recalled. And someone held her hair back whilst she was vomiting in the toilet. *No, please tell me it wasn't him.* Then she froze. Someone was in her room, she could hear them breathing. Slowly she pulled back the quilt and turned her head to the source of the sound. She blinked hard, hoping the figure crammed into the chair in the corner was an illusion, but it wasn't. Guy Miller really was asleep in her bedroom, his arms folded, his neck at a very crooked angle.

What the f . . .

The involuntary groan that came from deep in her throat jerked Guy awake. They both sat bolt upright in their respective sleeping quarters.

'Hi,' he said sleepily. 'How are you feeling?' His neck ached like a beast.

Floz suddenly became aware that she was fully dressed. Oh no, he'd put her to bed. She looked down. She never wore this shirt. When had she put it on? *Had* she put it on? Or had he done it for her? *Oh please no.*

'Oh God,' she vocalized her horror. Her head was being

bombarded with snapshots. It was like the worst photo album in the world: *Floz throwing up*, *Floz trying to act sober* and her personal favourite, *Floz weeing all over the carpet and Guy washing her down*. Which bits were real, which bits weren't? *Nooo!* But she did distinctly remember a cloth. She gulped. Hang on, he wiped her face, she remembered now. Closing her eyes and rubbing at them did nothing to blot out what she remembered. If anything, their colours were brighter against the darkness. Why didn't she have a headache? She wanted one. She wanted to be in Headache Land, where it was too painful to think about other things. Things that she wanted so badly to blot out. In fact, she wanted to blot out her whole life. Not die, just in case she woke up to suffer eternity feeling exactly the same as she did now. She wanted not to exist.

'Floz, you got drunk. We've all done it.'

'I was sick, wasn't I?' she cringed. *Yes, you were*, said some irritating little swine of a voice in her head. *He was holding your hair back whilst you were throwing up over the bathroom floor, REMEMBER?*

'A bit.' Guy held up his hands in a gesture of 'so what'.

Remember sitting on his knee? taunted the voice. *Bet you can't remember what you said to him, you dirty bitch.*

'Was I saying anything?' said Floz, hands still pressed over her eyes.

'Only "bleurghh".'

God, did that make it better or worse?

'Floz, you got drunk, you cried, you were sick,' said Guy, sounding not unlike Julius Caesar. 'I gave you some water so you would have less of a headache and put you to bed. End of story. You didn't do anything wrong. Unless you count the topless dancing.'

Floz's eyes enlarged to saucers.

Guy held out his hands. 'No, sorry, wrong thing to say. Just trying to lighten you up a bit. Honestly. You didn't do any dancing at all. Sorry.'

'Did I ring you?' Surely she didn't. Why would she ring *him*?

'No, *I* rang *you* to see if you were okay. After all that . . . Nick business.'

Ask him why you're wearing that shirt, said the evil voice within.

Did she have her old bra on? The comfy white one that she threw in with any colour wash? Had he seen it?

'Look, I'll go and make you some tea.' Guy stretched out the stiffness in every part of his body which spending a whole night being crunched in that tiny chair had caused.

'No, it's okay. You've done enough for me.'

'I insist.'

'No, please.'

'Floz, pretend I'm Juliet who doesn't take no for an answer, okay?'

Floz sighed then nodded slowly in agreement. She waited until he had half-limped out of the room before stepping out of bed. Or stepping off a roundabout, which is how it felt. She didn't need the mirror to tell her how dreadful she must look. But, being a self-torturing bint, she stole a glance at herself. Surprise! No black circles, amazing! Or any make-up at all. Her fringe was stuck up at an alarming angle, mind, and there were nice bags under a lovely cyclamen-pink pair of eyes. All set off beautifully by the hideous psychedelic shirt, which she kept forgetting to put into the charity bag. But relief and joy flooded her as she noticed how drunkenly buttoned up it was – she must have done it herself.

She tiptoed out with an armful of fresh clothes to the bathroom and had a shower. She felt a bit wobbly and slightly queasy, seeing as she had nothing at all in her stomach. A splash of water and bit of make-up later, she felt almost human.

Guy was frying bacon. Her sick-empty stomach responded to the smoky smell with a primal growl.

'You look a bit less lime-green in the cheeks.' He smiled at her and pulled out the chair underneath the table, where he had set a place for her, complete with mug of tea. His eyes were grey and twinkly and his face so much more handsome for not glowering at her. 'Sit,' he commanded. 'Now eat.'

He placed a sizzling sandwich in front of her. Floz couldn't remember a man ever making her breakfast before. Nick had promised that when he came over, he was going to cook her a real Canadian hunter's breakfast. *Nick, who didn't exist.*

Guy had trimmed all the fat off the bacon, she noticed. She hated fat. He'd somehow known that and acted on it. He didn't seem like the same Guy who wouldn't let her in the flat. Then she twigged. *That's when they were looking at your computer.*

And it was Guy who had trawled through the net and found out the truth behind Nick/Chas for her. And looked out for her last night. He wouldn't have done that if he didn't like her, would he? How could she have got everything so very wrong? Before she knew it, tears were falling faster than she could wipe them away.

Floz bit down on the sandwich to stifle the sob more than to satisfy her hunger. Guy heard her sniffing behind him but busied himself cutting bread for his own sandwich and humming. She knew he was pretending not to hear to save her a little dignity.

'Thank you for finding out about – you know,' she said quietly. 'I half-wish you hadn't though. It would have been better to carry on believing he was real than hear the truth.'

Guy took his bacon sandwich over to the table and sat down.

'Floz, there are some very flawed people out there. Hanging onto that image of a perfect man who never existed would have affected your life too much. No one in the future would have lived up to the fantasy.'

Floz thought of Nick – tall, with just the right amount of lean muscle, gentlemanly and intelligent with a soft Canadian drawl. A character who had moulded himself over time to her ideal spec. Guy was so terribly right. Chas Hanson had a nice voice, if his phone calls were anything to go by . . . but he was a much older man than he purported to be – and God knows what he looked like. She didn't know if the pictures he had sent her of himself were old ones or even of him at all. No wonder he took the relationship right up to the point of the possible meet before he bailed out.

'And how much would a trip to Canada have cost you? Not just in money, but in more wasted emotion?'

'I feel such a fool,' said Floz wearily. Her nerves felt like she had just disembarked from a very long and wild roller-coaster.

'You're not a fool,' said Guy. His hand was so close to hers on the table. It was huge. She imagined Nick having hands like that – long fingers that stroked and held. *Nick Nick Nick*. 'Floz, the most intelligent of people get drawn in by these weirdos. For the record, having seen the letters, I would bet anything that this guy cared for you. He knew you were the genuine article and I think he got himself wrapped up in a fantasy that he so wanted to be real. I also think the death of his son totally screwed him up and he was trying to claw his way back into the past. I . . .'

'Please, no more,' said Floz. She was so hideously embarrassed to think that anyone could have seen what was in her heart. Guy especially – the person most likely to think her a total tit. She had poured out her heart in those letters, believing they were for Nick's eyes only, and now loads of people had seen them. They all knew now that not even her own parents loved her.

'I had a friend once,' began Guy. He couldn't believe he had started to tell this story, but as he thought it would help Floz, he was prepared to go to that dark place again. 'We only went out a couple of times before we split up. She wasn't the type I usually go for, she was so small and fragile and I wanted to protect her, but boy was she hard work. She was hooked on the drama of dysfunctional men treating her badly and she couldn't cope with the fact that I respected her – so it ended. But we managed to stay friends. Her name was Lacey. Lacey Robinson. We trained at the same cookery college.'

He stopped then, wondering if Floz wanted to hear this tale of damned misery, but she nodded at him to go on.

'She was obsessive when she fell in love: that person became the centre of her being. It wasn't healthy. The man would finish it – or disappear – then she'd turn to me as the only friend in her life and cry on my shoulder. Then one day she hooked up with this Jamie bloke – on the net – who was "perfect". He ticked every box. He was *the* Mr Right. He lived in Durham so they didn't get to see each other that much, and that's why it kept the flame alight. They'd meet in romantic restaurants for lunch – never at his house, and she never stayed overnight. She was planning to leave her life here and go up there to live with him.

'Then one day he just stopped contacting her. He wouldn't answer his phone, texts, emails . . . She nearly went crazy, ripping herself to shreds trying to work out what she had done to cause him to do that. So she drove up there. How the hell she didn't crash I don't know. He wouldn't come out of the house, so she sat outside it for hours – then his girlfriend arrived. Seems that Mr Loverman was really a Mr Love-rat, thriving on the excitement of reeling girls in and then cutting them loose when they got too close. He got off on the chase and didn't give a toss what heartache he caused in the process. Needless to say, Lacey was devastated. She rang me when she got home to tell me all about it, but she sounded all right, as if she was handling it okay. She said that finding out the truth had released her from him and that she was fine. Totally fine. I shouldn't have believed her, because she was never fine. But I was working hard, and tired, and I didn't check up on my hunch and drive over. That night she filled herself with pills and alcohol, slit her wrists and killed herself.'

'Oh, Guy, surely you couldn't blame yourself for that?'

'I could have saved her if I'd gone over,' said Guy, coughing down the rising emotion in his throat. 'I still dream about the pain she must have suffered, killing herself like that. I went off the rails a bit, to be honest. Steve has babysat me, wrestled bottles of vodka off me and put me to bed more times than I care to remember. Trust me, Floz, you can't drown your sorrows because they're bloody Gold Medallist Olympic swimmers, and no one knows that better than me. I lost my job, got arrested for fighting, totally lost my way in the world. Kenny Moulding might have taken his pound of flesh from me over the years, but he gave me a job when no one else would.'

'You mustn't blame yourself for her death,' Floz repeated gently. 'Some people are born with a self-destruct button, and once it is activated, there is nothing you can do to override it.'

'I wish I could believe that.'

Floz thought for a moment before speaking.

'I know I'm right, Guy, because I knew someone once who was like that.' She paused. 'He had a wife and his own business and a nice house. Then . . .' *So many dark days. So much going wrong. So much sadness.* 'His business started to fail. He needed to plough money into it to rescue it, but he didn't have it and he couldn't raise it. So, when the banks rejected him, he turned to gambling, hoping for that one big win that would rescue him.' *He enjoyed the gambling. The excitement blotted out all the sadness.*

'I'm presuming he didn't get the win,' said Guy.

'Actually, in the beginning he was very lucky. Maybe if he hadn't had that initial luck, things might have been different. Then that luck changed – but he was convinced that it would come back, that his one big win was just around the corner. Guy, he ended up gambling away everything they had. His wife just couldn't reach him. He's one of the town drunks now. One of the idiots who sits on the bench outside the public toilets with cheap cider and strong beer.' *That's why I don't go into town much, in case I see him. In case I see my ex-husband.* 'I used to look at those drunks and wonder how they got to that place in life, where they came from, what they once were. They weren't born swigging from cans.'

'He didn't kill himself though, Floz. There's a difference.'

'No, but he disappeared into himself, didn't care about anyone but himself – and he *is* killing himself, only his method is a much slower one. No one could stop him, his button was pressed and there was no turning back. His wife lost everything too, but she chose to carry on and survive. It's very hard trying to protect someone who is hell-bent on harming themselves. But they are locked in a world of one person and they throw away the key.' *And until recently I never appreciated that slope would be so easy to slide down.*

Guy's hand closed over hers and he squeezed it. It was large and safe, she thought. Hers was small and chilled, he thought. There was a comfortable silence in the room, a sweet air of calm.

Floz said in a humbled voice: 'Please don't tell Juliet or Steve about any of this.' His hand was still on hers and she liked it. His thumb made a single tentative stroke against her wrist.

'I wouldn't do that,' said Guy. 'Our secret, eh?'

His eyes were kind and warm as a grey wolf's coat. Floz realized then how Lacey could have found brief respite from her heartbreaks, being folded and held in his arms. She wanted them to fold around her. She wanted to be held. She wanted to be held against the protective bulk of Guy Miller.

Then Juliet and Steve crashed into the flat and their hands sprang apart.

'Hellooo, it's only us. Ooooh . . .' Juliet spotted Guy. 'What are *you* doing here at this time?' Her eyebrows rose.

'Oy, nothing like that,' said Guy. 'I just popped in to see if . . .' Oh bloody hell, he couldn't think of a viable excuse why he was there alone with Floz at this hour.

'. . . if you were back,' Floz jumped in. 'Because Guy wanted to see Steve about . . . er . . . the suits for the wedding.'

'Yes, I did,' said Guy, mouthing 'thank you' at Floz when Juliet turned to look at Steve.

'I hope you're not just going to go out and get something without coordinating with me,' said Juliet, planting her hands firmly on her waist.

'No,' said Guy. 'But suits in our size aren't going to be easy to find off the peg, so I thought we'd better get cracking on some research sooner rather than later.'

'There's that seamstress on Lamb Street.'

'Seamstress?' said Guy and Steve together.

'If you let me finish,' growled Juliet. 'She's married to a tailor and they turn stuff around really quickly. She stuck her neck out for women's lib and got a Thai husband.'

'Good idea,' said Steve. 'Shall we take a drive out now whilst you're here, Guy?'

'Why not.'

Steve dropped Juliet's suitcase and hurried Guy out.

'Right, mate,' he said. 'What's going on with you two then?'

Sometimes men were worse than women for gossip.

'You all right?' asked Juliet, as softly as she was able with her gruff smoky voice. 'I was thinking about you.'

'Yes, I'm good,' said Floz, pouring Juliet a cup of tea from the pot. 'Guy told me about Lacey.'

'He's too kind about her,' said Juliet. 'She was a self-obsessed bitch. I could have zapped her back to life and killed her all over again for what she put Guy through. Did he tell you that she wrote *No one loves me* and *I hate you all* and other lovely things all over her walls? She wanted to hurt the bloke who dumped her far more than she wanted to live. In her case it was a total waste because he didn't give a toss. She ended up crucifying Guy instead, because he was the one who drove over to her house and found her.'

Floz's hands shot up to her mouth. 'No, he didn't tell me that.'

'I never really gave Steve credit for what he did for Guy during those years when my brother fell apart,' said Juliet. 'He was the only one big enough to drag him out of fights and throw him into bed when he was off his head on booze. I was too busy seeing the Steve I wanted to see, not the lovely, kind man he is. I got too used to not liking him. Thank God I came to my senses because I really am so lucky that he is my man.'

'You are,' said Floz with a wide smile.

'I wish you could find your own Steve, Floz,' said Juliet, her eyes looking glassier with every second.

'Me too,' said Floz.

'Jesus, these bloody hormones!' Juliet half-laughed, half-sobbed as she reached for the tissues.

That night Floz tossed and turned in bed, the whole Nick Vermeer story tumbling heavily around in her head. She knew she had to end this for herself – write to him and tell him exactly what she thought.

I should have suspected as soon as you sent me the fictitious birth-date – because you once told me it was October, I remembered. What a very convincing liar you are. What an absolute twisted sick bastard. I hate you . . .

Her heart was pounding, expletives were pumping out of her brain, then a vision of Lacey's Jamie crashed into her head. Like Lacey, she so wanted to hurt Chas Hanson back. But what guarantee was there that would happen? What good would it do? He had to know he was a sick man without the need for her to spell it out to him. She thought of the violent way his son had killed himself. How big must the wound be inside him to have raised a child and loved him and then have to bury him after he took his own life in such a terrible and violent and wasteful way?

Floz vented her spleen onto the page, cleansed herself of all she would have said to Chas Hanson, had he appeared before her. Then, after she had filled in the last full stop, she hit the delete button. The charge of the words remained in the air somewhere but they would not be delivered to Chas to add to his pain.

Chapter 79

'Well?'

Juliet emerged from the dressing room looking like an over-sized toilet-roll cover. She made a gypsy bride look subtle. Floz tried not to laugh, but Coco had no such qualms and the pair of them fell onto each other giggling.

'I told you I'd look a twat!' Juliet's lip was pulled back over her teeth. 'And I don't want white. I want something a bit different, a bit *me*.'

'This is the best fun I've had in years,' said Coco, wiping the tears from his eyes. 'It's funnier than the Morecambe and Wise André Previn sketch!'

'If I might suggest something like this,' said the lovely lady who ran the shop. Her name badge said *Freya* and she was tall and elegant, with a calming effect like Prozac upon nervous brides.

Freya held out a long, plain, sleeveless dress which flowed outwards. It was the palest shade of gold, and Juliet's party all gasped in unison.

'Now that is gorgeous.' Juliet took the hanger and sighed at the colour.

'Very autumnal, don't you think?' Freya smiled. 'And we can dye the shoes and veil to match.'

Juliet zipped the dressing-room curtain shut, after telling Freya that she didn't need any help. Minutes later she emerged, the perfect vision of a bride in her own mould. The smile on her face was bigger than a new moon.

'How bloody gorgeous am I in this?'

Coco's eyes filled up with tears and he started flapping his hands like a deranged seal.

'Oh, that is the one! Ju, you look stunning.'

Juliet looked at herself in the mirror. Her stomach would have grown with the baby when she got married – in twenty-seven days' time – but that didn't matter because the style of the gown would disguise her bump. She felt beautiful in that dress and she so wanted to look beautiful for Steve. Her husband and the father of her babies. She used the plural because she knew she was carrying twins. Not officially – but she *knew*. In the same way she had secretly known she was pregnant before the test picked it up.

'Right, we need to sort out my bridesmaids,' said Juliet, as Freya unzipped her. 'We'll start with the female one.'

When Freya suggested a brown dress for Floz, Coco and Juliet wrinkled up their noses, but they should have trusted the lady. She brought out three gowns in deepest chocolate. The first was too fussy and made Floz look rather dumpy, but the second, a shoulderless gown with a matching bolero jacket, totally complemented her lovely curvy shape.

'Oh Floz, I just want to lick you,' said Coco. 'Not in a sexual way – I'm not on the turn, don't worry – but you look as if you are made out of Dairy Milk.'

Floz's red hair looked on fire against the deep brown of the material. Freya visualized her with tiny leaves threaded into her hair rather than a headdress. Again, she was right. She loosely caught up Floz's hair with tiny leaf-decorated pins. She said she could replicate those leaves by stitching tiny ones onto Juliet's veil, but then Juliet spotted a tall golden tiara reflecting more light than a disco ball – and the deal was sealed.

Juliet was ecstatic because everything was coming together

faster than she expected. Coco chose a huge dandy cravat in
a matching shade of chocolate. He had a sudden vision of
himself in that and a green suit, so the next stop was the
town-centre tailors where he was fortunate to find an off-
the-peg number and a shirt that wouldn't have looked out of
place on Mr Darcy.

Juliet sighed, looking at the rack of men's jackets and trousers. She thought of Steve in a suit, she thought of him taking
that suit off on his wedding night and commanding that she
strip off immediately. He was so domineering in private. She
held that image in her mind for a minute, then rang to tell him
and Guy to get their arses down to the White Wedding shop
in Maltstone to check out the dark brown cravats. They were
out getting measured for their suits today.

As they left the menswear shop, Juliet noticed how edgy
Floz was in town, looking around her as if she expected someone to leap out at her. Floz, she had noticed, rarely came into
the centre of Barnsley. If she needed to shop, she always went
to Meadowhall.

'What's up, Floz?' Juliet laughed. 'Are you trying to avoid
someone?'

'Yes,' said Floz. She felt it was time to trust her friends. She
took a deep breath. 'My ex-husband. I don't want to bump
into him.'

'I don't blame you,' said Juliet. 'I've seen Roger a couple of
times in town with Hattie and not enjoyed the experience. Isn't
it funny how people who were once so close to you can become
such strangers?'

Floz nodded, then she took a deep breath before diving into
a big lake of trust. 'Remember that drunk we saw once, singing, the one the police took away? That was my ex-husband.'

'Bloody hell,' said Coco. 'No wonder you ran off for
chocolate.'

'I bet you're nearly as sick thinking that you once shagged

him as I am about Roger.' Juliet pulled a revolted face, making Floz chuckle.

There, that wasn't so hard, was it – letting people in?

'Let's go to the Yorkshire Rose and have lunch,' suggested Coco.

'How about we go to that little bistro at the side of Hobbyworld instead,' countered Floz.

'But I'm starving now!' Coco's bottom lip protruded.

'We'll be there in fifteen minutes, and it's lovely,' pressed Floz.

'I agree,' said Juliet. 'Let's do that. Floz doesn't want to bump into her ex so let's not force her to stay in town.'

'Sorry, Floz,' said Coco. 'You being comfortable is way more important than my stomach. Let's drive to Sheffield.'

After lunch they poured into Hobbyworld to source table decorations. Floz found some darling little heart-shaped golden favour boxes and some tiny firework embellishments. They bought place-name cards and table confetti and serviettes patterned with leaves because the manager of the Oak Leaf had said that if they wanted anything other than white serviettes, they would have to supply them. It was by far one of the nicest shopping days that Juliet had ever spent.

And tonight they were all going out with Steve's wrestling lot after the matches had finished. He was the good guy tonight – complete with big angel wings. Juliet quite fancied making love to an angel. She made a mental note to remind him to bring that costume over to the flat afterwards.

Chapter 80

The Centennial Rooms were half-empty that night. The *South Yorkshire Herald* had failed to put an advert in to drum up a crowd, Steve had texted her earlier. It didn't recognize wrestling as a true sport, apparently, and so wouldn't support it. Juliet was furious when she walked in and saw so many vacant seats. 'Snotty bastard incompetent paper,' she said to Floz. 'They won't cover an event like this, but if you grow the biggest tomato in Wombwell, you'll be on the damned front page.'

Juliet watched Steve climb into the ring and she hurt for him. He loved wrestling so much. He would have been in his element, had he been born into its heyday in Britain. But he wasn't and could only perform in front of a few die-hard fans and some golden oldies.

'Go, Steve!' yelled Floz. Then clamped her hand over her mouth. She'd gotten quite carried away then. The old man next to her was looking at her and she felt as if she should apologize.

'Sorry about shouting. Hope I didn't deafen you,' she said.

'Not at all,' he said. She couldn't work out if he was from Yorkshire or America – he had a very odd accent.

'It's just that I know him – the Angel,' Floz went on. 'He's marrying my friend next month. He's such a sweet man.'

'He's a very good wrestler,' said the old man.

'He lives and breathes it,' said Floz, while Juliet stood and issued a few choice expletives as Jeff Leppard got her lover in a head-lock. Floz added with a whisper, 'Mind you, I think I'd rather face Steve in a ring than his missus.'

The old man laughed. 'What's his day job?' he asked.

'He's a plasterer,' said Floz. 'And a very good one. He's a damned hard worker.'

'Bastard!' yelled Juliet at Jeff.

'They're friends really,' explained Floz. 'Jeff Leppard is coming out for a drink afterwards with all the other lads, to celebrate Steve and Juliet's engagement. You'd be welcome to join us. It's not a private party.'

'Ah, that's nice.' The old man folded his arms. 'Where are you all going?'

'The pub just across the road. The Lamp,' said Floz. 'They're putting on some sandwiches and nibbles, I heard.'

Floz was not to know what repercussions that conversation would cause.

There was no way the lads were going to let Steve have just a little wrestlers' engagement party. Behind Steve and Juliet's back they had clubbed together and arranged a feast 'for a Feast'. There was more food than at a Roman orgy, and a few bottles of fizz for the ladies, although the men stuck to their pints. And Guy, who was unfortunately having to work in Burgerov that night, had made and sent over an enormous cake of a wrestling ring, complete with a fondant-Steve with his wings on and Juliet dressed as a sexy demon.

'Wonder how odd Guy felt, modelling his sister's tits out of icing,' laughed Juliet. She was so touched by the warmth in the room. And during Steve's speech, in which he praised his good mates and praised the wrestling, Floz noticed that the old man who had been sitting next to her had come over to the pub and was watching the proceedings. He was almost squashed by the door flying open when Chianti Parkin entered like a storm-cloud, her dad and uncle at her heels.

It was the first time Floz had seen the legend that was Chianti. She was tall with long swishy hair that she kept ruffling with her hand and tossing back over her shoulders. She had a fatless body, nipped-in waist and thin legs which looked six foot long in the pin-heeled thigh-length boots she wore. But Floz was mostly fascinated by her face. It should have been pretty, since it had all the elements beauty needed – almond-shaped eyes, tiny nose, cheekbones that could have sliced metal, but her mouth was thin and puckered up like a tightly closed drawstring bag. Instead of pretty, she looked hard and characterless, and her true soul showed in that mouth. Her beauty, it was obvious to Floz, was a very thin veneer. Especially when she looked across at the lovely, bouncy Juliet at the other side of the room, grinning with her plump full lips, light dancing in her grey eyes and pulsing out joy and happy vibes as she talked to Alberto Masserati and the Pogmoor Brothers – Kerry and Hilary – who had learned to fight from an early age because they were called Kerry and Hilary, Juliet had told her.

Chianti swept up a glass of wine and sank it with such speed it was as if she were punishing her throat. Then she reached for another. Whilst her father and uncle were mingling, Chianti was staring malignantly at Steve, and slightly tottering on her heels. Then, when Steve threw back his head and laughed, it seemed to trigger off something in her. She strode purposefully over to Steve, and before he could register what was happening, she threw a full glass of the fizz in his face.

'And you know what that's for, don't you?' she smiled smugly. 'If anyone does the dumping, it's me.'

Steve didn't react in any other way than to wipe the wine from his face with his large hand, which seemed to infuriate Chianti more. She wanted a fight, not some dignified show of indifference from this stupid, thick idiot who had *dared* to end a date to go and meet with someone else. *And what a someone!*

'So where's your big, fat, ugly *fiancée* then?' sniggered Chianti.

'If you mean me, I'm here,' said Juliet from behind her. Then she grabbed Chianti's brassy hair, pulled back her head and poured a full pint of beer straight onto her face.

'Me extensions!' yelled Chianti. A few of them, which hadn't been glued on properly, came away in Juliet's hand.

'Juliet!' yelled Steve. But his formidable fiancée would not be silenced and no one – not even Alberto Masserati – was brave enough to wade in.

'How dare you and your fake hair come in here and ruin our party,' Juliet was snarling as she propelled Chianti towards the door. 'Don't you ever attack my man again or the next time I'll pull your fake fingernails out and stick them in your fake knockers!'

Chianti gave a startled yelp as her butt landed on the pavement outside and Juliet brushed her hands.

She bounced back into the pub just in time to see Little Derek lift his finger to Steve.

'Don't you ever ask me for work again, lad,' he growled before slamming his unfinished pint down on the table. Then he marched out of the pub, followed by his brother.

'Oh, flaming great,' said Steve with a massive sigh. 'What the heck did you have to wade in for, Ju?' Had he been alone he thought he might have cried. Little Derek was the only promoter he knew. He wouldn't be able to wrestle in shows any more if Little Derek didn't give him a job.

'He'll come round, lad,' said Fred Zeppelin, giving Steve a squeeze on the shoulder, but the tone of his voice said anything but, because they all knew that Little Derek was a right nasty beggar when he wanted to be, and no one upset his precious girl and got away with it.

'Oh God,' said Steve, dropping his eyes to look at his boots.

When he lifted his head, the old man with the strange accent was in front of him and smiling. And holding out his hand.

'May I introduce myself,' he said. 'My name is Patrick Milburn. You might know my son, at least by name – William Milburn.'

Steve shook the old man's hand, out of courtesy.

'I'm sorry, I don't think I know your—'

Patrick Milburn reached into his pocket and handed over a business card. Steve read it. Then he read it again and he felt little cells in his brain explode. The card had Patrick's name on it, below three large letters in white and red – GWE. *Global Wrestling Enterprises. William – Will – Milburn. The billionaire head of GWE. And this was his dad.*

'I'm on a talent-scouting mission,' said Patrick Milburn. 'Son, how would you like to come over to America in the next couple of weeks and talk contracts?'

Chapter 81

Steve was severely hungover the next morning, as were Jeff Leppard, Fred Zeppelin, Tarzan and the enormous and hirsute Apeman, Klondyke Kevin and Big Bad Davy. The Pogmoor Brothers had to take turns in carrying each other home. The party that followed Patrick Milburn's announcement put the party before Chianti's entrance fifty miles into the shade.

But now, as Steve lay in bed, his headache wearing off thanks to the tablets and water that Juliet had given him, reality was intruding on his dream.

'Nice to be asked,' he said, putting his arm around Juliet. 'But I can't go. Not really.'

Juliet shrugged him off. 'What do you mean, you can't go?'

'I wouldn't go without you. And I wouldn't ask you to leave your family.'

'You are going, Steven Feast. And I'm coming with you.'

'What about the baby? It will kill your mum and dad if they can't see the baby grow up.'

Juliet fell back against him. 'Steve, I don't know how all this will play out. All I know is that you've wanted this chance all your life and you are going to take it. I imagine you'll be on the road quite often; I'll come home then and stay with Mum and Dad. And when I'm away from them – and you – there's always Skype. We'll work it out. Somehow. Other people do.'

'I'd love to do it, Ju. Just for a few years.'

'You are going to. Don't argue with me. You're always telling Guy to go for it, and now it's your time to shine, honey.'

'You are so deliciously bossy, Juliet Miller. I love you more than wrestling, do you know that? So what do you have to say to that then?' Steve kissed her softly on her lovely, bossy mouth.

And for once, Juliet Miller, who knew that if Steve Feast loved her more than wrestling, he loved her a hell of a lot, didn't want to say anything.

Floz drove to the newsagent's to get the Sunday papers, but didn't drive straight home. Instead she took a long detour out into the country, through Maltstone and out on the Higher Hoppleton Road. It was a farm-heavy area and some of the fields still had huge rolls of harvested hay in them. Scarlet poppies were out in force, standing tall, reverently still and silent. She passed a trio of old ladies picking the last of the fat blackberries from the hedgerows to make lovely apple and blackberry pies with, so she imagined. Floz wasn't sure where the cottage was so drove quite slowly, but then she spotted the *For Sale* notice cancelled out with a diagonal *Sold* sticker. She pulled in, curious to see why Hallow's had gotten under Guy's skin so much.

She pushed open the gate and had to walk down the drive for a while before the house came fully into view, as the grasses in the garden were thick and huge. But as soon as her eyes closed on the house, she could see exactly why Guy Miller had coveted this cottage since he was a child.

Like Guy, she didn't see the peeling paintwork on the windows, and when she looked through the glass, the crumbling plaster and awful carpet didn't register. She saw a roaring fire in the huge inglenook, she saw herself reading and sprawled out on a huge squashy sofa with an old black friendly cat like lovely Stripies purring on her knee. She saw Guy Miller in his chef's whites, bringing out a big tray of cheese and bread and pâté for them to share. Floz gasped. Where had that thought come from? Why was she thinking about sharing a house with Guy Miller of all people?

Floz felt quite wobbly as she walked back to the car.

Chapter 82

First thing Monday morning, Guy got a call from his solicitor to say that all the paperwork on the restaurant was now complete. Burgerov was officially his to close up, gut, fumigate and raise magnificently like a Phoenix from the ashes. He walked into work early with renewed vigour, ready to do battle. And because he walked in early, he found Varto sliding a bottle of vodka from the bar into his locker.

'Good morning, Varto,' smiled Guy. 'Whilst you're in that locker, get your coat and all your belongings and leave my restaurant. You're sacked.'

Varto turned to him with a cocky sneer on his face. 'You know you can't sack me,' he said. 'It's not your restaurant. It's Mr Moulding's restaurant and I think he have something to say if you try to sack me. He very friendly with my mama, you understand.'

Guy was stunned. Varto really had no idea that the ownership of Burgerov had been transferred. He thought some gossip might have leaked out, but Varto appeared to know nothing. Mentally Guy clapped his hands together, and prepared to enjoy himself.

'So you didn't know that I'm the new boss? Kenny never told "your mama" that he's sold Burgerov to me – and as your new boss, I'm sacking you for stealing that vodka?'

'Ees lies,' said Varto. 'You are not the owner.' Guy noted that he never mentioned it was lies that he was caught nicking the vodka.

'You go and ask Kenny then. Oh, sorry you can't. You see, I'm presuming that by now Kenny will be on a flight to Spain. With Mrs Moulding. Goodbye, Varto. I'll have your P45 sent on.'

Varto started spouting very dramatic East European at Antonin; the latter returned it, then addressed Guy with the same arrogant mask on his face.

'If Varto go, I go.'

'Burgerov then,' said Guy calmly, but with a giggle in his head.

'And Igor and Stanislav will come as well. You will have no one to run your stinking restaurant.'

Well, if that was a blackmail technique, it didn't work. Guy stood with his arms folded and a grin of high amusement.

'I'll take that as your formal resignation, shall I?' he said. 'Gina, you'll be a witness to that?'

'I will,' said Gina, who was delighted to hear that Guy was taking over and welcomed the new regime with her whole heart.

After much slamming of locker doors and presumably swearing, Igor, Stanislav, Varto and Antonin stormed out of the restaurant, pausing by the gate to give Guy a chance to calm down and call them back, offer them a pay rise and apologize on bended knee. They didn't expect to see Gina stick a hand-written note in the window announcing that Burgerov would be closed until further notice.

The morning was spent cancelling the few reservations that had been made and ringing the builders to ask if they were able to come any sooner than they were booked to do. Since all Guy's staff had walked out, he might as well start the transformation before the end of the month. Obviously he would keep Gina on, and Sandra the accounts lady and old Glenys the cleaner, and pay them whilst they were off. It couldn't have worked out better for him. Kenny hadn't bothered to ring him and let him know that the transaction had been completed far earlier than anticipated, but then Kenny had been mentally free of the restaurant and all its worries since the morning when Guy had offered to take it off his hands. Now Burgerov was no more. In a couple of months' time, it would be called by another name, have keen and clean staff and a menu that would call people like a siren.

The King was dead. Long live the King.

Chapter 83

Floz was on Guy's mind. He wasn't stupid – he'd realized, of course, that Floz had been talking about her husband when she told him the story about the man with the self-destruct button. Then he thought of her beautiful letters to the fictitious Nick, and how much love she obviously had inside to give. She must have a harvest of it, great store cupboards of it saved for someone very special. He wished he could have been its recipient. He'd return that love ten-fold to her.

Her lovely face was in his head constantly, seared on his frontal lobe. He knew he just had to come right out with it and ask her to dinner – no messing. He didn't want to give fate a chance to screw things up for him again. He went to bed that night with a very simple plan formed in his brain.

The next morning Guy stood by the outside doors of Blackberry Court. He had rehearsed at least a million times what he was going to say, and a million times he had stuttered and given a more rubbish variation of what he had said before. It was a beautiful day, crisp and bright, with just enough breeze to nudge the bronze leaves that still clung stubbornly to the trees.

'Come on, Guy,' he egged himself on. His arm came out and pressed the buzzer. Nothing happened for an eternity. Ironic, he laughed, that he had found the guts to take this one step further and she wasn't in. Then he heard her sweet voice: 'Hello.'

'Oh, hi, it's Guy. Floz, can I ask you a favour?'

'Come up,' she said and buzzed the lock open.

Stage one complete. He took the stairs three at a time. She was just opening the door. She was wearing jeans and a red top and her hair was loose and messy around her shoulders.

'Come in, Guy,' she said, feeling ever so slightly shivery. He was wearing a blue shirt, unbuttoned at the neck, and dark chest hairs were just visible at the base of his throat.

'Hi Floz,' he said. 'Look, er . . .' *Go for it, Guy.* 'I wonder if you could spare me half an hour. I need to go over to Hallow's and . . .' Shite, he couldn't remember what he'd thought of as an excuse to get her there. 'I could really do with someone's opinion on . . .' *think, think, you berk* 'the best layout before the builders start knocking walls down.' *Phew*.

'Course,' smiled Floz. 'I'd love to see inside anyway. Not sure I'll be much help, but happy to have a nosy. I'll get my coat.'

Stage two accomplished.

Guy's leg was doing a nervous shake on the clutch. He could have done a formidable Elvis impression from the waist down. He kangaroo-ed round the corner and apologized.

'Sorry, I've only been driving for twenty-three years,' he said.

'It's the extra weight you're carrying today,' said Floz. 'It's obviously affected something technical under the bonnet that I couldn't possibly know the name of.'

They drove on in silence. Guy felt he should really say something sparkling and witty. 'Lovely weather today.' *Oh FFS, Guy!*

'I love autumn,' said Floz as they passed a field bursting with red poppies. 'It's such a beautiful season.'

'All the best conker trees were round here when I was a lad,' smiled Guy. One day he'd help his own children land the prickly cases. Then they would open them, pull out the brown shiny conkers, take them home and soak them in vinegar to harden them up for contests at school, just as Perry had done with him.

Guy pulled onto the land of Hallow's Cottage. The owner had no qualms about lending Guy the keys for the house so he could measure up and invite his builder friends in. Guy pushed open the creaky door and they walked into the stale, slightly damp air of the cottage.

'Oh wow,' said Floz, turning full circle in the space. It was so much nicer being inside than peering through the dirty windows. It was a huge room – and that fireplace . . . She saw it in her mind's eye full of crackling logs and orange flames.

'Do you think it's too big?' asked Guy, feigning consternation. 'Do you think it should be divided into two rooms?'

'No, not at all,' said Floz. 'It's beautiful exactly as it is. I can just see it with a big leather Chesterfield . . .'

'. . . big leather Chesterfield,' said Guy at exactly the same time, which made them both chortle.

'And a huge Chinese rug,' said Floz.

'Red,' said Guy, seeing the same room that Floz did. 'Huge logs on the fire . . .'

'And *that* is the ideal spot for your Christmas tree,' smiled Floz, pointing to the corner where the stairs were overlooked by a galleried landing. The space could have easily accommodated a thirteen-foot tree.

Guy saw it, all the presents around the base of it, rocking horses, teddy bears, candy canes, a puppy snuffling out his bone-present.

They both laughed and turned to each other and when their eyes locked the moment was somehow too intense.

'Come and look at the kitchen.' Guy strode in and showed

Floz around. It needed a total refurb, obviously, but it was a lovely square shape.

Opposite to the kitchen was a smaller room, with huge windows giving a view of what might one day be a flowery cottage garden and the farm fields beyond. Floz imagined herself sitting at a desk by this window, the scent of honey-suckle drifting in as she wrote some lovely Valentine's verse that flowed out of her because she was so loved up.

Guy beckoned her up the stairs. He was like a giddy kitten. It was all going too well. His brain had raced ahead. He was way past the stage of asking Floz out on a date. He was carrying her up these stairs in her bridal gown and her fingers were already working on his shirt buttons.

He pushed open the door to the largest bedroom with windows in two walls and knobbly beams running across the ceiling. Floz sighed at its loveliness. She saw a four-poster and Guy throwing her playfully onto it. She was dressed in a white bridal gown, laughing as she kicked off her shoes.

She knew she was blushing and turned away to the door which he took as a sign to move to the next room, a smaller, but not by much, L-shaped bedroom with built-in old oak cupboards a foot and a half deep. Guy saw two children in here, books and toys on the shelves, GWE duvet covers and curtains with Steve's face on them.

Next door was a darling country cottage bathroom with a hideous avocado suite in it, and down two steps another bedroom with views over the countryside.

Floz realized she had probably been sighing for ten full minutes. She laughed at herself.

'And that concludes the guided tour of Hallow's Cottage.' Guy smiled and bowed.

'It's gorgeous.' Floz gave him a burst of applause, following him back downstairs to the lounge. She was amazed that she wasn't in some chocolate-box Dorset village but on the edge

of an industrial northern town. 'I'm so glad you're buying it.
It's going to be stunning.'

'Sorry I can't offer you a cup of tea,' he said. 'I should have
brought a flask, shouldn't I?' Damn, why didn't he think of
that sooner?

'Ah, don't worry.'

'You'll have to come back when I have electricity,' he said.
Ooh, nice. He hadn't planned to say that, but it was a lovely
little opener.

'Thank you, I will,' Floz nodded. Her heart gave a thrilled
little skip inside her. *Yeeesss!*

'I can't wait to finish it and move in,' said Guy. 'I can't wait
to cook in that kitchen and sleep in that bedroom upstairs. I
can't wait to fall asleep in front of that log fire. I can't wait to . . .'

'Have a bath in the avocado suite,' giggled Floz.

'Yeah right, like I'm going to leave that in,' laughed Guy.

His eyes are so warm and bright, thought Floz. She wanted
to drag her fingers through the waves of his thick hair and pull
his lips down to hers.

'And boy, I can't wait to see that Christmas tree,' said Guy.
He caught her eyes again. They were so green, he thought.
Green as that Christmas tree they would have one day in the
corner.

'Can you imagine this place at Christmas!' said Floz.

'What kid is not going to believe that Santa comes down the
chimney and out of that fireplace? Can't you just see a row of
stockings hanging up there?'

Floz turned to look at the fireplace. She had her back to him
when she said, 'Children would love this house. They'd have
such wonderful memories of it when they grew up.'

Guy felt overjoyed that Floz was so much on his wavelength.

'I've never wanted them myself,' she added, still facing away
from him. 'I'm happy for Juliet, of course, but motherhood
isn't for me.'

Guy raised his eyebrows. He didn't see that one coming. He hadn't time to fully process what she had said because she carried on speaking.

'In fact, I'm looking forward to getting my own flat for one when I move out. Being around Juliet and Steve has made me totally realize how much I want to be on my own for the considerable future. No flat-mates or relationships.'

'Really?' said Guy, his voice hardly louder than a whisper.

'Yep,' she said. 'I've been thinking that I may go and live somewhere warm and abroad for the winter. The good thing about my job is that I can work anywhere in the world really, so long as I have some internet access to send my stuff over. I'm a careerwoman and in the next few years I'm going to give my writing total focus. In fact, that reminds me, I'd better get home because I've got a deadline to meet.'

She turned back to him and smiled, but it didn't reach her eyes.

'Yes, of course,' said Guy. 'Well, thanks for coming. I did need a woman's advice on what I should do with the lounge – if I should divide it up or not.'

'Don't do it.' Floz strode towards the door. She looked like a different person from the one who had been standing in the room with him minutes before. This one was much colder, missiling vibes of untouchability. It couldn't have been more obvious that she suspected he was going to ask her out and was trying to stop him making a tit of himself. It was no less a rejection for him, her not actually saying the words.

He put a brave face on as he drove her back, appearing friendly but not really able to work out what he had said to make her slam down the shutters on him.

He dropped her off at the flat and waved goodbye. There was no apparent awkwardness between them, but some bridge that connected them had collapsed. Guy felt all the lovely pictures of the cottage's future burn at the edges, and crumble into ash.

Floz closed the door of the flat and stood behind it. Maybe she had unwittingly spoken the truth. Maybe she should move away, put everything she had into driving her career forward, put in more hours, write more copy. She would have to, to kill those pictures of Guy Miller and Christmas trees and log fires that were dancing in her brain.

Chapter 84

'Well?'

'It's a no go,' said Guy.

'Oh you are frigging joking!' Steve could have thrown the phone against the wall. 'How come?'

'I honestly don't know.' Guy had torn the conversation apart so many times but couldn't pinpoint what he had said to make Floz back off. He'd concluded that he would never know. He had driven himself half-nuts trying to work it out. Probably full-nuts.

'Maybe she didn't realize you were flirting with her,' tried Steve, but it sounded weak even to him.

'Believe me,' said Guy. 'She knew I was about to say how I felt, and she didn't want to hear it. There's nothing else it could be.'

'At least you've not fallen out,' Steve tried. He was *so* crap at making people feel better.

Guy just said, 'Aye.' But it was no comfort to know that somewhere out there was a man for Floz to love and it wasn't him. Nor would he have any future chance of it being him if she did as she said she might, and moved abroad. 'Anyway, never mind about me. Are you ready for the off tomorrow?'

'Oh yes,' grinned Steve. He was in the middle of packing his suitcase because the following day he was flying off to the headquarters of Global Wrestling Enterprises in Connecticut to meet with Will Milburn himself. He was spending four days there in all and he couldn't wait. He was more excited than a kid going over to Disneyland.

'Have a great time, mate,' said Guy, genuinely pleased that Steve was getting his overdue break.

'I will,' nodded Steve. 'And look, as far as Floz is concerned, don't write it off until the fat lady sings.'

Alas, Juliet picked that very moment to come out of the bathroom behind him, trilling, 'I'm leaving on a jet plane.'

Chapter 85

Juliet was moping around the flat. Steve had only been gone for two nights and she could hardly bear the separation.

Floz threw a bridal magazine at her.

'Here, look at some pretty pictures and take your mind off Steve,' she said.

'He's having a ball, bless him,' smiled Juliet. 'He said that Will Milburn really likes his persona and wants to put him on contract. This is all his Christmases rolled into one. But I don't half miss him. My bed feels huge and empty at night. I used to think when people said that, they were exaggerating. I loved it when Roger was away on business and I had the bed to myself. But I hate going to bed without Steve.'

'Aw,' said Floz, with a soppy grin. 'It must be love.'

'It is,' nodded Juliet. 'Did you used to like sleeping with your husband?'

Floz shook her head to get rid of the mental image of herself in bed with Chris. She could no longer remember him as the man she married, only as the scraggy drunk making a fool of himself in town.

'Sorry,' Juliet apologized.

'It's fine,' Floz said. 'I must have, I suppose. Once upon a time.'

'Was he an alcoholic when you met him?' Juliet asked.

'No,' replied Floz. 'He liked a drink, but nothing excessive.

It was only when his shop started to go downhill that he turned to the bottle. He said the oblivion gave him some mercy.'

'From his financial troubles?' pressed Juliet.

'Yes.' *And his heartbreak.* Floz took a deep breath.

'Floz, do you fancy coming shopping with me tomorrow for some more baby things?'

'I'd love to,' lied Floz, 'but I can't. I've got a deadline to meet. I can't let Lee down.'

'No worries,' sighed Juliet, reaching for her bottle of Gaviscon to relieve some heartburn. 'I'll have to take my mother then.'

'She'll enjoy that,' said Floz. 'Right, back to the job in hand. Flowers. What colour and how many?'

Chapter 86

Steve came back home like a new man. He was beaming from ear to ear at all the schmoozing he had been doing in America with Will Milburn and his men. He had signed a two-year contract with GWE which would officially start on 1 January, and he'd be earning more money than he dreamed of. He was to be introduced as *The Archangel* – long-lost angelic brother of the Gravedigger, who was *the* big name at GWE. It was all going to take some getting used to, but with Juliet at his side, he reckoned he could manage it. She made him feel that he was capable of achieving anything – give or take a Physics A-level. He couldn't wait to marry her. He drove like a madman over to her flat to see her after landing home. Within minutes, she had dragged him off to bed for reunion sex. Juliet's pregnancy hormones had made her more insatiable than ever.

Over the next couple of weeks, in between all the love-making, Juliet and Steve were running around like headless chickens organizing flowers and invitations and a wedding photographer. Floz, meanwhile, was busy writing card briefs. Ploughing all her mental energies into her work stopped her thinking too much about having to leave Blackberry Court – and Guy Miller. Why hadn't she just explained things to him when he took her over to Hallow's Cottage? He had been about to ask her out, she knew. But instead of turning frosty and confusing him, she should have told him straight why they couldn't cross a barrier and start a relationship. She hadn't seen him since. He was too busy supervising the changes in the new restaurant. It seemed each of them was grateful to have something on which to focus.

Floz had just taken a break from looking for flats on the internet. There was a possible on Greenfield Lane that she had made an appointment to see at six o'clock, but it wasn't filling her with excitement. She was brewing a pot of tea when she heard voices outside the flat door. Two seconds later, Juliet, Grainne and Coco fell in laden with boxes.

'Hiya!' yelled Coco with exhausted breaths. 'It's us. We've been shopping, can you tell?'

'Mum won't let me bring the cot up,' said Juliet, dropping the parcels and feeling her muscles sigh with relief. 'One: it would break my sodding back and two: she says it's bad luck. Have you ever heard anything so daft as it being bad luck?'

'I'm with your mum on this one,' said Floz, getting out extra cups and adding more water and an extra tea bag to the teapot. 'Don't risk flying in the face of superstition.'

'Floz, do you remember when you said you didn't use that storage cupboard in your room?' said Juliet. 'Is that still the case?'

'Yep,' said Floz, 'why?'

'Do you think I could put some baby stuff in it?' asked Juliet. 'I've run out of space. Everything is so damned bulky.' She pointed to her new purchases which she had picked up from Babyworld on the way home – an activity gym and a car seat. She had just bought the one for now but she knew her forthcoming scan would tell her she needed two.

'Course,' said Floz.

'Ta, you're a love. Can you imagine strapping a little tiny baby in here?' beamed Juliet.

'Yes,' said Floz, but she didn't let her imagination go down that particular avenue.

Chapter 87

Number 27, Greenfield Lane was a neat little semi-detached house on the outside, made up of two flats. The one being advertised was on the top floor. The landlord, Mr Selby – a sweaty, portly man who huffed and puffed all the way up the stairs – wasn't in the least embarrassed that the entrance and staircase needed a good vacuum and a couple of containersful of Shake 'n' Vac.

'Bathroom, bedroom, lounge, kitchen,' he pointed, looking as if he were making a horizontal sign of the cross.

The bathroom was a decent size, but smelly. The water in the loo was yellow and stinky, as the last person to wee in it hadn't flushed it. There were no pictures floating around Floz's head of how it could be transformed. The kitchen was basic, ancient MFI's cheapest units. The floor was carpeted and thick with grease. The lounge was small and square and characterless. It had a sofa in it that looked as if it had been dragged out of a skip. The bedroom wasn't much better. The thought of going to sleep on that stained mattress made Floz feel slightly queasy. Like the princess with the pea, she rather thought she would feel that stain however many undersheets she had.

'Gas and electricity on a meter,' said Mr Selby. 'Like I said on the phone, two months in advance, all breakages to be paid for. I take a five-hundred-pound bond an' all. Refundable when you leave if you haven't broke owt.'

'When can I let you know?' said Floz, smiling and trying not to look as if the thought of moving in here made her want to cry.

'Now if you can,' said Mr Selby. He seemed surprised that she wasn't instantly taken with it.

'Well, I've got another place to see first,' fibbed Floz.

'Where's that then?'

'Oh, er . . . Bretton.'

Please don't ask me where in Bretton, prayed Floz. But he didn't. He just shepherded her down the stairs and said, 'Right then. I can't hold it for you. If someone gives me a definite, they can have it, you know.'

'I perfectly understand,' said Floz. 'Thank you so much.'

But Mr Selby had turned away from her after the 'Thank'. He could obviously sense that she would rather cut off her own ear than lived in his stinky, grotty flat, which would probably not be half-bad for a good scrub and a few new carpets.

Floz sat in her car and rested her head on the steering wheel. She had never liked change, hated being ripped away from houses after daring to grow a few roots. The trouble was that being ripped away from the Miller family felt more than an uprooting. It felt like pulling out her heart.

She made a plan that as soon as Juliet had got married, she would move into the first place she could find – even if it was just for a little while. And if Greenfield Lane was still on the market, she would take a deep breath, buy a supermarket aisle's-worth of cleaning products and rent it.

Chapter 88

Three days later Guy stood in the restaurant and wondered again what the hell he had taken on. The main walls were all newly plastered, and big wet patches where it hadn't yet dried made it look as if it was riddled with damp. The old drapes had been pulled off the windows in a storm of dust and cobwebs. All the cheap tables and chairs had been removed, the disgusting lamp-shades skipped, and the space looked vast and more like a cavernous – and grotty – dance hall.

He tried to imagine it after the decorators had been in and painted the walls in subtle green and creams, with the new light fittings added, the heavy, beautiful drapes at the window . . . but today he couldn't. He was tired. And he wanted to do all this *with* someone and *for* someone – and there was no one, not even someone he could dream about. Sandra's voice called him to the office. She had found some very prom-ising possibles for new staff. Oh, and she showed him a letter that said Varto was suing them for five million pounds.

He was laughing when he picked up the phone to find his sister on the other end of the line in tears, begging him to come to their parents' house, where she was now heading from work. She wasn't making much sense on the phone. All he could ascertain was that no one was ill, it wasn't a medical emergency.

Guy dashed into his parents' house to see Alberto Masserati crammed into Perry's giant armchair with Stripies on his knee. He was stroking the cat with one hand, and the giant fingers of his other were holding a dainty china cup of tea. Although he wasn't a tall man, Alberto looked as if he had swallowed a wardrobe and always wore his trademark leather coat which seemed to double that width. He was a fearsome animal in the ring, but sitting in Guy's mum and dad's front room, he looked rather as if he was about to cry.

'The bloody Oak Leaf has gone into liquidation!' sobbed Juliet, throwing herself on her brother. 'Where the hell can I have my wedding reception now?'

'Alberto's daughter is supposed to be having her reception there tomorrow,' added Grainne. 'He just went up there to pay the balance and found it closed up. He can't even get to the wedding cake that they took up at the beginning of the week.'

'I knew that Steve was having his reception there as well,' said Alberto. 'The long and the short of it is there's no place free.'

'Why don't you have it in the pub?' asked Guy. Alberto ran a tiny inn in Little Cawthorpe: the Grapevine.

'I've got one hundred and twenty guests coming. I can't seat that lot in my gaffe. Our Lulu's in a right state.'

'There must be somewhere free,' said Guy.

'Me and the missus have rung everywhere. Which means Juliet and Guy are probably stuffed as well.'

'What the hell's going on?' Steve crashed into the room, still in his plastering whites. He'd driven like a nutter over to the Millers' house after Juliet rang him in tears and told him to meet her there.

'I've a good mind to go round to that bloody landlord at the Oak Leaf and smash his face in,' said Juliet.

'Trust me, if that had been an option, I'd have done it,' said Alberto. 'But he's nicked the stock and done a runner. No doubt our deposits have filled up his petrol tank.'

'I don't know what to say,' said Guy, hunting around in his brain for a solution.

'I do. I had an idea,' said Alberto. 'Guy, if you can arrange the catering for me at your restaurant, I'll do it for your sister at my pub. You can even have the beer garden for fireworks at night.'

'I would, Alberto, but one, I've no staff and two, the place has just been plastered. It looks a right mess.'

'My son has a textile shop,' said Alberto. 'We were going to drape all the walls in the Oak Leaf with black net. My daughter's one of them Goths, hence the Hallowe'en theme.'

'That's doable,' nodded Guy. 'The old kitchen hasn't been completely stripped out yet, thank goodness, but I've still got the problem of no staff.'

'I can give you a couple of waitresses,' said Alberto, visibly sweating. 'I can't give you the chef because he's the bloody groom.'

'You've got us,' piped up Grainne with a grin. 'I can be a waitress, if not a cook.'

'I can help in the kitchen,' said Perry. 'And I'm sure Steve will.'

'And I will,' said Juliet. 'And I'm sure Floz will as well.'

'I'll ring around the wrestling lads, see if any of them are free. Oh please, Guy,' begged Alberto, as Stripies reached up and rubbed his head against Alberto's stubbly face, finding it as desirable as a central-heated scratching post.

'Gina will help, I'm sure,' Guy decided. He looked up to see a crescent of dear expectant faces. His sister's wedding, as well as Alberto's daughter's, depended on this. Then he clicked into action. 'Right, Alberto, we're on.'

'So you've given me paid leave but you've changed your mind and want me to come in and work instead. I don't know!' said Gina with mock-annoyance.

'Trust me, this is a big emergency and if you turn around and say no, I won't hold it against you,' said Guy on the other end of the phone. 'Obviously I'll pay you for that as well.'

'Of course I will,' said Gina, who would probably have given Guy that answer if he had asked her to sever her own head and stick it on a pikestaff outside Buck House.

'Thank you so, so much,' Guy said gratefully. 'I owe you.'

'Owe me what?' tried Gina, seizing her big chance. 'I should insist on dinner at Four Trees for this.'

Guy swallowed, because he didn't know how to get out of that one without hurting her feelings. But then, was the thought of taking Gina out on a date so bad? Floz couldn't have made it clearer that she didn't want him; Gina was crazy about him. Maybe he should move on and forget Floz and accept that it wasn't to be, after all. Maybe if he and Gina went out, his feelings might start to grow in her direction. A sea-change had happened to Steve and Juliet, so it wasn't that far-fetched an idea – and really, how convenient would that be?

'Okay. How about a couple of days after Alberto's daughter's wedding, say the second of November? I know the maître d'hôte. I'm sure he can squeeze us in.'

'Lovely!' said Gina, sighing in the manner of someone who couldn't believe her luck and would have fainted had she said more.

Guy put down the phone but, try as he might, he couldn't find an image in his brain of Gina and him making love in front of that log fire in Hallow's Cottage.

Chapter 89

Within the hour, Burgerov was full of people. Jeff Leppard had arrived with a truck full of lads to make some temporary frames to hang the black drapes from. The Miller family and Floz were ripping the packaging off the hired tables and chairs, and Guy was ringing around suppliers trying to order stocks. Saturday afternoon was not the best time to do this.

'I don't care if we have to have fish and chips,' said Alberto. 'Just do your best, mate. It doesn't have to be the full beef dinner shebang.'

Just then, Big Bad Davy walked into the madness. 'Oy, ugly,' he called at Alberto. 'I've got a vanload of fruit and veg here for you if you want it. I heard on the grapevine, if you'll excuse the pun, that you were in the shit.'

'You legend,' said Alberto, encasing him in a bone-crushing hug that had him screaming for mercy.

'It's going to be a bit of a squash on some tables, Alberto,' said Guy.

'Doesn't matter,' said Alberto. 'The wife's side are all skinny bleeders. You can fit twenty of them on the end of a pin.'

'Do you need meat?' asked Davy. 'My brother's a butcher. Stay away from me, Alberto,' he warned, seeing the wide man's arms come out again. 'I'll ring him, if you don't come any closer.'

The moon was out by the time all the temporary drapes had

been hung, the tables arranged, the tablecloths, cutlery and glasses put out, the serviettes folded and place-names distributed.

'I won't forget this,' said Alberto, giving Guy a tearful man-hug, though Guy's solid bones were only slightly bruised. 'I'll make sure your sister's day is as special as my girl's will be tomorrow.'

Guy waved everyone off. He had an early start in the morn-ing so he would sleep on the sofa in his office. But before he could call it a night, he had a cake to make.

Chapter 90

When the motley crew of kitchen staff arrived early that Sunday morning, Guy had already had two espressos. Not that he needed the extra kick because the adrenalin coursing through his arteries could have generated all the electricity for the ovens.

The kitchen was filled with the delicious aroma of beef. Guy was just putting the finishing touches to a four-tiered black-iced wedding cake with some sugar-spun cobwebs. It was a bizarre concept for a wedding cake, but stunning. There was a collective 'ahhh' from everyone when they entered the kitchen and saw it.

'Morning,' smiled Guy. 'Help yourself to aprons, Gina will show you where they are.'

'Morning, everyone,' chirped Gina, who had arrived an hour before. For all that delicious time she and Guy had been in the kitchen alone together. He had broken off icing the cake to make her a coffee. From the way she had melted at the attention, it was as though he had presented her with an engagement ring.

Gina had been walking on air since talking to Guy the previous day. Her feet hadn't touched the ground and she had gone to sleep imagining the date to come, then the wedding to come, then the children and grandchildren who would follow.

She knew better than to mention anything about the date that morning though, because when he had his whites on, he was no longer Guy, he was 'Chef' and focused on food and service and nothing else. And *GOD* was he sexy when he locked into his duties.

Floz, Juliet, Perry, Steve, Grainne, Coco and Gideon all fastened on their aprons. They had just started on peeling vegetables when Jeff Leppard's wife and daughter arrived, then Alberto's two waitresses turned up with the flower arrangements which Tarzan, who by day was Dave Ward the florist, had been up since the crack of dawn arranging, surprisingly daintily, with his big fingers.

It was the first time Floz had been in contact with Guy since the day they had driven out to Hallow's. She had tried so hard to put him out of her mind, because she couldn't be the woman he wanted. But thoughts of him and that cottage had kept pushing through – especially in her dreams, when her defensive barriers were down.

Now they were here in the same room and she could barely look at him, because every time her eyes fell on him, her heart started quickening. But other than a brief nod of greeting, he had totally ignored her, and that hurt more than she could have imagined. She really should have told him the truth. Seeing him now made her realize that. She owed him that at least, then he would see why he shouldn't get involved with her.

This Guy in whites, creator of the Hallowe'en cake, was a different man to the clumsy, shy Guy she knew. He was assured and in control, and so very sexy.

'Gina, check the beef will you, please.'

'Yes, Chef.'

He even sounded different. The TV chefs, including the smouldering Spanish Raul Cruz, weren't anything as desirable as Guy Miller in his chef's outfit.

Guy swore under his breath as the tiny fondant black cat which he was moulding tumbled to the floor. *Focus, you idiot, focus.* It was the first time he had been in the same room as Floz since they had driven out to Hallow's, when she had pulled up her drawbridge. He had thrown every bit of energy and thought into the restaurant, and drawing up plans for the cottage. He had tried not to think of her, but she kept breaking through, especially at night in his dreams.

He couldn't look at her without his heart cracking just a little bit more. She didn't want what he had to offer, a heart brimming with love. He growled and told himself to concentrate on the job in hand.

With the cake finished, he strutted around his kitchen-kingdom checking on all the preparations.

'Floz, who told you to slice those carrots like that? I don't want them sliced, I want them roasted whole,' he barked at her.

'Sorry, Chef,' said Floz. 'Shall I start again?'

'Of course. Unless you have some magic carrot glue and can join them back together again.'

'No, Chef.'

Gina's eyes jerked to the short red-haired woman. *One Floz equals all of my back catalogue and yours put together* – that's what she had overheard Guy say to his friend that day when he visited. So this was *her*. This was *Floz*.

There was something about that little interchange that intrigued Gina. Chef wasn't usually that snipey, not even with Varto. And he hadn't made eye-contact with this Floz person when he told her off. Nor had she lifted her eyes to him.

Floz tipped the carrots she had sliced into the bin. Gina watched Chef's eyes follow her across the kitchen, a look so warm and soft and totally at odds with the way he had just spoken to her. And her intuition clicked on and she knew that Guy liked this woman a lot. And he wouldn't have needed to be put on the spot to ask *her* out to dinner. She blinked away the tears that prickled at the back of her eyes. She knew she was being ridiculous, imagining all this from a few seconds of watching Guy's expression, but still, she also knew she was right.

Gina picked up another bag of carrots and delivered them to Floz's workspace. 'Don't mind him, he's a pussycat really.'

'Thanks,' said Floz. 'I know he's under pressure.'

'He eats and drinks pressure,' said Gina sweetly. 'Are you a friend of the family?'

'I'm Juliet's flat-mate.' Floz ran her scraper quickly down the side of a carrot.

'Ah. So all this madness is going to be repeated in a few days' time again,' laughed Gina. 'Seems like romance is in the air.'

'For some anyway.' Floz's eyes lifted when Guy shouted for assistance to move the cake.

Gina leaned in closer to Floz. 'I hope he doesn't bawl like that in Four Trees when we go out to dinner. I'll die of embarrassment.'

Gina watched Floz momentarily freeze. Yes, she had been right, there was something between Floz and Guy. Something that she wanted to smash into smithereens. Chef was as good as Gina's; she couldn't get so close to him after all this time and not totally snare him.

'It's supposed to be very nice there,' said Floz, the trace of a tremor in her voice.

'We've held off the date for so long with all the restaurant and wedding stress because he's been too busy. I'm sure it'll be worth waiting for. Call me over if you need any help, won't you?'

Gina saw again that wounded look in Floz's eyes before she turned and strolled back to the dessert station. She just had to hold on for two more days then she would make Guy hers. Once she was under his skin, she would drive 'Floz' totally and utterly out.

Chapter 91

Lulu Masserati was one inch taller in her heels and only marginally less wide than her father. Not that it stopped her from choosing a black meringue of a dress, against all the rules of what a woman with her shape should wear. She was big, bouncy and milkmaid-bonny and had a huge bright-red smile when she walked into Burgerov with her groom who, in his top hat, looked more like an undertaker than a newly-wedded spouse. Steve hoped he'd make Lulu happy. He wouldn't have liked to have been Alberto's son-in-law if he ever messed her about. The short, wide man was a sweetheart outside the ring, but he had the potential to be truly terrifying.

They were greeted by Grainne and the waitresses bearing glasses of Buck's Fizz, with a splash of green food colouring in as instructed. Whilst they were mingling, Floz and Coco circulated with trays of canapés: dates stuffed with cream cheese, smoked salmon and dill on tiny peppered crackers, crostini with chorizo and bean pâté, sticky king prawns, curry-filled pastries – to name but a few.

'Is the wine on the table? Are the pumpkins lit?' barked Guy.

'Yes, Chef,' replied Perry, cheerfully relishing his role as Commis Chef.

'Everyone's nearly seated, Chef,' said Steve, who was now wearing a suit and operating front of house.

'Then let's get these starters out!'

One hundred and twenty red-pepper soups were delivered to the tables, then one hundred and twenty empty bowls were collected and washed and dried by hand, seeing as the dish-washers had all been stripped out during the refurb. Meanwhile the miniature Coquilles St Jacques were served in scallop shells.

'Are those sorbets finished? If they are, get them out now, please!' yelled Guy, watching his team of total amateurs some-how work together in a harmony he wished he'd been able to see in Varto, Antonin and the rest of his ex-staff. One hundred and twenty champagne sorbets were ferried out.

The main was roast beef, horseradish mash, roasted maple carrots, creamed parsnip, cauliflower in a Stilton and white wine sauce, red onion and port gravy, 'a ménage à trois' of green vegetables and the crispest, puffiest Yorkshire puddings that it was possible to imagine.

Guy had no time to listen to the praising comments that the waitresses and Steve brought back. He was too busy checking the towers of heart-shaped raspberry shortcakes and chocolate mousse trifles that were lined up for dessert.

Floz watched how he checked every single one, rejecting one for having a misshaped swirl of cream on it, another for having a deformed heart shape drawn around the plate rim in raspberry coulis.

The waitresses marched out with hands full of dessert plates. As the last one was set on the table, everyone in the kitchen dared to let out a sigh of relief.

'I don't know how you bloody did it, but you did, lad,' said Perry, with a beaming smile of pride on his face.

'Because he's a genius,' said Gina. She put her arm around Guy's waist and hugged him, and saw Floz turn away as if the sight of her touching Guy burned her eyes.

She'd been an idiot, Floz could see that now. And she'd missed her chance because now Gina had claimed him and he

was taking her out – to Four Trees of all places. Leggy, blonde
Gina, whom he was bound to fall in love with because she was
so golden and pretty and more than likely able to give him
what he most wanted. So Floz didn't see how quickly Guy
pulled away from Gina, only heard that he clapped his hands.

'Come on, we haven't finished yet. Don't rest on your laurels.
Where are those home-made mints? Where's the cake-knife?
Didn't I ask someone to tie that black ribbon around the handle?
Sharon, Janice, put the water through the coffee machines, please.'

Over coffee, the wedding speeches were made. Alberto
delivered his with so many tears that people who didn't know
him might have been fooled into thinking he was soft. At least
he could take the Mick out of himself and warned his new son-
in-law never to climb in a wrestling ring with him, not even as
a joke. Alberto made Guy come out and take a round of
applause. Guy was followed into the restaurant by his impromptu
kitchen staff to see him take his moment of glory.

'It's more down to these guys,' said Guy, casting his hand
towards the others behind him. 'They've had to put up with
me shouting at them all morning, throwing orders at them,
when they could have been sitting at home enjoying their
weekend. I must especially thank my second-in-command –
Gina – who always does every job to perfection.'

Gina beamed at the accolade and the applause. She heard
love, hope and promise in every one of Guy's words. She
couldn't help but flash a victorious look at Floz who was clapping dutifully but her eyes were downcast.

After the meal the wedding party began to drift off. Some
had travelled a long way and had to get home for work the
next day, the bride and groom were being driven off to the
airport to catch an early evening plane to the Bahamas, and the
rest were going back to Alberto's pub for a nightcap.

'You are all welcome to join us,' said Alberto, shaking Guy's
hand with his usual bone-crushing vigour.

'Thanks, mate, but I'm knackered,' said Guy. That was the response of them all. They just wanted to put their feet up and have a totally easy Sunday night.

'We'll make it up to you on Friday – I'll be in touch during the week,' said Alberto. 'I can't thank you enough. I even think if we had a fight in the ring, I'd let you win.'

'Aye, course you would,' scoffed Guy. Not for a minute did he believe that one.

November

'Autumn, the year's last, loveliest smile.'
William Cullen Bryant

Chapter 92

Gina went to the loo for the fourth time in as many minutes. To say she was nervous about this evening was an understatement. She had started her primping and preening at lunchtime, but her preparations for this night had begun much sooner. For over a year the lingerie, which she was now wearing, had been bought and stored in tissue paper in her drawer awaiting a date with Guy Miller: a black basque and matching g-string, stockings with seams and little bows at the thigh. The black dress over the top of it was new, chic and very expensive. She sprayed herself with her lucky perfume and stood back to view herself in the mirror and smiled. She was now as ready as she would ever be to put her first step on the road to being Mrs Gina Miller. *It all comes to she who waits.*

When she heard Guy's car draw up outside her front door, her heart went into a crazy rhythm. She slipped on her new black velvet heels, her new panther-black faux-fur coat, and blew herself a good luck kiss in the hall mirror. She looked good and she felt good, because before the end of the night she knew she would have felt Guy Miller's lips on her own.

Guy watched Gina come out of her front door. She looked lovely. Her hair was glossy, sleek and golden-blonde, her legs slim and long in those killer heels, but his heart-rate stayed constant – there was no skip, no kick, just a steady regular beat.

But Floz, cutting up carrots in a huge white apron, had made it race like Red Rum towards the last fence.

'Hi,' said Gina, buckling herself up. Her eyes were shining, her smile was soft and hopeful, and Guy knew then that this was a mistake.

He drove on, making conversation about Alberto's wedding and the enquiries he'd had since from two of the guests about holding functions in the new restaurant when it opened.

When they got to Four Trees and he opened the car door for Gina, he knew she was reading so much more into it than mere automatic gallantry. He had intended to order them champagne at the table but he couldn't, because she would see that as more evidence of romance, and by the end of the night he was going to have to let her down very gently.

They went to their table and he felt Gina staring at him whilst he was looking at the wine list. He knew her eyes would be big and doe-innocent, pupils dilated to max aperture. It make him feel slightly suffocated and he pulled at his collar.

'Any preference – red or white?' he asked.

'White for me, please,' replied Gina. 'Have they got a Pinot Grigio?'

Guy looked down the list. 'Er, yep. That's fine for me too. So what do you fancy for starter?' he asked.

'How about you choose for me?' smiled Gina. She had seen that on films many times and it always looked so romantic.

Guy cursed himself. He hadn't realized she had it this bad for him. He dreaded the thought of hurting her, but he had to get through the evening. Maybe she would deduce his non-interest during the course of the meal if he gave off just enough of a chill for her to get the message and save her dignity. Like Floz had done with him.

'I don't know what you like though,' said Guy.

'Anything,' said Gina.

Balls.

Gina was seeing them with different dishes. If he ordered her the scallops, she would take that as a sign that he wanted her to spear one with a fork and pass it through his lips so he could taste it. He would do the same for her, that's what happened between flirting couples.

He ordered scallops. True love, she thought. For himself, the mussels. They sounded a macho and sexy thing to request.

'And the Pinot Grigio,' Guy told the waiter.

'Which one, sir?' The waiter was fairly new. He wasn't that familiar with the listings.

'It's number . . . er . . .' Guy opened the wine menu; *oh God, it just had to be, didn't it?* '. . . sixty-nine.' He slammed the menu shut and handed it quickly over. He reached for some bread and busied himself ripping bits off and dipping it in olive oil.

Gina did a lot of silent smiling at him whilst they waited for the starters to arrive. It occurred to Guy that he had never socialized with Gina in all the three years they had worked together. He didn't know what she was like when she was free of her duties. From the looks she was giving him, he would have been forgiven for thinking that in between shifts, she worshipped at a shrine of him. In Burgerov she was all innocent blue eyes. Now, those eyes looked borderline feral.

He refilled her empty wine glass.

'That's a lovely wine,' she said. 'You must be an expert.'

'Hardly,' laughed Guy bashfully.

'French, isn't it? I like France so much,' said Gina. 'I wish I could have gone there this summer but it's hard to holiday solo, don't you think? I miss going away with someone.'

'It's harder for a woman to do that, I often think,' Guy replied, filtering his reply for come-ons.

'Lots of things are,' Gina sighed like Snow White at the Wishing Well. She was fishing for a 'Like what?' which Guy felt obliged to give.

'Well, take for instance, asking a man out.'

Oh shite.

'Women have to wait around for years sometimes until a man asks her out. Otherwise she's "forward" and a bit butch, don't you think?'

Guy made a series of hand expressions, eyebrow formations and huffs to indicate that he wasn't sure about that one. He could have snogged the waiter, who rescued them by delivering the starters.

'How're your scallops?' asked Guy, immediately regretting it as Gina picked one up with her fork and held it to Guy's lips. To take it would have been suggestive, to refuse it ungentlemanly and churlish. He tried to take it from her fork as unsexually as possible.

'Lovely,' he said.

'How're your mussels?'

'They're good, thank you.'

'Can I try one?'

'Sure.'

He felt obliged to reciprocate the fork thing. Gina closed her mouth slowly around the mussel and chewed seductively. 'Fabulous,' she said.

'What are you doing with your time off then, Gina?' Guy asked, when the waiter had cleared the plates. He hadn't bargained for conversation to be this laboured between them. Gina had turned into a love-struck teenager. Her eyes were almost pumping out cartoon hearts in his direction and it all felt very intense and uncomfortable.

'Ooh, not much,' she replied, smiling and sighing again.

He wouldn't have been surprised if she had spent the time off just practising writing the name 'Gina Miller'. He couldn't have imagined she was so enamoured. He felt dreadfully guilty now that there would be no second date.

'It's nice in here, isn't it?' asked Guy, looking around because the heat of Gina's gaze was burning him.

'We'll have to come again. My treat next time.' Gina's smile was so wide the ends were almost touching at the back of her head.

Guy was stuck how to answer. He couldn't say yes because that would have been setting her up for more disappointment; he couldn't say no because that would crush her. He plumped for needing the loo and excused himself. The mains were on the table when he came back. Guy waited for the inevitable forking-of-food ritual to begin: he didn't have to wait long.

'Are you looking forward to your sister's baby arriving then?' Gina popped the last of her pâté-stuffed steak into her mouth.

'Yes, I am, very much,' replied Guy. 'I love children.'

'So do I,' nodded Gina with great enthusiasm, pleased to have found yet another way in which she and Guy were compatible. She wouldn't be able to stop herself choosing four suitable names that went with 'Miller' when she got home. Four male and four female just in case they had all boys or all girls.

'I bet the wedding will be lovely in Alberto's Inn,' said Gina, sure that any moment Guy was going to ask her to partner him.

'I think he'll do a grand job,' said Guy, knowing exactly why the wedding subject had been brought up. 'We'll all be crammed though. It's a very tiny room.'

'They always seem to be able to squeeze one more in though, don't they?' Gina said with a tinkly laugh. 'I bet it will be lovely and cosy with everyone squashing up.'

The waiter cleared away the plates and brought dessert menus. Guy stared at his, hoping for a change in subject.

'Ooh, look at these for two to share!' Gina shrieked with delight, draining her glass of wine.

'Not for me.' Guy patted his stomach. 'You feel free – I think I'll just have a coffee. I'm not really a dessert person.' It was a huge lie. He knew that if Floz was sitting opposite to him, he would have been the first to suggest a pudding to share.

It was as if a cloud had fallen over Gina's face. Having so much power over her emotions was a heavy responsibility, one that Guy really didn't want to shoulder.

Gina ordered a panna cotta whilst the waiter filled up her wine glass. She was full but didn't want the meal to end.

'How do you get on with that Floz?' she asked. The 'that' before the name was telling, Guy thought.

'She's – she's a nice person. I don't really know her that well,' he said.

'You're not setting her on in the restaurant, are you?'

'Floz?' he laughed, and Gina saw the genuine warmth in his eyes when he said her name; it pained her. She gulped back her wine. 'No, she's a writer.'

'I've never heard of her.' Gina couldn't keep the snipe out of her words.

'Not books – she's a copywriter for greetings cards,' he replied, thanking the waiter then for delivering his coffee and Gina's dessert.

'She doesn't like you very much, does she?' Gina stabbed her spoon into the panna cotta.

'I don't know,' replied Guy, feeling a real moment of *ouch*.

'All those arty types are strange,' Gina went on, her tongue loosened by the wine. 'I went out with a journo once. Writers should only ever go out with other writers, they're so strange. Teachers should only go out with teachers, doctors with people in the medical profession and chefs with other chefs. We should stick to our own. Don't you think?'

Guy sipped his coffee and shrugged his shoulders by way of an answer. He felt so guilty for thinking it but he couldn't wait for this date to end. He had been wrong to think that affection could be forced; chemistry had no master.

Gina had no intention of letting Guy go early though. She ordered a Napoleon coffee and persuaded him to have another espresso to keep her company whilst she was drinking.

'I can't wait to get back to work,' said Gina. 'I've missed being in the kitchen with you so much.'

'I've missed working too,' said Guy.

'With me?'

'Sorry?' Guy coughed.

'Have you missed working with *me*?' Her eyes were bright with tears or booze, he couldn't tell which.

'Yes, yes of course,' Guy said, not returning the love-heart eye stare he knew would be waiting for him if he lifted up his head. He collared a passing waiter and asked for the bill. He hoped he'd be quick and fished out his credit card in readiness.

'It's been lovely, thank you, Guy,' said Gina softly, moulding herself into another personality, hoping that this one would beat down the walls of his defences. She felt his distance, knew that this date would not lead to another. This had been a thank-you dinner that she hadn't managed to convert to a romantic one. She drained the coffee in one, felt the hit of brandy in her stomach.

'Thank you for your company, Gina.'

'I really like you, Guy.' Gina's eyes were brimming with water. There was only a direct proposition left to try. She didn't mind if he used her for a night. Maybe then, in between her legs, he would find that there was a connection between them.

'I . . .' The blessed waiter arrived with the credit-card machine and Guy and the waiter tried to complete the transaction whilst not making mention that Gina was dabbing at her eyes with the cloth serviette.

Gina's tears flowed faster, knowing she would not be coming back to this restaurant with Guy or becoming engaged to him. He would not be saying to her, 'Do you remember our first date here?' and on the anniversary of this first date, dropping to his knees and proposing to her. Her future and dreams were pulling away from her, out of her grasp, disappearing into the distance. She *had* to make him interested. She had loved him for so long. She didn't know what she would do if he turned her down. They had crossed a barrier that couldn't be uncrossed.

She threaded her arm through Guy's as they walked across the car park, enjoying the fantasy that this was her man. Guy opened the door for her and she climbed into the car as seductively as she could, flashing a long leg clad in a finely woven stocking, but he didn't even dip his eyes for a micro-second.

The air in the car on that drive to Gina's house was so heavy, it needed extra lung-strength to breathe in. Gina sat defeated, fighting back tipsy-tears, half-hating Guy for being so impervious to her but knowing she was still going to try and seduce him on her doorstep. One ex-boyfriend had told her that her perfume was half Poison, half-desperation.

Guy pulled up outside her house, got out of the car and opened the door for her.

'Well, thank you for a lovely dinner, Gina.'

She turned big watery eyes up to him. 'What's wrong with me, Guy?'

'Nothing's wrong with you, Gina. Nothing at all.'

'Will you stay the night?'

Gulp.

Guy sighed. 'No, Gina. Thank you, but no.'

She stayed resolutely in the car, sobbing now. 'Oh no, I've ruined everything. I shouldn't have said that. I like you so much, Guy. Can we go out again, can we start again?' Tears were streaming down her face.

Guy knew that being soft now would be cruel, giving her false hope.

'No, Gina,' he said, trying to keep all emotion out of his voice. 'I think that would be the wrong thing to do.'

Gina's features hardened. 'Fine!' Guy tried not to let her hear the sigh of relief as she suddenly propelled herself up and out of the car. 'Maybe if I was *Floz* with her love-sick eyes, things might be different!'

'Love-sick? What do you mean?' said Guy.

' "Oh, Guy, I'm trying not to look at you whilst I'm cutting up my carrots all wrong!" ' scoffed Gina in a puerile baby voice. 'And you trying not to look at her in the same way! I won't be back to work in the restaurant, Guy.' She walked two wobbly steps forward and dropped her keys on the ground. Guy picked them up for her because she almost toppled, bending down to retrieve them.

'Gina, don't be daft . . .'

She snatched them out of his hands, anger coating her like a suit of armour. Love dictated the rules to people, not the other way round. It would not be swayed by long legs in black stockings and blue eyes full of devotion. It had laughed at her efforts and chosen a short red-head who couldn't cut up carrots to be Guy's object of desire.

'Thanks, but no thanks,' she snarled.

And her house door opened and slammed shut so hard it was a wonder the glass panels didn't shatter.

Chapter 93

Two days before her wedding, Juliet lay on the sonographer's bed shaking with excitement.

The sonographer pulled down Juliet's trousers a few inches and smeared her tummy with gel.

'Jesus, that's cold!' yelped Juliet.

'Sorry,' smiled the woman, taking a seat and lifting up the probe. 'So, your doctor has sent you up for an early scan. You're not having any problems, are you?'

'No, touch wood,' replied Juliet, 'but I'm a fifth-generation twin. He said you can tell quite early on if I'm carrying more than one baby.'

'That's right,' said the sonographer, falling silent for a while, moving the probe around Juliet's fast-growing stomach, studying the screen in front of her, Steve behind her trying to work out what the moving blobs were.

'Yep,' she said eventually and pointed something out to Steve. 'There you go – twins.'

She twisted the screen around to Juliet, who promptly burst into tears a second behind Steve.

'You're expecting sixth-generation twins. Congratulations to you both!'

Chapter 94

Floz arrived at the White Wedding boutique a little before Juliet.

'Good morning,' said the lovely Freya. 'Final fittings today. Where's the bride?'

'She's on her way,' replied Floz. 'She's just having a scan today. To see if she is carrying twins.'

'How lovely,' said Freya, taking Floz's beautiful chocolate bridesmaid's dress out of the plastic case and helping Floz slip into it. It still fitted perfectly.

'It's so beautiful,' said Floz. 'I would never have thought of having this colour for a bridesmaid.'

'It suits the season and your colouring so well,' said Freya. 'I think one day you'll be an autumn bride yourself. Autumn is your lucky season, I would have said.'

'I wish,' said Floz quietly. 'I was a spring bride last time.'

'I have been a spring bride and an autumn bride,' said Freya, looking over Floz's shoulder at her reflection. 'Autumn was much luckier for me.'

She fitted the pretty headdress of leaves onto Floz's head.

'I think I'm only destined to be a bride once,' sighed Floz. 'I don't really have a lot of luck in that area.'

'My dresses all have a little magic in them for the wearer.' Freya pulled strands of Floz's fiery hair, arranging it around the headdress. 'Maybe you'll be surprised. It's not for you to say that you won't find love. Love decides whether to make itself available to you or not.'

'It would be nice if it did,' said Floz, but not believing for a second that it would hunt her out again.

Chapter 95

'Thanks for coming with me,' said Steve, pulling up in the car park. Tomorrow he would be coming here for a much happier reason, but today he had a duty he wanted to perform.

'Don't be daft,' said Guy. 'Of course I want to be here for you.'

They had just picked up their wedding suits and a large bouquet of pink flowers from the florist next door to the tailor.

'I wish I could have bought her flowers for her birthday when she was alive,' said Steve. 'She didn't want anything she couldn't drink.' He coughed down some tears that threatened to show themselves, and Guy patted him on the back.

They got out of the car and walked down the church path.

'You'll be here tomorrow, wondering what the frig you've let yourself in for,' laughed Guy.

'I don't think so,' smiled Steve. 'I can't wait.'

The Reverend 'Gossip' was standing at the church door and waved. 'Hello, Steven, ready for your big day tomorrow?' he asked.

'Hello, Rev Glossop,' said Steve. 'Just come to put these on my mam's grave. She'd have been fifty-five today.' He felt sad at the waste of those years and all that she should have had to come.

The vicar gave him a comforting pat on the arm. 'Seems there are a few birthday remembrances today,' he said. 'Lady over there, in the children's graveyard – can you see?'

Steve saw a blur of a woman in a blue coat in the distance and nodded.

'She lost three babies at this time of year. All of them stillborn.'

Steve couldn't imagine how he would feel if a tragedy like that happened to him and Juliet.

'And the poor lady had an unfortunate series of miscarriages too. Such a tragic story,' the vicar went on.

'She didn't go on to adopt then?' asked Guy.

'Her husband . . . well,' the vicar, gossipy as he was, wondered if he had told too much of the story already and abridged the version, 'didn't cope very well with it all and his business collapsed. They lost everything. So very sad. Such a lovely woman.' He nodded towards the lady as if sending her his best vibes, then he turned back to Steve. 'Anyway, must get on. We shall see you and Juliet tomorrow, Steven.'

'Aye, see you tomorrow, Rev.'

He and Guy walked on towards Mrs Feast's grave. Steve had ordered a stone for her, but the ground needed to settle for a few months before it was erected. For now there was just a simple cross there which he had made from driftword and whittled into it the words *Love you, Mum*. He and Guy bent and ripped out a couple of weeds which had started to poke out of the soil.

'Can you imagine what that poor cow's gone through?' said Steve, the image of his babies fresh in his mind. He didn't want to think it could happen to anyone. Especially not to Juliet. That she would feel babies grow inside her over and over again and never get to feel them breathing.

'No, I can't,' said Guy, 'I really can't.'

'It scares me to even hear stories like that,' shivered Steve, taking the flowers out of the wrapping and putting them in the vase that stood in front of the cross. He looked up to see Guy staring over the top of the next gravestone.

'What's up?' he asked.

'Steve – look.'

Steve swung his head around to where Guy was pointing. The *poor cow* in the blue coat was walking out of the graveyard. And it was Floz.

They threaded their way to the corner of the churchyard where teddy bears and balloons sat amongst the flowers.

'Here,' said Steve, pointing to a gravestone of an angel. Upon it were the words:

Let your children be as so many flowers, borrowed from God.
If the flowers die or wither, thank God for the precious loan of them.

James Christopher Cherrydale b. d. 4 November 2002
Elisabeth Jane Cherrydale b. d. 14 October 2004
Eleanor May Cherrydale b. d. 2 November 2005

Sleep in Peace, Our Little Ones
We Shall Meet Again
Love Always, Mummy and Daddy

'Oh my God, that's why!'

Then Guy understood. Everything made sense. Why Floz had suddenly gone cold on him that day in Hallow's. When he had been talking about having lots of children – children that she could never bear him. Gina had said that Floz couldn't keep her eyes off him on the day of Lulu Masserati's wedding – she *did* like him, after all. He didn't know what he was going to do with this information yet. All he did know was that he wasn't going to give up on Floz.

There was hope and he was going to seize it and run with it.

Chapter 96

'My, my, you three ladies – and Raymond, of course – don't you look a picture?'

Perry grinned, taking in the sight of his wife in her bronze suit, Floz in her beautiful chocolate dress, Juliet in her classy golden gown holding a teardrop of gold flowers and leaves, and Coco, smart in his suit. The girls had stayed with the Millers the night before the wedding, and had been regally fussed over by them. Coco and Gideon had come along too with dips and nibbles and cakes, and Perry had mixed some of his speciality home-made port-soaked-punch and in the end it had turned into a rather jolly mixed-sex hen party.

'I can't believe I'm getting married,' said Juliet, looking at herself in the mirror. She grinned for the millionth time. Alberto was giving them one of the inn's hotel rooms as a honeymoon suite, and Juliet couldn't wait to dive into bed with her husband as Mrs Feast. Boy, was she going to feast on him tonight.

'I can't either,' croaked Coco, patting his choked-up chest. 'I think it's marvellous.'

Floz nodded and smiled, but her heart felt so heavy. As much as she was looking forward to the wedding, she was dreading seeing Gina cosying up to Guy. She would just have to try very hard not to look at them.

'The weather's holding,' said Grainne, looking out of the window at a fine, if chilly day, with a faint hint of mist above the grass. The trees were bare now, the last of the leaves ripped from their branches in the winds of the night; the blackberries were long gone, poppies slumbering under the soil, and the conkers had all fallen and were engaged in battles in the schoolyards. The rusts of autumn's hair would be turned to white soon enough.

Perry handed out long flutes of champagne and raised his own to his daughter.

'My darling girl, may you and Steven be as happy as your mother and I have been and continue to be.'

Floz toasted her grinning friend and enjoyed the warmth that this lovely family generated. She wished she could store it, for she felt cold winter was only a breath away.

'Ready?' asked Guy.

'I'm crapping myself,' said Steve. 'Can you say "I'm crapping myself" in church?'

'I'm sure God would forgive you this once.' Guy adjusted Steve's golden rose in his buttonhole.

The organist was playing the equivalent of church Musak as the pews filled up with aunties and wrestlers.

'Yes, I'm sure I've got the rings.' Guy patted his pocket as Steve opened his mouth to ask the same question yet again.

'No, I won't say anything to Juliet about Floz,' Steve said, as Guy opened his mouth in turn. 'I know Ju would be upset, thinking of all those times she press-ganged Floz into going shopping with her for baby stuff.'

The organist switched tunes. Der-der-der-der; der-der-der-*derrrr*. The first bars of 'Here Comes the Bride'. She was here.

'Oh fuck,' said Steve. 'Sorry, God.'

'Good luck, mate,' said Guy.

'And you, for later,' said Steve, with a wink.

★

Alberto Masserati and his family and staff had done the wedding
party proud. The dining room in the inn was draped in materi-
als in autumn shades, the linen on the table matched, and
confetti of tiny leaves had been scattered everywhere. Even the
waitresses were in brown dresses with white aprons and leaf
crowns in their hair, giving the impression they were part-time
Roman Empresses.

As they drank Buck's Fizz, Floz felt as if she were being
stared at. She was right. She turned to the side to see Guy's
eyes upon her, grey and intense. He was blatant in his interest
and didn't turn away after being discovered staring, but merely
smiled and tipped his glass towards her. She smiled back a little
and swung her eyes away, feeling a blush spread over her
cheeks – and wondered why there was no Gina with him.

He was in a funny mood today. As they were leaving the
church, the bride and groom walking down the aisle, the best
man and bridesmaid behind, he had held out his arm for her
to take.

'You look beautiful, Floz,' he had said.

'Oh . . . oh, thank you,' she had replied.

'Like a wood nymph.'

'Not a gnome then?' she had chuckled.

'Oh no, most definitely a nymph.'

'Wait till I start flying about later,' she had joked bashfully.

'I'd love to make you feel as if you were flying, Floz,' he had
replied smokily, under his breath but still loud enough to be
heard. *What the heck had he meant by that?* Although the tone he
had used had left her in no doubt really that he wasn't planning
on taking her paragliding. It had made her legs very quivery.
She was glad to be at the other end of the top table, in between
Coco and Perry and away from Guy's gaze.

Alberto served up asparagus wrapped in prosciutto for
starter, then 'Autumn soup' which was a rich, thick broth
made of root vegetables and served with leaf-shaped toasts.

Lime sorbet followed and preceded a main course of pork medallions in a mustard sauce. Dessert was toffee-apple brûlée, each one with a tiny heart-shaped sparkler fizzing away on it.

Perry stood up then to deliver his short and sweet speech. He was a shy man and didn't relish standing up in public.

'I'm not very good at the speeches,' he began, to a rousing chorus of encouraging applause. 'But I'd like to thank Alberto and his family and his staff for doing this lovely reception for us. Come out and take a bow, my friends.'

To a splendid ripple of applause, Alberto and his equally shy gang of staff came out to be publicly acclaimed before disappearing back to the sanctuary of the kitchen. On stage Alberto reaped attention; off it, he made Perry look like Peter Mandelson.

'And thank you to all the relatives who've travelled to see my little girl get wed. All I'll say is that I would have been delighted to welcome Steve into our family, except he's already been in it for thirty years. That means that he knows what he's getting with my daughter and he's a very brave man.'

There was a loud rumble of laughter at that, especially as Juliet put her hands on her hips and pretended to look affronted.

'I'll say to you both what Gron's dad said on our wedding day.' Perry coughed and the room hushed to pin-drop silence.

> 'May your day be touched by a bit of Irish luck,
> Brightened by a song in your heart and warmed by the smiles
> Of the people you love.
> May the Good Lord watch over you
> As you grow in love.
> May the light of friendship guide your paths together.
> May the laughter of children grace the halls of your home.
> May the joy of living for one another trip a smile from your lips,
> A twinkle from your eye.

'Ladies and gentlemen, would you please raise your glasses and toast my beautiful Juliet and her Romeo – Steven. The new Mr and Mrs Feast.'

'The bride and groom!' everyone chorused and clapped. Grainne gave Perry a big kiss on the cheek. Now he could relax and enjoy himself at last.

Guy stood up. He looked even larger in this tiny room with the low ceilings. Floz felt her heart do a bit of a gallop at the sight of him in that black morning suit and waistcoat, chocolate cravat at his neck, shirt white and crisp, golden rose bright and tightly budded in his buttonhole. He was going to make someone a lovely husband one day, some children a wonderful father. 'Ladies and gentlemen,' he began, swinging his eyes around the room, locking with Floz's yet again before moving on. 'I was going to tell you an embarrassing story about Steve, but there were so many I didn't know where to start.'

The wrestlers began shouting that they had loads too.

'I'm just glad that my best friend is my sister's Mr Right,' Guy said with such tenderness in his voice that Steve was forced to start gulping to stop tears racing to his eyes. 'What she doesn't know is that he's fancied her from school.'

'Have you?' gasped Juliet.

'Yep,' said Steve.

'Why didn't you tell me then?' she said.

'I daren't,' he said. 'I might have fancied you, but you scared the living daylights out of me as well.'

'Oy, you two, shut up!' called Guy as everyone laughed. 'Steve has been the best friend anyone could have. And I know he and Juliet will be happy, because he'll be her best friend too as well as her husband.'

'Aw!' came a chorus. Alberto Masserati was peeping out of the kitchen, blowing his nose.

'And I'd like to thank Juliet's beautiful *bridesmaids* for supporting her and being there for her. Coco has been Ju's friend forever, and though Floz has only come into our lives this autumn, we all feel we've known her as long.'

He smiled at her, and she smiled back, feeling hot and light-headed and self-conscious and honoured all at the same time.

'Please, raise your glasses to Floz and Coco.'

'Floz and Coco.'

Guy winked at Floz and she coughed. She was glad when he sat down and the spotlight of his attention was switched off for a bit whilst she caught her breath.

Then Juliet stood up to a roomful of chuckles.

'I know what you're all thinking,' she said. 'That I'm going to be doing the speech instead of Steve, but marriage has mellowed me. Temporarily anyway. Ladies and gentlemen, may I present my husband – the groom.'

There was a lot of applause and laughter as Steve stood up and looked totally dumbfounded.

'Well, thank you, Wife,' he said. 'Back to the kitchen with you.'

'Don't push it, love,' said Juliet, emptying her glass of orange juice.

Steve grinned. 'I'd like to thank you all for coming and seeing my first wife and I married today.'

Everyone laughed heartily, Juliet included.

'Seriously. The Millers have been my family for as long as I can remember. So this day means more to me than I could say. And wherever we end up living – whether it's here or America for a few years or both – you know I'll look after her and our children with everything that I've got. I've always loved her. And I always will. I'll have to, because she'd kill me otherwise.'

'I don't know whether to laugh or cry,' said Coco, alternating between sobbing and giggling at the speeches.

'Ladies and gentlemen, please raise your glasses to my lovely missus. Juliet – the bride.'

'The bride!'

Coco collapsed into his hankie. 'Oh, Floz, we're all falling apart. She's off to America with Steve and you're off to God knows where.'

Floz put her arm around him. It felt very much like the end of a lovely era to her too. She daren't even think of the week to come, packing up, possibly moving into that awful house with the smelly carpet and the wheezing landlord.

'Fireworks after the coffee, everyone,' announced Alberto as his waitresses starting busying around with cafetières.

'Are they those Chinese ones Steve got last year from Robber Johnny?' asked the Grim Reaper.

'Yep,' yelled Steve overhearing him. 'And he's got me a "Big Bugger" as well.'

'Chuffing hell. I'll get the ambulance standing by,' laughed Grim.

'You must not be a stranger to us, dear Floz.' Perry poured out a coffee for Floz. 'You must come for lunch on Sundays or pop around whenever you want.'

'Thank you,' said Floz, pressing down the emotion rising in her throat.

'We'll go out for lunch as well sometimes,' said Coco, nudging her from the other side. 'I feel like I've had you in my life forever, Floz.'

'Don't,' said Floz, blowing out her cheeks. She looked around at the jolly throng and hoped she wouldn't make a clot of herself by crying. The Pogmoor Brothers were arm-wrestling, the Grim Reaper had his giant arm around his tiny girlfriend's shoulder as he was deep in conversation with Jeff Leppard and Big Bad Davy and their wives, Klondyke Kevin was flirting with Amanda, Daphne and her husband were chuckling at something, Juliet and Steve were talking quietly to each other, holding hands. Guy had his back to her as he talked to Fred Zeppelin and his missus. His black curly hair just covered his collar, and Floz wondered what it would feel like in her fingers.

'Ladies and gentlemen, get your arses outside for the fireworks!' yelled Alberto.

He had lit patio heaters and strung fairylights outside in the chilly beer garden.

'Stand well back, for frig's sake!' said Mrs Masserati, herding those members of the wedding party who had strayed past a chalked white line on the ground.

'Wait, I need to throw my bouquet,' said Juliet, turning around and tossing it high into the air. It sailed a good foot over Floz's outstretched hand and landed straight into Coco's.

'Oh my GOD!' he joked. 'Gid, you'll have to marry me now.'

Gideon thought for a moment. Then he made Coco's mouth drop to his shoes. 'Okay. Why not? Bit more of a whirlwind than I'm used to in my life, but it feels right. Coco – will you marry me? Really?'

Coco went into paroxysms of noisy glee until he was shocked into silence by the bang of the first firework. Steve had a feeling that Robber Johnny had got them from the IRA. The noise was thunderous, the reverberations would have made the space station wobble in the sky. Someone had to go and get Aunt Clara's heart pills out of her coat pocket. The men were in a state of orgasmic delight.

Floz stood at the back of the crowd gazing into a sky that was suddenly flashing with coloured crackles and fizzles, the air full of that familiar end-of-autumn fire smoke. Jeff Leppard was passing around sparklers and like big kids the wrestlers were attempting to write their names in the air with them. Everyone was standing in couples, arms round each other, or leaning on each other, or holding hands. It was touching and warm, yet she felt as if she were stood in some cold lonely shadow at the edge.

Then she felt *him* behind her. She did not need to turn to know it was Guy.

'Lovely but mad, aren't they?' he said. She didn't know if he meant the guests or the fireworks, not that it mattered for the answer was the same for both.

'Yes,' she said.

'Are you cold?' He noticed her shivering.

'A little.'

His arms closed around her, his breath was warm on her neck as he leaned over her and felt her delicious gasp of shock.

'Dear Floz,' he said, his cheek upon hers. 'I think I'm in love with you.'

She twisted to face him. He saw the flicker of firework sparks reflected in her eyes.

'Oh, Guy, I'm not the woman for you.'

He lifted up her hand and kissed the back of it. Her skin was scented with those dear, familiar strawberries.

'I think you are every inch the woman for me,' he said. 'I don't care if you can't have children. Yes, I know about it, Floz. You're all I want. Anything else would be a bonus.'

He cupped her face in his big hands, lowered his head slowly and kissed her on the lips. His arms came around her and she felt like the perfect shape against him and he knew that all the pictures he'd had in his head of her and Hallow's Cottage and stupidly tall Christmas trees and that huge log fire were wonderful scenes waiting to happen.

'Watch out, everyone, I'm lighting the "Big Bugger",' said Alberto.

The massive explosion went off with a defeaning *whoosh*. Everyone stood reverently still as the 'Big Bugger' rocketed moonward then it burst into a magnificent chrysanthemum of rainbow fire, blossoming across the sky with a boom that was off the Richter scale. And still it couldn't be heard above the fireworks going off in Floz Cherrydale's and Guy Miller's hearts.

Epilogue

The *South Yorkshire Herald*, 7 November:

WOMAN GIVES BIRTH TO BROTHER'S TWIN CRACKERS

A Barnsley woman and wife of GWE Superstar wrestler Archangel has given birth to her brother's children, for whom she was a surrogate. The twin boys were born in Barnsley District General Hospital on 5 November and are the natural children of Mrs Florence Miller and Mr Guy Miller, the Michelin-starred chef and owner of the nationally acclaimed Firenze restaurant in Lower Hoodley, Barnsley.

Mrs Juliet Feast, who gave birth on her fortieth birthday, is herself a mother of twin boys and twin girls.

'It went like a dream and I wasn't surprised that I had twins for them — there are now six generations of them in our family,' said Mrs Feast. 'Alas, my sister-in-law is unable to have children and I suggested that I act as surrogate for them. They took a lot of persuading, but I am a very hard woman to say no to.'

Mrs Miller, who suffered a series of devastating miscarriages and stillbirths, was understandably jubilant.

'I still can't believe it,' she said. 'My sister-in-law has also been my best friend for years. She has given us the world.'

The boys, Julius and Steven, weighed in at a whopping 8lbs 14oz and 8lb 8oz.

Acknowledgements

There are a few people I'd like to thank for helping me with this book.

Firstly the wonderful, funny, warm UK wrestling community – especially my mates 'Tarzan Boy Darren' Ward and Klondyke Kate, Sam 'Dwight J Ingleburgh' Betts, Ray Robinson, Tony Kelly and the late greats: Gordon 'Pedro the Gypsy' Allen, Arthur 'Butcher Goodman' Betton, Herbert 'Wilson Sheppard' Craddock and George 'Joe Williams' Hubbard for inspiring this story – and giving me so many anecdotes. I just wish I could put them all into print, but I'd be arrested under the indecency act.

To the fabulously friendly WWE, especially the lovely Heather Sanford, who arranges for me to cuddle huge wrestlers twice yearly, freeze-frame the moment in photographic form – and thus thoroughly embarrass my sons Tez and George.

To my gorgeous agent Lizzy Kremer and everyone at Simon & Schuster who sorts me out and looks after me, especially my brilliant editors Suzanne Baboneau and Libby Yevtushenko and my long-suffering publicist and friend Nigel Stoneman – all of whom are a constant source of support despite the fact I must drive them barmy.

To Joan 'Eagle-Eye' Deitch who works her magic on my manuscript and is my good luck charm.

To Jill Craven at our lovely library – a lady who never fails to shove my name out there and has no concept of the words 'switching off from the job'. To all the Yorkshire press who have been with me from the beginning and helped my career blossom – you've been smashing.

To the utterly delightful Daphne Butters who won the Supreme Cat competition to name the moggy in this book. What a pleasure it was to meet you.

To my ace family and friends who keep me on the right side of sane – and insane.

To my solicitor David Gordon at Atteys who answers all my obscure research questions with such grace.

To Jackson Taylor whose daft little idea about an autumn book didn't half bear some fruit.

And to the fantastic greetings card companies who have given me a wage over the years and allowed me to afford school clothes, a roof over my head – and gin: Emotional Rescue, Wishing Well, Quitting Hollywood, Carlton, Paperlink – and to the late Chris Douglas-Morris at Statics who started that enchanted ball rolling. The golden days of joke-writing were the best fun I ever had.

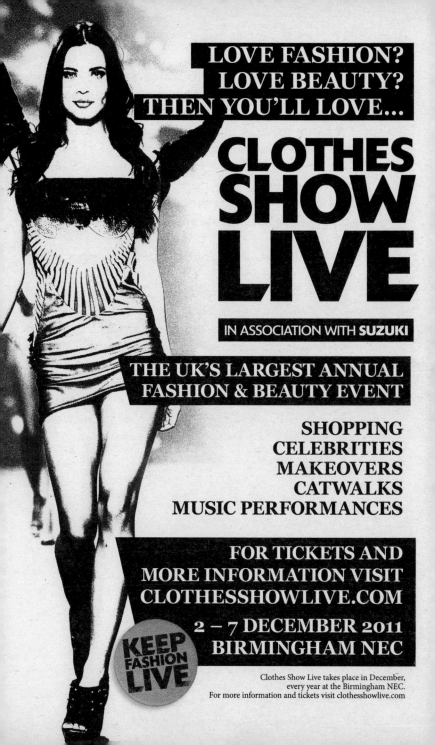